PRAISE FOR

The Broken Girls

"[*The Broken Girls*] mixes a creepy supernatural tale . . . with a gripping mystery. [It] also works well as a story about unshakable friendship, parenting issues, obsession, and sexism folded into a satisfying plot that straddles two eras of time."   —The Associated Press

"Clever and wonderfully chilling. It held me hostage in a very modern ghost story until the early hours."
—Fiona Barton, *New York Times* bestselling
author of *The Suspect*

"Part hauntingly Gothic and part suspenseful crime drama, *The Broken Girls* is a bona fide page-turner. [A] story of friendship, revenge, and redemption."
—Karen White, *New York Times* bestselling
author of *Dreams of Falling*

"Haunting and memorable, *The Broken Girls* is a mesmerizing blend of past and present, a sometimes heartbreaking and always compelling quest for the truth about secrets that shouldn't stay buried. Masterfully done!"
—Karen Dionne, international bestselling
author of *The Marsh King's Daughter*

"St. James's riveting genre-blender combines a supernatural tale with intertwined mysteries from the 1950s and today. . . . Frighteningly believable, peopled with feisty characters, and features top-notch dialogue."

—*Booklist* (starred review)

"A creepy supernatural mystery. . . . In this page-turner, the secrets Fiona uncovers lead to a terrifying conclusion that has less to do with the paranormal and more to do with the evil that men do." —Shondaland

"Chilling, disturbing, and gripping, this is a well-written, modern-day Gothic tale about facing our darkest fears."

—Tessa Harris, author of *The Sixth Victim*

"An intense, genuinely creepy novel that links the ghostly, Gothic strands of a sixty-year-old murder with secrets about to be unearthed in the present day. . . . With a ghostly setting and an addictive plot, St. James's story is as haunting as it gets—poignant, evocative, and difficult to forget." —*BookPage*

"St. James is a unique author who usually combines elegant writing with a mystery to be solved that is complicated by ghostly elements. Spooky and Gothic but fascinating, too." —*Kirkus Reviews*

"[A] creepy supernatural thriller." —*Publishers Weekly*

ALSO BY SIMONE ST. JAMES

The Haunting of Maddy Clare

An Inquiry into Love and Death

Silence for the Dead

The Other Side of Midnight

Lost Among the Living

The Sun Down Motel

the Broken Girls

Simone St. James

BERKLEY
New York

BERKLEY
An imprint of Penguin Random House LLC
penguinrandomhouse.com

ISBN: 9780593201497

Berkley hardcover edition / March 2018
Berkley trade paperback edition / November 2018
Berkley premium mass-market edition / November 2020

Printed in the United States of America
1 3 5 7 9 10 8 6 4 2

Cover photos: Woman © Ingrid Michel / Arcangel Images;
Ghosted building © Alexandre Cappellari / Arcangel Images
Cover design © Sarah Oberrender
Book design by Laura K. Corless

This book is for my mother, the greatest heroine of my life.

I love you, Mom.

the Broken Girls

prologue

Barrons, Vermont
November 1950

The sun vanished below the horizon as the girl crested the rise of Old Barrons Road. Night, and she still had three miles to go.

The air here went blue at dusk, purplish and cold, a light that blurred details as if one were looking through smoke. Squinting, the girl cast a glance back at the road where it climbed the rise behind her, the breeze tousling her hair and creeping through the thin fabric of her collar, but no one that she could see was following.

Still: *Faster,* she thought.

She hurried down the slope, her thick schoolgirl's shoes pelting stones onto the broken road, her long legs moving like a foal's as she kept her balance. She'd outgrown the gray wool skirt she wore—it hung above her knees now—but there was nothing to be done about it. She carried her uniform skirt in the suitcase that banged

against her legs, and she'd be putting it back on soon
enough.

If I'm lucky.

Stop it, stupid. Stupid.

Faster.

Her palms were sweaty against the suitcase handle.
She'd nearly dropped the case as she'd wrestled it off the
bus in haste, perspiration stinging her back and armpits
as she glanced up at the bus's windows.

Everything all right? the driver had asked, something
about the panic in a teenage girl's face penetrating his
disinterest.

Yes, yes— She'd given him a ghastly smile and a wave
and turned away, the case banging her knees, as if she
were bustling off down a busy city street and not making slow progress across a cracked stretch of pavement
known only as the North Road. The shadows had grown
long, and she'd glanced back as the door closed, and
again as the bus drew away.

No one else had gotten off the bus. The scrape of her
shoes and the far-off call of a crow were the only sounds.
She was alone.

No one had followed.

Not yet.

She reached the bottom of the slope of Old Barrons
Road, panting in her haste. She made herself keep her
gaze forward. To look back would be to tempt it. If she
only looked forward, it would stay away.

The cold wind blew up again, freezing her sweat to
ice. She bent, pushed her body faster. If she cut through

the trees, she'd travel an exact diagonal that would land her in the sports field, where at least she had a chance she'd meet someone on the way to her dorm. A shorter route than this one, which circled around the woods to the front gates of Idlewild Hall. But that meant leaving the road, walking through the trees in the dark. She could lose direction. She couldn't decide.

Her heart gave a quick stutter behind her rib cage, then returned to its pounding. Exertion always did this to her, as did fear. The toxic mix of both made her light-headed for a minute, unable to think. Her body still wasn't quite right. Though she was fifteen, her breasts were small and she'd started bleeding only last year. The doctor had warned her there would be a delay, perfectly normal, a biological aftereffect of malnutrition. *You're young and you'll recover,* he'd said, *but it's hell on the body.* The phrase had echoed with her for a while, sifting past the jumble of her thoughts. *Hell on the body.* It was darkly funny, even. When her distant relatives had peered at her afterward and asked what the doctor had said, she'd found herself replying: *He said it's hell on the body.* At the bemused looks that followed, she'd tried to say something comforting: *At least I still have all my teeth.* They'd looked away then, these Americans who didn't understand what an achievement it was to keep all your teeth. She'd been quiet after that.

Closer, now, to the front gates of Idlewild Hall. Her memories worked in unruly ways; she'd forget the names of half the classmates she lived with, but she could re-member the illustration on the frontispiece of the old copy of *Blackie's Girls' Annual* she'd found on a shelf in the dorm: a girl in a 1920s low-waisted dress, walking a romping dog over a hillside, shading her eyes with her hand as the wind blew her hair. She had stared at that illustration so many times she'd had dreams about it, and she could recall every line of it, even now. Part of her fascination had come from its innocence, the clean milkiness of the girl in the drawing, who could walk her dog without thinking about doctors or teeth or sores or scabs or any of the other things she had buried in her brain, things that bobbed up to the surface before vanishing into the darkness again.

She heard no sound behind her, but just like that, she knew. Even with the wind in her ears and the sound of her own feet, there was a murmur of something, a whisper she must have been attuned to, because when she turned her head this time, her neck creaking in protest, she saw the figure. Cresting the rise she'd just come over herself, it started the descent down the road toward her.

No. I was the only one to get off the bus. There was no one else.

But she'd known, hadn't she? She had. It was why she was already in a near run, her knuckles and her chin going numb with cold. Now she pushed into a jog, her grip nearly slipping on the suitcase handle as the case banged against her leg. She blinked hard in the descending darkness, trying to make out shapes, landmarks. How far away was she? Could she make it?

She glanced back again. Through the fog of darkness, she could see a long black skirt, the narrow waist and shoulders, the gauzy sway of a black veil over the figure's face moving in the wind. Unseen feet moving beneath the skirt's hem. The details were visible now because the figure was closer—moving only at a walk, but already somehow closing in, closer every time she looked. The face behind the veil wasn't visible, but the girl knew she was being watched, the hidden gaze fixed on her.

Panicked, she made an abrupt change of direction, leaving the road and plunging into the trees. There was no path, and she made her way slowly through thick tangles of brush, the dead stalks of weeds stinging her legs through her stockings. In seconds the view of the road behind her disappeared, and she guessed at her direction, hoping she was heading in a straight line toward the sports field. The terrain slowed her down, and sweat trickled between her shoulder blades, soaking into the cheap cotton of her blouse, which stuck to her skin. The suitcase was clumsy and heavy, and soon she dropped it in order to move more quickly through the woods. There was no sound but the harsh rasp of her own breathing.

Her ankle twisted, sent sharp pains up her leg, but still she ran. Her hair came out of its pins, and branches scraped her palms as she pushed them from her face, but still she ran. Ahead of her was the old fence that surrounded Idlewild, rotted and broken, easy to get through. There was no sound from behind her. And then there was.

Mary Hand, Mary Hand, dead and buried under land . . .

Faster, faster. Don't let her catch you.
She'll say she wants to be your friend . . .

Ahead, the trees were thinning, the pearly light of the half-moon illuminating the clearing of the sports field.

Do not let her in again!

The girl's lungs burned, and a sob burst from her throat. She wasn't ready. She *wasn't*. Despite everything that had happened—or perhaps because of it. Her blood still pumped; her broken body still ran for its life. And in a moment of pure, dark clarity, she understood that all of it was for nothing.

She'd always known the monsters were real.

And they were here.

The girl looked into the darkness and screamed.

chapter 1

Barrons, Vermont
November 2014

The shrill of the cell phone jerked Fiona awake in the driver's seat. She lurched forward, bracing her palms on the wheel, staring into the blackness of the windshield.

She blinked, focused. Had she fallen asleep? She'd parked on the gravel shoulder of Old Barrons Road, she remembered, so she could sit in the unbroken silence and think. She must have drifted off.

The phone rang again. She swiped quickly at her eyes and glanced at it, sitting on the passenger seat where she'd tossed it. The display glowed in the darkness. Jamie's name, and the time: three o'clock in the morning. It was the day Deb would have turned forty if she'd still been alive.

She picked up the phone and answered it. "Jamie," she said.

His voice was a low rumble, half-asleep and accusing,

on the other end of the line. "I woke up and you were gone."

"I couldn't sleep."

"So you left? For God's sake, Fee. Where are you?"

She opened her door and swung her legs out into the chilly air. He'd be angry, but there was nothing she could do about that. "I'm on Old Barrons Road. I'm parked on the shoulder, at the bottom of the hill."

Jamie was quiet for a second, and she knew he was calculating the date. Deb's birthday. "Fee."

"I was going to just go home. I was." She got out of the car and stood, her cramped legs protesting, the cold air slapping her awake and tousling her hair. She walked to the edge of the road and looked up and down, shoving her free hand into the pocket of her windproof jacket. Back the way she'd come, she could see the road sign indicating thirty miles to Burlington and the washed-out lights of the twenty-four-hour gas station at the top of the hill. Past the hill, out of her sight, she knew there was the intersection with the North Road, with its jumble of fast-food restaurants, yet more gas stations, and a couple of hopeful big-box stores. In the other direction, ahead of the car's hood, there was only darkness, as if Old Barrons Road dropped off the face of the earth.

"You didn't have to go home," Jamie was saying.

"I know," Fiona replied. "But I was restless, and I didn't want to wake you up. So I left, and I started driving, but then I started thinking."

He sighed. She could picture him leaning back on the

pillows, wearing an old T-shirt and boxer shorts, the sleek muscles of his forearm flexing as he scrubbed a hand over his eyes. He was due on shift at six thirty; she really had been trying not to wake him. "Thinking what?"

"I started wondering how much traffic there is on Old Barrons Road in the middle of the night. You know, if someone parked their car here and left it, how long would it be before someone drove by and noticed? The cops always said it wasn't possible that Tim Christopher could have left his car here for so long, unseen. But they never really tested that, did they?"

And there it was: the ugly thing, the demon, coming to the surface, spoken aloud. The thing she'd become so good at keeping buried. The idea had been niggling at her for days as Deb's birthday approached. She'd tried to be quiet about it, but tonight, as she'd lain sleepless, her thoughts couldn't be contained. "This isn't healthy," Jamie said. "You know it isn't. I know you think about your sister a lot. I know you mourn her. But actually going to Idlewild—that's different, Fee."

"I know," Fiona said. "I know we've been over this. I know what my therapist used to say. I know it's been twenty years. I've tried not to obsess about this, I swear." She tried to keep the pleading from her voice, but it came out anyway. "Just listen to me, okay?"

"Okay," he replied. "Shoot."

She swallowed. "I came here and I parked by the side of the road. I sat here for"—she checked her watch—"thirty minutes. Thirty *minutes*, Jamie. Not a single car passed by.

Not one." By her calculations, she'd been here for forty-five minutes, but she'd been asleep for fifteen, so she didn't count those. "He could have parked here and done it. The field at Idlewild Hall is only ten minutes through the trees. He would have had plenty of time."

On the other end of the line, she heard Jamie breathe. They'd been together for a year now—a fact that still surprised her sometimes—and he knew better than to say the usual empty words. *It doesn't matter. This won't bring her back. He's already in prison. It was twenty years ago; you need to move on.* Instead, he said, "Old Barrons Road wasn't the same in 1994. The old drive-in was still open on the east side of the road. It didn't do much business by the nineties, but kids used to party there, especially around Halloween."

Fiona bit back the protest she could feel rising in her throat. Jamie was right. She swiveled and looked into the darkness across the road, to where the old drive-in used to be, now an abandoned lot. The big screen had been taken down long ago, the greasy popcorn stand razed, and now there was only a dirt clearing behind the trees, overgrown with weeds. She remembered begging her parents to take her and Deb to the drive-in as a kid, thinking with a kid's logic that it would be an exciting experience, a sensory wonder. She'd soon learned it was a fool's quest. Her intellectual parents would no sooner take them to the drive-in to see *Beverly Hills Cop II* than they would take a walk on the moon. Deb, three years older and wiser, had just shaken her head and shrugged at Fiona's disappointment. *What did you expect?* "There wouldn't have been many kids at the drive-in on a Thursday in November," she said.

"But there *were* kids there," Jamie said with the easy logic of someone whose life hadn't been ripped apart. "None of them remembered seeing Christopher's car. This was all covered in the investigation."

Fiona felt a pulse of exhaustion behind her eyes, countered by a spurt of jagged energy that wouldn't let her stay still. She turned and paced away from the hill and the lights of the gas station, toward the darkness past the hood of her car at the other end of Old Barrons Road. "Of course you think they covered everything," she said to Jamie, her voice coming out sharper than she intended. "You're a cop. You have to believe it. In your world, a girl gets murdered, and Vermont's greatest minds come together to solve the case and put the bad guys away." Her boots scuffed the gravel on the side of the road, and the wind pierced through the legs of her jeans. She pulled up the collar of her coat as a cold shudder moved through her, an icy draft blasting through the layers of her clothes.

Jamie wasn't rising to her bait, which was one of the things that drove her crazy about him. "Fiona, I *know* they covered everything because I've been through the file. More than once. As have you, against all the rules and regulations of my job. It's all there in the murder file. In black and white."

"She wasn't your sister," Fiona said.

He was quiet for a second, acknowledging that. "Tim Christopher was charged," he said. "He was tried and convicted of Deb's murder. He's spent the past twenty years in a maximum-security prison. And, Fee, you're still out there on Old Barrons Road at three o'clock in the morning."

The farther she walked, the darker it got. It was colder here, a strange pocket of air that made her hunch farther into her coat as her nose grew numb. "I need to know how he did it," she said. Her sister, age twenty, had been strangled and dumped in the middle of the former sports field on the abandoned grounds of Idlewild Hall in 1994, left lying on one side, her knees drawn up, her eyes open. Her shirt and bra had been ripped open, the fabric and elastic torn straight through. She'd last been seen in her college dorm thirty miles away. Her boyfriend, Tim Christopher, had spent twenty years in prison for the crime. He'd claimed he was innocent, and he still did.

Fiona had been seventeen. She didn't much like to think about how the murder had torn her family apart, how it had affected her life. It was easier to stand on the side of the road and obsess over how Christopher had dumped her sister's body, something that had never been fully understood, since no footprints had been found in the field or the woods, no tire tracks on the side of the road. The Idlewild property was surrounded by a fence, but it was decades old and mostly broken; he could have easily carried the body through one of the gaps. Assuming he came this way.

Jamie was right. Damn him and his cop brain, which her journalist brain was constantly at odds with. This was a detail that was rubbing her raw, keeping her wound bleeding, long after everyone else had tied their bandages and hobbled away. She should grab a crutch—alcohol or drugs were the convenient ones—and start hobbling with the rest of them. Still, she shivered and stared into the trees, thinking, *How the hell did he carry her through there without leaving footprints?*

The phone was still to her ear. She could hear Jamie there, waiting.

"You're judging me," she said to him.

"I'm not," he protested.

"I can hear it in how you breathe."

"Are you being serious?"

"I—" She heard the scuff of a footstep behind her, and froze.

"Fiona?" Jamie asked, as though he'd heard it through the phone.

"Ssshh," she said, the sound coming instinctively from her lips. She stopped still and cocked her head. She was in almost complete darkness now. Idlewild Hall, the former girls' boarding school, had been closed and abandoned since 1979, long before Deb died, the gates locked, the grounds overgrown. There were no lights here at the end of the road, at the gates of the old school. Nothing but the wind in the trees.

She stiffly turned on her heel. It had been distinct, a footstep against the gravel. If it was some creep coming from the woods, she had no weapon to defend herself with. She'd have to scream through the phone at Jamie and hope for the best.

She stared into the dark silence behind her, watched the last dying leaves shimmer on the inky trees.

"What the fuck?" Jamie barked. He never swore unless he was alarmed.

"Ssshh," she said to him again. "It's no one. It's nothing. I thought I heard something, that's all."

"Do I have to tell you," he said, "to get off of a dark, abandoned road in the middle of the night?"

"Have you ever thought that there's something creepy about Old Barrons Road?" she asked. "I mean, have you ever been *out* here? It's sort of uncanny. It's like there's something . . ."

"I can't take much more of this," Jamie said. "Get back in your car and drive home, or I'm coming to get you."

"I'll go, I'll go." Her hands were tingling, even the hand that was frozen to her phone, and she still had a jittery blast of adrenaline blowing down her spine. *That had been a footstep. A real one.* The hill was hidden through the trees from here, and she suddenly longed for the comforting sight of the fluorescent gas station lights. She took a step, then realized something. She stopped and turned around again, heading quickly for the gates of Idlewild Hall.

"I hope that sound is you walking toward your car," Jamie said darkly.

"There was a sign," Fiona said. "I saw it. It's posted on the gates. It wasn't there before." She got close enough to read the lettering in the dark. ANOTHER PROJECT BY MACMILLAN CONSTRUCTION, LTD. "Jamie, why is there a sign saying that Idlewild Hall is under construction?"

"Because it is," he replied. "As of next week. The property was sold two years ago, and the new owner is taking it over. It's going to be restored, from what I hear."

"Restored?" Fiona blinked at the sign, trying to take it in. "Restoring it into what?"

"Into a new school," he replied. "They're fixing it up and making it a boarding school again."

"They're *what?*"

"I didn't want to mention it, Fee. I know what that place means to you."

Fiona took a step back, still staring at the sign. *Restored*. Girls were going to be playing in the field where Deb's body had lain. They would build new buildings, tear down old ones, add a parking lot, maybe widen the road. All of this landscape that had been here for twenty years, the landscape she knew so well—the landscape of Deb's death—would be gone.

"Damn it," she said to Jamie as she turned and walked back toward her car. "I'll call you tomorrow. I'm going home."

chapter 2

Katie

Barrons, Vermont
October 1950

The first time Katie Winthrop had seen Idlewild Hall, she nearly cried. She'd been in the backseat of her father's Chevy, looking between Dad's gray-suited shoulder and Mom's crepe-bloused one, and when the big black gates loomed at the end of Old Barrons Road, she'd suddenly felt tears sting her eyes.

The gates were open, something she soon learned was rare. Dad had driven the car through the entrance and up the long dirt drive in silence, and she had stared at the building that rose up before them: the main hall, three stories high and stretching endlessly long, lined with peaked windows that looked like rows of teeth, broken only by the portico that signaled the front door. It was August, and the air was thick and hot, heavy with oncoming rain. As they drew closer, it looked uncannily like they were traveling into the jaws of the building, and Katie had swallowed hard, keeping straight and still as the hall grew larger and larger in the windshield.

Dad stopped the car, and for a moment there was no sound but the engine ticking. Idlewild Hall was dark, with no sign of life. Katie looked at her mother, but Mom's face was turned away, looking sightlessly out the passenger window, and even though Katie was so close she could see the makeup Mom had pressed onto her cheek with a little sponge, she did not speak.

I'm sorry, she'd suddenly wanted to say. *Please don't make me stay here. I can't do it. I'm so sorry . . .*

"I'll get your bags," Dad said.

That had been two years ago. Katie was used to Idlewild now—the long worn hallways that smelled like mildew and girls' sweat, the windows that let in icy drafts around the edges in winter, the wafts of wet, mulchy odor on the field hockey green no matter what the season, the uniforms that hadn't been changed since the school first opened in 1919.

Katie was the kind of girl other girls tended to obey easily: dark-haired, dominant, beautiful, a little aggressive, and unafraid. She wasn't popular, exactly, but she'd had to use her fists only twice, and both times she'd won easily. A good front, she knew, was most of the battle, and she'd used hers without mercy. It wasn't easy to survive in a boarding school full of throwaway girls, but after swallowing her tears in those first moments, Katie had mastered it.

She saw her parents twice a year, once in summer and once at Christmas, and she'd never told them she was sorry.

There were four girls per room in Clayton Hall, the
dormitory. You never knew whom you would get. One
of Katie's first roommates, a stringy-haired girl from
New Hampshire who claimed to be descended from a
real Salem witch, had the habit of humming relentlessly
as she read her Latin textbook, biting the side of her
thumbnail with such diligence that Katie had thought it
might be grounds for murder. After the Salem witch
left, she was replaced by a long-legged, springy-haired
girl whose name Katie had never remembered, and who
spent most of her nights curled up in her bunk, quietly
sobbing into her pillow until Charlotte Kankle, who was
massive and always angry, rolled out of her bunk and
told her, *Stop crying, for the love of Jesus Christ, or I promise you these other girls will hold you down while I give you
a bloody nose*. No one had contradicted her. The sobbing
girl had been quiet after that, and she'd left a few weeks
later.

Charlotte Kankle had since moved down the hall—
after she and Katie got into a fistfight, one of Katie's
victories—and now she had a set of roommates here in 3C
that, she had to admit, might not be a total failure.
Idlewild was the boarding school of last resort, where parents stashed their embarrassments, their failures, and their
recalcitrant girls. Hidden in the backwoods of Vermont, it
had only 120 students: illegitimate daughters, first wives'
daughters, servants' daughters, immigrant girls, girls who
misbehaved or couldn't learn. Most of them fought and
mistrusted one another, but in a backward way, Katie felt
these girls were the only ones who understood her. They

were the only ones who just shrugged in boredom when she told them how many times she'd run away from home.

She sat up in bed after curfew one night and rooted beneath her pillow for the pack of cigarettes she'd stashed there. It was October, and cold autumn rain spattered the single high window in the dorm room. She banged on the bunk above her. "CeCe."

"What is it?" CeCe was awake, of course. Katie had already known it from the sound of her breathing.

"I want to tell you a ghost story."

"Really?" There was a muffled sound as CeCe slid over on her bunk and looked over the edge, down at Katie. "Is it Mary Hand?"

"Oh, no," came a voice from the top bunk across the room. "Not another story about Mary Hand."

"Ssh, Roberta," CeCe said. "You'll wake Sonia."

"I'm awake," Sonia said from beneath her covers on the bunk below Roberta. When she was half-asleep, her French accent was more pronounced. "I cannot sleep with all of your talking."

Katie tapped a cigarette from the pack. All four girls in the room were fifteen years old—Idlewild had long ago grouped girls of the same age, since the older girls tended to bully the younger ones when they roomed to-gether. "Mary Hand is in my Latin textbook," she said. "Look."

She pulled the book—which was decades old and musty—from beneath her bed, along with a small flash-light. Flashlights were forbidden at Idlewild, a rule that every girl flouted without exception. Holding the flashlight steady, she quickly paged through the book until she came to the page she wanted. "See?" she said.

CeCe had climbed down from her bunk. She had the biggest breasts of any of the four of them, and she self-consciously brought a blanket down with her, pulling it over her shoulders. "Oh," she said as she stared at the page Katie had lit with the flashlight. "I have that in my grammar book. Something similar, at least."

"What is it?" Roberta was lured from her top bunk, her sleek calves poking from the hem of her outgrown nightgown, her brownish blond hair tied into a braid down her back. She landed on the floor without a sound and peered over CeCe's shoulder. Katie heard her soft intake of breath.

Along the edge of the page, in the narrow band of white space, was a message in pencil.

Saw Mary Hand through the window of 1G, Clayton Hall.
She was walking away over the field.
Wednesday, August 7, 1941. Jenny Baird.

Looking at it gave Katie a blurry, queasy feeling, a quick pulse of fear that she refused to show. Everyone knew of Mary Hand, but somehow these penciled letters made her more real. "It isn't a joke, is it," she said—a statement, not a question.

"No, it's not a joke," CeCe said. "The one in my grammar book said *Toilet, third floor, end of west hall, I saw Mary there.* That one was from 1939."

"It's a message." This was Sonia, who had gotten up and was looking over Roberta's shoulder. She shrugged and backed away again. "I've seen them, too. They have never changed the textbooks here, I think."

Katie flipped through the musty pages of the Latin textbook. Its front page listed the copyright as 1919, the year Idlewild opened. She tried to picture the school as it had been then: the building brand-new, the uniforms brand-new, the textbooks brand-new. Now, in 1950, Idlewild was a time machine, a place that had no inkling of atomic bombs or *Texaco Star Theatre* on television. It made sense, in a twisted way, that Idlewild girls would pass wisdom down to one another in the margins of their textbooks, alongside the lists of American Revolution battles and the chemical makeup of iodine. The teachers never looked in these books, and they were never thrown away. If you wanted to warn a future girl about Mary Hand, the books were the best place to do it.

Through the window of 1G, Clayton Hall. Katie struck a match and lit her cigarette.

"You shouldn't," Roberta said halfheartedly. "Susan Brady will smell it, and then you'll catch hell."

"Susan Brady is asleep," Katie replied. Susan was the dorm monitor for Floor Three, and she took her job very seriously, which meant that no one liked her. Katie switched off the flashlight and the four of them sat in the dark. Roberta tossed a pillow on the floor and sat with her back against the narrow dresser. Sonia quietly moved to the window and cracked it open, letting the smoke escape.

"So," CeCe said to Katie. "Have you seen her?"

Katie shrugged. She wished she'd never brought it up now; she knew these girls, but not well enough yet to trust them. Looking at the penciled messages in her Latin book again had unsettled her. The fact was, she wasn't entirely sure what had happened to her, and she wished that it had been as simple as seeing Idlewild's ghost in the bathroom. It had seemed real at the time, but to put it into words now felt impossible. She swallowed and deflected the subject. "Do you think she was really a student here?" she asked the other girls.

"I heard she was," Roberta said. "Mary Van Woorten, on the field hockey team, says that Mary Hand died when she was locked out of the school on a winter night and lost her way."

"It must have been years ago." CeCe had crawled onto the bunk next to Katie and propped up the pillows against the headboard. "I heard she knocks on the windows at night, trying to get in. That she begs girls to come outside and follow her, but if you do it, you die."

CeCe was the roommate Katie had had the longest, and the one she knew the most about, because CeCe was an open book. She was the illegitimate daughter of a rich banker, sired on one of the housemaids and packed off to one boarding school or another for most of her life. CeCe, amazingly, held no animosity toward her father, and was close to her mother, who was now a housekeeper for a family in Boston. She'd told Katie all of this on their first meeting, as she'd hung up her Idlewild crested jacket and put away her hockey stick.

"You can sometimes hear her singing in the field

when the wind is in the trees," Roberta added. "A lullaby or something."

Katie hadn't heard that one. "You can hear her?"

Roberta shrugged. She had been at Idlewild for only a few months, whereas the other girls had been here for at least a year, and Sonia for three. Roberta was smart, a natural athlete, though she didn't talk much. No one knew anything about her home life. Katie couldn't figure out what she was doing here of all places, but from the hooded look that she often saw in Roberta's eyes—that look of retreat, of watching the world as if from behind a wall, that was common to a lot of Idlewild girls—she guessed there was a reason. "I've never heard her myself, and I'm at practice four times a week." Roberta turned to Sonia, as she often did. "Sonia, what do you think?"

If CeCe was the easiest to understand, Sonia was the hardest. Pale, thin, quiet, flitting in and out of the crowds and the complicated social cliques, she seemed apart from everything, even for an Idlewild girl. She was an immigrant from France, and in the aftermath of the war, where so many of the girls had lost a father or a brother or had men come home ragged from POW camps, no one asked her about it. She'd been at Idlewild the longest of any of them.

Sonia seemed completely self-contained, as if whatever was happening inside her own head was sufficient for her. For some reason Roberta, who was swift and fit and graceful, had become smitten with Sonia, and could often be seen by her side. They were so easy together, it made Katie want that, too. Katie had never been easy with anyone. She'd always been the girl with admirers, not friends.

Sonia caught Katie's eyes briefly and shrugged, the gesture cool and European even in her simple white nightgown. "I have no use for ghosts," she said in her sweet, melodious accent, "though like everyone else, I've heard she wears a black dress and a veil, which seems a strange outfit if you are outside in the snow." Her gaze, resting on Katie in the darkened gloom, missed nothing. "You saw something. Did you not?"

Katie glanced at the cigarette, forgotten in her fingers. "I heard her," she said. She tamped out the smoke against the brass back of the sophomore achievement medal someone had left behind, and ground the butt with her thumb.

"*Heard* her?" CeCe asked.

Katie took a breath. Talking about Mary Hand felt like speaking of a family secret somehow. It was one thing to tell ghost stories in the dark, and another when you opened your locker before gym class and felt something push it closed again. There were always small things, like a feeling of being watched, or a cold patch in a hallway, that you were never quite sure you'd experienced, and you felt stupid bringing up. But this had been different, and Katie had the urge to speak it out loud. "It was in the common, on the path that goes past the dining hall."

The girls nodded. Idlewild's main buildings were arranged in a U-shaped square around a common, dotted with unkempt trees and weedy flagstoned paths. "That section scares me," CeCe said. "The one by the garden."

It scared Katie, too. No one liked the garden, even though the curriculum included Weekly Gardening, when they had to reluctantly dig through its damp, rotten-smelling earth. Even the teachers gave the garden a wide berth. "I was sneaking a cigarette after dinner, and I left the path so Mrs. Peabody wouldn't see me—you know she smokes her own cigarettes out there, even though she's not supposed to. I was beneath the big maple tree, and I just felt something. Someone was there."

CeCe was leaning forward, rapt. "But you didn't see anything?"

"There was a voice," Katie said. "It was—I didn't imagine it. It was right there next to me, as if someone was standing there. I heard it so clearly."

She could still recall that moment beneath the maple tree, standing on a bed of old maple keys, her cigarette dropping to the ground, the hair standing up on the back of her neck when a voice somewhere behind her right ear had spoken. Idlewild was an old place, and the fear here was old fear. Katie had thought she understood fear until that moment, but when the voice had spoken, she'd understood fear that was older and bigger than she could imagine.

"Well?" Roberta prompted. "What did she *say*?"

Katie cleared her throat. "'Hold still,'" she said.

They were all quiet for a moment.

"Oh, my God," CeCe said softly.

Strangely, it was Sonia that Katie looked at. Sonia was sitting on the floor, against the wall beneath the window, her thin legs drawn up, her knees to her chest. She was

very still, bathed in shadow, and Katie couldn't tell if Sonia's eyes were on her or not. Far off, a door slammed,
and something tapped, like dripping water, in the ceiling.

"Why?" Sonia asked her, the French lilt soft. "Why did
she say that to you?"

Katie shrugged hard, the muscles wrenching in her
shoulders, even though it was dark and the other girls
couldn't see it. "I don't know," she snapped, her voice
growing sharp before she tempered it. "It was just a voice
I heard. That's all I know."

A lie, a lie. But how could some old ghost even know?
Hold still. She couldn't talk about that. Not to anyone. Not yet.

"What did you do?" Roberta asked.

This was an easier question. "I ran like hell."

Only CeCe, leaning against the headboard, gave a
quick *tut* at the language. She'd been raised prim for an
illegitimate girl. "I would have run, too," she conceded.
"I saw a little boy once. At the Ellesmeres'." The Ellesmeres were her rich father's family, though CeCe hadn't
been given the family name. "I was playing in the back
courtyard one day while Mother worked. I looked up and
there was a boy in an upper window of the house, watching me. I waved, but he didn't wave back. When I asked
my mother about it, about why the boy wasn't allowed
outside to play, she got the strangest look on her face. She
told me I'd been seeing things, and that I should never
say anything about that boy again, especially in front of
the Ellesmeres. I never did see him again. I always wondered who he was."

"My grandmother used to tell me about the ghost in her attic," Roberta said. "It moved all the furniture around up there and made a racket. She said there were nights she'd lie in bed listening to trunks and dressers being dragged across the floor. Mum always said she was just an old lady looking for attention, but one summer I spent two weeks at my grandmother's house, and I heard it. It was just like she'd said—furniture being dragged across the floor, and the sound of the old brass floor lamp being picked up and put down, over and over. The next morning I asked her if it was Granddad's ghost doing it, and she only looked at me and said, 'No, dear. It's something much worse.'" She paused. "I never went back there. She died at Christmas that year, and Mum sold the house."

"What about you, Sonia?" CeCe asked. "Did you ever see a ghost?"

Sonia unfolded her thin legs and stood, then gripped the window and pulled it shut. The draft of cold air from outside ceased, but still Katie shivered.

"The dead are dead," she said. "I have no use for ghosts."

Katie watched her silhouette in the near darkness. It had sounded dismissive, but Sonia hadn't said she didn't believe in ghosts. She hadn't said she'd never seen one. She hadn't said they weren't real.

She knew, just as they all did.

The rain pelted the window again. *Hold still,* the voice in Katie's head said again. *Hold still.* She hugged herself tightly and closed her eyes.

chapter 3

Barrons, Vermont
November 2014

"Jonas," Fiona said the next morning as she walked into the cramped offices of *Lively Vermont*. "Did you know that Idlewild Hall is being restored?"

The main room was empty, but Jonas's door was ajar, and she knew he was in there. He always was. She wove past the mismatched desks and the cardboard boxes that littered the main room and headed toward *Lively Vermont*'s only private office, the lair of the magazine's owner and editor in chief.

"Is that you, Fiona Sheridan?" came a voice from inside. "I haven't seen you in days."

She reached the door and looked in at him. He was bent over his desk, staring closely at a photograph print, the computer blank and ignored behind him. Typical Jonas. "I guess it's a good thing I don't work for you, then," she said.

He looked up. "You're freelance. It counts."

Fiona felt herself smiling. "Not when it comes to health insurance."

He gave her a poker face, but she knew he was teasing. Jonas Cooper was fiftyish, his gray-brown hair swept back from his forehead in neat, impressive wings, his eyebrows dark slashes over his intense eyes. He wore a red-and-black-checkered shirt open at the throat over his waffle-weave undershirt. He and his wife had bought *Lively Vermont* over a decade ago, and since their divorce last year he'd been trying to keep it going. "Do you have a story for me?" he asked.

"No," Fiona replied. "I gave you one on Friday. You told me that blew the budget."

"For this issue, yes. But there's always another one."

For now, she thought. *Lively Vermont* was just one of several local magazines she wrote for, and it was struggling just as hard as the rest of them. "What is that?" she asked, gesturing to the photo.

"Local photographer," he replied. He glanced down at the picture again and shrugged. "She lives in East Charlotte. The work isn't bad. I might do a feature, if I can find a writer."

"No. Absolutely not."

"Why not?" Jonas leaned back in his vintage office chair and tossed the photograph onto a pile.

"Because I just did a story on artisanal cheese. That's my pound of flesh for this month."

Jonas gave her a look that said, *I know you're lying.* She was. Fiona excelled at writing fluff—she had no pretensions to creating great journalism. She didn't want to do an article about a photographer because photographers always asked her about her father. "Consider it," he said. "If this pans out, I might dig some money out of the sofa to pay for it. Now, what is it you were shouting about when you came in?"

Fiona felt her heart speed up, as if she were about to ask about something forbidden. "Idlewild Hall," she said. "I hear it's about to be restored."

Jonas looked wary, then nodded. "The new owner."

"Who is he?"

"She. Margaret Eden. Wife of the late investment whiz Joseph Eden. Does the name ring a bell?"

It did—something to do with the economic meltdown in 2008. She'd seen his face in the news. "So he bought the property?"

"No. He died, and the widow did. She's come up from New York to oversee the restoration, I think."

Fiona was stung, somehow, that Jonas knew. "The Christophers owned that land for decades," she said. "Ever since the school closed in 1979. No one told me it was sold. Or that it was going to be restored."

A look of sympathy came over Jonas's expression. "It wasn't my place," he said softly. "And the restoration has been nothing but talk until now. I didn't think anyone would actually go ahead with it."

"Well, it's going ahead. I saw the construction signs on the fences when I was there last night."

Jonas was quiet. He hadn't been living here in 1994— he'd moved here only when he bought the magazine—but he knew about Deb's murder, about her body dumped at Idlewild, about Tim Christopher going to prison for the crime. Everyone knew about it. There was no privacy in Barrons, not for the family of the victim of the town's most famous murder. Even Jonas knew there was something unhealthy about Fiona visiting the Idlewild grounds.

"Don't say it," Fiona warned him. "Just don't."

He held up his hands. "Hey, it's your business. I just run a magazine."

She stared at him for a minute as the familiar jittery energy from last night ran through her blood. "So, do you really want a story from me?" she asked. "A feature?"

"Why do I have the feeling I'll be sorry if I say yes?"

"Idlewild," she said. "That's the story I'll write. I'll interview Margaret Eden. I'll look at the plans for the school. I'll tour the property, get photographs, everything."

"Oh, Jesus," Jonas said. "I don't know, Fiona."

"It's local color," she said, feeling her cheeks heat up. "A new school, a revival, local jobs. No one else is covering it. It beats a feature about a photographer. Isn't that what you want for *Lively Vermont?*" She looked straight into his eyes. "I'm fine with it, Jonas," she said. "I swear, I'm fine."

To her relief, she saw the wariness leave his eyes and his calculating editor's side take over. He and his ex-wife, Emily, had bought *Lively Vermont* for its cachet as an independent Yankee think tank, but under Emily's direction they'd turned it into a soft-toothed lifestyle magazine, the kind that ran ads for eighty-dollar candles and five-thousand-dollar handmade quilts. Jonas had always been unhappy with that—he'd wanted more, which was why he continued to hire Fiona, hoping she'd show the same journalistic chops as her famous father. "I admit it's interesting, but I don't have the budget for a piece that big."

"I'll write it on spec," she said. "I'll take my own pictures. You don't even have to buy the piece. Just let me say I'm working for *Lively* when I call up Margaret Eden. It'll get my foot in the door faster."

"I see. And what do I get for letting you use the name of my magazine?"

"I'll give you first refusal on it." She waited as he thought it over, suddenly impatient. "Come on, Jonas. You know it's a good deal."

He looked like he wanted to be convinced, but he said, "You're about to ask for something else, aren't you?"

"I am," Fiona said, letting out a breath. "I want to start with history. Can you let me into the archives?"

Lively Vermont had first published off a photocopier in 1969, and every issue was kept in a bank of scarred wooden file cabinets that had followed the magazine through every office move. They now sat against the back wall of the office, where someone had left a plate with the stale remains of a doughnut atop them, alongside an ice-cold coffee cup.

"You could go to the library, you know," Jonas offered skeptically as Fiona pulled open the oldest drawers. "They'd have more about Idlewild than we do."

"Everyone at the library knows who I am," Fiona said. The files had a musty smell that made her briefly happy. "If they know what I'm researching, it won't be a secret anymore."

It was true. Malcolm Sheridan, the famous journalist, was a local legend in Barrons, and Fiona, his one remaining daughter, had distinctive red hair. The Barrons library staff was dedicated but extremely small, and because of Fiona's many research visits over the years, they all knew who she was.

"Okay," Jonas said. "And why is this a secret, exactly? Don't tell me there's high competition for this story."

She turned and gave him a look over her shoulder.

He gave her a look back. "I've never met a journalist who's afraid of librarians."

"You've never met a journalist with my family history," Fiona replied, trying to make it sound casual, easy. "I hate gossip. I can find other sources, especially online."

There was a pause of silence behind her as she pulled out the files from 1969 to 1979. "If you're looking for more sources, your father would have them," he said. "You know that."

"I know." Fiona banged the drawer shut. "I'm due to visit him soon anyway. I'll ask him about it."

"Fine. Just bring my files back intact. And, Fiona . . ." Jonas shrugged. "Like I say, it's your business, but there are going to be references to the Christophers in there. It's unavoidable."

He was right. Before their son had gone to prison for murder, the Christophers had been the richest and the most prominent family in Barrons. It was very likely there was something about Tim's parents in the file she was holding. But she'd cross that bridge when she had to. "Like I said," she told Jonas, "I'm fine."

Jonas looked as if he was considering saying something else, but all he said was "Say hello to your father for me."

"I will." Malcolm Sheridan was Jonas's journalistic idol, and it was that admiration that kept her employed at *Lively Vermont*. "I'll be in touch," she said, and she waved the files gratefully at him as she turned for the door.

It was a blustery gray day, the sun fighting to be seen from behind the clouds. The leaves had turned from vibrant colors to faded brown and had mostly left the trees. A handful of maple leaves, blown by the wind, had landed on Fiona's windshield, and she brushed them off as she got in her car.

She glimpsed her face briefly in the rearview mirror as she started the car—red hair, hazel eyes, pale skin, the beginnings of crow's-feet testifying to her thirty-seven years—and looked away again. She should probably bother with makeup one of these days. She should probably expand her wardrobe beyond jeans, boots, and a zip-up quilted jacket, too, at least until full winter hit. She tossed the files on the passenger seat and headed for downtown Barrons.

Barrons consisted of some well-preserved historic buildings in the center of town, used to draw the few tourists who came through, surrounded by a hardscrabble population that hoped those same tourists didn't notice their falling-down porches and the piles of firewood in their driveways. Fiona drove past the clapboard library and, half a mile up, a spray-painted sign advertising fall pumpkins, though Halloween was weeks ago. In the square at the center of town, she passed the old city hall and continued down New Street to the police station.

She parked in the station's small lot and picked up the files from the passenger seat. There was no one around, no movement in the squat square building, which had been built sometime in the 1970s, when Barrons finally became big enough to warrant a police force. Two picnic tables sat beneath the old oak trees in front of the station, and Fiona sat on one of the tables, swinging her feet onto the seat and pulling out her phone. She texted Jamie: *Are you in there?*

He made her wait five minutes. She had begun leafing through the first file when he texted back: *I'm coming out.*

Fiona tucked the phone back in her pocket and went back to the files. He took his time, making his point—he was still mad about last night—but eventually the front door of the station swung open and Jamie emerged, shrugging on a late-fall parka over his uniform.

Fiona glanced up and watched him. It was hard not to, she had to admit. Jamie Creel of the Barrons police, son and grandson of Vermont police chiefs, had dirty blond hair, dark blue eyes, and a scruff of beard on his jaw that grew in honey gold. He was younger than Fiona—twenty-nine to her thirty-seven—and he moved with easy grace as he huddled into his coat against the wind.

"Were you busy?" Fiona asked as he came closer.

He shrugged. "I was typing reports." He had left off his hat, and the wind tried to tousle his hair. He stopped a few feet from her picnic table, his hands in his pockets and his legs apart, as if braced.

"I came to apologize," she said.

He raised his eyebrows. "For what?"

"For freaking you out last night. For leaving."

His eyes narrowed. "You're not actually sorry," he observed.

"Still, I'm apologizing," she said, holding his gaze. "I mean it. Okay?"

He didn't answer, but gestured to the files in her lap, where she held a hand to them to keep them from blowing away. "What's that?"

"Files from *Lively Vermont*. I'm looking for a history of Idlewild Hall."

Jamie's posture relaxed and he scrubbed a hand over his face. "This has to do with last night, doesn't it? Fiona, come on."

"This is good," she protested. "I'm going to do a story."

"About Idlewild?"

"About the restoration, the new school." She watched his face. "It's a good idea."

"Maybe for someone, yes. For you?"

"Don't worry—I'm a big girl. I can handle it."

"You couldn't handle it last night," he said. "You were a basket case."

It *had* been sort of a strange episode, but she didn't regret it. That trip to Old Barrons Road had shaken something loose. Idlewild had always loomed silently in the back of her mind, a dark part of her mental landscape. She'd done her best not to talk about it for twenty years, but talking about it out loud now was like bloodletting, painful and somehow necessary at the same time. "I'm better today," she said, and she patted the table next to her. "Come sit down."

He sighed, but he stepped toward the table. Fiona watched with the surreal feeling she still got sometimes when she looked at Jamie, even now. A year ago she'd had a bad night—lonely, wallowing in self-pity and grief for Deb—and found herself at a local bar, drinking alone. Jamie had pulled up the stool next to her—handsome, muscled, glorious in a jaded way, a guy who looked like he'd been a college athlete before something had made him go as quiet and wary as a wild animal. Fiona had put down her drink and looked at him, expecting a line, waiting for it, but Jamie had taken his time. He'd sipped his beer thoughtfully, then put it down on the bar. *Hi*, he'd said.

There was more, but that was all, really—just *hi*. Two hours later they'd ended up in his bed, which had surprised her but somehow fit her mood. She'd assumed it was a one-night stand, but he'd asked for her number. When he called her, she'd swallowed her surprise and said yes. And when he'd called her again, she'd said yes again.

It didn't make sense. Cops and journalists were natural enemies; they should never have mixed. And in many ways, they didn't. Jamie didn't introduce Fiona to his colleagues or take her to any of their social functions. She never went inside the station when she wanted to see him during work hours, waiting for him outside instead. He had introduced her to his parents exactly once, a chilly conversation that was over in minutes. On her part, Fiona had brought Jamie to meet Malcolm, but only because Malcolm had insisted. He'd been worried when he heard his daughter was dating a cop, even though he never intruded in her love life. The meeting had been awkward, and she still had no idea what the two men had made of each other.

And yet Jamie's job was part of the reason she liked him, as was the fact that he'd been born in Barrons and had it in his blood. With every relationship, she'd had the hurdle of explaining her past, explaining Deb, rehashing what had happened and why. Most men tried to be understanding, but Deb was always *there*, a barricade that Fiona couldn't quite get past. She had never needed to explain with Jamie: He knew who she was when he approached her in that bar; his father had been police chief when Deb was murdered. She'd never had to tell him anything because he already knew.

So, despite the difficulties, it was easy with Jamie. Easy in a way Fiona was prepared to sacrifice for. He was smart, quietly funny. What he saw in her, she was less sure of, and she didn't ask; maybe it was the sex—which was particularly good—or companionship. All she knew was that she'd rather amputate her own arm with a rusty handsaw than have the *where are we going?* conversation.

Now he sat next to her on the picnic table and folded

his long legs. "You want something else," he said matter-of-factly. "Go ahead."

"The Idlewild property," she admitted. There was no point in prevaricating. "What do you know about it?"

"I only know what's common knowledge."

"Liar. You know everything. Start from the beginning."

Jamie's father and grandfather had both been chiefs of police in Barrons. The Creels had been a vital part of this area for decades, and they knew every family in Barrons, from the richest on down. In a way that felt alien to Fiona, Jamie was dedicated to this place, and he had an intelligent brain that never forgot a detail when it came to his town. So she waited for him to call up the information from somewhere in his circuitry, and then he started talking.

"Let's see. Idlewild was built just after World War One, I think, for girls who were veterans' orphans. It passed into different hands over the years, but enrollment went lower and lower. The Christopher family bought it when the school closed in 1979." He didn't glance at her when he spoke the family name of her sister's killer, so she knew he was absorbed in the history. "The Christophers were buying land like crazy around that time," he continued. "They planned to be real estate barons, I guess. Some of the properties they bought were profitable, and others were not. Idlewild was definitely in category two."

"Why?" Fiona asked. She knew some of this, but she let him talk.

Jamie shrugged. "Everything they tried fell through. Partners backed out; funding disappeared. They couldn't get anyone on board. The school has always been rumored to be haunted, which sounds silly when you're talking about a development deal, but I think the Christophers miscalculated. The fact is, Idlewild has always scared the people here. No one really wants to go near the place. The Christophers had other deals that were making them rich—or richer, I should say—so they eventually focused on those and let Idlewild sit as a white elephant."

Fiona remembered Idlewild from when she was growing up—kids telling stories at sleepovers, teenagers daring one another to go onto the property after dark. She'd never really believed in ghosts, and she didn't think any of the other kids did, either, but there was no doubt the abandoned remains of Idlewild Hall were unsettling. A crumbling portico, overgrown vines over the windows, that kind of thing. But for all its spookiness, it was just another place until the murder. "And then Deb died," she prompted Jamie.

"That was the end of the Christophers here," Jamie said. "Their years as the most prominent family in Barrons were over. After Tim was arrested, his father, Henry, started pulling up stakes almost right away. By the time Tim was convicted at trial, the family had sold off what they could and moved to Colorado. They're still there, as far as I know."

Fiona stared down at her hands. Deb had been so excited when she'd started dating Tim Christopher; he was tall, good-looking, from a rich and important family. Deb had never been happy as the child of middle-class intellectuals. "But they didn't sell Idlewild."

"They couldn't. The buildings are so run-down they're nearly worthless, and the land isn't worth much, either. The crash in 2008 didn't help. The family must have been pretty happy when this new buyer came along."

"Margaret Eden," Fiona said. "Who is she?"

"That I don't know." Jamie gave her an apologetic smile. "She's not local—she's from New York. I hear she's an elderly widow with a lot of money, that's all."

"I want to meet her."

"Dad says she's a recluse. Her son handles all of her business."

"Then I want to meet him."

"Fee." Jamie turned toward her, twisting his body so he could look at her. His knee brushed hers, and she tried not to jump. "Think about what you're doing," he said. "That's all I ask. Just think about it."

"I have thought about it," Fiona said. She held up one of the files. "What I want to know is, why restore Idlewild Hall now? There can't be any money in it."

"People still send their kids to boarding school," Jamie said.

"Around here? You know as well as I do what the average salary is in this part of the state. Who is sending their kid to an expensive boarding school, one that has already required millions to rebuild? Margaret Eden can't be financing everything by herself. If she has investors, who are they? How do they expect to make money?" *Money talks* had always been one of her father's tenets as a journalist. *Someone, somewhere, is almost always making money.*

"You think there's something else going on."

"I think that the place is a money pit. Maybe she's batty, or she's being taken advantage of. Don't you at least find it weird?"

He stepped off the table and stood facing her again. "All right," he admitted. "It's weird. And it's probably a good story. And no one has covered it." He looked at her triumphant expression and shook his head, but his features had relaxed, and she knew she'd convinced him. "Let me know how it goes when you track down Anthony Eden."

"Anthony is the son?"

"Yes. They live in one of the town houses on Mitchell Place—the big one on the corner. You could have found all of this stuff out yourself, you know."

"I know," Fiona replied, and she felt herself smiling at him. "But it's more fun to get information from you."

"I have to go back inside," he said. He caught her gaze, and there it was, the arc of electricity between them that never seemed to quit. Fiona felt the urge to touch him, but whoever was watching them from the station windows—and there was almost certainly someone—would never let him live it down.

"I'll call you later," she managed.

"Maybe," he replied. He took a step back, then turned and walked toward the station, giving her a wave over his shoulder. As he put his hand on the door, he stopped. "Tell your father," he said. "Don't let him find out from someone else." And then he was gone.

chapter 4

Roberta

Barrons, Vermont
October 1950

It was raining, a fine, cold mist descending over the hockey pitch, but still the girls played. At seven o'clock in the morning the sun was barely rising and the light was watery and gray, but the girls put on their thick uniforms and laced up their leather sneakers, then lined up beneath the eave outside the locker room with sticks in hand, waiting for the signal.

This was Roberta's favorite time. The quiet, the chill of the leftover night air, the cold seeping into her legs and her feet, waking her up. The trees around the edges of the pitch were black against the sky, and from one of them three ravens took flight, rising stark and lonely against the clouds. Their calls echoed faintly back to the girls as they stood, their breaths puffing, one girl coughing into her hand the only answering sound.

Ginny Smith and Brenda Averton were the team

captains, and they conferred quietly just outside the eave, the rain gathering in drops in Ginny's frizzy hair. Roberta was good enough to be team captain—she was a better field hockey player than either Ginny or Brenda—but she had been at Idlewild for only a few months, and neither Ginny nor Brenda was budging. Roberta didn't mind—all she wanted, really, was to play.

"Team Seven," Ginny said, turning to the girls, waving an arm, and trotting to one end of the hockey pitch.

"Team Nine," Brenda echoed, leading off the other half of the girls.

There weren't nine field hockey teams at Idlewild; the numbers came from the archaic team schedule, written in a pencil schematic and pinned to the wall of the locker room by some long-ago team captain, the graphite fading after years of display. Roberta was Team Nine, and she trotted after the other girls, stick in hand, as Brenda, her thick legs making an audible chafing sound beneath her hockey skirt, shouted strategy at them.

Then, finally, she got to run.

These were the elite field hockey players at Idlewild— the girls who chose the game as their class elective, the one part of the curriculum that was not mandatory. Twenty-two girls, no alternates, each with a stick except for the goalies. Though they'd seemed half-asleep a minute ago, as soon as the game began, they ran with teenage vigor, following the play of the ball back and forth over the field, circling, hemming, cutting one another off. There was no real reward for the winning team, no league that Idlewild could play in, no other schools to beat. Idlewild was an island on its own, just as it was in everything else, so the girls only played one another. Yet they still did it with all the energy of a team aiming for a championship.

This was where Roberta's mind stopped, where it all went away and she was just inside her body, every part of her moving in sync. There were no chattering girls on the hockey pitch, no cliques or alliances, no gossip or lies. The girls played in near silence in the gloom, their breath huffing, their expressions intent. She stopped feeling homesick, remembering her bedroom, its view out the window down their neat, tidy street, the quilt on her bed that her grandmother had sewn, the jewelry box on her dresser that her mother had given her as a thirteenth-birthday present. She hadn't had the heart to bring the jewelry box with her to Idlewild, where it could get stolen by the other girls, strangers who could put their hands all over her private things in their shared room.

Pat Carriveaux passed her the ball, and Roberta quickly handled it down the field, dodging girls coming at her right and left, her shoes squeaking and squelching in the grass. Her hair in its braid was soaked, the rain running down her neck into her collar, but the cool felt good on her heated skin. She circled the goal, but Cindy Benshaw made a fast move, leaning in to steal the ball nearly from the end of her stick, and Roberta jerked back to avoid tangling with her. Cindy ran with the ball, and Roberta steadied herself and ran after her.

Now she was flying, her body fully warm, barely feeling her feet as they hit the ground, the breath raw and painful in her lungs. She was unstoppable. She no longer pictured the face of her uncle, Van, her father's brother, who had come to live with them last year after his wife left him and he lost his job. Uncle Van, who had fought on the beaches of Normandy and now could not sleep or work, who carried a terrible scar down the side of his neck that he did not talk about, whose big, calloused hands always seemed lethal, even when they were curled in his lap as he listened to the radio hour after hour. She did not think about how she had opened the door to the garage one day and found Uncle Van sitting there, alone, hunched over in his chair, how she had seen—

The birds called overhead, and a spray of water hit Roberta's face, mixing with the sweat rolling down her temples. Her body was burning, the sensation pure pleasure. She never wanted to stop.

She had screamed that day, after she opened the garage door, and then she hadn't spoken again. For days, and then weeks, and then months. She would open her mouth and her thoughts would shut down, a curious blankness overtaking her, wiping the words clean from her mind. Her concerned parents had taken her to a doctor at first, wondering if something was physically wrong. Then they'd taken her to another doctor, and finally—to their burning shame—to a psychiatrist. Roberta had sat through it all in numb silence. She knew that everyone wanted her to be her old self again, to do something, to *say something*, but all Roberta saw was the garage door opening, over and over again, and the blankness. She couldn't explain to all of them that her words had left her and she had nothing to say.

And so she'd come to Idlewild. Her parents didn't know what to do with a stubborn teenage girl who wouldn't speak, except get her out of the house. Roberta was silent for her first week at Idlewild, too, and then one day a teacher asked her a question and she answered it, her voice as rusty as an old bucket in a well. Her first words in months, spoken at this horrible boarding school that every girl hated so much.

It had felt miraculous, saying those words, and yet it had felt natural, too. She had seen the garage door in her head less and less. And on the hockey field the garage door disappeared entirely and the quiet was the peaceful kind as her body took over.

Brenda whistled through her teeth and called a break when the first half of the game ended, and the girls began to leave the field. Roberta dropped her stick for a moment and leaned down, her hands on her knees, catching her breath as the other girls trotted past her. Something caught the corner of her eye, a swish of fabric, and she turned her head, expecting to see another girl holding back as she was, but there was nothing there. She turned back and stared at the ground, panting. Her roommates were probably getting up now, shuffling with the other girls down the hall to the communal bathroom, bumping into one another as they dressed for class.

Roberta could talk when she was with her roommates. She'd grown used to them, had come to depend on their constant closeness, their little annoyances. She could picture them clearly now: Katie's sultry beauty and *I don't care* attitude, CeCe's softer physique and trusting kindness, bone-thin Sonia's toughness, which hid something damaged underneath. She could talk to these girls, in this place, yet when her mother had come to visit—alone, without Dad—Roberta had been tongue-tied and awkward, forcing her words again. *Now is not a good time to come home,* her mother had said.

The movement came in the corner of her eye again, and now she straightened and turned. There was still nothing there. Roberta swiped at her forehead and temple, half-heartedly thinking that a strand of hair had gotten loose, though the movement had not looked like hair at all. It had looked like the swish of a skirt, moving as a girl walked past. She'd even thought she'd heard a footstep, though that wasn't possible. The other players had all left the field.

She turned to look at the huddle of girls milling beneath the eave to get out of the rain. Ginny gave her a narrow-eyed look, but didn't outright command Roberta to get moving. Roberta felt suddenly rooted in place, despite the rain soaking her, despite her wet feet through the leather shoes, despite the sweat cooling uncomfortably beneath her wool uniform. Something was moving on the field—something she couldn't quite see. And Ginny, looking straight at her, didn't see it.

There came a sound behind her, a quick, furtive footstep, and then an echo of a voice came from somewhere in the trees. Singing.

Oh, maybe tonight I'll hold her tight, when the moonbeams shine . . .

The sweat on Roberta's temples turned hot, and her arms jerked. She turned again, a full circle, but saw only the empty, rainy field. Ginny had turned away, and all the other girls stood quietly gossiping and catching their breath, their backs to her.

Oh, maybe tonight I'll hold her tight . . .

Roberta made her legs move. They creaked and shuddered like rusty old machine parts now, but she took one step, and then another. She knew that song. It was one of the songs they played on KPLI, on the *Starshine Soap GI Afternoon*, the show Uncle Van had listened to every day that played music from the war. It was called "My Dreams Are Getting Better All the Time," and it had been playing on the radio that day, its sound echoing off the bare walls and the concrete floor, when she had opened the garage door.

. . . when the moonbeams shine . . .

It wasn't a radio, or a record playing. It was a voice, coming from the trees—no, from the other end of the pitch—a snippet of sound just barely heard before it blew off in the wind. Roberta began to jog toward the others, fear jolting down her spine. She kept her eyes on the line of sweater-clad backs, huddled out of the rain, as her pace picked up and her legs moved faster.

Uncle Van. Sitting on a chair in the garage, bent forward, the gun pressed to his sweating skin, that pretty song playing, Uncle Van weeping, weeping . . .

She felt her words disappear, the blankness rising.

Away. Just get away. Don't think about it—just run . . .

Ginny turned and looked at her again as Roberta entered the damp, woolly crowd of girls, inhaling the miasma of rain and damp sweat. "What took you so long?" she snapped.

Roberta shook her head, numb. She remembered Mary Van Woorten's story about Mary Hand haunting the hockey field, singing lullabies in the trees. Mary Van Woorten was standing a few feet away, unaware, her cheeks red with cold, her blond hair tied back in a neat ponytail, shifting from foot to foot like a racehorse waiting for a signal. Lullabies, she'd said, not popular songs.

But Mary had sung a popular song this time. One just for her.

Roberta clutched her stick, crossed her arms over the front of her sweater, and moved in closer to the rest of the girls, seeking warmth. She thought of her roommates again, their familiar faces, their voices, their bickering laughter. And then she made the words come out.

"It's nothing," she said to Ginny. "Nothing at all."

chapter 5

Within a week the work had started at Idlewild, construction vehicles moving in alongside workers and trailers. The old, mostly broken fence was replaced with a new, high chain-link one, laced with signs warning trespassers. The view inside was obscured by trees, trucks, and the backs of Porta-Potties.

As she waited for one of her many calls to Anthony Eden to be returned, Fiona finally made the drive to her father's house, on a winding back road just outside the town lines. Fiona's parents had divorced two years after Deb's murder, and her mother had died of cancer eight years ago, still broken by her elder daughter's death. Malcolm Sheridan lived alone in the tiny bungalow they'd lived in as a family, withdrawing further and further into the world inside his formidable brain.

There were gaps on the roof where shingles had become detached, Fiona saw as she pulled up the dirt driveway. The roof would have to be done before winter, or it would start to leak. Malcolm probably had the money for it stashed somewhere, but the challenge would be finding it. Fiona was already running through the possibilities in her head as she knocked on the door.

He didn't answer—he usually didn't—but his old Volvo was in the driveway, so Fiona swung open the screen door, toed open the unlocked door behind it, and poked her head into the house. "Dad, it's me."

There was a shuffling sound from a back room, a creak. "Fee!"

Fiona came all the way through the doorway. The shades were drawn on all the windows—Malcolm claimed he couldn't work in bright sunlight—and the house smelled dusty and a little sour. Books and papers were stacked on every surface: kitchen counters, coffee tables, end tables, chairs. Fiona blinked, adjusting to the dim light after the bright fall day outside, and made her way across the small living room, taking note that the run-down kitchen looked as unused as ever.

Malcolm met her at the door to the back room he used as his office, wearing chinos so old they were now sold in vintage stores and a plaid flannel button-down shirt. Though he was over seventy now, he still had some brown in his longish gray hair, and he still exuded the same vitality he always had. "Fee!" he said again.

"Hi, Daddy." Malcolm took her up in a hug that squeezed her ribs, then let her go. Fiona hugged him back, steeped in the complicated mix of happiness and aching loss that she always felt in her father's presence. "I don't see any food in the kitchen. Have you been eating?"

"I'm fine, just fine. Working."

"The new book?"

"It's going to be . . ." He trailed off, his thoughts wandering back to the book he'd been writing for years now. "I'm just working through some things, but I think I'm very close to a breakthrough."

He turned and retreated into his office, and Fiona followed. The office was where her father really lived. This was where his mind had always been as Fiona was growing up, and since her mother had left, she suspected it was where his physical body spent most of its waking hours. There was a desk stacked with more papers, a Mac computer probably old enough to go into an Apple museum, and a low bookshelf. On the wall were two framed photos: one of Malcolm in Vietnam in 1969, wearing combat fatigues, posed on one knee in the middle of a field ringed with palm trees, a line of military trucks behind him; the other of Vietnamese women in a rice field, bent low over their work as four American helicopters loomed in menacing black silhouette above them. One of Malcolm's award-winning photographs. Fiona was always glad he hadn't had the other famous photo framed and posted; it depicted a Vietnamese woman gently wrapping her dead six-year-old son in linen as she prepared to bury him. Fiona's mother had drawn the line at displaying that photo in the house, claiming it would disturb the girls to look at it every day.

Does it ever bother you, one of Fiona's therapists had asked after the murder, *that your father was so absent when you were growing up? That he was never home?*

Seventeen-year-old Fiona had replied, *How is Dad supposed to save the world if he's sitting at home with me?*

It wasn't just the war, which was finishing as Malcolm's daughters were born. It was the aftermath: the books written, the prizes won, the trips to Washington, the speaking tours and engagements. And always, with her father, there had been marches, protests, and sit-ins: women's rights, black power, stop police brutality, abolish the death penalty. Malcolm Sheridan always protested, even well into the nineties, when the other hippies had long sold out and protests were no longer cool. He *had* wanted to save the world. Until Deb died, and all that protest spirit died with her.

Now he stacked some of the papers on his desk. "I didn't know you were coming. Some tea, maybe . . ."

"It's okay, Dad." She felt a jolt of worry, looking at him. Did those broad shoulders, which had always been so powerful, look narrower, weaker? Did he look pale? "Did you go see the doctor like I told you to?"

"Warburton? I don't trust that old hack anymore," Malcolm retorted. "He just prescribes whatever the pharmaceutical companies tell him to. Does he think I don't know?"

Fiona gritted her teeth. "Dad."

"Thank you, sweetie, but I'll handle it." He closed the document he was working on almost hurriedly, as if afraid she would read it over his shoulder.

"When are you going to let me read the manuscript?" she asked him. He'd been working on a new book, about the 2008 financial crisis. The problem was that he'd been working on it for five years, with apparently no progress.

"Soon, soon," Malcolm said, patting her on the shoulder. "Now, let's go to the kitchen and you can tell me about your day."

She followed him meekly into the kitchen, where he fussed at the clutter on the counters, looking for the kettle. This was the way it always happened with her: stark courage when she wasn't in her father's presence, and lip-biting worry and lack of confidence when she was actually here, watching an old man make tea. There was too much history in this old house, too much pain, too much love. Her mother had bought that kettle, bringing it home one day in her station wagon after one of Dad's royalty checks came in.

Still, she blurted it out. "I'm working on a new story."

"Is that so?" Her father didn't approve of Fiona's chosen work, the stories about the right yoga poses for stress and how to make mini apple pies in a muffin tin. But he'd stopped voicing his disapproval years ago, replacing it with an apathy that meant he was tuning her out.

Fiona looked away from him, at the old clock on the wall, pretending he wasn't there so she could get the words out. "It's about Idlewild Hall."

The water was running in the sink, filling the kettle, but now it shut off. There was a second of silence. "Oh?" he said. "You mean the restoration."

"What?" She snapped back to look at her father. "You knew about that?"

"Norm Simpson called me—oh, two weeks ago. He thought I should know."

Fiona blinked, her mind scrambling, trying to place the name. Her father knew so many people, it was impossible to keep track. "No one told me about it."

"Well, people are sensitive, Fee. That's all. What's your story angle?" He was interested now, awake, looking at her from the corner of his eye as he plugged in the kettle.

"I want to talk to this Margaret Eden. And her son, Anthony. I want to know their endgame."

"There's going to be no money in it," Malcolm said, turning and leaning on the counter, crossing his arms. "That place has always been a problem. City council has debated buying it from the Christophers three times since 2000, just so they can tear it down, but they never got up the gumption to do it. And now they've lost their chance."

Fiona suppressed the triumph she felt—*Yes! He agrees with me!*—and turned to open the fridge. "That's what I think. But I can't get Anthony Eden to return my calls, even when I say I'm writing for *Lively Vermont*."

The kettle whistled. Her father poured their tea and looked thoughtful. "I could make some calls," he said.

"You don't need to do that," she replied automatically. "Dad, it's—it's okay with you that I'm writing this?"

For the first time, his face went hard, the expression closed down. "Your sister isn't there. I told Norm Simpson the same thing. She's gone. You sound like your mother, still worried every day that you're making Deb unhappy."

"I don't—" But she did. Of course she did. Leave it to her father to get to the heart of it with his journalist's precision. Her parents had divorced two years after the murder, unable to carry on together anymore. Her mother had gone to work at Walgreens after the divorce, even though she had a Ph.D. She'd said it was because she was tired of academia, but Fiona always knew it was because Deb had been embarrassed by what she referred to as her parents' nerdiness. She'd been uncomfortable with Malcolm's fame as a journalist and an activist— twenty-year-old Deb, who had wanted nothing more than to fit in, be popular, and have friends, had thought she had all the answers. She'd been so young, Fiona thought now. So terribly young. The attitude had affected their mother, yet no matter how Deb had scorned him, Malcolm refused to apologize for the way he led his life.

But when Fiona looked around their childhood home now, at the clutter and disorder that hadn't been touched in years, she wondered if her father felt as guilty as the rest of them did. There had been arguments that year before Deb died—she'd been in college, barely passing her classes while she socialized and had fun. She'd been drinking, going to parties, and dating Tim, to their parents' hurt confusion. Fiona, at seventeen, had watched the rift from the sidelines. And then, one November night, it had all been over.

Still, Malcolm Sheridan was Malcolm Sheridan. Two days after she'd visited him, Fiona received a phone call from Anthony Eden's assistant, asking her to meet Eden at the gates of Idlewild Hall the next morning for a tour and an interview. "I can't do it," she said to Jamie that night, sitting on the couch in his small apartment, curled up against him and thinking about Deb again. "I can't go."

"Right," he said. "You can't go."

Fiona pressed the palms of her hands over her eyes. "Yes, I can. I can go. I'm going."

"This is the most ambitious thing you've ever written, isn't it?" he asked. He'd finished a long shift, and they were sitting in the half-dark quiet, without even the TV on. She could feel his muscles slowly unknotting, as if his job kept him in some unbearable level of silent tension he could only now release.

"Is that a dig?" she asked him, though she knew it wasn't.

"No," he said. "But since I've known you, all you've written are those fluff pieces." He paused, feeling his way. "I just get the feeling you're a better writer than you let on."

Fiona swallowed. She'd gone to journalism school—it had been second nature to follow in Malcolm's footsteps, and she was incapable of doing anything else—but she'd freelanced her entire career instead of working in a newsroom. She told herself it was because she could do bigger and better things that way. But here she was. "Well, I guess I'll find out. They say you're supposed to do something that scares you every day, right?"

Jamie snorted. He was probably unaware she'd read that motto on a yoga bag. "It's a good thing I'm a cop, then."

"Oh, really?" It was one of her hobbies to test how far she could push Jamie. "Directing traffic at the Christmas parade? That must be pretty terrifying."

In response, he dropped his head back, resting it on the back of the sofa and staring at the ceiling. "You are so dead," he said with a straight face.

"Or that time they were fixing the bridge. You had to stand there for *hours*." Fiona shook her head. "I don't know how you handle it every day."

"So dead," Jamie said again.

"Or when we get a big snowfall, and you have to help all the cars in the ditch—"

She was fast, but he was faster. Before she could get away, he had pulled her down by the hips and pinned her to the sofa. "Take it back," he said.

She leaned up and brushed her lips over his gorgeous mouth. "Make me," she said.

He did. She took it back, eventually.

Fiona stood next to the tall black gates to Idlewild, leaning on her parked car, watching Old Barrons Road. It looked different in daylight, though it was still stark and lonely, the last dead leaves skittering across the road. There was no movement at the gas station, no one on the hill. Birds cried overhead as they gathered to go south before the brutal winter hit. Fiona turned up the collar of her parka and rubbed her hands.

A black Mercedes came over the hill, moving as slowly as a funeral procession, its engine soundless. Fiona watched as it pulled up next to her and the driver's window whirred down, showing a man over fifty with a wide forehead, thinning brown hair, and a pair of sharp eyes that were trained on her, unblinking.

"Mr. Eden?" Fiona said.

He nodded once, briefly, from the warm leather interior of his car. "Please follow me," he said.

He pressed a button somewhere—Fiona pictured a sleek console in there, like in a James Bond film—and the gates made a loud, ringing *clang*. An automatic lock—that was new. A motor purred and the gates swung open slowly, revealing an unpaved dirt driveway leading away, freshly dug like an open scar.

Fiona got in her car and followed. The drive was bumpy, and at first there was nothing to see but trees. But the trees thinned, and the driveway curved, and for the first time in twenty years she saw Idlewild Hall.

My God, she thought. *This place. This place.*

There was nothing like it—not in the Vermont countryside full of clapboard and Colonials, and perhaps not anywhere. Idlewild was a monster of a building, not high but massively long, rowed with windows that dully reflected the gray sky through a film of dirt. Brambles and weeds clotted the front lawn, and tangles of dead vines crawled the walls. Four of the windows on the far end of the building were broken, looking like eyes that had blinked closed. The rest of the windows grinned down the driveway at the approaching cars. *All the better to eat you with, my dear.*

Fiona had last been here four days after Deb's body was found. The police hadn't let her come to the scene, but after they'd cleared everything away, she'd come through the fence and stood in the middle of the sports field, on the place where Deb's body had lain. She'd been looking for solace, perhaps, or a place to begin to understand, but instead she'd found a litter of wreaths, cheap bundles of flowers, beer bottles, and cigarette butts. The aftermath of the concerned citizens of Barrons—and its teenagers—conducting their own vigil.

The building had been in ruins then. It was worse now. As Fiona got closer, she saw that the end of the main building, where the windows were broken, actually sagged a little, as if the roof had fallen in. The circular drive in front of the main doors was uneven and muddy, and she had to take care to keep her balance as she got out of the car. She strapped her DSLR camera around her neck and turned to greet her tour guide.

"I'm sorry about the mess," the man said as he walked from the parked Mercedes toward her. "The driveway was overgrown, the pavement cracked and upended in parts. We had to have it redug before we could do much else." He held out his hand. His expression was naturally serious, but he attempted a smile. "I'm Anthony Eden. It's nice to meet you."

"Fiona Sheridan." His hand was warm and smooth. He was wearing a cashmere coat, in contrast to the jeans, boots, and parka she'd worn in preparation for touring a construction site.

"I only have an hour, I'm afraid," Anthony said. "Shall we start with the main building?"

"Of course." As they started walking, Fiona pulled out her pocket MP3 recorder. "Do you mind if I record what you tell me? It helps to make the quotes more accurate."

Anthony briefly glanced down at the recorder, then away again. "If you like." An electric security console had been installed on the main door, and he punched in a code. The console beeped, and he opened the door.

"You've worked fast," Fiona commented, thumbing on the recorder. "I noticed the new fencing and the electric gate as well."

"Security was our first measure. We don't want the local kids treating this place as a free hotel room anymore." He had walked into the main hall and stopped. Fiona stopped, too.

It was a massive space, musty and dim, lit only by the cloudy sunlight coming through the windows. The ceiling rose three stories high; the floor was paneled in wood of a chocolate color so dark it was nearly black. In front of them rose a staircase, sweeping up to a landing on the second floor and another landing on the third, lined with intricate wood railings, the balconies on the upper floors spinning away from either side of the staircase like a spider's web, fading back into the darkness. There was no sound but a silent hush and the rustle of a bird's wings somewhere in the rafters. The smell was mildewy like wet wood, underlain with something faintly rotten.

"Oh, my God," Fiona murmured.

"You are now looking at the main hall," Anthony Eden said. She was beginning to see that his manner was more than stodgy politeness—he didn't want to be here. Likely his mother had made him do this. "The building dates from 1919, and all of the wood is original. Much of it cannot be saved, of course, but we plan to restore the original wood wherever we can."

"Is that even possible?" Fiona asked, raising her camera and snapping a shot.

"The wood experts arrive next week. There is a drainage problem on the east side of the property, so we've had to focus on that this first week, to halt the progress of the damp in all of the buildings."

The staircase, as old as it was, had held, and they climbed it to the second floor, where Eden led her down a hallway littered with debris. "This was a functioning girls' boarding school until it closed in 1979," he said, beginning his tour guide speech. "We intend to restore it to its previous condition and reopen it to students again."

"Girls only?" Fiona asked.

"That is the intent. My mother believes that girls should be given their own chance at a better education in order to give them a start in the world."

They entered a classroom. "This still has desks in it," Fiona said.

"Yes. Most of the rooms in these buildings still contain the original furniture. The school was nearly bankrupt by the time it closed, and it was mostly abandoned as the owners tried to sell off the land."

Fiona moved into the classroom. The desks were solid wood, very old. Most of them had words and names scratched into them by generations of girls. The blackboard was still here, covered in unreadable chalk scrawls, and there were birds' nests in the rafters. Plaster had fallen from the ceiling over time onto the floor. A poster on one wall, faded, its edges curled, depicted a line drawing of a row of happy, rosy-cheeked girls in uniforms sitting at desks, with the caption GOOD GIRLS MAKE GOOD MOTHERS!

Fiona took more shots. It smelled less musty in here than it had downstairs, but there were other smells—rotten wood and something coppery, possibly from the old pipes in the walls. Fiona moved closer to the blackboard, stepping around the empty chairs and desks. There were layers of scrawls on it—graffiti from the kids who had wandered in here. Names. Swearwords and crude drawings. There were crumbs of smashed chalk on the floor. But the blackboard was filmed over and cloudy, coated with dust mixed with old chalk dust, as if no one had been here in years.

Fiona took a few more pictures and turned to the windows. Two of the panes were cracked and broken, the sills rotted through where rain and snow had come in. The third window was intact.

"Let's move on," Anthony Eden said behind her. He was still in the doorway; he hadn't come into the room.

Fiona turned, and the sunlight coming through the intact window illuminated the writing on it, etched into the grime coating the glass, the lettering thin and spidery.

GOOD
NIGHT
GIRL

Fiona frowned at it. The words were fresh, the letters in the glass clear, not clouded over like the blackboard was. It had been written with something scratchy, like a fingernail.

"Miss Sheridan?" Eden said.

Fiona stared at the words for a long moment. Had someone been in here today? Had they gotten past the new locks? Who would come all the way here, bother to break in, to write graffiti like that? Why *Good Night Girl*? It made her think of Deb, lying on the field outside, her shirt and bra ripped open, the wind blowing over her unseeing face.

"Miss Sheridan." Anthony Eden broke into her thoughts. "We really should move on."

Tearing her gaze from the window, she followed him out of the room. They toured another classroom, and another. Except for the damage—water had run down the walls in one room, and a section of wall was crumbling in another—it was as if those girls had left yesterday, just stood up and walked away. Fiona paused at another broken window and looked out over the view of the common and the grounds beyond. "What's that out there?" she asked.

Eden was in the doorway, impatient to leave again. His face had gone pale, and as Fiona watched, he pulled a large handkerchief from his pocket and mopped his forehead. He glanced past her shoulder at the construction equipment that was moving busily in the distance. "That is the crew hired to deal with the drainage problem. They need to dig up an old well, from what I understand. I think we have the idea of the classrooms, don't we? Let's move to the dining hall."

She followed him down the corridor again. "Mr. Eden—"

"Anthony, please." His voice was tense.

"All right, thank you. I'm Fiona. Anthony, how long do you see the restoration taking?"

He was walking quickly toward the stairs, barely waiting for her. "It may take some time, especially to repair the fallen-in ceilings. But we are prepared to do it properly."

"This restoration was all your mother's idea?"

A definite chill at that. "Yes, it was."

"I wonder if I could interview her."

"Unfortunately, that won't be possible. My mother doesn't wish to speak with journalists."

We'll see about that, Fiona thought. They had descended the stairs and he turned left, taking her through the atrium. No way was she going to be deterred from interviewing the mysterious Margaret Eden. "Why not?" Fiona asked. "Is your mother ill?"

"My mother is in perfect health. She does not wish to answer questions from reporters, that's all."

Fiona kept at it. "Why did she choose Idlewild? Was she a student here?"

"No. My mother is from Connecticut. My father is from Maryland."

"Your father was an investor," Fiona said. "Was this one of his projects? Your mother is carrying it on now— is that it?"

They had reached a back door, and Eden turned to face her. Some of the paleness had left his face, but the flush that replaced it was no healthier. "Not even close," he said. "In fact, my father did not approve of this project at all, and forbade my mother from attempting it. He said it would lose money. It's only now that he's died that my mother has gone ahead."

So that was it, then. Anthony was on his father's side on this, and disapproved of his mother's going against her husband's wishes. It explained why he looked so pained to be here, so eager to keep moving. She tried for a little softening. "I'm very sorry about your father," she said.

He stayed stiff for a second. "Thank you, Fiona." Then he turned and opened the back door, leading her out into the common.

The cold air slapped her in the face, dispersing the close, damp smells she'd been inhaling inside. The sunlight, even in its indirect, clouded-over form, made her blink after the dimness. What the hell, she wondered, would possess Margaret Eden, a woman who was not local, to be so determined to sink her money into Idlewild Hall?

They crossed the common. In Idlewild's heyday, this would have been a manicured green spot, made for strolling and studying in the soft grass. Now it was harsh and overgrown, the grass flattened and going brown as winter approached. The wind bit Fiona's legs through her jeans.

They were behind the main building, thankfully facing away from the sharp-toothed mouth of the front façade. To the left, a gloomy building of gray stone and broody windows sat silent. "What is that?" she asked Anthony.

He glanced over briefly. "That is the teachers' hall. It was flooded, I'm afraid, and I can't give you a tour because the floors are too rotted and dangerous. The dining hall got off more lightly, so we can go inside."

They were headed for the right-hand building, this one with large windows and double doors. "The school's buildings all look very different," Fiona said as they picked their way over the broken path. "Do you know anything about the architecture?"

"Almost nothing," he replied. "There are no records still in existence of who the architects were." He stopped on the path. "If you look here, and here"—he motioned with a black-coated arm to the roof of the main building and the roof of the dining hall—"you can see that the buildings are strangely mismatched. In fact, the southernmost windows of the dining hall provide only a view of the brick wall of the main hall. It's a curious construction."

"You think it was hastily planned?"

"I have no idea," he said. "We're still debating what to do. There is a garden in the wedge between the two buildings, so at least the school tried to put something there. But sunlight must be a problem. We're not sure what they grew, or tried to grow."

Fiona peered into the space between the two buildings as they passed. There were the remains of an overgrown garden, tangled with weeds that were brown and wet. The sunlight hit the spot at an oblique angle, making the shadows beneath the dead leaves dark as ink. The windows from both buildings stared blankly down.

There was an electronic keypad on the dining hall door as well, and Anthony punched in the combination. Fiona realized as she walked inside that she'd been picturing something *Harry Potter*–like, with high Gothic ceilings and warm candlelight. But Idlewild's dining hall was nothing like that. The plaster ceilings were damp with rot and mold, the walls streaked with water stains so dark they looked like blood in the half-light. Heavy, scarred wooden tables lined the walls, some of them jumbled together, one turned on its side, the legs jutting out like broken bones. The sunlight coming through the uncovered windows was gray and harsh, raising every ruined detail. The classrooms had looked abandoned; this room looked postapocalyptic, as if the last thing to happen in here had been too horrifying to contemplate.

Fiona walked slowly into the middle of the room. The hair on the back of her neck felt cold. Suddenly she didn't want to take pictures. She didn't want to be here at all anymore.

She glanced at Anthony and realized he felt the same way she did. His expression was almost nauseated with distaste.

He cleared his throat, pulling the handkerchief from his pocket again, and began to speak. "The kitchen is quite usable. The appliances will need updating, of course, and the floors and walls need repair. But the basics are there. We should be able to create a functioning cafeteria in here for the students."

Fiona walked to one of the windows. Did he actually think any students would want to eat in here? The thought made her queasy. *The school has always been rumored to be haunted,* Jamie had said. It was just an abandoned building, like a million others, but standing here, looking at this ruined room, she could easily see how the rumors had started. Where the stories had come from. If you believed in that sort of thing.

She raised her camera to take more pictures—it was time to wrap up; she was in agreement with Anthony on that—but was distracted by motion through the window. The angle was different, but this was the same view she'd seen from the classroom in the main hall, of another building and then the construction crew digging—tearing up an old well, Anthony had said. The glass was grimy, and without thinking, Fiona curled her fingers and touched the side of her palm to it, wiping a swatch of dirt away for a clearer view. She immediately regretted touching anything in this room, and dropped her hand to her side.

"I have another appointment," Anthony said from the doorway. He hadn't come fully inside any room they'd been in. "I'm sorry we couldn't spend more time."

"I haven't asked all my questions," Fiona said, distracted by the scene at the construction site. The backhoe had stopped moving, and two men in construction helmets were standing on the green, conferring. They were joined by a third man, and then a fourth.

"We can try to reschedule, but I'm quite busy." He paused. "Fiona?"

"You have a problem," Fiona said. She pointed through the rubbed-clean streak to the scene outside. "The crew has stopped working."

"They may be on a designated break."

"No one is taking a break," Fiona said. Now the fourth man had a phone to his ear, and a fifth man came around from the sports field, jogging in haste to join the others. There was something alarmed about his quick pace. "I think that's your foreman," Fiona pointed out. "They're calling him in."

"You can't possibly know that."

There was a chill of foreboding running through Fiona's blood. She stared at the men, gathered with their heads together, their postures tense and distressed. One of them walked away into the bushes, his hand over his mouth.

In the damp emptiness of the dining hall, Anthony's cell phone rang.

Fiona didn't have to watch him answer it. It was enough to hear his voice, short at first, then growing harsh and tense. He listened for a long moment. "I'll be there," he said, and hung up.

She turned around. He was drawn and still, his gaze faraway, a man in a long black cashmere coat in a ruined room. He put his hands in the pockets of his coat, and when he looked at her, his face was pale again, his expression shaken.

"There's been—a discovery," he said. "I don't— They've found something. It seems to be a body. In the well."

The breath went out of her in an exhalation as the moment froze, suspended. She felt shock, yes. Surprise. But part of her knew only acceptance. Part of her had expected nothing else.

Of course there are bodies here. This is Idlewild Hall.

"Take me there," she said to him. "I can help."

chapter 6

CeCe

Barrons, Vermont
October 1950

She wished she weren't always hungry. At fifteen, CeCe was hungry from morning to night, her body empty as a hollowed-out log. Idlewild fed them three meals per day, but everything CeCe ate seemed to vanish as soon as it passed her lips. It was embarrassing, not because she was fat—she wasn't; she was round, that was all—but because it made her look forward to meals in the dining hall. No one looked forward to meals in the dining hall, because the dining hall was horrible.

It was the supper hour, and CeCe followed Katie from the counter through the throng of girls toward a table. Even in the Idlewild uniform, Katie looked pretty. You could put a scratchy plaid skirt, a cheap white blouse, and a thick winter cardigan on her, and she still looked like Hedy Lamarr. CeCe knew that her rounder face and short dark hair were pretty enough, but she felt like a yeti next to Katie's glamour. Katie knew everything, and she was scared of nothing, which was exactly how CeCe wanted to be. Since CeCe was one of the few girls Katie didn't hate, CeCe clung to her like glue and brought her tidbits of gossip when she found them.

Today she had a good one, and she was excited. "Guess what I'm getting tonight," she said in a conspiratorial voice as they slid onto a bench at one of the tables, bumping two other girls down. She leaned closer to Katie's ear. "Pat Claiman's copy of *Lady Chatterley's Lover*."

Katie stared at her, fork in midair, her dark-lashed, sultry eyes wide. Pat Claiman's brother had smuggled her the book on Family Visit Day two months ago, and it had been passed from girl to girl ever since. Every girl at Idlewild was crazy to get her hands on it. "You're kidding," Katie said. "How did you do it?"

"It wasn't easy. I had to give Pat ten dollars."

Katie's eyes went even wider. "Ten *dollars*? CeCe, where did you get that?"

CeCe shrugged. "My father sends me money, you know. It was either that or read Sandra Krekly's stack of *Life* magazines, but those are all two years old."

Today's dinner was beef, mashed potatoes, creamed corn, and a sticky-sweet bread that CeCe thought was supposed to be corn bread, but tasted like nothing at all. Katie picked up a scoop of potatoes on her fork and put it in her mouth, her expression thoughtful. CeCe watched as Katie's gaze roamed the room, her eyes narrowing and calculating. She always saw things going on around them that CeCe was too stupid to see. "You'll have to read us the good parts aloud," Katie said.

"I can't." CeCe blushed. "No way. When I get to the racy bits, I'll give the book to you."

"Fine, I'll read it." Katie tossed her hair and poked at her potatoes again. "It's probably nothing I haven't seen anyway."

This was Katie's usual line. She came across like she was experienced with men, but CeCe was starting to notice that she never gave any details. She didn't care. "I hear it's juicy," she said, trying to keep Katie strung along. "Pat says there are even bad words in it. And they *do* things."

But Katie's attention was drifting. In the back corner, Alison Garner and Sherri Koustapos were arguing at their table, their heads lowered. Sherri had an angry snarl on her lip. Katie watched them warily. She seemed to have a radar for trouble, as if she could detect it from any quarter.

CeCe tried to distract her. "Hey, there's Roberta."

Roberta was crossing the room, carrying her wooden tray with her dinner on it. She sat at a table with her field hockey team, the girls jostling and giggling while Roberta was quiet. CeCe looked down at her plate and realized she'd already eaten everything on it, so she put down her knife and fork.

"Do you ever wonder," Katie said, "why Roberta is here? Her grades are good, and she's an athlete. She doesn't seem to belong."

"Oh, that's easy," CeCe said without thinking. "Her uncle came home from the war and tried to kill himself. Roberta walked in on him doing it, so they sent her away."

"What?" Katie stared at CeCe, and CeCe realized

she'd scored an even bigger point than she had with *Lady Chatterley's Lover*. "How do you know that?"

"Susan Brady isn't just the dorm monitor, you know," CeCe told her. "She knows *everything*. She heard Miss Maxwell telling Mrs. Peabody about it, and then she told me."

Katie seemed to process this. "That doesn't make any sense. If the uncle is crazy, why was Roberta the one who was sent away?"

"Maybe she saw blood," CeCe said. "Maybe she had a nervous breakdown or something. If I saw something like that, I'd want to get as far away as possible."

It was a fair point. They looked at Roberta, who was eating her dinner in silence, her face pale. "Keep your head down," Katie warned after a minute. "Here comes Lady Loon."

The argument at the back table had escalated, and Sherri Koustapos had jumped up, shoving the bench with the backs of her knees. Alison was still sitting, eating her creamed corn, but her face was red with silent fury. CeCe had felt Alison's wrath only once, in her first month at Idlewild—Alison had called her a "fat cow" and hit her with one of the broken badminton rackets from the locker storage room—and she never wanted to feel it again. Alison hated everyone, and when she hit, she hit hard.

Striding across the room, heading for the commotion, was Miss London, the teacher everyone knew as Lady Loon. Her dirty blond hair was frizzing loose from its topknot, and the armpits of her flowered polyester dress were damp. She was in her twenties, Idlewild's youngest teacher, and after only six months of teaching here she was still woefully unprepared. The girls' moods drove her crazy, their dramas riled her up, and their lack of discipline always enraged her. With over a hundred teenage girls, most of them unsalvageable, riding her nerves every day, she spent most of her time in a crazy rage that would have been funny if it didn't have an echo of hopelessness about it.

"Ladies!" CeCe heard her say over the din of the fighting rabble of girls. "Ladies. Sit *down*!"

The girls didn't notice. With a gasp, CeCe watched Sherri lean over and spit on Alison's plate. Alison barely paused before she jumped off her bench and hit as hard as she could, her heavy, waxy fist making contact with Sherri's nose with an audible *crack*.

The other teachers, who had stood milling at the edge of the room, reluctantly began to move, muttering. Lady Loon—it was her habit of calling the girls *ladies* that gave her the title—wrenched Alison by the arm and dragged her from the table. The din was deafening. Girls were shouting, Sherri was screaming and bleeding, and the teachers were moving in as a group. CeCe couldn't hear her voice, but she could see Lady Loon's lipsticked mouth forming the words: *Calm down, ladies! Calm down!* She watched as blood dripped between Sherri's fingers and spattered on the floor, and she inched a little closer to Katie. "I hate blood," she said.

She followed Katie's gaze, which had left the melee and focused on something else. Sonia was standing in front of one of the large windows, behind a knot of excited girls. The French girl was still, her face pale. How had CeCe never noticed how small she was? Sonia always seemed so strong, like a blade, narrow but impossible to break. Yet she was shorter than all the American girls around her, and when one of them bumped past her to get a better view, Sonia was knocked almost off-balance, like a rag doll.

But it was her face that made CeCe sit up in alarm. Sonia's expression was empty, as blank as a piece of notepaper, her lips slack. Her usual look of quick, quiet intelligence, as if she was thinking fascinating things without saying them, had vanished. Her hands dangled at her sides. Her eyes, which were normally observant and a little wry, were open and seeing—they must have been seeing—but they contained nothing at all.

Lady Loon was restraining Alison, who was kicking and screaming now. Sherri had sagged to her knees, and one of her friends had fainted. The teachers had descended on the group, tugging at Sherri, trying to clear space around the fainted girl. Mrs. Peabody held Alison's other arm, and CeCe could hear her booming voice. "It's Special Detention for you, my girl. Do you hear? Get moving. *Move!*"

CeCe looked back at Sonia. She was watching, watching. Her skin had gone gray.

From the other corner of the room, CeCe saw Roberta get up from her table and try to make her way across the room toward Sonia, her face tight with fear.

"Katie," CeCe said over the noise. "Is Sonia sick?"

Katie touched CeCe's wrist. "Quick." She rose from her chair and CeCe followed, the two of them winding their way through the sweaty, excited crowd of girls to-

ward Sonia. Roberta was coming from the other direction, but her progress was slower, impeded by a thick
section of her hockey friends.

Katie dodged expertly through the cloud of wool
uniforms, using her elbows and her knees. CeCe followed in her wake, thinking of the color of Sonia's face.
There's something wrong with Sonia, she thought. *How
did we not know? How did we not see that there's something wrong with Sonia?*

Sonia was still by the window, unmoving. Katie
swooped past her, took her hand, and tugged it. Without thinking, CeCe took Sonia's other hand so the girl
was protected from both sides.

When CeCe was a girl, her rich father had sent her a
Christmas present at her first boarding school: a baby doll.
The baby had unsettling marble eyes, a hard skull, and
two hard hands, molded into tiny fingers that formed into
an impossibly adult shape. Sonia's hand reminded CeCe of
one of those hands now—small, cold, folded in on itself,
alive but somehow dead. CeCe kept hold of it as she and
Katie maneuvered the French girl out of the room. From
the corner of her eye, she saw Roberta following, her long
legs eating the ground to catch up to them easily, her braid
swinging, her forehead stamped with worry.

Sonia made no sound, no protest. Her feet stumbled
between Katie and CeCe, but her hands and arms did not
move. They left the dining hall and came out into the wet
air, the four of them moving as one toward Clayton Hall.
"It's all right," she heard herself say to Sonia, even though
she didn't know what was wrong. "It's all right."

"Should we get her to the infirmary?" Roberta asked. The infirmary was across the common, in the teachers' hall.

"No." Katie's voice was flat. "We're not taking her to Nurse Hedmeyer. She can't help anyway. Just get her to the dorm. Keep walking."

"We should tell someone," CeCe said.

"Tell who?" Katie turned to her as they walked, and her eyes were so angry that CeCe felt herself pale in shock. "Lady Loon? Mrs. Peabody? About this? They'll just discipline her. Have you lost your mind?"

"Shut up, Katie," Roberta said. "She's trying to help."

CeCe looked at Sonia's ashen face, her half-closed eyes. There was something going on she didn't understand. She was always so stupid, so stupid. "What's wrong with her?"

No one answered. They entered Clayton Hall, and they helped Sonia up the stairs to the third floor. Sonia tried to walk between them, but her ankles buckled and her head sagged. She said something in French that sounded like a recitation, the words spilling automatically as her lips moved.

None of the other girls knew French, but CeCe watched Sonia's lips as the four of them hit the third-floor landing. "I think she's praying."

"She isn't praying," Katie said.

In their room, they put Sonia to bed in her bunk, laying her on top of the covers and pulling off her shoes. Sonia muttered again, and this time there were English words mixed in with the French. CeCe put her ear to Sonia's lips and caught some words: *Please don't take me there. Please don't. I'll be quiet.* She was repeating it under her breath. Finally, the girl rolled over on her back and put her shaking hands to her face, shutting them out, her thin legs sticking out from beneath her rucked-up skirt.

Roberta sat at the edge of the bed. Katie stood, looking down at Sonia with an impenetrably dark expression on her face, and then she said, "I'll get a glass of water," and left the room.

CeCe looked at Roberta, her long, plainly pretty face, her blond hair tied back. Roberta's expression when she looked at Sonia was troubled, but deep with understanding. She didn't think anyone wanted her to talk, but she couldn't help herself. "How did you know what was happening?" she asked. "How did you know what to do?"

Roberta shook her head. "I didn't."

"You've seen her do something like this before, haven't you?"

The pause before Roberta spoke was a beat too long. "No."

Roberta's expression slowly closed down, the emotion leaving it. She became as impassive as a statue. Maybe it was Roberta who had had a fit like this, after her uncle tried to kill himself. Maybe, beneath her quiet demeanor, Roberta wasn't as calm and confident as she seemed. "What does it mean?" CeCe asked her. "Is she sick?"

"CeCe, shut up."

But she couldn't. When CeCe was afraid, when she was nervous, she found it hard to shut up. "Katie knew, too. She's seen this before."

"No, I haven't." Katie was in the doorway, a glass of water in her hand. "I just think on my feet. She's had a shock of some kind, and she was about to faint. We had to get her out of there so the teachers wouldn't see. Sonia, drink this." She reached down, pulled one of the other girl's hands from her face, tilted her head back, and looked into her eyes. "Listen to me," she said clearly. "People saw us leaving. It's over if you don't get ahold of yourself. Girls who faint get sent to Special Detention for being disruptive. Now *sit up*."

CeCe opened her mouth to protest, but to her amazement Sonia swung her legs over the side of the bed and sat up. She swayed for a second, then held out her hand. "Give me the water," she said, her voice a rasp, her French accent sharpened by exhaustion.

A knock came on the door. "Ladies." It was Lady Loon. "What is going on in there?"

Katie nodded to Roberta, and Roberta stood and opened the door. "Nothing, Miss London," she said. "Sonia had a fit of dizziness, but she's well now."

Sonia had been gulping the water, but she lowered the glass and looked at the teacher. "I hate blood," she said clearly.

Lady Loon ran a hand through her disastrous hair. "Afternoon class starts in twenty minutes," she said. "Anyone not in attendance will be noted for detention. Is that clear?"

"Yes, Miss London," CeCe said.

The teacher looked helplessly up the hallway, then down again, then wandered off toward the stairwell.

CeCe looked at the faces of the three other girls. What had happened in the dining hall had nearly given Sonia a nervous breakdown. What could be so horrible that it could be brought back by the sight of two girls fighting? She usually felt like the stupid one, but she thought maybe she was starting to see. She didn't know everything about her friends, but these were Idlewild girls. Idlewild girls were always here for a reason. They were rough, like Katie, or impassive, like Roberta, because something had made them that way. Something they instinctively understood in one another. They hadn't known what exactly was wrong with Sonia—they still didn't know—but they had recognized it all the same.

Please don't take me there, Sonia had said. CeCe didn't know what it meant, but it was something terrible. Maybe more terrible than anything the rest of them had seen.

CeCe hadn't been wanted, not by either her father or her mother, but she'd always been safe. She'd never been in the kind of danger that she thought Sonia was seeing behind her eyes. She'd never had anything really bad happen to her. Not *really* bad.

Except for the water. That day at the beach with her mother, years ago, swimming in the ocean. Looking up through the water, unable to breathe, and seeing her mother's face. Then nothing.

But the water had been a long time ago. And it had been an accident.

And as CeCe's mother had told her, girls had accidents all the time.

chapter 7

It was a twenty-minute walk over the hardened, muddy ground to the well. Fiona walked behind Anthony Eden, glancing at his black-clad back as he scrambled in his expensive shoes. She kept her hand on her camera so it wouldn't bounce against her chest, and she was grateful she'd remembered to wear her hiking boots. She had simply followed him from the dining hall after he got the call, without a word, and so far he was so flustered he hadn't yet thought to send her away.

Through the gaps in the trees she glimpsed the sports field, where Deb had been found. There was nothing there now but empty, overgrown grass. Closer were the indoor gymnasium and girls' lockers, the building dilapidated and falling down. In the eaves of the overhang at the edge of the building, she could see tangles of generations of birds' nests.

The workmen were gathered in a knot. One of them had pulled out a large plastic tarp of cheerful, incongruous blue and was attempting to unfold it. The others watched Anthony as their foreman stepped forward.

"Are you certain?" Anthony said.

The man's face was gray. "Yes, sir," he said. "It's pretty clear."

"It isn't a hoax? Teenagers have been using this property to scare each other for years."

The foreman shook his head. "Not a hoax. I've been in this business twenty years and I've never seen anything like it."

Anthony's lips pursed. "Let me see."

They led him around the rise. There was a digger of some kind and a backhoe, both of them parked and silent. Dug into the slope of the rise was a huge ragged hole, the edges of mud and crumbling brick. Though it was full daylight, the center of the hole was pitch-black, as if it led into the depths of somewhere light could not go.

"In there," the foreman said.

There was a smell. Wet, rancid. Digging into the back of the brain, traveling down the spine. Anthony took a large flashlight from one of the workmen and approached the hole, carefully climbing over the mud and the broken bricks in his leather shoes. Swallowing the smell, Fiona followed at his shoulder.

He clicked on the flashlight and shone it into the blackness. "I don't see anything."

"Lower, sir. You'll see it." The foreman paused. "You'll see her."

Her.

Fiona stared at the circle of light, watching it move down the well. The far wall was still intact, the bricks damp and slimy. Her hands were cold, but she couldn't put them in her pockets. She couldn't move as the light traveled down, down.

And then, *her.*

She was not a hoax.

The girl was folded, her knees bent, tucked beneath her chin. Her head was down, her face hidden, as if bowed with grief. Rotten strands of long hair trailed down her back. One hand was dropped to her side, hidden in the darkness; the other was curled over one shin, nothing but a translucent sheen of long-gone skin over dark bone. The shin itself was a mottled skeleton. Her shoes, which had probably been leather, had long rotted away, leaving only rubber soles beneath the ruins of her feet. But there were ragged remains of the rest of her clothes: a thin wool coat, mostly decayed away. A strip of fabric around her neck that was the last of what had once been a blouse with a Peter Pan collar. A skirt, discolored with mold. Threads dangling from her skeletal legs that had once been wool stockings.

"There's no water in the well." This was the foreman's voice, low and strangled. "It dried up, which was why it wasn't in use anymore. The water, it drained away down . . ." He trailed off, and Fiona wondered if he was pointing or gesturing somewhere. Neither she nor Anthony was watching. "So it's damp in there, sure, but—she's just been sitting there."

Fiona swallowed and said to Anthony, "Give me the flashlight." He seemed to have shut down; he handed the light to her immediately. She hefted it, swung it down to the girl's skirt. "The color is bleached away," she said. "Idlewild uniforms were navy blue and dark green." Her research last night had drawn up more than one class picture, girls lined up in rows, wearing identical skirts and blouses. "I can't tell if she's got the Idlewild crest."

"She's a student," Anthony said. His voice was low, his words mechanical, as if he was not thinking of what he was saying. "She must be. Look at her."

"She's small," Fiona said, traveling the light over the body again. "She looks like a child."

"Not a child." His voice was almost a whisper. "Not a child. A girl. This is a disaster. This will end us. The entire project. Everything." He turned and looked at her, as if remembering she was there. "Oh, God. You're a journalist. Are you going to write about this? What are you going to do?"

Fiona tore her gaze from the body in the well and stared at him. Something was crawling through her at the sight of the body, crawling over her skin. Not just revulsion and pity. Something big. Something that had to do with Deb and the words scrawled on the window. *Good Night Girl*. "I don't know," she said. "Maybe she fell. But it's part of the story."

She watched his jaw clamp shut, his mind work. He was thinking about lawyers, nondisclosure agreements, gag orders. None of it mattered. Fiona was already standing here, looking at the body, and the cat was already out of the bag. "You can't possibly be such a jackal," he said finally.

"I'm not sure what I am," she told him, "but I'm not a jackal. I'm a writer. And this"—she motioned to the gaping hole in the well, the girl inside—"can be handled with respect." She thought of Deb, the news stories from twenty years ago. "I can do it. I might be the only one who can do it right."

He was silent for a long minute. "You can't promise that. The police—"

"I can help with that, too." She pulled out her cell phone and dialed. "Listen."

It rang only twice before Jamie's voice came on the other end. "Fee?"

"Jamie, I'm at Idlewild. We're going to need some police."

He paused, surprised. She'd called his personal cell phone. "What are you talking about? What's going on?"

"They've found a body here."

"Shit. Shit, Fee. Call nine-one-one."

Fiona remembered that she'd used the wrong terminology in this case. "It isn't a fresh body. It's remains, definitely human, probably decades old. We'll need a coroner, some police. But can it be quiet? It might be . . . an accident. She might have just fallen."

"She?"

"Yes. The owners want it quiet until she's identified and it's sorted out. Can that be done?"

He paused for a second. "All right," he said. "I'll take care of it. We're on our way."

"Your help is admirable," Anthony said as she hung up. "But futile."

"Don't be so sure."

He put his icy hand over hers on the flashlight and aimed it at the back of the dead girl's head. "Look at that," he said. "Now tell me she fell."

Fiona stared. *Who are you?* she thought. *What happened? Who are you, and how did you get here?*

Even after so many years, with the blood long gone, it was clear in the light. Beneath the strands of hair, the back of the girl's head was smashed, a section of the skull nothing but shards of broken bone.

The day stretched long, over the cold light of afternoon and the early descent of evening. By six o'clock the crew on scene had set up lights beneath the two tents they worked in—one over the ruins of the well, the second to receive and photograph the body. The crew was small. Fiona had memories of crowds of people in the news footage after Deb's body was found— uniformed cops pressing back rubberneckers, detectives and crime scene techs scurrying in and out, more uniformed cops spreading out to look for footprints. But this was different. There was a handful of people moving back and forth between the tents, talking as quietly as if they were working in a library. There were no rubberneckers except Fiona, who was sitting on a pile of broken stone from the well, sipping a hot cup of coffee. Anthony Eden was gone, probably to report to his mother, and the only uniform on the scene belonged to Jamie.

He exited the tent with the body in it and crossed the grass to sit next to her, wearing his heavy cop's parka. His hair looked darker in the onset of dusk, his trim beard of lighter gold. "We're almost done," he said.

Fiona nodded and made room for him to sit next to her. "Thanks for the coffee."

"It's nothing. You've been sitting here all day. You must be freezing."

"I'm fine." Her toes were a little frigid in her hiking boots and her ass was numb, but it wasn't anything she couldn't handle. She'd long ago put her camera back in her car, since pictures were out of the question. "Can you tell me anything?"

He stared at the lit tent and seemed to think it over. "Is this off the record?"

"Jamie, for God's sake."

"I know. I have to ask. It's my job."

She drew a thumbnail along the top of her coffee cup. "Fine. It's off the record."

"She was a teenager," he said, appeased. "Fourteen, fifteen, thereabouts. Small for her age, but based on the bones, Dave Saunders is certain."

"The cause of death?"

"It's preliminary until the autopsy is done, but you saw her head. Saunders says a blow with something big and blunt, a rock or the end of a shovel."

"She couldn't have hit her head on the way down the well?"

"No. The bricks in the well are the wrong shape, the wrong size. Too smooth."

She'd been expecting it, but still she felt something heavy in her stomach. Her glance wandered off through the trees toward the sports field, where Deb had lain. *Two girls dead, four hundred feet apart.* "How old is the body?"

"Based on the decomposition, at least forty years. According to Saunders, she's reasonably well preserved because she's been in the well, though not in water. The body is too old to test whether she was raped. No animals have been at her, and she's been mostly protected from the elements. But she's decomposed. She's been there a long time."

This girl had been here, long dead, curled inside the well, on the night Deb was murdered. And after Deb was dead and before her body was found on the field, Idlewild had been the resting site for two murdered girls, decades apart. There was no way Fiona could be impartial about this, no way she could avoid crossing the lines. "I've seen pictures of the Idlewild uniforms, and they were navy blue and green. She isn't wearing a uniform, is she?"

Jamie said nothing, and Fiona turned and looked at him. He was still staring at the tent where the body lay, his jaw set.

"What?" Fiona said. "You know something else. What is it?"

He paused. "We can't be sure. And if I tell you, you have to stay out of it at least until we notify the family."

Fiona felt the hair on the back of her neck stand up. "You've identified her?"

"There's a tag sewn into the collar of her blouse," he said. "A name tag."

"Tell me."

"Fee, you've been on the other side of this. If she has family, and the slightest thing is handled wrong, we make this worse."

Fiona knew. She remembered the day the cops had knocked on their door, the minute she had seen their faces and known that Deb wasn't missing anymore. She pulled a notebook and pen from her back jeans pocket. "Just tell me."

"I'm warning you: Don't go digging. Give us a few days at least. This is a police investigation."

"I know." Fiona stared at him, waiting. "I *know*. Jamie. Tell me."

He scrubbed a hand over his face. "Sonia Gallipeau," he said. "I don't recognize the name—I don't think it's a local family. She may have been a student from away. It doesn't ring a bell for me, any missing girl with that name, but I already have Harvey digging into the files back at the station. He'll call me any minute. And we don't even have confirmation that this girl is Sonia Gallipeau—she could just be wearing Sonia's blouse. She could have stolen or borrowed it, or bought it second-hand."

Fiona scribbled the name down in her notebook. "I'll do my own search," she said, holding up a hand before he could speak. "Just on the Internet. No phone calls. And I'll ask Dad."

Jamie's mouth was open to speak, but he thought better of it and closed it. He might not like it, but he was smart enough not to turn down help from Malcolm if it could aid the case. "I want to know what he says. And what you find."

"I'll come by later." She pocketed the notebook and pen, then flung an arm around his neck, leaning in close to his ear, feeling the tension in his shoulders even through his parka. "I'll bring takeout, and we'll trade. *Quid pro quo*. How does that sound?"

He still stared ahead, but a red flush moved up his cheeks. "You do this to me," he said, shaking his head. "Fuck it. Bring beer."

"I will." She could have kissed him, but she didn't. Instead, she got up and headed back over the muddy track toward her car, without looking back to see if he was watching.

chapter 8

Sonia

Books were her salvation. As a child, she'd had a shelf of childhood favorites that she loved enough to read over and over again. But after, during the hospital stay and the long voyage and the cold days in Idlewild's dreary hallways, books became more than mere stories. They were her lifeline, the pages as essential to her as breathing.

Even now, sitting in class, Sonia touched her finger to the yellowed pages of her Latin textbook, as if its texture could calm her. At the blackboard, Mrs. Peabody droned on about verb conjugation as the ten girls in the room fidgeted in their chairs. Charlotte Kankle peeled at a hangnail on her thumb, watching from under her angry lowered brows as a bead of blood came out. Cindy Benshaw shifted in her chair and scratched her ear, the motion of her arm revealing the circles of sweat stains on the armpit of her blouse, like the rings of an old tree. It was cold outside, but it was suffocating in here, the room airless, the smells of unwashed girls' bodies and chalk dust trapped in a bubble.

Sonia already knew this Latin lesson. She had read ahead in the textbook ages ago; she couldn't help it. Books were in short supply at Idlewild. There was no library, no literature class, no kindly librarian to take *My Friend Flicka* from the shelf and hand it over with a smile. The only books at Idlewild were sent by friends or family, dropped off on rare Family Visit Days, or brought back by the lucky girls after Christmas holiday visits home. As a result, every book in Idlewild, no matter how silly or dull, circulated through a hundred hungry hands before finally disintegrating into individual pages, which were often held together by an elastic band until the pages themselves began to disappear. And when there were no other books to be had, the most desperate girls read textbooks.

Barely listening to the lecture, Sonia flipped the pages of the textbook over, looking for the handwriting. Pencil writing, just as Katie had shown them in her own book under the light of a flashlight. She turned to the first page of the textbook's index and stared at the writing in the margin.

Mary hates the teachers more than she hates us.
Jessie Dunn, January 1947.

Sonia turned away from the page again and looked up at Mrs. Peabody. She was writing on the blackboard, her wide rear end on full display, her thick waist pinched painfully by her ill-fitting girdle beneath her polyester dress. Idlewild's polite fiction that its girls would leave educated, ready for great things—Bryn Mawr, Yale, Harvard—was one that no one believed, not even the teachers.

Her temples pounded, an aftereffect of yesterday's episode in the dining hall. The details were shaky and juddery in places, like a film coming off its reel. She had frozen at supper, watching the girls fight, listening to the angry shouts from the teachers. Her friends had taken her back to their room while she'd fought the memory of something awful and terrifying, a thing she didn't want to look at or touch anymore.

Charlotte Kankle was sucking the side of her thumb, licking the blood off. She watched Mrs. Peabody with a sort of hypnotized focus, a half-asleep concentration. Sonia envied her, the way she could turn her brain off, think about absolutely nothing. It was a trick Sonia herself had never learned. That was what books did—they turned off your thinking for you, put their thoughts in your head so you wouldn't have your own. Her own treasure was her copy of *Blackie's Girls' Annual*, found on a shelf in the dorm, left by some previous occupant and quickly squirreled away so she could stare at its thirty-year-old plates and read its strange stories of English schoolgirls' picnic outings over and over again.

Books, Sonia had decided, were what she would live with when she finally left this place. She would work in a library—any library, anywhere. She'd sweep the floors if she had to. But she'd work in a library, and she'd read the books every day for the rest of her life.

Sonia's chair jerked: Katie, kicking her from the desk behind. Sonia had never seen a girl who got bored as fast, or as dangerously, as Katie. Roberta had the ability to be still, and CeCe rarely got bored at all, but behind Katie's tilted, dark-lashed eyes lurked a restless intelligence that sometimes looked for trouble.

Sure enough, seconds later a scrap of paper sailed over Sonia's shoulder and landed on her desk. Sonia uncrumpled it to see a crude drawing of Mrs. Peabody, wearing a witch's hat, sporting a wart on her nose, riding a field hockey stick, her black skirt hiked up and a pelt of dark hair visible on her knobby legs. The caption beneath the drawing read, *SPORTSMANSHIP, GIRLS! SPORTSMANSHIP!*

Sonia stifled a laugh. Sportsmanship was Mrs. Peabody's hobbyhorse, the lecture she gave out regularly, whether the topic was test marks or proper ways to line up in the dining hall or actual sports. Lack of sportsmanship, in Mrs. Peabody's view, was the root of most problems with Idlewild girls. Like Lady Loon's constant use of *ladies* or Mrs. Wentworth's spitting as she spoke, it was a tic that became more noticeable with the suffocating familiarity that was life at a boarding school, and it made for good satire. The sportsmanship lecture was unavoidable for any student who spent years in Mrs. Peabody's class.

Sonia slipped the paper into her textbook just as Mrs. Peabody turned around. "Miss Winthrop," the teacher said with dark intent.

"Yes, Mrs. Peabody," came Katie's voice from behind Sonia.

"You are disturbing my class for the third time this week."

Though she wasn't facing her, Sonia could imagine Katie's lip curling. "I didn't do anything."

Mrs. Peabody's eyes went hard. She was a fiftyish woman with a face pockmarked with old acne scars. She handled the girls with more dignity than Lady Loon, but she was tough as nails and usually mean, her fingers and teeth yellowed with nicotine. Sonia wondered what had caused Mrs. Peabody, like the other teachers, to take a job at Idlewild instead of at a normal school. "Your rudeness is only making it worse for you," she said to Katie.

"I didn't *do* anything, you old hag," Katie snapped back.

Sonia felt clammy sweat on her back, beneath her blouse. Charlotte Kankle had stopped sucking her thumb, and Cindy Benshaw was staring, openmouthed. *Stop shouting,* Sonia thought. She remembered having the same thought in the dining hall yesterday.

"Katie Winthrop!" Mrs. Peabody picked up a ruler and smacked it hard on the desk, making all the girls jump. "You are the most disobedient—"

Next to the blackboard, the classroom door flew open and hit the wall with a *bang*.

The girls jumped again, including Sonia. The sound was as loud as a gunshot, the doorknob crashing into the wall. There was no one in the doorway, nothing to see beyond it but an empty hall.

Let me in, a voice said.

Mrs. Peabody dropped her ruler. There was a breath of

silence in the room, a waft of cold air down the back of Sonia's neck. She slid down in her chair, her body wanting to fold in on itself. *What was that?* Sonia looked around. Rose Perry had her hand over her mouth, her eyes wide. Charlotte Kankle was gripping the sides of her desk with a white-knuckled hold. Had everyone heard it? Or was it just her?

"What is this?" Mrs. Peabody nearly shouted, her voice harsh and shrill. Fear, Sonia realized. She recognized fear. It was crawling through the depths of her own stomach right now. "Is this some kind of prank?" The teacher stared at them, her eyes blazing.

The room was silent. Even Katie didn't speak. Someone giggled, the sound terrified and completely devoid of humor. Someone else whispered, "Shh." Sonia stared at the open square of doorway. *What if something is coming? Right now? Down the hallway toward the door, slow and steady, closer, and when it reaches the door, it will—*

"Fine," Mrs. Peabody said into the silence of the room. "Since no one will confess, Miss Winthrop, get up. You're going to detention."

"That's unfair!" Katie shouted. "I didn't *do* anything."

Mrs. Peabody marched out from behind her desk and up the classroom aisle. Her face was red now, her cheeks mottled. "Get up," she said. "Right now." She yanked Katie out of her seat by the arm, jerking her upward in a bruising grip. Katie's limbs jumped like a marionette's, and her face set in an expression hard as granite. As Mrs. Peabody yanked her mercilessly back down the aisle, Katie caught Sonia's eye and her look was cold.

The girls watched as Katie was taken from the room, her shoes clapping uneasily on the old wood floor as she tried to keep her balance in Mrs. Peabody's grip. Then both of them were gone, and the air was heavy with silence. Not one girl breathed a word.

I should have done something, Sonia thought softly to herself, staring down at her textbook again. *I should have stood up. It's too late now.*

And suddenly, she felt like crying.

chapter 9

Barrons, Vermont
November 2014

At ten o'clock that night, Fiona arrived at Jamie's. She brought her laptop, her notebooks, and the promised six-pack of beer.

Jamie lived on the top floor of a duplex in downtown Barrons, an old Victorian house that had been restored—to a degree—and rented. The lady who owned it was more than happy to rent the top unit to a cop, and the family with two small children who lived in the bottom unit were happy to have him for a neighbor. The street was a treelined lane that had been wealthy a hundred years ago, when Barrons had seen better days. Now its big Victorians were split into apartments for blue-collar parents and retirees, and rusty bikes and abandoned kids' toys littered the half-mowed lawns.

He was sitting at his own laptop at the kitchen table, wearing worn jeans and a gray T-shirt, when she came in. There was a single light on overhead, the rest of the apartment in darkness. He didn't look up from the file he was reading when she closed the door behind her. "You eat?" he said. "There are leftovers in the fridge."

She dropped her things on the table across from him and hesitated. She hadn't eaten. He knew that. She probably should, but her brain was buzzing with everything she'd found, and she wanted to get to it.

Jamie looked up at her as if reading her mind. "Eat, or this doesn't get done," he said.

She sighed. "Fine."

He waved her away and went back to his file. She knew exactly how he felt. She dug in the fridge and found pasta and meat sauce, cold. She dumped some into a bowl, added a spoon, pulled two beers from the six-pack, and walked back to the table.

"Who's first?" she asked, sitting down and sliding his beer over to him.

"I'll go." Jamie cracked his beer and took a drink. "Sonia Gallipeau, age fifteen, was reported missing in early December 1950. She was an Idlewild student with no local family. She left to visit a great-aunt and great-uncle in Burlington. She left after a day without their permission—ran away. She got on the bus back to Barrons. She never got there, and she was never seen again."

"So it is her," Fiona said. "Not just a borrowed blouse."

"It seems so, yes." Jamie riffled through his stack of papers. "We have no trace of dental records and no trace of any living relatives. The great-aunt and great-uncle are long dead, no descendants. So at this point we can't match her, even with DNA."

Fiona took a bite of her cold pasta. "Where was she last seen?"

"Burlington, getting on the bus, by the ticket taker."

"What did the bus driver say?"

"No one interviewed him. No one even found out his name." Jamie pulled an old folder out of his pile and held it up. "You see this? This is the missing persons file." It had two or three pieces of paper in it, tops. "She was a boarding school girl, and she was fifteen, so she was presumed a runaway. Case closed."

"Who reported her missing?"

"The headmistress at Idlewild. One Julia Patton." Jamie put the file down again. "She died in 1971, so that's a dead end. I can't get a line on Idlewild's student records, because the school has been closed for so long. And Anthony Eden won't return my calls."

"Aha." Fiona held up her spoon. "That's where I come in. He returned mine."

Jamie shook his head. "Of course he did."

"It pays to have a nosy journalist on your side," Fiona said. "But in this case, it's a dead end. Because get this: According to Anthony Eden, there *are* no Idlewild student records."

Jamie sat back in his chair. "They're gone?"

"Disappeared when the school closed, and were most likely destroyed. Sixty years of records."

"That's going to make things harder." He scratched

at his beard for a second, dismayed. "Do you think Eden is lying?"

"Maybe," Fiona said. She took another scoop of the pasta. "It's always possible. But I can't see the angle. He wants this squared away fast, not drawn out. I can't picture him carting dozens of moldy old file boxes out of there and hiding them. And I can't figure what he would be covering up, since this happened before he was born."

"Neither can I. But I'm going to run a check at local storage places to see if he's rented a space. That many records would need room."

That was fine with her. She'd promised Anthony to handle the story quietly, not to keep him immune from police probing. "What else did you find?" she asked Jamie.

"We did a basic check on the name," he replied. "She was only fifteen, so there wasn't much. No medical or dental that we could find. She'd never been in the system before, as either a juvenile delinquent or a runaway. And no birth certificate, either—she wasn't born here."

That surprised her. They were a few hours from Quebec, and French names were not that uncommon. "She was from Canada?"

Jamie shook his head. "France."

Damn. Damn. She should have thought of that angle, instead of assuming and looking locally. *Never make assumptions,* her father admonished in her head. "You found immigration records?"

He nodded, his expression haunted. "She came in 1947."

It hit her. Arriving from France in 1947, age twelve,

no family. "Shit," she said. "You mean she was a refugee."

"Yes."

She put down her spoon and rubbed her fingertips over her eye sockets, thinking. "So Sonia spent her childhood in France during the war. Nazi-occupied France. She lost her parents, her family. And she came here, only to—"

"Only to be murdered and dumped in a well," Jamie finished for her.

They were silent for a minute. It had happened over sixty years ago, but something about it was still nauseating, as if she could smell that rotten stench from the blackness of the well once again. She pressed her fingers harder, then dropped her hands. It was done; Sonia Gallipeau was dead, no matter how unjustly. She couldn't change it, but maybe she could do something about it. "What about her records from France?" she said to Jamie. "Can you get those?"

He was sitting back in his chair, staring blankly at his laptop screen as if it might give him answers. He listlessly picked up his beer and drained it. "I've put the request out," he said. "It'll take a day or two. The only reason I was given permission to do it at all was in case she had living relatives in Europe that we can inform. Maybe someone, somewhere, was left to look for her."

Fiona stared at him. She knew how a small police force worked, and she knew even more now that she'd spent a year with him. "How long do we have?" she asked.

Jamie shook his head. "Not long. We don't have many detectives, Fee, and there was a murder in Burlington last week. We can spend some resources on it, but this girl has no family, and the likelihood is that whoever did this is dead."

"But it's a murder," she protested. "Once the coroner confirms it, it's an open case."

"A cold one. Cold before we even touched it. We'll do our due diligence—we'll investigate. But our resources are limited. There are fresh cases we have to work. If nothing comes up quick, we move on."

Fiona realized she hadn't touched her own beer yet. She cracked it open and took a drink. "Can your father help?" Jamie's father was a retired chief of police, and he still had cronies in the department who held considerable sway.

"I already asked him," Jamie said. "He said there's no point." He held up Sonia's slim missing persons file again. "This is from Granddad's time; he was one of the cops who interviewed the headmistress. Granddad died in 1982. The cop who took down this report is dead, too."

"We need people who were young at that time," she said. She opened her laptop and powered it up. "They're more likely to be alive now. How tired are you?"

"I'm not tired," he said. He looked tired, but she knew that, like her, he'd never sleep. They'd never done this before, she realized—worked together on something. Usually their work took them in separate directions, which was how she'd thought they liked it. But it was good, working with Jamie. "What do you have in mind?" he asked.

She circled her thoughts back to the task at hand. "It'll take some searching, but if we split it up, it won't take as long," she said. She opened her e-mail and called up a message from her in-box. "There's almost nothing about Idlewild online," she said. "Most boarding schools have alumni associations or something, but Idlewild was different. When it shut down, it just disappeared."

"Not the usual kind of student bonding," Jamie said.

"It wasn't a happy place for most of those girls, I think. They were sent there because they were problem kids. As far as I can tell, no one has ever planned a reunion, or tried to. Facebook gave me nothing, either. So I called the local historical society."

The Barrons Historical Society, it turned out, consisted of two old widowed sisters who kept copies of newspapers and random other papers willed to the society in a rented office that was open for only four hours a week. They might have seemed like dotty eccentrics on the surface, but Hester, the sister Fiona had talked to, had knowledge of Barrons that rivaled Jamie's.

"I've never been there," Jamie said.

"You'd probably love it," Fiona told him. "However, they had next to nothing about Idlewild Hall—only a few class photographs. I had the woman I talked to scan and e-mail them to me." Fiona had been prepared to drive to the office and do that herself instead of asking an elderly woman to do it, but Hester had surprised her, saying that she and her sister were in the process of trying to digitize the entire archive. "The pictures are interesting, but not particularly useful. Except one." She called it up in her e-mail and turned her screen so he could see. Eleven girls stood on the lawn in front of Idlewild, each girl holding a field hockey stick. They wore field hockey uniforms, and they were carefully posed, the girls on each side angled inward, their shoulders overlapping. Despite the sports uniforms, they all looked formal: unsmiling white girls of varying shapes and sizes, staring into the lens, waiting for the picture to be taken. At the left end was a woman who was obviously a teacher, though she looked to be only in her early twenties. Neat handwriting across the top stated: *Idlewild Girls Field Hockey Team, 1952.* Two years after Sonia's death.

Fiona let Jamie look at the photo, and then she clicked to the next attachment. It was a scan of the back of the photo, which was covered in the same neat handwriting, the ink only slightly faded over time.

Jamie leaned forward. "Shit," he said. "This is a list of their names."

"It's the only photo with handwriting," Fiona said. She clicked back to the photo itself and pointed to the pixels of black and white, the blur of girls' faces. "One of these girls must have known Sonia. And if we dig, somebody must still be alive."

It was nearly one o'clock when they found her.

The beer was long gone, and Fiona's eyes hurt, moving dryly in her skull as if they were made from the cracked volcanic ash of Pompeii. She was no stranger to Internet searches; she was something of an expert at them, in fact. A journalist had to be in this day and age. But she was soft, she realized. She'd spent too much time looking up gluten-free brownie recipes and ways to use egg cups to make Christmas decorations, and she'd never tried to find this many people from so long ago.

Most of the girls in the photograph, as far as they could tell, were dead. Four of the eleven, frustratingly, had such common names that it was impossible to pin down who they might be; since few Idlewild girls were local, they could have been born anywhere, so records searches were no good. One girl, Roberta Greene, a tall, pretty girl with a braid of pale hair, had possibly become a lawyer in New Hampshire under a married name. That was interesting, and Fiona wondered how an Idlewild girl had ended up with an expensive law school education. But it was Jamie who hit the jackpot, and he hit it with the teacher.

"Sarah London," he said. "Never married. Retired teacher, member of the East Mills Ladies' Society." He turned his laptop toward her, showing her the society's Web page complete with photo, and gave a tired smile that even this late, even with her ashy eyes, made Fiona's stomach flutter. "Thank God for old spinsters," he said. "I'll get an address from the DMV tomorrow."

It was a lucky break. They went to bed at last, and even though they were both exhausted, they pulled each other's clothes off in silence. Fiona didn't need any words as she slid her fingers through his hair, as he kissed the tender skin along her jawline and just below her ear, as he flexed his arms around her and pulled her in tight. As she hooked her legs over the backs of his thighs and smelled the scent of his skin and let all her thoughts spiral away as sensation took over.

After, Jamie dressed and curled up against her back in his T-shirt and boxers, asleep before his head hit the pillow. Fiona lay on her side with her knees up, her eyes open, feeling the weight of his arm over her waist and the deep, soothing rhythm of his breathing, and as she did so often, she thought about Deb.

Fiona had been at Tim Christopher's murder trial, sitting in the front seats reserved for the victim's family. She'd thought she'd get an argument when she said she wanted to go, but by the time of the trial it felt like her parents had been snatched by aliens that inhabited their bodies, leaving them silent and apathetic, barely able to look her in the eye. Maybe a seventeen-year-old girl shouldn't have been there, but it didn't matter. She'd gone.

The trial, she realized later, had been her full initiation into adult life, even more than the murder had been. Afterward, she'd no longer been able to pretend that this was happening to someone else, or that Deb had just died naturally and peacefully in her sleep—both fantasies she'd used while lying in bed at night, wishing frantically that it would all go away. The trial was where they had talked of blood and hyoid bones and scrapings from beneath Deb's fingernails. Of Deb's sexual activity, or lack of it, analysis of when her sister had had sex and how often. Strands of Deb's long black hair had been found in Tim Christopher's backseat, and a discussion had ensued about exactly how a girl's hair might get into her boyfriend's backseat: Was she lying there because they were having intercourse? Or was she lying there because he'd strangled her and she was already dead?

Fiona had always thought herself worldly because of her father's career. But the clear forensic debates by strange men in suits, in front of a crowded courtroom, of the contents of Deb's vagina—no one had ever said the word *vagina* in their house—had shocked her deeply, sickeningly. She had looked around the room and known that every person there was picturing smart, sleek, handsome Tim Christopher atop her sister in his backseat, grunting away. That, right there, had been her first clear understanding that adulthood was going to be nothing like she'd thought it would be.

There had been testimony, one day, from one of Tim Christopher's college friends. He had seen Tim the morning of the murder. They had shot hoops between classes. They had talked about nothing special, the friend recalled—except for one thing. There had been mention of a girl they both knew who had unsuccessfully tried to commit suicide the week before. The friend had been shocked, but Tim Christopher had just shrugged, throwing the ball at the hoop. *Some girls should just be dead*, the friend remembered Tim saying, his voice cold. *There's nothing that can be done*.

Deb, dead in that cold field. Sonia Gallipeau, curled up in the well four hundred feet away.

Some girls should just be dead.

Fiona thought of her sister's long, beautiful black hair, and closed her eyes.

chapter 10

Barrons, Vermont
November 2014

It snowed overnight, just a light dusting that gathered in the cracks and crevices, blowing in the wind like packing peanuts. Fiona drove over roads more and more remote and rutted into East Mills, a tiny town that didn't seem to offer much more than a gas station, a few grimy shops, and a Dunkin' Donuts. Trucks blasted by as she traveled the main street, either on their way to Canada or on their way back. The sky was mottled, the sun coming and going behind swift-moving clouds.

Sarah London lived in an old Victorian with missing shingles and a postage-stamp front lawn that was thick with dead weeds. Fiona had tried to call first, but had gotten only a phone that rang and rang on the other end, with no answering machine, and she hadn't had a signal on her cell at all for the last half hour. She pulled the phone out of her pocket now, as she sat in the driveway, but saw that she had no bars. Fine, then. She would wing it.

She got out and walked to the wooden porch, her boots loud on the damp, sagging steps. According to the DMV record Jamie had pulled, Sarah London was eighty-eight years old, which made the house's neglect logical, especially if the old woman lived alone.

Her first knock on the storm door wasn't answered, but her second knock brought a faint shuffling from within. "Miss London?" she called. "I'm not a sales-person. My name is Fiona Sheridan, and I'm a journalist."

That brought footsteps, as she'd known it would. The inner door swung open to reveal a woman with a stooped back, her thin white hair tied back. Though her posture was crouched and she was wearing an old housecoat, she still gave off an air of offended dignity. She narrowed her eyes at Fiona through the screen. "What does a journalist want with me?"

"I'm doing a story on Idlewild Hall."

In an instant the woman's eyes lit up, a reaction that she quickly struggled to mask as if she thought Fiona was leading her on. "No one cares about Idlewild Hall," she said, suspicious again.

"I do," Fiona said. "They're restoring it. Did you know that?"

For a second the woman swayed in utter surprise, her gaze so vacant with shock that Fiona wondered if she'd have to barge inside and use the landline to call 911. Then she gripped the doorframe and unlatched the storm door. "My God, my God," she murmured. "Come inside."

The house's interior mirrored the exterior: a place that had been cared for, but was now sinking into neglect with the age of its owner. An unused sitting room sat primly on the right, old figurines and knickknacks growing dust on its fussy shelves. The floor of the front hall was lined with a plastic runner that had probably been placed there in the early eighties. Fiona politely paused and unlaced her boots as the woman proceeded into the kitchen.

"I don't—I don't have anything," the woman said as she looked around the kitchen, where the newspaper she'd been reading was neatly set on the kitchen table. "I wasn't expecting . . ."

"It's okay, Miss London," Fiona said. "I don't need anything. Thank you."

"What did you say your name was again?"

"Fiona Sheridan. Call me Fiona, please."

Sarah London nodded, and Fiona noticed she didn't return the invitation. "Have a seat, Fiona."

Obediently, Fiona pulled out a kitchen chair and sat on it. *Once a teacher, always a teacher,* she thought. She folded her hands in front of her on the table.

That seemed to please the old woman. She pulled out her own chair and lowered herself. Her hands were twisted and gnarled with arthritis, the knuckles pearly gray. "Now, please tell me about this restoration. As you can see, I've been reading the newspaper, which I do every day. I've never read anything about this."

"That's why I'm writing the story," Fiona said.

Miss London seemed to consider this. "Who—who in the world is mad enough to restore Idlewild?"

It was a sentiment that so closely mirrored Fiona's own thoughts that she paused. But there was a tinge of nerves on the edges of Miss London's expression, on the edges of her words. "A woman named Margaret Eden," she said, "aided by her son, Anthony."

Miss London blinked and shook her head. "I've never heard of such people."

Fiona had a list of questions in her head that she'd planned to ask, but on an impulse she skipped all of them. "Why do you think it's mad to restore Idlewild?" she said.

"Well, of course it's mad." Miss London's voice shook a little, but she maintained her composure, sitting with ramrod posture. "Of course it is. That old building . . . that old place." She waved a twisted hand, as if Fiona should surely know what she was talking about. "Are they making it into a school?"

"Yes."

"Oh, dear God." The words were spoken swiftly, softly, as if they'd escaped from the woman's mouth. Then she recovered and said, "Well, I wish them luck."

"You were a teacher there for a long time, were you not?"

"Twenty-nine years. Until the school's last day."

"You must have loved it there."

"No one loved it there," the older woman said bluntly. "Those girls were trouble. They made life miserable for all of us. They weren't good girls. Not at all."

Fiona felt her eyebrows rise. "And yet you stayed."

"Teaching is all I know, Fiona," Miss London said, her expression growing stern. "It's what I do. Or what I did, at least."

"Was Idlewild the only place you ever worked?"

"I worked at a few other schools after Idlewild closed, until I retired. I'm local." That hand wave again, as if there was no need to say all of this aloud. "Born not even half a mile from where we're sitting now. A Vermonter all my life. I never saw the need to leave."

In the pasty light of the kitchen, Sarah London looked much older than she had at first, her eyes watery, the corners of her mouth drooping. She was a tough old Vermonter, but that didn't mean she'd had an easy life. "I have a photograph," Fiona said. "Would you like to see it?"

"I suppose," Miss London said carefully, though the gleam of interest in her eyes was a dead giveaway.

Fiona pulled a printout of the field hockey photograph from her pocket and smoothed it out over the table. Miss London looked at it for a long time. "That's me," she said finally. "Took over the team the year Charlene McMaster quit to get married. She barely lasted eight months. I didn't want to do it, not one bit. But we did as we were told in those days."

"Do you remember these girls?" Fiona asked.

"Of course I do. We didn't have all that many students. And my memory hasn't gone yet, praise God."

Fiona glanced down at the photograph, the girls lined

up in their uniforms. *They weren't good girls.* "You even remember their names?"

"Yes, probably. Why do you ask?"

"This was taken two years after the disappearance of a student named Sonia Gallipeau," Fiona said. "Do you remember that?"

The room rang with deafening silence.

"Miss London?" Fiona asked.

"The French girl," Miss London said quietly, almost to herself. She shook her head. "I haven't heard that name in over sixty years."

"Something happened to her," Fiona said. "In 1950."

"She ran away, they said." Miss London's hand went to her face, the gnarled yet elegant old fingers stroking her cheek in an absent, thoughtful gesture. "I remember that day. My first year. She went off to see relatives and never came back."

"What do you remember?" Fiona prompted softly.

"Everything." Miss London's fingers stroked her cheek again, automatic. "We searched for her, but not for long. There wasn't much to do about a runaway girl. I never said anything, because the case was closed and we all moved on. But I always thought she was dead."

"Why did you think she was dead?" Fiona asked.

"Don't get me wrong. We had girls who ran away." Miss London shook her head. "One just the year before Sonia. There's nothing you can do about a bad apple. But I never thought Sonia would do it. She had nowhere to go, for one. She wasn't even American. She was plain, quiet as a mouse. She wouldn't go off hitching rides or running away with some boy. She didn't have it in her."

"So you don't think she ran away."

"I thought at first—the relatives must have done it. It's the obvious choice, isn't it? No one knew them. They came to see her once a year at Christmas, but that was all. Then she goes to visit and she never comes back. But they checked out the relatives and said no. They were just a couple of old people who felt sorry for her, but didn't want to take in a girl. The wife had nagged the husband into the visit—said she felt bad, leaving the girl there for so long, with a visit only once a year. The husband didn't want to do it—he wasn't interested in a teenage girl, though eventually he gave in. But she'd changed her bus ticket and run away from them, too."

Fiona waited. Miss London's eyes were open, but she was seeing nothing, nothing but 1950. There wasn't even a clock ticking in this house; it was so silent.

"They found her suitcase," Miss London continued. "In the woods right off the edge of Old Barrons Road, where it meets the school gates. They found it in the weeds."

Now it was Fiona's turn to freeze in shock. *Right where I was walking,* she thought. *Right where I was standing, talking to Jamie on the phone, and listening to a shuffling sound in the gravel that was just like a footstep.*

The old teacher kept talking, the words spilling out. "What girl runs away with no suitcase? I ask you. Her friends were beside themselves, but the Winthrop girl left a few years later, and that girl, the Ellesmeres' girl, left after that. I don't know what happened to them. I don't know what happened to any of them."

"Wait a minute," Fiona said. "They found her abandoned suitcase, and still everyone thought she'd run away?"

"You weren't there," Miss London argued. "You weren't living with those girls. In that place. We had a girl run away the year before I came. They'd thought for sure she was dead. Then she turned up at her grandparents' in Florida with some hoodlum in tow." Her eyes met Fiona's, eyes that were aged and watery but somehow hard. "Sonia ran away from her own relatives, so it was decided. I couldn't say anything. I was new, but even then I understood."

"Understood what?"

"You can sit there and judge. But *you* spend twenty-nine years at Idlewild. I was on edge every day. It's a hard place, an awful place. I had to stay because it was my job, because I needed the money, but sometimes the girls . . . they ran. And deep down we didn't blame them."

"Why not?"

"Because we were all so horribly afraid."

The back of Fiona's neck was icy cold. "Afraid of what?"

Miss London's lips parted, but there was a smack on the front storm door, followed by the bang of the inner door. "Aunt Sairy!" came a woman's voice, roughened by cigarette smoke. "It's me."

Shoes clomped up the hallway runner, and Fiona

twisted in her chair to see a woman in her late forties come to the kitchen door, her lank blond hair in a ponytail, her wide hips pressed into yoga pants beneath her parka. She was scowling. "Oh, hello," she said, her voice darkening with suspicion.

Fiona pushed her chair back and stood up, figuring she was once again being mistaken for a salesperson, probably in the midst of snowing an eighty-eight-year-old woman into some kind of scam. "I'm Fiona Sheridan," she said, holding out her hand. "I'm a journalist writing a story about Idlewild Hall."

The cloud left the woman's face, and she looked at Miss London for confirmation. "Okay, then," she said ungraciously, shaking Fiona's hand briskly in her freezing-cold one. "I saw your car outside. Aunt Sairy almost never has visitors."

"Cathy is my sister's daughter," Miss London said from her seat at the table. She had recovered her brisk teacher's manner.

Fiona's chance was gone. There was no way to get back what had just been about to be said—whatever that was. But she wasn't ready to leave yet, Cathy or no Cathy. "Miss London, I'll get out of your hair, but can I ask you a few quick questions first? Nothing too complicated, I promise."

Miss London nodded, and Cathy banged into the kitchen, noisily doing something with the dishes in the sink. *I'm watching you,* her every movement said.

Fiona quickly lowered herself into a chair again. "First of all, the records from Idlewild haven't been located. Do you remember anything about where they might have gone when the school closed?"

"I don't know anything about any records," the old woman said, as Cathy banged a glass especially loud on the counter behind her.

"Okay," Fiona said. "You mentioned Sonia's friends. Can you tell me anything else about them?"

"Those girls were her roommates in Clayton Hall, the dorm," came the answer, called straight up from the old woman's memory. "They were together often. It was hard for her to make friends, I suppose, since she was quiet and not pretty. I remember thinking it was unusual to see girls like that become friends. They didn't fit."

"Didn't fit? How?"

"Oh, Lord." She waved a hand again, and Cathy ran the water in the sink in a rushing jet, nearly drowning her out. "The Winthrop girl, for one. She was trouble through and through. She was a bad influence. The Greene girl was nice enough, but we all knew she'd had a mental breakdown at home and stopped talking for months. Quiet, but touched in the head, that one. The Ellesmere girl came from a good family, but not properly, if you know what I mean. She was stupid, too. Not like Sonia."

Fiona pulled her notebook and pen from her pocket, the first time she'd done so. "What were their names? Their full names? Starting with the Winthrop girl?"

"It was a long time ago," Cathy complained from the sink. "Aunt Sairy shouldn't have to remember names."

"I *do*," Miss London insisted, her teacher's voice so

icy that Cathy was immediately silenced. "The Winthrop girl's name was Katie. Her people were from Connecticut, I think—good people, though their daughter had gone bad. She was a discipline problem from the day she arrived until the day she left."

"Where did she go? Home?"

"No. God knows. I think she found a boy or something. It wouldn't surprise me. She had that kind of look—the kind that boys go crazy for. Beauty, but not the wholesome kind." She shook her head. "The one that was touched in the head was Roberta Greene—she was on the field hockey team." She pulled the photo printout toward her and stabbed a finger at one of the girls. "That's her right there."

Fiona nodded, trying not to show how excited she was. Roberta Greene was the girl she and Jamie thought might have become a lawyer. She couldn't have been too "touched in the head" to get through law school and pass the bar. "She had a breakdown, you say?" Maybe there were medical records somewhere.

"Stopped talking. There was a suicide in the family, I believe, or an attempted one, and she witnessed it."

"That's terrible."

Miss London shrugged. "We didn't have social services or child psychologists in those days. We didn't have *Oprah* or *Dr. Phil*. Parents just didn't know what to do. They were at the end of their rope, and they sent her to us."

"Okay." Fiona steered the old woman's memories back. "The last girl, the stupid one. You said her name was Ellesmere?"

Behind her, Cathy finally gave up and stood watching them, her arms crossed tightly over her chest. Miss London answered, "The Ellesmeres were a prominent family in those days. The girl—Cecelia was her name; I have it now—was the daughter of Brad Ellesmere, but born on the wrong side of the blanket, if you know what I mean."

"Right." Fiona caught Cathy's eye, and they exchanged a brief look. The generation of people who used phrases like *born on the wrong side of the blanket* was rapidly disappearing, Fiona thought with a pang. "So she was Mr. Ellesmere's child, but she didn't have his name."

"That's right." Miss London lowered her voice a little, as if someone could still overhear this bit of juicy gossip. "She was the housekeeper's daughter. He let her have the child, but he packed her away. There was something about the mother going away for a while, too— went crazy from having a child out of wedlock, or so I heard. Brad Ellesmere didn't have children inside his marriage, but he had more than one bastard child. It was a scandal in those days, but we kept quiet about it. It was private business. It wasn't like now, when everybody's business is all over the Internet, for the world to see."

Fiona wrote down the name *Cecelia*. "And what was her last name, then?" she asked. "Her legal one?"

"Oh, goodness." Miss London stroked her cheek again, but this time it was for show. She was having a good time, and she wanted to draw it out. Fiona waited patiently, her pen poised. "We all thought of her as the Ellesmere girl. There was no secret about it—Brad Ellesmere himself dropped her off at the school. She used to follow the Winthrop girl around; it was a natural pairing, the strong, pretty girl with the weaker, pudgier one. Ah yes—Frank. That was her last name. I told you there was nothing wrong with my memory."

"No." Fiona smiled at her. "There certainly isn't."

"Okay, Aunt Sairy," Cathy broke in. "You need a rest."

"Thank you very much for your help, Miss London," Fiona said.

"You're welcome. What does Sonia Gallipeau have to do with a story on the school's restoration?"

"Part of the article is about some of the newsworthy events in the school's past," Fiona said smoothly. "Sonia's disappearance is one of them. I thought that if I could track down a few of her friends, one of them might be able to give me a memory of her."

"You're going to have a tangle," Miss London said practically. "Most of the girls disappeared when they left school. No one knew where they went, and frankly, there was no one who cared."

There was a second of silence in the room as these harsh words came down. Then Cathy moved to the kitchen door. "Don't get up, Aunt Sairy. Fiona, I'll show you out."

Fiona followed her through the house's stuffy hall. At the front door, she put her boots back on and dug a business card out of her pocket, putting it in Cathy's hand. "I appreciate you letting me talk to her," she said. "If she remembers anything else, or if I can come back and see her again, please give me a call."

Cathy gave her a baleful, suspicious stare, but took

the card. "No one cares about Aunt Sairy anymore," she said. "No one ever has. She's a good woman. If you publish one bad word about her, I'll come find you and sue you."

It was as good a farewell as she was going to get, so Fiona took it. As she started her car and pulled out of the driveway, she wondered why Sarah London's niece felt it was so important to insist, after all these years, that her aunt was a good woman.

She was five miles out of East Mills before she got a cell signal again, her phone beeping and vibrating on the passenger seat. She was on a back road heading to the paved two-lane that would eventually turn into Seven Points Road, her car shuddering over old potholes, but she pulled over beneath an overhang of trees and picked up the phone. In these parts, it was always best to take advantage of a signal when you could get one.

There was a message from Jamie: "Call me." She dialed him first, bypassing his office line and using his personal cell. He picked up on the second ring.

"Where are you?" he asked.

"Heading back from East Mills. I talked to the teacher."

"And?"

"I got a few names of Sonia's friends. I'll start tracking them. What about you?"

There was disappointment in his voice. There was a

low murmur of voices in the background, and she guessed he was inside the station, in the open desk area the cops used. "I have nothing, if you can believe it."

"Nothing?"

"The French police came back to me. They have a birth record of Sonia Gallipeau in 1935, and that's all. Nothing else."

Fiona felt her heart sink. She thought of the girl's body, curled in on itself in the well, her head resting on her knees. "No living relatives at all?"

"None. There's a death record for her father in Dachau concentration camp in 1943. Nothing about her mother, or any siblings."

Fiona stared out her windshield at a swirl of snow that had kicked up on the side of the road in the wind. Those words—*Dachau concentration camp*—had the power to give her a twist of nausea, a clammy, greasy chill of fear. "I thought the Nazis kept records of everything."

"So did I. But I think we're wrong. It's like Sonia was born, and then she and her mother disappeared off the face of the earth. Until Sonia appeared on the immigration records. Alone."

It was hard for her to make friends, Sarah London had said of Sonia, *since she was quiet and not pretty.* What sort of life had Sonia lived, the lone survivor of her small family in a strange country? Fiona felt outrage that she had died alone, her head smashed in, dumped in a well for sixty-four years. Deb had died alone, but she'd been found within thirty hours, buried with love at a funeral that had drawn hundreds of friends and family. She'd been grieved for twenty years, loved. Was still grieved. Sonia had simply been forgotten. "I guess we need to find the friends, then," she said to Jamie. "Miss London said the girls were roommates, and that they were close. One of them must remember her."

"I agree," Jamie said. "Listen, I have to go. Give me the names, will you?"

For a second, Fiona felt the urge to say no. She wanted to do this—she wanted to be the one to track these girls down, to talk to them, to do something for the dead girl in the well. But she couldn't do as much on her own as she could with the Barrons police force helping her. So she gave Jamie the names and hung up, staring at the deserted roadside with her phone in her lap, wondering why she felt like she'd just given the case away, let it slip from her hands.

She called her father, and the second she heard his voice, she began to feel better. "Dad, can I come by?"

"Fee! Yes, of course." She heard the rustle of papers, the beep of the outdated computer. He was working, as always. "How far are you? Let me put tea on."

"Give me twenty-five minutes."

"You have something to run by me, don't you, my girl?"

"Yes, I do."

"That's my daughter," he said, and hung up.

The trees waved in the wind, the bare branches over-hanging the car wafting like a sultan's fan. Fiona shivered and sank farther into her coat, unwilling to move for the moment. She had done this the other night, too—sat in her parked car at the side of the road, staring at nothing and thinking. There was something soothing and meditative about the side of a road, a place most people passed by. As a child she'd spent car rides looking out the window, thinking of the places they passed, wondering what it would be like to stop there, or there, or there. It had never been enough for her just to get from one place to another.

Now she watched as a crow landed on a stark branch on the other side of the road, its big black body gleaming as if coated with oil. It cocked its black beak at her and was soon joined by a second bird, the two of them edging cautiously along the branch the way birds do, each foot rising and falling with careful precision, the talons flexing out and curling in again as they gripped the branch. They stared at her with their small black eyes, so fathomless yet so knowing, as if they were taking in every detail of her. Near the end of the branch, having found a good vantage point, both birds were still.

The phone shrilled and vibrated in Fiona's lap, making her jump. She didn't recognize the number, but it was local. She answered. "Hello?"

"Okay, fine." The words were brisk, not bothering with a greeting. Fiona recognized the voice only because she'd just heard it twenty minutes ago—it was Cathy. "Aunt Sairy's napping, and she can't hear me, so I guess I'll tell you. But you have to promise she won't get in trouble."

Fiona felt her heart stutter in her chest, the back of her neck prickling. "What do you mean, get in trouble?"

"She had good intentions," Cathy said. "You have to understand that Aunt Sairy has a good heart. She meant well. She's been paranoid ever since she did it. That's why she didn't tell you. But she's getting old now, and we're going to get rid of the house soon. She's moving in with me. We might as well tell you as anyone."

"Cathy." Fiona was sitting up in the driver's seat now, her mouth dry. "What are you talking about?"

"The records," Cathy said. "From the school. She took them, the last day. They were going to destroy them—sixty years of records. There was nowhere to put them, nowhere to store them. No one wanted them. The Christophers had bought the land and were going to put the records in the landfill. So Aunt Sairy volunteered to take the records to the dump, but instead she brought them home."

"Home?"

"In the shed out back," Cathy said. "They're all there. They've been there since 1979. We'll have to get rid of them when we sell the house. Give me a few days to talk Aunt Sairy into it, and you can come and get them. Hell, they're worthless. You can have every single one of them for all I care."

chapter 11

Katie

Barrons, Vermont
October 1950

Katie had never been to Special Detention before, not
even when she got into a fistfight with Charlotte Kankle.
That fight had been broken up by Sally D'Allessandro, the
dorm monitor for Floor Three before she'd left Idlewild
and nosy Susan Brady had been appointed instead. Sally
had had an oddly languid manner for a dorm monitor, and
she'd never sent anyone to Special Detention—she'd just
halfheartedly dressed them down as she'd stood in front of
them with her droopy posture and bony arms. *Hey, just
stop it, okay?*

Katie followed Mrs. Peabody across the courtyard,
her hands still jittering in nervous fear. What had just
happened? Had that been real? The door banging open?
The voice? She hadn't heard the words exactly, but she'd
heard *something*. High-pitched, plaintive. The other girls
had looked as scared as she was. Katie watched Mrs. Pea-

body's polyester-clad back, looking for a sign, a reaction, anything from a grown-up. All she saw was the teacher's furiously angry stride, the swish of her dress loud in the silence.

Mrs. Peabody led her to a room on the first floor at the end of the teachers' dorm. She pointed to a stack of Latin textbooks, accompanied by blank paper and a pen. "The conjugation exercises," she said succinctly. "Do them until the detention is finished. I will be checking your work."

Katie stared balefully at the stack of books. "The exercises from which one?" she asked.

"All of them," Mrs. Peabody replied. "Think twice before you talk back to me and you pull a prank like that again."

"It wasn't a prank," Katie protested. How was that even possible? How could she have made the door slam open?

But in an angry flash of understanding, she knew it didn't matter. Because Mrs. Peabody already knew. This was all a fiction to make the teacher feel better. "It was Mary," she said to the older woman, the truth hard and satisfying as she watched Mrs. Peabody recoil. "It was *Mary*—"

Mrs. Peabody lunged forward and grabbed Katie's arm so fast, so hard, that Katie cried out. "I will hear no more of this nonsense!" she hissed, her face so close Katie could smell sugary peppermint on her breath. Her eyes were hard with fear. She shook Katie once, her fingers digging into her arm. "Conjugation exercises. One hour." She let her go and left, shutting the door with a click.

"*It wasn't a prank!*" Katie screamed at the closed door, as loud as she could. "*It was Mary!*"

There was no response.

Stupid, stupid. She was still shaking. Time to get herself together. Katie did a circuit of the room. A dusty chalkboard; a grimy window looking out toward the woods; a stack of old local newspapers, mostly rotted; a single desk and chair, the desk stacked with the books, papers, and pen. Katie tried the door; it was locked. She yanked at the window, but got a shower of old paint flakes in her hair for the effort. She got on her stockinged knees and inspected the desk, looking at all the initials carved by girls locked in Special Detention over the years. Disappointing—she didn't recognize any of the initials, nor had anyone carved anything good into the hard wood. A riffle through the blank notepaper showed nothing there, either.

Then she looked at the stack of textbooks. Books that stayed permanently in this room.

Teachers are so stupid.

She sat in the hard ladder-back chair and leafed open the top book. The verb conjugation answers were written in the margins; doing the exercises would be easy. The book was full of other messages left over the years, including an entire story about a unicorn written in pencil over the empty back pages, complete with drawings. The story started innocently, and got progressively dirtier, until the final illustration was so rude even

Katie had to laugh. Whoever the author was—the story was unsigned—Katie approved of her heartily. There were other messages in the book's margins, some of them barely literate, some of them rude, some of them potentially useful.

Mrs. Patton pretends she has a husband but she doesn't. Interesting. Mrs. Patton was Idlewild's headmistress, often spoken of but rarely seen. Katie filed this tidbit away.

Mary Hand walks on Old Barrons Road at night. She sucks blood. Maybe true, probably not, and not very interesting either way.

There is a baby buried in the garden.

Katie had heard this one before. It was one of Idlewild's myths, though she had no idea if it was true. Everyone hated the garden, which they were all forced to use in weekly sessions called Weekly Gardening. There was no one reason the garden was so hated, though the strangely slimy soil and the pervasive chill created by the shadows of the two buildings that bordered it were part of it. The garden never drained properly, and it always had an odor of rotting vegetables to it, mixed with something more pungent. Every once in a while someone resurrected the dead baby story, probably to scare the freshman girls.

Katie looked up when she noticed movement on the wall. A spider was crawling down from the ceiling, its legs rippling gracefully, its body fat and black. Katie stared at it for a long minute, transfixed and shuddering. Idlewild had a lot of spiders—and mice, and beetles, and bats under the eaves outside the locker rooms. But the spiders were the worst. If she killed it with her shoe, she'd be stuck looking at its dead black smear for the rest of Special Detention. Reluctantly, she looked down at the books again.

The next textbook had other bits of wisdom: *If you call for Mary Hand at dusk under a new moon, she rises from the grave.*

Beneath this, a different girl had written in bold, black pen: *Tried it not true*

The conversation was continued by a third girl, writing along the bottom of the page: *She is real. Died in 1907 after miscarriage. It is in the records.*

A debater chimed in: *Idlewild was not opened until 1919 stupid*

To which was returned: *This house was here then look it up. Her baby is buried in the garden*

The baby in the garden again. Katie glanced up at the spider, which was halfway down the wall now, intent on its spider business. There was a second one in the far corner of the ceiling, still and curled. She could not see a web. *Maybe I should kill them after all,* she thought. Feeling like she was being watched, she forced her gaze down and reached forward to turn the page.

Hold still, a voice said in her ear as a spider, black and cold, crawled over the edge of the desk and skittered over the back of her hand.

Katie screamed, upending the chair and backing away, shaking her hand. The spider dropped out of sight, but she could still feel the touch of its tiny legs on her skin, the feather pokes of its feet. Her heart was pound-

ing so hard her vision blurred, and she heard deep, gasping breathing that she realized was her own. She put her
hands to her ears.

Hold still, the voice said again.

Her teeth chattered. She struggled to inhale a breath
that tasted like old chalk and something acid, sour. She
backed up against the wall, her shoulders bumping it,
then too late remembered the spider she'd seen. She
looked up to find it poised several feet above her left
ear, utterly still, clearly watching her. It began a slow,
deliberate pace toward her, somehow intent. The other
spider was still in the corner of the ceiling, curled,
though its legs were now waving helplessly, as if it
couldn't move.

Katie tried the locked door again, her clammy hand
slipping on the knob. Then she lunged to the desk,
picked up one of the textbooks, and smashed the spider
on the wall.

She couldn't look at the mess it made. She dropped
the textbook and picked up the next one, holding it up,
maneuvering back toward the door. Somehow the door
seemed the safest place. Her hands were shaking. She
nearly put her back to the door, then realized there could
be more spiders—*spiders*—and stood several inches from
it instead, the textbook under her arm. The silence beat
in her ears. There was no movement.

"Fuck," she said into the silence. It was an awful
word—the worst curse she knew, the worst word in her
entire vocabulary. Her mother would have slapped her if
she'd heard her speak it. It felt good, somehow power-

ful, coming from her mouth right now. "Fuck," she said again, louder. *"Fuck!"*

There was no answer. She spun in a circle, still keyed up and shaking, the textbook raised, her gaze skipping over the disgusting smear on the wall. Everything was still. The thing in the top corner had stopped moving.

She let out a shaky breath. There were cold tears on her cheeks, she realized, though she had no memory of shedding them. She looked down at the textbook in her hands and opened it. Written in pencil, the lines of a familiar rhyme looked back up at her:

Mary Hand, Mary Hand, dead and buried under land. She'll say she wants to be your friend. Do not let her in again!

She stared at it, her head aching. Her eyes burned. Those two words: *Hold still*. She wanted to cry again.

She'd met Thomas when she was thirteen. He was sixteen, with big, heavy shoulders, eyes that drooped sleepily, and a curious smell of mothballs. He'd lived on the other side of the block. He'd liked to flirt with her, and she'd loved the attention: tickling, chasing, wrestling. More tickling. He had given her silly nicknames, teased her, made fun of her. She'd played along, breathless, feeling special, singled out among the other girls. He was *sixteen*!

And then, an afternoon in July: the air hot, the sky high and blistering blue, the two of them in the empty school yard, chasing each other around the playground, abandoned in the summer heat. He'd caught her behind the slide, which was too hot to touch that day, the slide that was so familiar to her with its nonsensical words painted down the side: BIG SLIDE FUN!

Thomas had pinned her to the ground, shoved at her skirt. *Hold still*, he'd said.

He'd knocked the wind out of her, and for a second her eyes focused on those bright yellow words—BIG SLIDE FUN!—in confusion, the letters crossing over one another. Then she'd felt his fingers on her, and she'd fought him. She'd bitten him, scratched him, thrashed him with her feet. He'd hit her—*hit* her—and thumped her to her knees on the ground when she'd tried to run, his big hands on her, his mothball smell in her nose. *Hold still.* Yanking her cotton underpants off, his only words to her for those few frantic, hot minutes: *Hold still.*

She'd managed to run. She wasn't faster than he was, with his big, long legs, but he gave up quickly, not wanting to chase her publicly through the neighborhood. She remembered coming through the front door of her house and seeing herself in the eyes of her mother, who was just then coming down the stairs: disheveled, her stockings ripped, her underwear gone, dirt in her hair, blood on her knees, a red mark on her cheek. Her mother had stared at her in shock for a moment and descended the rest of the stairs in one quick motion, gripping Katie by the arm.

"For God's sake, get cleaned up," she'd said. "Do you want your father to see you like this?"

"I don't—"

"Katie." Her mother's grip was painful. She was wearing a flowered silk blouse and a dark green skirt, stockings, heels. Katie could smell her mother's familiar smell, the Calgon soap she used and the Severens Ladies' Pomade she used in her hair. She could see the familiar look in her mother's eyes: anger, wretched fear, bone-deep disgust. *You're going to get in trouble,* her mother had warned her countless times, hissed angrily when her father was out of range, when she'd tried to run away yet again. *I don't know what's the matter with you. I've never known. You're going to get in trouble.*

"Go," her mother said, shoving her toward the stairs.

They blamed her, of course. They never even asked who the boy was, not that she would have told them. The low, murmured conversations behind closed doors were almost expected after that. Katie thought about running away again, but instead she'd been dropped off at Idlewild three weeks later, the mark on her cheek faded, the scrapes on her knees healed.

The Special Detention room was still. The air was thin, stale. The spider in the corner had quieted. But Katie was not fooled.

Somewhere here, breathing. A quiet sound, some-where she couldn't see.

And then a breath of voice, pleading. *Let me in . . .*

Katie felt her legs tense. She squeezed her bladder, trying not to let it go.

Let me in. More clear now, coming from the direc-tion of the window. *Please. Please, I'm so cold. Let me in!*

"No," Katie said. She made herself shout it. "No! I'm not letting you in! Go away!"

Please. The voice was high, pitiful, pleading. *I'll die out here.*

Katie was shaking. "You can't because you're already dead." She stared at the window, saw nothing, and turned in a full circle, her eyes panicked and staring. "I'm not letting you in, so go away! I mean it!"

Let me in, came the plaintive cry again—and then her mother's voice, close to Katie's ear, spoken like an expert mimic. *You're going to get in trouble.*

She exhaled a long terrified breath. She waited, but no more voices came, not for the moment. But they would come again. She already knew she was going to be in here for a while.

She stepped to the desk, picking up the pen and tapping it experimentally, looking for hidden spiders. Then she retreated to her spot next to the door. She balanced the textbook on her other arm and managed to write with cold, stiff fingers:

I am trapped in Special Detention with Mary Hand and I can't get out

She stilled for a long moment, waiting. Waiting.

Then she added: *Mary knows.*

She lowered herself to the floor and crossed her legs beneath her skirt as something faint and weak scrabbled at the window.

chapter 12

Malcolm Sheridan listened patiently, sipping his tea, as Fiona told him about the girl in the well. As she talked, he got quietly excited, evidenced by the quick jittering of his knee.

"Does the coroner have her?" he asked when she finished.

He meant the body. Sonia's body. "Yes."

"That'll be Dave Saunders. Can you get the results through Jamie? If not, I can call him."

Fiona sat back in her mother's old flowered chair, thinking. "I don't think the report will have any surprises," she said. "I saw the girl—her skull was clearly smashed in. I can probably get the report from Jamie."

"That's a damned lucky break with those records," her father said, his mind already flying past hers, following its own track. He had put down his cup and was staring at the glass coffee table, his brow furrowing. This was what he was like when a story was brewing, she thought. She hadn't seen this in a long time.

"What I want," she said, trying to steer his formidable brain, "is to know if there's something we're missing in France. Family, history. Something more than a birth certificate."

"You mean something from the camps," Malcolm said.

"Yes. Jamie found her birth record, but—"

"No, no, no," Malcolm interrupted. He got out of his chair and started to pace. "There are other places to look. Libraries, museums, archives. The government record is the smallest part of the picture. Was she a Jew?"

Fiona shook her head. "I don't know."

"It's possible she wasn't. She would have been so young during the war—not all the camps took children, or kept them alive if they did. If her father was in Dachau, she was likely imprisoned with her mother. We'll have a better chance of finding her through a search for the mother."

Fiona looked at her notes. "The mother's name was Emilie. Emilie Gallipeau."

"But no death record?" Malcolm picked up his cup and carried it into the kitchen. His voice traveled back to her. "It could have been any of the camps. Ravensbrück took women, and children, too, I think. So many of the records were sealed for decades, but a lot of them are coming unsealed now. And of course, many records were completely lost. The war was a great mess of data, you know, before computers. Full of human hubris and error. A different time. I have reference books, but some of them are outdated already. In some ways, right now is an exciting time for historians, if you can catch the last survivors before they die."

"Okay," Fiona said. A pulse of excitement beat in her throat, but she tried to push it down. Most goose chases like this ended up with nothing, she reminded herself. "Since I can't go to France and search every archive and library, what do I do?"

Her father reappeared in the doorway. His eyes crinkled with amusement. "You talk to someone who can. Or who already is."

"The police—"

"Fee, Fee." He was clearly laughing at her now. "You've spent too long with that policeman of yours. The police don't have all the answers, and neither does the government. *The people* are where you find things. Like those records you just found. The people are the ones who keep the memories and the records the powers that be would rather erase."

"Dad." If she didn't stop him now, he'd launch over his favorite ground, the political lectures that used to amuse her mother before Deb died. Once a hippie, always a hippie. "Okay, okay. We can go through whatever channels you want to find information. I promised Jamie we wouldn't interfere with the police investigation, that's all."

"No. The police will do an autopsy, do a search for living relatives, then put the file in a cold case box and move on. They won't be going anywhere near France in 1945. But we can find her, Fee. We can find out who she was."

For a second, emotion rolled up through Fiona's

throat, and she couldn't breathe. Her father had been like this, once upon a time. The man in the photo on the wall in the other room, the man on the ground in Vietnam in 1969, had been complicated and demanding and often absent, but he had been so painfully, vibrantly alive it had almost hurt to be around him. The air had crackled when he walked into a room. Malcolm Sheridan had never done small talk—he was the kind of man who looked you in the eye on first meeting and said, *Do you enjoy what you do? Do you find it fulfilling?* If you had the courage to answer, he'd listen like it was the most fascinating thing he'd ever heard. And in that moment, it always was. He was a brilliant dreamer, a relentless intellectual, and a troublemaker, but the thing that always struck you about Fiona's father was that he was truly interested in *everything*.

It had been twenty years since she'd seen that man. He'd vanished when Deb's body had been found on the field at Idlewild. When Tim Christopher had murdered his daughter, Malcolm had folded in on himself, disappeared. The man who had emerged from that experience had been subdued, unfocused, his anger scattershot, bubbling up and disappearing into apathy again. Fiona's mother, who had been so tolerant of his larger-than-life personality before the murder, had simply shut down. She'd severed herself from his interests, from their friends. After the divorce, she'd been determined not to be that woman, Malcolm's wife—Deb's mother—anymore.

But this Malcolm, the one Fiona was seeing a shadowy glimpse of right now—this Malcolm was the man people still spoke reverently of twenty years later, the man people still dropped everything for when he phoned. The man who had inspired such awe that his name had still gotten Fiona hired at *Lively Vermont*.

But she couldn't say any of that. They never talked about it, about what had happened after Deb. It was too hard. Fiona gathered up her notes, trying to keep her expression and her voice level.

"Okay," she said to him. "I'll leave it with you. I have to stop by *Lively Vermont*. And I'm going to find these girls, these school friends of Sonia's."

"I'll call you later," he said, turning back toward the kitchen. He called out: "Make sure that boy of yours doesn't screw up the investigation!"

As Fiona was on the road to the *Lively Vermont* offices, her phone buzzed. Anthony Eden. She ignored it. She'd update him later. Starving, she stopped for a burrito, then drove through downtown Barrons to the boxy old low-rise whose cheap rent was the kind that *Lively Vermont* could afford. Though it was only five o'clock, the sun was sinking fast in the sky, reminding her that winter in its full force was coming, with its whiteouts and snowdrifts.

She was too late to see Jonas—he must have left on time today, which was rare for him. Fiona got the janitor to let her in. The offices were empty, Jonas's door closed and locked. Instead of bothering him at home, Fiona took a piece of scrap paper from a handy desk and wrote, *Came by to give you an update. Not much yet, but it's good. Trust me. I'll call tomorrow. F.* She folded the paper and slipped it under his door.

She had the file she'd pulled from the archives under her arm, so she walked to the scarred old cabinets on the wall to replace it. But with the drawer open and the file in her hand, she paused.

There are references to the Christophers in there, Jonas had warned her.

He was right. She'd seen it when she read the file: a photograph from the opening of the Barrons Hotel in 1971, showing Henry Christopher, dubbed a "prominent local investor and businessman," standing next to the mayor, wearing a tuxedo and shaking hands while smiling at the camera. He was young, his resemblance to his future son sharp and distinct. At his shoulder was a cool, pretty blond woman in a shiny silk dress, smiling tightly at the camera. In true 1971 style, she was listed in the caption only as "Mrs. Christopher." *Ilsa,* Fiona thought. *Her name is Ilsa.*

She stared at the two faces, both young and attractive, a couple who was married and rich and had it all. Their son, who would grow up to kill Deb, would be born in three years, an only child. When Tim went to prison for murder, Henry and Ilsa left Vermont.

Fiona had glossed over this picture when she'd first seen it, flinching away as one does when seeing an unexpected picture of something gory or dead, but now she made herself look at it. She waited for some kind of emotion to overcome her—hatred of these two people, or re-sentiment, or grief. None of that happened. Henry kept smiling from his chiseled, handsome face and Ilsa kept looking slightly uncomfortable, and Fiona felt nothing but a churning in her gut.

Henry Christopher looked at ease next to the mayor, as if they knew each other well. The Barrons Hotel had closed after barely four years, unable to stay afloat.

Henry Christopher and the mayor, selling Barrons a bill of goods and smiling about it.

She should quit this, but instead she closed the file and moved two cabinets down, to the files from the 1990s. She dug out 1994, the year of Deb's murder, and opened it.

She had never read *Lively Vermont*'s coverage of the murder, assuming it had been covered at all. In the 1990s the magazine hadn't gone through its lifestyle phase yet and was still trying to be a newsmagazine, though it did its best to be the splashy kind that was in favor at the time. They'd changed the format to *Rolling Stone*–like larger, thinner paper and tried to put sexier stories on the cover. *Ah, the last days of magazine glory,* Fiona thought wistfully, looking through the year's issues, *when everyone was still making money.*

She could not have explained why she was doing this any more than she could explain why she'd walked Old Barrons Road, watching the patterns of cars, in the middle of the night. Maybe it had to do with seeing a spark of Malcolm's old spirit earlier. Whatever the reason, it was a compulsion. Her blood started prickling as she paged through the issues of the magazine, the back of her neck tightening as it had the other night. *I can't stop this. I can't.*

The murder wasn't a cover story—that was too tabloidy for *Lively Vermont*—but they had covered the story after Tim Christopher's arrest in a longish piece entitled "No Peace: Murder of a Local Girl Puts an End to Innocence in Rural Vermont." Fiona winced at the headline at the same time her eye caught the piece's byline: It had been written by Patrick Saller, a former staffer Fiona was familiar with who had been cut loose in one of *Lively Vermont*'s many staff purges and still freelanced the occasional story.

It wasn't a bad piece; Saller had done his homework. There was a timeline of Deb's disappearance and murder that was correct, including the clothes Deb had last been seen in (white blouse, dark green cotton pants, light gray raincoat, black knit hat) and the fact that her roommate, Carol Dibbs, had been confused about the time she'd last seen Deb because of clocks that gave two different times in their shared apartment.

The photos, too, were better than the ones taken from the wires in every news story of the day: the outside of Deb and Carol's dorm building, looking forbidding and cold; a portrait of Deb cropped from a photo of her twentieth birthday two weeks before the murder, her hair flying, her face relaxed in a laugh. Their parents had released photos of Deb to the media when she went missing, but everyone used the more formal one, showing Deb sitting demurely with her hands in her lap; the snapshot Saller had picked was blurrier but, Fiona thought, showed Deb's true personality better. The biggest shot was of the field at Idlewild Hall, as Fiona herself had seen it days after the body was removed, littered with wreaths and garbage.

It was as if Saller had gotten a shot of Fiona's own memory, and she stared at it for a long time, remembering what it had felt like to stand there, wondering what the hell she had expected to see, her feet freezing in her sneakers, snot running onto her upper lip. The memory brought a wave of nausea with it, as if Fiona were temporarily seventeen again, in the middle of that dark tunnel with no way out, with strangers for parents and teachers who gave her meaningful looks. For the rest of that school year—which she'd barely passed—she'd been That Girl, the one whose sister had been murdered. It had been a year of therapy sessions and irrational anger and a sort of blank, terrifying grief, accompanied— thank you, adolescence—by a skin breakout that had refused to go away.

It's over, she reminded herself. *It's over.*

Yet twenty years later, she was sitting at a desk in the magazine's empty offices, reading the story.

But as she scanned the article, something jumped out at her. Something she had never seen before.

It was buried in an account of the evidence, pieced together from various sources, since the trial had not yet happened. The facts were familiar. In Tim's defense, there were no witnesses to the murder; Deb had not been raped, and had no skin cells or bodily fluids on her; though he wasn't a straight-A student, Tim was known as a decent, good-looking guy from a good family who wasn't violent. Counteracting this were the hairs in his backseat, the fact that he was the last person seen with her, the fact that he and Deb had fought loudly and often, including on the day she was murdered, and—most damningly—a smear of her blood on the thigh of his jeans. The blood was likely from Deb's nose, since blood had been found in her nostrils as if she'd been hit, and it had probably been wiped there absently from Tim's hand when she'd bled on him.

The biggest question was that of Tim's alibi. At first, this was a blank in the narrative of Deb's last night, like a passage that had been blacked out; but Patrick Saller had interviewed the owner of Pop's Ice Cream, an ice-cream parlor on Germany Road, twenty minutes from the university campus. "He was here that evening," Saller quoted the shop's owner, Richard Rush, as saying. "Just after nine o'clock. He was alone. He ordered a cup of Rocky Road and stayed here, eating it, until we closed at ten." Rush claimed that Tim was the only customer in the shop for much of that time, and therefore no one else had seen him. Deb's time of death had been placed at sometime between nine and eleven o'clock.

Fiona stared at the paragraph, reading it over and over. The words blazed in front of her eyes, then blurred again.

None of this had been mentioned at the trial, or in any other coverage of the case. At trial, Tim had had no alibi for the time of the murder, claiming he had gone home alone after dropping Deb off after a fight. He admitted to hitting her and making her nose bleed, but nothing else. His lack of alibi had been part of what had brought a conviction. Tim's testimony had never mentioned Pop's Ice Cream at all.

If Richard Rush was his alibi, at least until ten o'clock, why hadn't it been presented in court? It wasn't complete, but it cast reasonable doubt on the timeline. What the hell had happened? Why would a man fighting a murder charge not present testimony like this? Had it been discredited somehow?

Leave it. Even as she was thinking it, Fiona had put the magazine down and was reaching for the phone on the empty desk she was sitting at. *Leave it.* She Googled Pop's Ice Cream on her cell phone and saw that it was still in business, still on Germany Road. She used the landline to dial the number, in case the place had a call display.

"Pop's," said a voice on the other end of the line.

"Hi," Fiona said. "I'm looking for Richard Rush."

It was a long shot, but she had nothing to lose by trying. "Um," said the voice, which was teenage and so far indistinguishable between male and female. "Does he work here?"

"He used to own the place," Fiona said.

"Oh, right. Um. Let me get the owner."

Fiona waited, and a minute later a thirtysomething male voice came on the line. "Can I help you?"

"Hi. I'm looking for Richard Rush, who used to own the shop in the 1990s. Do you know who I'm referring to?"

"I should." The voice gave a flat laugh. "That's my dad."

"Is Mr. Rush still working, or is he retired?"

"Dad is retired. Gone to Florida," the man said. His tone was getting cooler now, guarded. "Who am I speaking to?"

"My name is Tess Drake," Fiona said. Tess Drake was the receptionist at her dentist's office, and she'd always liked the name. "I write for the magazine *Lively Vermont*. I'm doing a follow-up story to a piece we did in 1994."

"Well, I'm Mike Rush," the man replied, "and I'm surprised. I don't think *Lively Vermont* has ever done a piece on us. I've worked here since I was sixteen."

Score again. Fiona should have been playing the slots with that kind of luck. "It wasn't a piece about Pop's, exactly," she said. "It was a story about a murder that happened in 1994. A college student. Your dad was interviewed. It's the twenty-year anniversary, and we're doing a follow-up piece."

"You're talking about Deb Sheridan," Mike said. "I remember that."

Fiona's throat seized for a brief, embarrassing second. She was so used to everyone tiptoeing around Deb in her presence that it was strange to hear this man, who had no idea who she was, say the name so easily. "Yes. That's the one."

"Horrible," Mike said. "I remember that night."

"You do?"

"Sure, I was working here. I told you, I started when I was sixteen. Dad had me working the store with him that night." Mike paused, as if something uncomfortable was coming back to him. "I never really knew what to think."

"You saw Tim Christopher in the shop that night? The night of the murder?"

"He was here, yes."

There was a hesitance in his voice that tripped Fiona's wires. "But?"

He sighed. "Listen, Dad would be furious if he knew I was telling you this. What the hell? I'm thirty-eight, you know? I have kids of my own, teenagers. And he's in Florida, and I'm still worried about what my dad would say if he heard me."

"I know," Fiona said. "I can sympathize. I really can. But he isn't here, Mike. And I want to hear what you have to say."

They were the right words. She knew it, even as the line was quiet for a moment, as he thought it over. Twenty years, and no one had ever wanted to know what eighteen-year-old Mike had seen that night, what he thought, how it had affected him. How it had frightened him.

Because it had. That twenty-year-old fear was buried deep in the tenor of his voice, but Fiona could hear it. It was like a whistle on a dog's frequency, that fear. Only someone who felt the same would know.

"Tim Christopher came into the shop while I was working," he said, unaware that he was slicing Fiona with every word, making her bleed. "Dad was here, too. Tim had on a red flannel shirt and jeans and a baseball cap. He was a big guy, football player size, handsome, with hands twice the size of mine. He was by himself. He ordered Rocky Road ice cream, and I took his money. Then he ate it and left. That's a fact. That's what happened. Except the thing is, it happened at four o'clock in the afternoon."

Fiona's mind calculated wildly. She knew the timeline in detail by memory. At four o'clock in the afternoon, according to the official record, Tim Christopher claimed to have been taking a walk after his last class of the day, alone. He had had a beer with friends at five thirty, the next time any witnesses could vouch for him. At seven thirty, he'd gone to Deb's dorm room to pick her up, and the two of them had argued, with Carol Dibbs in her bedroom listening through the walls, looking at a clock that was wrong. At seven fifty, they'd left together, and Carol had watched through the window as Deb, still angry, had gotten into Tim Christopher's car. By eleven o'clock, she was dead and lying on the field at Idlewild.

Tim claimed their argument—Deb was irrationally jealous, he said, and accused him of cheating on her—had gotten so tense that she asked him to drop her off on a downtown street. She didn't want to be in the car with him anymore, he claimed. He'd dropped her off and driven away, angry. He pinpointed the spot to police. But despite a widespread request in the media, the investigation had never found a single witness who had seen Deb after Carol watched her get in Tim's car, and now Tim was in prison, serving time for her murder.

A witness who had seen him from nine to ten o'clock, alone, would have made all the difference.

"I don't understand," Fiona managed into the phone.

"Me, neither," Mike agreed. "I know what I saw. I

know what time it was, and I damned well know the difference between four o'clock in the afternoon and nine o'clock at night. But Dad was here when Chief Creel came—I wasn't on shift then. Dad told the chief what he'd seen, and he said nine o'clock. No one ever asked me anything—no one. When I saw that article and asked Dad about it, he got angry. My dad only ever gave me the belt three times in my life, and that was one of them. He told me never to ask about it again."

Chief Creel. That was Jamie's father. Fiona's throat was dry while her hand was clammy on the receiver. "But that testimony never made it to trial."

"I know. I don't know what happened. Dad shut me out of everything, and like I said, no one ever asked. That was a bad time. Dad was really weird for a while. I knew it wasn't a mistake—Dad never made mistakes like that. He never forgot anything, not the prices of his ice creams or my mom's hair salon appointments or his kids' birthdays. He knew four o'clock, just like I did. But then I finished school, and I moved out to go to college, and the trial was months later. And I figured Dad must have told Chief Creel he'd made a mistake, because there wasn't anything said about Tim coming into the shop at all."

"Okay," Fiona managed. "Okay, I see. Should I ask your father about it?"

"He won't talk to you," Mike said. "And he'll be mad as hell at me."

It wasn't an answer. "You're not going to give me his number, are you?"

"No, I'm not, Miss Drake. You can get it yourself. And I'll give you a word of advice."

"What is it?"

"This case," Mike said. "If you're writing a follow-up about it twenty years later, you need to add that people here haven't forgotten. That's more important than the timeline or the trial—Tim was convicted because he killed that girl. I believe that. That day, I served ice cream to a man who went on to murder his girlfriend and dump her like a piece of trash. I can still see his face. I still wonder what I could have done. It affected a lot of us, even eighteen-year-old clueless punks working in ice-cream stores that nobody wanted to talk to. My sister was thirteen, and after she read the news reports, she had nightmares. My mother wouldn't let her out alone. You have to remember what it was like in 1994. No one was on the Internet—no one had grown up looking at this stuff. My kids are growing up inured somehow, less scared than I was. But in 1994, we were *scared*."

So was I, Fiona thought. "Thank you, Mr. Rush. I appreciate it."

She hung up the phone—the receiver was slick with her sweat—and stared at the wall, unseeing. Her head throbbed. Her jaw ached. Unbidden, Sarah London's words came back to her, the ones she'd spoken right before Cathy had come in and interrupted them.

We were all so horribly afraid.

Sonia.

Deb.

It was time to go back to Idlewild.

chapter 13

Fiona waited until dawn, when the sky had turned cold slate gray and the first neighbors in her building had begun to leave for work. She'd stayed home from Jamie's last night, begging off with an excuse when he'd texted her. He hadn't pushed.

So she'd stayed home, done her laundry, thrown out some of the more disgusting remnants in the fridge, and replaced them with fresh groceries. Her apartment was in a low-rise building on the south end of town, on a smattering of old residential streets that had once been intended as a suburb perhaps, but had frozen in size as Barrons itself had stopped growing, like a bug in amber. The rent was cheap, the building was ugly—they made nothing beautiful in the early 1980s—and the apartment itself was functional, filled with secondhand furniture she'd scoured from her parents' spare rooms and off Internet listing sites. The only artwork on the walls was a framed Chagall print Jamie had bought back in the summer and put up himself. Fiona had wanted to argue with him about it until she saw how the print looked on the wall, with its dreamy figures floating upward, looking into one another's eyes. She had to admit then that it was the best thing in the entire apartment, and she'd left it up.

She barely slept, and when the sky began to turn light, she rolled out of bed, showered, and pulled on jeans, a T-shirt with a gray flannel shirt buttoned over it, and her hiking boots. She zipped up her heavy late-fall coat and tucked her damp hair into a knit cap against the cold. Then she took the elevator down to the building's small lot, got in her car, and drove toward Old Barrons Road.

She parked on the side of the road, at the bottom of the hill, near where she'd stopped the car a few nights ago. She'd studied the Idlewild property lines more than once, trying to figure out Tim Christopher's path with her sister's body. The west side of the property, past the woods on the other side of the sports field, bordered government land, sealed off with a high fence. The north side contained all the school's buildings—the main hall, the dorm, the gymnasium and old locker rooms, the teachers' hall, the cafeteria, the support buildings. Past that, the land dropped off in a slow tangle of thick, weedy brush, wet and muddy, nearly impossible to walk, three miles toward the nearest back road. The south side likewise had no access, deep with brush and freezing mud, spattered with trees, bordered by old overgrown fields. This place, on the east edge where Old Barrons Road twisted up toward the gates of the school—this place was

the fastest way to get from a car to the Idlewild grounds
if you weren't driving through the front gate. If you
knew your way through the gaps in the old fence.

Fiona swung her legs out of the car and got her bear-
ings. The wind howled a gust straight down the hill,
dense with early cold, and too late she realized she'd forgotten gloves. She shoved her hands in her pockets and
walked toward the trees.

It was dark in the thicket of trees, even though the can-
opy of leaves was gone. The trunks were narrow, packed
dense, hard to see past. As the light came through the
other side of the trees, Fiona saw Anthony Eden's new
fence, a high chain-link with signs posted warning trespassers to keep away. Keeping the kids out, as well as the
vagrants and the curious people and any other locals who
had been using this land since the school closed in 1979.

Gritting her teeth at the cold metal against her bare
hands, Fiona climbed the fence. By the time she got to
the top, she was sweating beneath her coat. Normally
she ran for exercise, a route she did around her neighborhood and back, but lately she'd fallen off the wagon.

From her high vantage point, she could see across the
grounds. The main school building loomed off to her left,
its teeth bared at her in the dim light. *I see you,* it seemed
to leer. Behind it were the shapes of the school's other
buildings, blurred in shadow. Farther toward the other
end of the property she could see the ruins of the well,
indicated by the last strips of police tape that had cordoned
off the site. Beneath her was the edge of the sports field.
There was no one in sight, and no cars sounded on the

road behind her through the trees. Fiona swung her leg over the top of the fence and started down the other side.

What the hell are you doing here, Fiona? The question came as her hiking boots hit the ground. It was Jamie's voice, as clear as if he were standing at her shoulder, shaking his head. She walked across the field and toward the buildings as the wind buffeted her hat. She shoved her hands in her pockets again.

She had no interest in getting inside any of the buildings, even though she'd watched Anthony key his security code into the main keypad and memorized it in case she needed it later. She skirted past the main building, forcing herself to stop and look up into its grim face, to stare at its blank windows and sagging roof. She tried to picture Sonia here, standing where she was right now, having escaped an unknown hell in Europe only to come to a strange country and face this forbidding building, her new home. Had she felt relief, or had she been just as frightened here as she'd been in some godforsaken concentration camp?

Past the main building, she followed the same path she and Anthony had walked, toward the dining hall. As she passed the garden, icy cold in its dank shadows between buildings, her phone vibrated with a text. Fiona took out her phone and swiped it with a numb finger. It was Jamie.

Why do I have the feeling you're not home in bed right now?

Fiona stopped, staring down at the words. How the hell did he know? She wiped tears of cold from her eyes and typed a reply. *Wrong. I'm snug under my covers, asleep.*

His reply was immediate. *Oh shit. Where are you?*

Fiona blew out a frustrated breath. She didn't mean to make him worry; she really didn't. He didn't have to. She could handle it. She *was* handling it. She quickly typed *I'm fine* and sent it, then dropped the phone back into her pocket.

From the corner of her eye, a shadow moved in the garden.

She turned and looked. It was an animal, perhaps—a fox or a rabbit. Gone now. But from the corner of her eye, the shape had been . . . strange. Nothing like an animal. Smooth, sinuous, like something bent, bowing its head to the ground.

Over the silence came a faint high-pitched sound. Fiona turned back, facing the way she'd come, listening. Voices? No, not voices, exactly. Music. Someone was playing a song, back out past the main building, in the direction of the field.

She started toward it. She couldn't catch the tune, exactly, though it sounded familiar—it was too far away, the wind whipping it and dispersing it. Who the hell was at Idlewild, playing music at this hour? Some teenager with an MP3 player? She started to jog as she rounded the side of the main building, her heart speeding up. Someone was here, messing around—there was no reason to be afraid. But there was something about the music—the familiar rhythm and cadence of it, which her brain hadn't quite placed—that made her wonder if she was alone here. That made her realize she was armed with absolutely nothing with which she could defend herself.

There was no one in front of the school, no one visible

on the muddy half-dug road or in the dark stand of trees. No one at the gate. The music didn't come from there anyway—it was coming from the direction of the field.

There was someone in the field.

Fiona stopped dead when she saw the figure. It was a woman, small and slight—a girl, perhaps. She wore a black dress that was long and heavy, a costume from a bygone era. She faced away, looking off at nothing over the field, utterly still.

What the hell was going on? There had been no one in sight when she'd straddled the fence minutes ago. Fiona approached the girl, consciously making noise so she wouldn't startle her, noting that the girl had no coat in the cold. "Hello?" she called as she started over the field, her boots sinking into the cold muddy grass. "Hello there?"

The girl didn't move. Wind bit into Fiona's hands, snaked down the neck of her coat, making her nose run. The girl didn't turn, didn't move. She was wearing some kind of hat or hood, black, so Fiona couldn't see the back of her head clearly. The music grew stronger, and sounded like it was coming from the trees. She recognized it now, the familiar tune sung in the familiar voice, a song she'd heard a thousand times: Gloria Gaynor's "I Will Survive." Deb's favorite song, the one she'd danced to in her room most often, mouthing the lyrics and doing hip-popping disco moves as her little sister, Fiona, watched and clapped.

Fiona slowed, hesitated. That song, with its peppy beat overlaid by Gloria Gaynor's vulnerable yet determined voice, had been difficult to avoid for the past twenty years. It was still a popular song, so much so that Fiona had trained herself to no longer think of Deb when she heard it. She made herself think of pink pantsuits and multicolored stage lights and fresh-faced girls wearing fake eyelashes and blush, instead of her sister in her pajamas, standing on the bed, pointing cheesily across the room. But why was this song playing now, over the cold landscape of Idlewild Hall at dawn on a November morning?

The sky seemed to lower, and as the sun came up behind the clouds, the morning light turned a strange white shade, turning the trees dark and the ground vibrant, every detail visible in sudden perfection. Fiona took a step and kicked something with the toe of her boot. She looked down and saw it was a wreath of plastic flowers.

That's it, she thought with certainty, listening to the wind flap in the fabric of the strange girl's dress over the strains of Gloria Gaynor's voice. *This is a dream.*

Because strewn over the grass between her and the girl was a litter of flowers, wreaths, cards, teddy bears—the detritus people leave at the site of grief. The same detritus that had been left in this place after Deb's body was found. Fiona looked around and realized, belatedly, that the girl was standing in the exact spot that Deb had lain with her coat open and her shirt torn, her eyes open to the empty air.

She looked down again. *ANGEL,* read one of the handwritten cards, the writing now blurred and soaked. She toed another cheap bouquet of plastic flowers, bright yellow daffodils and pink roses. Next to it was a crumpled cigarette package, cellophane winking in the light. The same garbage she'd seen when she'd come here at age seventeen. *It's a dream. A nightmare. I'm still in bed. I never got up.*

She raised her gaze to the girl again. She hadn't moved. Fiona was closer now, and she could see the girl's narrow shoulders, the weave of the thick fabric of her dress. The wind picked up a scrap of fabric, blowing it around her head, and Fiona realized it was a veil. Beneath it, Fiona caught a glimpse of golden brown hair tied tightly at the back of the girl's neck.

There was something otherworldly about her, but since this was a dream, Fiona decided not to be afraid. "Who are you?" she asked, thinking, *She looks so real, I can see her breathing.* "What are you doing here?"

No answer. No acknowledgment that the girl knew Fiona was there. Fiona had just lifted her hand to touch her—what the hell? It was a dream—when she heard her voice being called. A deep male voice shouting her name in the wind.

She turned. A man in a black coat was striding over the field toward her. Anthony Eden.

"Fiona!" he shouted.

Did he see the girl? Fiona glanced back over her shoulder and froze. The girl was gone. She looked down; the wreaths and cards were gone, too. Gloria Gaynor was silent.

"Are you trespassing?" he asked as he came closer. He was out of breath, flustered, his thinning hair blowing in the cold wind. "That is not a good idea. Security is just coming on shift. If they'd seen you, they would have called the police."

"I—" Fiona couldn't speak. She was still in shock from what she'd just seen—whatever it was. *Am I losing my mind?* "I was just—"

"For God's sake, let's get out of here." He took her arm and tugged her gently, pulling her across the field toward the main building. "It's a good thing I came by this morning to check on the progress and saw your car, or you would have been in trouble. I can't think of why you came. I hate this place, myself."

"Anthony," Fiona managed as they crossed the field. "I think I saw—"

But he tugged her, nearly unbalancing her, and suddenly she was so close her shoulder touched his. "Shh," he said, his voice lowered. "Please don't say it. I think she listens."

The words were so unexpected it took a moment for her to process them. By the time she did, he had let her go and was walking normally again without glancing in her direction, as if he'd never said a thing.

Numbly she followed his gaze to the dead, empty windows of Idlewild. It was watching them, watching her, laughing with its broken teeth. For a second her fear turned to defiance at the sight. *I see you,* she said to it. *I hate you.*

But Idlewild still grinned. *I hate you, too.*

When they reached the muddy drive, Anthony said, "I'll have security open the gates so you can leave. If you want to see the grounds again, Fiona, please call me so you don't end up in the back of a police car."

He motioned to a uniformed man who was getting out of a car marked with the logo of a private security company. The man nodded and pressed a button inside his car, and the gates began to swing open. Waiting for her to leave.

She wanted to run down the rutted drive and through

the gates. She wanted out. She wanted to be gone from here forever.

Instead she turned to Anthony and said, in a voice both quiet and clear, "Who is she?"

He shook his head. "That's my mother's specialty, I'm afraid. You'll have to ask her."

"Except I don't have an interview with her," Fiona returned, frustrated.

"You should have returned my calls," he said. "That's what I wanted to tell you. Mother has changed her mind. She's agreed to talk to you." He glanced at his watch. "She'll be getting up now, having her morning tea. I'll call ahead and tell her you're coming, shall I?"

It didn't matter that she was scared, cold, shabbily dressed, and worried about her own mental state. She was finally getting the chance to talk to Margaret Eden. "Yes, thank you," she said as politely as she could. "I'm on my way."

He gave her the address. "Let's not tell her about this incident," he finished, waving vaguely behind them, "or we'll both be in trouble."

"Will she be angry?"

To her surprise, that made Anthony laugh, a sound that was brief and polite, but still genuinely amused. "If you ever find that you can predict Mother, then you know her better than I do. And I've known her all my life."

That should have made her uneasy. Yet it didn't.

Fiona turned and walked down the muddy drive, preparing to take on Margaret Eden.

chapter 14

CeCe

Barrons, Vermont
October 1950

The last Sunday of every month was Family Visit Day at Idlewild, when families could come see the girls. The visits took place in the dining hall, with each girl getting a table to sit with her visitor. There were over a hundred girls in the school, but barely six or seven families showed up each Family Visit Day. The rest either didn't know about it or didn't care.

CeCe had put on a clean uniform and carefully brushed her hair. It was too much to expect that Mother would come; she lived in Boston, where she worked as a housekeeper, and to come back here on her Sunday off was impossible. Her father would not come, of course—she hadn't seen him since he'd dropped her off here. But she'd had a letter from someone else instead.

She watched, scanning each face as visitors came into the room. A set of parents. A mother with two children. It was nearly Halloween, and the two children had brought candy for their sister at school, which they were obviously reluctant to part with. Finally, a young man appeared, neatly groomed and wearing a navy blue seersucker suit. He was directed to her table. CeCe stood up and smiled.

He smiled back as he approached her. He had dark brown hair slicked back with pomade, and the white shirt beneath his suit jacket was starched and clean, his tie straight. He had gray eyes beneath bold, level brows and a thin face with high cheekbones. He was handsome, CeCe thought, except that his front teeth were just a little crooked. But otherwise he was decent-looking, classy. He looked to be about twenty.

"Hi," he said when he got close enough to speak. "Cecilia?"

"That's me," she said, jittery with nervousness. "Call me CeCe."

He shook her hand. If he noticed how clammy hers was, he didn't let on. "I'm Joseph."

"It's so nice," she said, then realized that she hadn't finished her sentence. "It's so nice to meet you."

"You, too." He gestured for her to sit, and he sat across from her and smiled again. "So, do you think we have a resemblance?"

They had none, not the slightest, but CeCe smiled at him and said, "I don't know. I guess."

"Well, since we have the same father, there must be some resemblance somewhere," he said. He looked her up and down, and she was painfully aware of the soft curves bulging beneath her uniform, the dark thick hair that was nothing like his. She'd been so excited to meet him, this boy. He was another illegitimate child of her father's by a different mother, though his mother wasn't a servant, like hers. His mother was the daughter of a banker, and Brad Ellesmere had helped her set up house when she'd gotten pregnant, given her support until she found a husband. He'd stayed close to Joseph, too— Joseph was the favorite child, the son. Though, as with CeCe, he hadn't given Joseph his family name.

Joseph had written her last week, asking to come and see her. They were family, he said, even if their family was on the wrong side of the blanket. He had no other legitimate brothers or sisters, and he was tracking down all of his father's other children with his father's blessing, hoping to find family where he had none. CeCe had no other brothers or sisters, either, and she'd replied to him enthusiastically, asking him to come.

"So," she said to him now, trying not to fidget. "Have you found any other siblings?"

"Sure," he said. "Two others, one in North Carolina and one in Baltimore. Dad sure did get around." He stopped and blushed bright red. "Oh, jeez, I'm sorry."

"It's okay." CeCe shook her head. "I've heard it before. I've heard everything by now, as I'm sure you have."

"It isn't always easy," Joseph agreed. "When I was a little kid, I used to lie in bed and dream about having normal parents."

"Me, too." CeCe felt her own face heating. There were other illegitimate girls at Idlewild, but she'd never talked to another girl about what it was like. "I used to daydream that Dad would come and sweep my mother off her feet and marry her."

"So did I." Joseph laughed. The sound was awkward, but CeCe liked it. It was exactly like her own awkward laugh. "I guess he can't marry everyone."

This was good, CeCe thought. This was really good. Having family that wasn't Mother. She couldn't believe he was being so nice to her when he didn't have to, that he wasn't embarrassed. "Who were the other two you found?" she asked. "Boys or girls?"

"Girls, both," he said. He put his hands on the table and tried to keep them still. "Dad says I'm the only boy. The other two didn't want to see me, though." He shrugged. "Their mothers got married, too, like mine, and they don't want anything to do with Dad or his other kids."

Sisters. I have sisters. She tried to keep her expression calm. "That's too bad."

"Yeah. Say, I got you something." He lifted a small cardboard box. "It's just a little thing. I didn't have time to get it wrapped or anything."

CeCe blinked at the box. "A gift? Joseph, really . . ."

"Hey, you're my sister, right?" he said softly. "It's the least I can do. Open it up."

She blinked hard and removed the lid from the box. Inside was a strange-looking cube of plastic, adorned with a knob and a lot of holes. "What, um," she said, feeling stupid, "what is it?"

"It's a radio," he explained. He lifted the square from the box and turned it. "You switch it on here, see, and you tune in to a station using this knob. This is brand-new, CeCe. A prototype. Dad got me one last month. It's the greatest thing."

"Okay," CeCe said cautiously. She'd seen radios before—the Ellesmeres had had one—but they were the size of cabinets. She'd never seen a radio so small. She was almost positive that such a thing was against Idlewild rules, but Joseph wouldn't know that. "So I can just turn it on and listen to music?"

"Or radio shows, or whatever is on," he said. "Sometimes there are symphonies, or operas, or big band shows. All kinds of things."

She looked up at him, blinking in amazement. This really was a nice gift. "Wasn't it expensive?"

He waved that away. "I wanted to get you something. You're trapped in this dusty old boarding school. Who wouldn't want a radio in a place like this?"

"That's true." CeCe laughed. She had no resentment that as the daughter of a housekeeper she'd been sent to boarding school, while he'd probably been given private tutors. That was just the way of the world. Besides, their father sent her money and presents sometimes, too. He hadn't forgotten her entirely. "Nothing much happens here. I'll have to hide it, though, or the dorm monitors will confiscate it."

He seemed surprised at that, but he promptly dropped the radio back in the box and closed the lid. "Am I making you break the rules?"

"I've done it before."

He grinned. "I like the sound of that." They smiled at each other for a second, and CeCe thought again,

This is good. "Listen," Joseph said. "Dad tells me your mother is a housekeeper in Boston."

"It's surprising he's been so open with you about all of this," she said. "Doesn't he worry people will disapprove?" She blushed again. "What about, um, his wife?" Her mother had never told her anything about her father's wife—not a single word.

"His wife is sick," Joseph said bluntly. "They never had any kids, you know, in the marriage. So Dad is behind me in this. He doesn't have any sons. Except me. I don't think he cares very much what people think. He wants his kids taken care of, even if they aren't his wife's. I mean, who is going to take over his business someday, if it isn't me?"

CeCe nodded and looked down at the box on the table in front of her, drawing her thumbnail along the lid. She didn't know her father well—barely at all, actually—but he'd never been unkind to her. It was other people who were unkind. And, of course, Mother was ashamed, while Father wasn't. That, too, was the way of the world.

She had the sudden feeling this visit had more to it than just friendliness from a long-lost half brother, though she couldn't quite figure out what it was. "I guess he's always been honest."

"He has." Joseph paused. "He told me about your mother and the time you almost died at the beach."

Her head jerked up. No one talked about that. Never. "That was an accident."

Joseph shook his head. "That's not what Dad says."

"He doesn't *know*," she said, the words coming out

forceful with her sudden anger. "He wasn't there. It was an *accident*."

But still he shook his head, so calm, so certain. A young man who had been told the truth by his father, undoubting. "Look, no one blames you. Not at all. But your mother—"

"She slipped." CeCe heard the rushing of water in her ears, and pushed the thought away.

"CeCe, you nearly drowned," he said. "Dad said they had to put your mother in a hospital for a while."

"That was *unfair*."

"The doctors said—"

"Stop," CeCe nearly shouted. The families at the other tables were looking over at them now, and the teacher on duty, Mrs. Wentworth, was looking concerned. "The doctors don't know her."

She had been six. Her mother had taken her swimming at the beach. She remembered the dark, damp sand between her toes, the slap of cold water. Watching the waves come and go, making the sand look slick as glass as the water receded. She'd touched it over and over, after every wave left, trying to feel the hardness of the sand-glass, watching the water curve around her fingers. Nothing else. She didn't remember her mother telling her to come into the water. She didn't remember the sky, or the voices of the other people on the beach, or the sound of seagulls calling, or the water rushing into her mouth. She only remembered touching the smooth sand, then looking up at Mother through the water.

And then someone was shouting, and she'd opened

her eyes to see a man with a huge mustache looking into her face. *Little girl, are you all right?*

Her mother had slipped, holding her in the water. She'd slipped and fallen and pinned CeCe beneath her by accident. But the police came, and though CeCe had no memory after that, just flashes of images here and there— a strange house she'd stayed at that had a puppy, a man who had made finger puppets sing a song and made her laugh—she knew what had happened. Her mother had assured her, years later. It had been an accident.

Her father hadn't been there; she and her mother had gone to the beach alone. Had he been involved when her mother went into the hospital? Had he had her locked up? She hadn't known that. It was unfair. Her mother had never had the chance to defend herself. She'd never gone back to work for the Ellesmeres after getting out. She'd gone to Boston and her father had dropped CeCe off at her first boarding school, the one that took younger kids, the one she'd been at before her father had come to get her again to move her to Idlewild.

"Dad was looking out for you," Joseph said. "He got your mother that job after she got out of the hospital, and he sent you to school. He says that now I'm grown, I have to look out for you, too."

"My mother looks out for me," CeCe said numbly.

"Gosh, I'm sorry," Joseph said. "I didn't come here to upset you." He *did* look rather sorry, his eyes sad and his chin drooping. "I just know things have been hard for you—you know, harder than they are for me. So I wanted to meet you and bring you a present. I wanted to let you know I'm here. If you ever need help, just let me know."

She blinked hard. She wanted to shout at him, wanted to stomp from the room. If she were Katie, she'd know some profanity she could say, something that would shock him and make him stop feeling sorry for her. No one ever felt sorry for Katie, while everyone always felt sorry for CeCe. She was sick of it.

But she stared at him, and she couldn't do it. She couldn't be mean. He'd tried to be nice to her, and he'd spent quite a bit of money on her radio. So she heard herself say, "Thank you for the present."

"Okay," he said. "Can I visit you again?"

She said yes, and he shook her hand and left. She took the radio back to her room and slid it under her mattress in its box, thinking she would forget about it, that she would never listen to it. *I don't need his stupid radio*, she thought. But late that night, when all the girls were in their nightgowns and lying in bed, she rolled over and looked down at Katie on the bunk below her. "I got a present today," she said, unable to help herself. Unable to stop herself from trying to please Katie, with her pretty black hair and mischievous tilted eyes.

Katie yawned, as if presents were old news. "What is it?"

"A radio."

"That's a lie," Katie said immediately.

"It isn't," CeCe said. She was smiling now. Maybe the radio would be useful after all. "My half brother came to Family Visit Day and brought it for me. He bought it. He has money."

"If you had a radio," Roberta said from her bunk across the room, "we'd be able to see it. Radios are big."

"Not this one."

Katie was watching her steadily from her witch dark eyes. "Fine, then," she said. "Show us."

So CeCe pulled the box out from beneath her mattress and climbed down. She took out the radio, flipped the switch, and rotated the dial, just as Joseph had shown her. "We can listen to music and everything," she said. "The news. Joseph said there are concerts."

The other girls got out of bed and huddled around, even Sonia, all four of them in white nightgowns like ghosts. "Keep the volume low," Roberta whispered, her braid flung over her shoulder. "If Susan Brady hears, she'll take it."

They were silent. CeCe turned the dial, and a twist of noise came out of the little box, a spike of unintelligible static. Then there were voices.

"What do you say, Charlie?"

"I don't say much!"

"That's not what I said. I say, Charlie, what do you say?"

"What's that?" Sonia whispered. "A radio show?" The voices drifted away, and CeCe turned the dial again. Violin music rose over the static and wafted tinnily through the room.

"Bach," Sonia said.

It was the last word they spoke for a long time. As the cold descended and the wind howled outside, they sat cross-legged and rapt, staring at the small square of metal and plastic in the center of their circle, listening.

CeCe thought about the world far away, waves through the air moving through the little box and turning into music. About her brother traveling back to Baltimore, her unknown sisters somewhere out there. She did not think about her mother's arms pushing her under the water. *It's all out there,* she thought. *If only I could go.*

chapter 15

Fiona arrived at Margaret Eden's home at Mitchell Place, a gated community of expensive townhomes built during the boom years before the 2008 crash. Even then, the neighborhood's existence had hinged more on hope than on actual local wealth; there wasn't much demand for "executive" homes for wealthy professionals in Barrons, and the houses had taken years longer to complete than planned.

Now Mitchell Place was stuck between the wishes of its few remaining residents and the reality of a community with not enough tenants. The homes were well kept, but the security guard at the entrance gate was a cheap rental from a local outfit in a polyester uniform, and the sign on his booth clearly stated that the gate was manned only by camera and alarm systems after seven p.m. The weeds on the grass leading up to the gate were overgrown, and past the wrought iron, Fiona could see the covered remains of a pool, drained and empty this time of year and possibly not reopening come summer.

Margaret Eden's door, however, was opened by a maid—a white girl in an immaculate uniform, her hair pinned back. Anthony must have called ahead, because the maid let Fiona in. The front hall was marble, its small confines chill and harsh, and Fiona felt like the wayward help as she handed the maid her coat. She rolled up her hat and shoved it into the sleeve of her coat self-consciously before the maid took it away.

She was led into a parlor, also marble. It was empty except for a few pieces of furniture in stark modern style. There was no sign of Margaret Eden, so Fiona circulated through the room, using her journalist's instincts without thinking. There were no books, no clutter. No personal items lying around. On the mantel over the fireplace was a framed photo of Anthony, much younger, wearing a graduation cap and gown and smiling. There was a second photo, this one of a man with distinguished white hair, obviously Anthony's father, standing on a golf course.

"So you're Fiona."

Fiona turned to see an elderly woman standing behind her. She wore a collared white blouse and slacks, a dark green cardigan over her shoulders. Her white hair was cut short and curled. She looked like a grandmother, except she stood as straight and elegant as a reed, her sharp gaze fixed on Fiona. She gave Fiona an up-and-down once-over that was blatant and assessing.

"Mrs. Eden," Fiona said.

"I'm Margaret," the older woman corrected her. "And

you were at Idlewild." She held up a hand. "Of course Anthony told me. He's never been able to keep a secret from me in his life."

"He was worried you'd be angry," Fiona said—though what Anthony had actually said was: *If you ever find that you can predict Mother, then you know her better than I do.*

"I'm not angry. I'm curious, though. I admit it. Climbed the fence, did you? Perhaps you're cold. Do you want some tea?"

"No, thank you."

"All right, then. Have a seat."

Fiona did, lowering herself onto one of the uncomfortable sofas. This was supposed to be her interview, she remembered. She opened her mouth to speak, but Margaret spoke first.

"This house is horrid," she said. "You don't have to say it—I can read it on your face. The only thing I can say for myself is that I didn't decorate it. It came furnished this way when the last people moved out."

"You don't own this place?" Fiona asked in surprise.

Margaret shrugged. "I didn't think we'd stay long. Just long enough to get the Idlewild project done."

"Were you an Idlewild student?" Fiona asked her.

"Never. I'm not even local, as I'm sure your research has told you. I'm from Connecticut, and I lived with my husband in New York."

"Then why?" Margaret's bluntness was rubbing off on her; Fiona bypassed small talk and asked the most honest question she had. "Why Idlewild? Why restore that place, of all places?"

Margaret leaned back in her seat and gave Fiona the assessing look again. "I could ask you the same thing," she said. "Why Idlewild? Why are you writing a story about it? Why did you climb the fence this morning?" She raised her eyebrows, as if waiting. "Hmm?"

Fiona said nothing.

"You have a history there, it turns out," Margaret said. "I know who your father is, that your sister was killed and left there. It's why I decided to meet you. At first, Anthony only asked me if I would talk to a reporter, and I said no. He didn't tell me *which* reporter. I learned this morning that you're Deb Sheridan's sister, Malcolm Sheridan's daughter, and of course I'd heard of the murder."

Even in New York? Fiona thought. "We're not talking about me," she said, the words coming out tight. "We're talking about you."

"Are we? Very well. I'm restoring Idlewild so that there will be a girls' school there again. So that future generations of girls will get a good education."

Fiona shifted on her bleak sofa. Her hands and feet were still cold. "No one in these parts can afford to send their daughters to boarding school," she said. "And I've seen the grounds. It will cost a fortune to make the buildings even habitable."

"You sound just like my husband." Margaret smiled, rubbing a finger absently over the bracelet on her other wrist. "He hated the idea of this project so much. With the heat of a thousand suns. So does Anthony. He's worried I'm going to flush away his entire inheritance."

"You don't seem very concerned about that yourself," Fiona said.

"Anthony will have plenty of money," Margaret said. "He always has. He's divorced, and he has no children, so there's just him and me. And I'm still breathing. So I bought Idlewild, and I'm going to do what I want with it."

I'm not in control of this conversation, Fiona thought. So she said, "Even after a body was found in the well?"

A flinch crossed Margaret's face and was gone. It was the first real emotion the older woman had shown. "If the police can't find the girl's family, I'll have her buried properly myself. And then the restoration project will continue."

"You can't." The words were out before Fiona could stop them. They came from somewhere deep inside her, from a well of something she almost never acknowledged. Grief, anger, outrage. *Get a grip, Fiona,* she thought, but instead she said, "No girl is going to want to go to school in that place."

"And yet girls did," Margaret said, unfazed by Fiona's outburst. "For sixty years." She looked Fiona over again, but this time her expression was softer. "Tell me something." Her voice lowered, became more intimate. "At Idlewild. Did you see her?"

Fiona's skin went cold. The girl in the black dress and veil, standing in the field. But no. That wasn't possible. "See who?"

"Mary Hand," Margaret replied.

Fiona had never heard the name before, but something about it made her stomach drop, made her brain do a lazy spin. "I don't—" She cleared her throat. "I don't know who that is."

But Margaret was watching her face, missing nothing. "Yes, you do," she said. "You've seen her. This morning, I think. Anthony said you were standing in the field."

Fiona blinked at her in horror. "Is that what this is?" she asked. "Is that what this whole thing is all about? You're some kind of ghost hunter?"

"She was wearing a black dress, wasn't she?" Margaret said. "She had a veil over her face. Did she speak to you?"

Their gazes were locked, and Fiona couldn't look away. From nowhere, she recalled the words etched into the glass of the classroom window: *Good Night Girl*. "Who is she?" she asked. "Who is Mary Hand?"

"She's a legend," Margaret replied. "I don't know if she existed, or who she was. I've spent money looking. I can't find a record of her. I don't know if she was ever real."

"A student?"

"Who knows?" Margaret shrugged and leaned back again, breaking the connection. "What I'd like, more than anything, is the Idlewild files so I can see for myself. But they weren't on the property when we bought it. Anthony says they're gone."

Fiona held still. She didn't think about Sarah London, or Cathy telling her aunt's secret, that the files were sitting in her shed. "Do you think that will answer your questions?" she asked Margaret. "You think that this ghost, Mary Hand, is in the files somewhere?"

But Margaret only smiled. "I think they'd be illuminating," she said. "Don't you?"

chapter 16

Barrons, Vermont
November 2014

Jamie insisted on coming with her to pick up the files from Sarah London's back shed. It was a Thursday, his day off shift, because as the police department's junior member— Jamie was twenty-nine, but the force was hardly swamped with new recruits—he worked all the weekend shifts. Like a man born from a line of true cops, he ignored Fiona's suggestion he take an actual day off, and drove her to East Mills to clean out the ancient shed filled with papers that had been sitting there for thirty-five years.

Fiona gave in, unable to resist not only Jamie but the use of his strong shoulders in hauling boxes, and his much bigger SUV. So they drove down the rutted two-lane blacktop off the highway as the sun climbed, slanting thin late-autumn light into their eyes even though it was after nine o'clock. The days were getting shorter, and soon they'd be in the dregs of winter, when the sun never warmed the air no matter how bright, and the light was gone by five.

They talked as they drove, Jamie in jeans and a thick flannel shirt over a T-shirt, his hair combed back, a Dunkin' Donuts coffee in one hand as he drove with the other. Fiona wore a pullover sweater and jeans, her hair in a pony-tail, and leaned against the passenger door, sipping her own coffee as they talked. It had been a while since they'd spent a day together—two weeks, maybe three. Jamie picked up as much overtime as the force's budget would allow, and Fiona's schedule was equally offbeat as she wrote one story or another. They usually kept their conversations light, but today it wasn't going to happen. She had too much on her mind. Jamie, as always, was a good listener, and before she knew it, the words were spilling out.

She told him about her visit to Idlewild. It hadn't been her finest moment, and she still didn't know what to make of what she'd seen on the field. But she forced the story out, trying to keep her voice matter-of-fact. Jamie didn't chide her about trespassing, or not answering his texts, and he took in her account of the ghost with surprised silence.

"Jesus Christ, Fiona," he said at last.

Fiona gulped her coffee. "Say it," she prompted him. "If you think I should go on meds, just say it."

He shook his head. "No meds," he said. "I can't say I know what you saw, but I don't think you're crazy."

She stared at him for a long time, waiting for more. But the silence stretched out in the car, the hum of the SUV's engine the only sound between them. "That's it?" she said. "You think I actually saw a ghost?"

"Why not?" he said, surprising her. "You want me to say it isn't possible? How the hell do I know what's possible or not? Kids have always said that place is haunted."

"Have you ever heard the name Mary Hand?" Fiona asked.

"No."

"Margaret Eden has," she said. "She says there's a legend about a girl named Mary Hand haunting the grounds. And yet Margaret also says she was never a student, and she isn't local." She paused, looking out the passenger window, unseeing. "She knew what I saw, Jamie. She knew."

"Is there any way she could have been repeating back something you'd already said?"

Fiona thought back over the conversation. "No. Margaret described the black dress and veil. I hadn't talked about that. I hadn't admitted anything."

"A girl with a veil," Jamie said, musing. "I haven't heard that particular story before. Then again, I never did a dare to go on the Idlewild grounds growing up. I was the straight-and-narrow kid, destined to become a cop. What about you?"

Fiona shook her head. "Deb was into friends and boys, not ghost-hunting dares. Which meant I wasn't, either." The words cut sharply, the memory still clear. Deb had been three years older, and Fiona had followed everything she did—she'd worn Deb's hand-me-down clothes, her old shoes, her old winter jackets. She was quieter and more introverted than her outgoing sister, but she'd tried her best not to be. Deb had been a road map of what to be, and when she'd died, that road map had vanished, leaving Fiona adrift. For twenty years and counting.

"If this . . ." It felt strange to talk about a ghost like it was actually a real thing. "If Mary Hand has been there all these years, someone must have seen her besides me. Sarah London told me that everyone at the school lived in fear of something. But she'd never heard of Margaret."

"So Sarah London knows," he said. "Maybe Mary Hand was a student. If so, there should be something about her in the records."

"That's what Margaret thinks." Fiona drained the last of her coffee. "She wants these records. She was a cagey old lady. I can't figure out what her game is—whether it's money, or ghosts, or something else she wants. But the records are definitely part of what she's looking for. I think she suspected that I know where they are."

"Well, we're one up on her, then," Jamie said, grinning. "Let's see what happens when she knows they're yours. Maybe she'll come to you with a different game."

Fiona smiled at him.

"What?" he said, glancing at her.

"You're sucked in," she said. "Just like I am. Admit it."

"Maybe."

"Maybe," she mocked him.

He pulled into Sarah London's gravel drive and turned off the ignition. Her heart gave a little pop, because she knew that look in his eyes. Still, she watched as he put his cup down, leaned over, and took her face in his hands.

He kissed her slowly, properly, taking his time. She

tried to stay unaffected, but he was oh so good at it; she felt the rasp of his beard and the press of his thumbs, and before she knew it, she was gripping his wrists and kissing him back, letting her teeth slide over his bottom lip as he made a sound in her mouth and kissed her harder. Sometimes their kisses were complicated, a kind of conversation on their own, but this one wasn't—this was just Jamie, kissing her in his car as the bright sunlight slanted in, making the moment spin on and on.

Finally, they paused for breath. "Come to dinner at my parents' tonight," he said, still holding her face, his breath on her cheek.

She felt herself stiffen. She'd met Jamie's parents once, briefly, and she was pretty sure a journalist was not whom they wanted for their precious son. "I don't think that's a good idea."

"Sure it is." He kissed her neck and she tried not to shiver. "We've been dating for a year, Fee. Having dinner with the parents is part of the deal."

It was. She knew it was. But a meet-the-parents evening— Jesus. She wasn't ready for this. "I'm no good at it," she warned him. "The girlfriend thing. I'm terrible at it, actually."

"I know," he said, and he laughed softly when he felt her stiffen in offense. "But they've been asking about you. My mother especially. She wants to feed you pot roast and ask leading questions about what your intentions are."

"Oh, my God." Fiona didn't even like pot roast. She'd had pretzels for dinner last night.

"I know we've taken it slow, Fee," he said. "I get it. I wanted to take it slow, too. But it's time."

Damn it. He was right. There was only so long she would have gotten away with putting this off. "Look, I can endure it, but if we do this, they're going to think we're serious."

She regretted the words—this could lead to the *are we serious* conversation—and thought he might argue, but Jamie just exhaled a sigh and leaned against the seat next to her. "I know," he said. "But I have to give them something. My mother actually asked me when I'm going to find a nice girl and settle down."

Fiona paused, surprised at how that alarmed her. The words bubbled up—*Is that what you want? To get married and settle down?*—but she bit them back. What if he said, *Yes, it is?*

They were not having this conversation.

It had been only a year. That wasn't long; this was 2014. People weren't expected to court and get married anymore like it was 1950. But Jamie was younger than she was, and he hadn't grown up with freethinking hippie parents. He didn't ask her for much. As much as she hated the idea of dinner with his parents, she could do it. For him. Just suck it up and go.

"Fine," she finally said, halfheartedly shoving against his chest. "I'll go, all right? I'll eat pot roast. Now let's get moving. You're going to give that old lady a heart attack if she's looking out the window."

He grinned and grabbed his coat from the backseat.

Miss London wasn't watching from the window. She

didn't come to the door, either, even after repeated knocking. Worried, Fiona pulled out her cell phone and walked to the end of the drive, looking for cell reception. She was partway down the street when she lucked into enough bars to call Cathy.

"I had to take Aunt Sairy for a checkup," Cathy said. "The doctor changed the time, and she can't miss her checkups. Just go around back to the shed. I left the key under the old gnome."

So they walked around the house to the backyard. Miss London had no neighbors behind her, and her backyard sloped away into a thicket of huge pine trees, stark and black now against the gray sky. Beyond that were a few tangled fields and a power station crisscrossed with metal towers. Crows shouted somewhere overhead, and a truck engine roared from the nearby two-lane highway.

Standing behind the old house was a shed covered with vinyl siding in avocado green. Fiona felt for the key beneath the garden gnome on the back porch while Jamie cleared the shed doorway of the snow shovel and the wheelbarrow leaning against it. The door was rusted, held shut by a padlock that was dulled with age and exposure. Fiona had a moment of doubt that the old lock would even work, but the key slid in easily and Jamie popped off the lock and swung open the door.

"Oh, hell," he said.

The shed was full—literally full—of cardboard file boxes, stacked from floor to ceiling, some of them collapsing beneath a quarter century of weight. Fiona's heart sped up. This was it: sixty years of Idlewild's history compacted into one old woman's shed. Somewhere in here was the answer to who Sonia Gallipeau was, maybe even where she'd come from. Somewhere in here were files about Sonia's friends, who might still be alive. Somewhere in here might even be a file about a girl named Mary Hand.

Unable to help herself, she tugged on the first box sitting at eye level and hauled it out, placing it on the cold ground and popping the lid off. Inside were textbooks, old and yellowed. The top was titled *Latin Grammar for Girls*.

Jamie read the title over her shoulder. "The good old days," he commented, "when apparently Latin was different if you were a girl."

Fiona agreed. She lifted the textbook and found a few others stacked inside. Biology. History. "It looks like Miss London wanted to keep the curriculum as well as all the records." She looked up at him. "Is all of this going to fit in your SUV?"

He glanced around, calculating. "Sure," he said. "The bigger question is, are you going to keep all of this in your apartment?"

"I have room."

He shrugged, picked up the box, and carted it toward the car.

It took them nearly ninety minutes to empty the shed. Considering how long the boxes had been sitting there, surprisingly few of them had water damage. Even when building sheds with vinyl siding, Yankees had taken pride in their craftsmanship in the seventies. They drove off with all of Idlewild in the back of Jamie's SUV, smelling like damp cardboard.

There were twenty-one boxes in all. Fiona tried to organize them once they had unloaded them into her small apartment, stacked in the living room. Some boxes contained tests and lesson plans; these were shoved against the wall as unimportant. Some contained financial records, like paychecks and supplier bills; these were stacked next as possibles. Some seemed to contain random memorabilia, probably scooped from classrooms on the school's last day before closing: a desk-sized globe, a slide rule, a rolled-up poster, the old textbooks. These Fiona set aside as fascinating but not necessary to the story. When she'd finished the article, she'd take pictures of them to add to the context of the story when it went to press.

The final five boxes were student records. Fiona and Jamie ordered Chinese delivery for lunch and split the last boxes, looking for the names on Fiona's list, as well as any other names that stood out as interesting. Jamie's box contained the *G* files, and the first folder he pulled out was Sonia Gallipeau's.

The first page listed Sonia's height, weight, age, uniform size, and date of admission to Idlewild. It listed her nearest family member as her great-uncle, Mr. Henry DuBois, of Burlington, a name Jamie recognized from his search for Sonia's relatives. Henry DuBois and his wife, Eleanor, were the people Sonia had visited for the weekend before she was murdered. The last known people who saw her alive. They were both dead, and had no children.

There was no photograph. Fiona found herself wishing she knew what Sonia had looked like.

There were a few pages listing Sonia's grades—all were

high. A teacher had written in pencil: *Bright and quiet. Adept at memorization. Physical fitness adequate.* Sonia's body was small; if she'd been in a concentration camp, she'd have been malnourished while she was supposed to be growing, but she would have had to be strong to survive at all. Fiona made a note to ask a doctor for an opinion.

There was a piece of notepaper slipped into the file signed by Gerta Hedmeyer, the Idlewild school nurse. *Student brought to infirmary November 4, 1950. Fainting spell during Weekly Gardening. No reason known. Student is slight; possibly iron deficient. Complained of headache. Gave student aspirin and instructed her to rest. Released to care of Roberta Greene, student's dorm mate.*

"There's Roberta," Jamie said as Fiona read over his shoulder. "Proof that they were friends. We need to talk to her."

Fiona stared at the note. Roberta Greene, who had brought her friend to the infirmary when she'd fainted sixty-four years ago, was at the moment the closest thing to family Sonia Gallipeau had. It was definitely time to meet Roberta.

"This is interesting," Jamie said, pointing to the nurse's note. "She says it's a possible iron deficiency."

"That's code," Fiona explained.

"What?"

"It means Sonia was having her period on the day she fainted. It was a polite way to refer to it back then. Our old doctor still used that when I was growing up."

"But this is the nurse's own notes," he protested. "In

an all-female boarding school. There wasn't a man for miles around."

"It doesn't matter. It was going in the file, where others could read it. She still had to be polite. It was a generational thing."

He shook his head. "That generation blows my mind. They didn't talk about anything at all. My granddad fought in the war and never talked about it, not even to Dad. An entire damn war, and not one word."

"It's true," Fiona said. "There's nothing in this file about Sonia being in a concentration camp. If she had come from one, the school nurse didn't even know. She would have lived with the experience and never talked about it. All of these girls—these Idlewild girls. Whatever they went through to end up sent off to boarding school, they probably never spoke of it. That wasn't how it was done."

The next page of the file, the final page, contained the entry about Sonia's disappearance. It was written by Julia Patton, Idlewild's headmistress, neatly typed on a page of letterhead.

December 5, 1950
IDLEWILD HALL

I, Julia Patton, headmistress of Idlewild Hall, state that on November 28, 1950, student Sonia Gallipeau was given weekend leave to visit relatives. She departed at 11:00 on Friday, November 28, intending to take the 12:00 bus to

Burlington. She wore a wool coat and skirt and carried a suitcase. She was seen walking up Old Barrons Road to the bus stop by several students.

I also state that Sonia Gallipeau did not return to Idlewild Hall, neither on the intended day of her return, November 30, 1950, nor any other day. I swear hereby that she has not been seen again by me, by any teacher in my employ, or by any other student in my care. On the morning of December 1, 1950, when I was informed by a member of my staff that Sonia had not returned, I placed a call to the Barrons police and reported her missing. I was interviewed by Officers Daniel O'Leary and Garrett Creel and gave a statement. I also helped police search the woods by Old Barrons Road when it was made known to police that Sonia had in fact boarded the bus leaving Burlington on November 29, 1950. We found a suitcase that I recognize as Sonia's, which now resides in my office.

It is my belief that Sonia ran away, likely with the aid of someone helping her, possibly a boy.

Signed,

Julia Patton

A note handwritten across the bottom of the page read:

Addendum, December 9, 1950: Suitcase now missing from my office.
Not located. JP.

Jamie put the file down and stood up, pacing to the window. He didn't speak.

Running a hand through her hair, Fiona turned to Julia Patton's statement and picked it up. She turned the paper over, noting the faint carbon marks on the back. "This was typed with carbon paper behind it," she said. "She probably gave a copy to the police." Though the police would not have received the handwritten addendum, which had been added later.

"It isn't in the missing persons file," Jamie said. "There's only a report from Daniel O'Leary."

"Is that weird?" Fiona asked him. "Pages missing from case files?"

"In a case sixty-four years old? I don't know. Probably not."

He went quiet again. He was possibly thinking about Garrett Creel Sr., his grandfather, who had apparently interviewed Julia Patton about the disappearance alongside his colleague, and what the file implied about him. Fiona let him wrestle with it for a minute.

"It was a different time," Jamie finally said, "but it's pretty clear that no one took Sonia's disappearance seriously." He paused. "Not even Granddad."

It was bothering him. Jamie was proud of his cop's lineage. "The judgment on Sonia is pretty harsh," Fiona agreed, "especially coming from the headmistress. I know she left her relatives', but to conclude that she ran off with a boy? This was a girl who lived under supervision in a boarding school. She was hardly out tearing up Barrons, seducing boys. And she had no suitcase."

"I don't understand it," Jamie said, still looking out the window. "How no one could have thought something bad could have happened to her. How it didn't even cross their minds. She was a fifteen-year-old girl who had dropped her suitcase and disappeared."

Unbidden, Malcolm's words came into Fiona's mind: *Was she a Jew?* There was nothing in the school's file about Sonia being Jewish, but what if she had been? Would the police have searched for a runaway girl who was a Jewish refugee with no family the same way they would have searched for a local Catholic girl?

And who had taken Sonia's suitcase from Julia Patton's office? Her killer had put Sonia's body in the well, which was nearly within view of the headmistress's office window. Had the killer taken the suitcase as well? If the suitcase contained a clue to the killer's identity, it would have to be disposed of. Could Julia Patton have known who Sonia's killer was? Could she have done it herself?

She read the headmistress's note again. "The fact that she left her great-aunt and -uncle's a day early bothers me. She'd gone all that way to visit them. Why did she turn around and leave?"

"We may never know."

Fiona put the file down. "Let's continue," she said. "We can't answer these questions now. Let's find the other girls' files."

"We don't have time," Jamie said, turning from the window and checking his watch. "We're due for dinner at my parents'."

"No, *no*. You've got to be kidding me."

Jamie shook his head. "You promised, so you're coming. These files will be here when we get back."

"I can't leave." She felt physical pain, staring at the boxes she wanted so badly to open.

"Yes, you can."

She got up reluctantly from her spot on the floor and brushed off the legs of her jeans. "Fine. But I'm not dressing up. And we're coming back here."

"After dinner," Jamie said. "I promise."

They were in Jamie's car, and he was pulling onto Meredith Street, when Fiona's phone rang. It was her father.

"I've got something," he said when she answered. "About your Sonia girl."

Fiona felt her mouth go dry. "What is it?"

"I had a professor friend of mine put me in touch with a student to do some archival research," he said. "She found her in a passenger manifest on a ship leaving Calais in 1947. Sonia Gallipeau, age twelve. Traveling alone. Same date of birth as your girl."

"That's her," Fiona said.

"The manifest lists her previous place of residence," Malcolm said. "An official took the information down, but it must have come from her."

Fiona closed her eyes to the blacktop flying by, to the stark trees and the gray sky, to everything. "Tell me," she said.

"I'm sorry, sweetheart," her father said. "Her previous place of residence was Ravensbrück prison."

chapter 17

Roberta

Of all the hated classes at Idlewild—and that was most of them—Weekly Gardening was the most despised. It had come, Roberta supposed, from some misguided idea that the housewives of the future should know how to grow their own vegetables. Or perhaps it descended from an idea that the school would subsist on its own produce, like a nunnery. In any case, every girl who attended Idlewild had to spend an hour every week in the communal school garden, digging hopelessly in the dirt and trying not to get her uniform muddy as she poked at the dead vegetables.

The month had slid into November, cold and hard. Roberta stood in a row with four other girls as Mrs. Peabody handed them each a gardening tool. "We are going to add lettuces to our planting next spring, so today we'll be digging space before the ground freezes." She indicated a chalked-off square of ground, filled with dead weeds and rocks. "One hour, girls. Get started."

Roberta looked at Sonia, who was standing next to her. Sonia was huddled into her old wool coat, her face pinched and miserable, her thin hands on the handle of her shovel. "Are you all right?"

"Bon." Sonia wiped her nose with the back of her hand. She reverted to French when she was tired.

Roberta buttoned her own coat higher over her neck and bent to her work. It wasn't the work that the girls loathed—it was the garden itself. It was placed in the crux of shadows between the main hall and the dining hall, and it was relentlessly cold, damp, and moldy, no matter the season. The windows of both buildings stared blankly down at the girls as they worked. There was a persistent legend at Idlewild that Mary Hand's baby was buried in the garden, which did nothing to add to the attraction of Weekly Gardening. Every time Roberta gardened in here, she expected to find baby bones.

The girls bent to work, their breath puffing in the morning air, the slanting November sunshine on the common putting them all in dark shadow. Roberta felt her shoes squish—the garden was always wet, with runnels of water pooling in the overturned dirt.

Mary Van Woorten raised her head and stared at Sonia. "You're not digging," she said, her mouth pursing in her pale round face.

"I am digging," Sonia said grimly, pushing her shovel into the dirt.

"No, you're not. You have to dig harder, like the rest of us."

"Leave her alone," Roberta said. She watched Sonia from the corner of her eye. The girl was gripping her shovel, wedging it into the wet dirt, but she wasn't lifting much. Her teeth were chattering. Sonia was small, but she was strong, and this wasn't like her. "Sonia?" Roberta said softly.

"I am fine." As if to illustrate this, Sonia pushed at her shovel again.

"You aren't even making a hole!" Mary persisted.

Sonia lifted her face and snapped at her. "You stupid girl," she bit out, her hands shaking. "You've never had to dig. You've never had to *dig*."

"What does that mean?" Mary said. "I'm digging right now."

"I think something's wrong with her," Margaret Kevin piped up. "Mary, be quiet."

"Shut up," Sonia shouted, stunning all of them. Roberta had never seen her friend so angry. "Just be quiet, all of you, and leave me alone."

They dug in silence. Roberta glanced back over her shoulder and saw Mrs. Peabody smoking a cigarette near the door to the teachers' hall, talking quietly with Mrs. Wentworth. They laughed at something, and Mrs. Wentworth shook her head. From the girls' place in the shadows, the two teachers looked bathed in sunlight, as if Roberta were watching them through a magical doorway.

She looked down at the space she was digging, the mottled, ugly clots of dirt. *Baby bones.* She always thought of baby bones here. Finger bones, leg bones, a soft little skull . . .

Don't think about it. Don't.

The blade of her shovel slipped, and for a second there was something white and fleshy speared on the metal, something pale and soft and rotten. Roberta flinched and dropped the shovel, preparing to scream, before she realized what she'd severed was a mushroom, huge and wet in the cold, damp earth.

She was trying to calm down when there was a huff of breath next to her, like a sigh. She turned to see Sonia fall to her knees in the dirt. She still clutched her shovel, her hands sliding down the handle as she lowered to the ground. Roberta bent and grabbed her friend by the shoulders.

"I can do it," Sonia said, her head bowing so her forehead nearly touched the ground, her eyes rolling back in her head.

"Mrs. Peabody!" Mary Van Woorten shouted.

"Sonia," Roberta whispered, clutching the girl harder.

Sonia's shoulders heaved, and she quietly threw up drops of spit into the dirt. Then she sagged, her eyes closing. Roberta held her tight. Her friend weighed almost nothing at all.

"Have you been sleeping?" Miss Hedmeyer, the school nurse, said. "Eating?"

"Yes, *madame.*" Sonia's voice was pale, tired.

Miss Hedmeyer jabbed her fingers up under Sonia's jaw, feeling her lymph nodes. "No swelling," she said. "No fever. What else?"

"I have a headache, *madame*."

Roberta bit the side of her thumb as she watched Miss Hedmeyer take a bottle of aspirin out of a cupboard and shake out a few large chalky pills. "I've seen this before," Miss Hedmeyer said. She had light blond hair that contrasted with a startling spray of freckles across her nose. When she wasn't treating the ailments of the Idlewild girls, she taught their meager science curriculum, which mostly consisted of the periodic table of elements and the process of photosynthesis, sometimes mixed with explanations of snow and rain. It was not assumed that the housewives of the future needed to know much about science. "It happens to some girls when they're asked to do physical activity during their time of month. Am I correct?"

Sonia blinked and said nothing, and even Roberta could see her abject humiliation.

"Get some rest," Miss Hedmeyer said. She tapped Sonia on the arm of her thick uniform sweater. "You need to be tougher," she advised. "Girls like you. There's not a thing wrong with you. We feed you good food here."

Sonia's voice was nearly a whisper. "Yes, *madame*."

"And less French, please. This is America." The nurse turned to Roberta. "I'll talk to Mrs. Peabody and get you the next hour free to make sure she doesn't faint again. Since you're on the field hockey team, she'll likely agree."

Roberta kept her eyes downcast. "Thank you, Miss Hedmeyer."

She took Sonia's hand as they left the room. She thought vaguely of putting the girl's arm around her shoulder and half carrying her to their room, but Sonia stayed upright, even climbing the dorm stairs, though she kept her cold, clammy hand in Roberta's, her gaze down on her feet.

In their room, Roberta helped her take off her mud-soaked stockings and shoes. They worked in silence, Roberta hanging the stockings over the doorknob to dry—dried mud was easier to get out in the sink than the wet kind—as Sonia pulled back her covers and lay in bed, still wearing her skirt and sweater. Sonia folded her hands over her chest.

Roberta kicked her own shoes off and sat on the edge of the bed, looking down at her friend's pale face. "Tell me," she said.

Sonia stared at the wooden slats that made up Roberta's bunk above hers. "It is a sad story," she said.

"We all have sad stories," Roberta countered, thinking of Uncle Van. Without thinking, she added, "Please."

The word seemed to surprise Sonia, who glanced at Roberta, then away again. Dutifully, she spoke. "My mother distributed pamphlets during the war," she said. "For the Resistance. She helped smuggle the pamphlets from the printers to the places they needed to go. I helped her."

Roberta bit the side of her thumb again. In France? she wondered. What sorts of pamphlets? Resistance against Hitler? Already she was lost. She knew so little—no one talked to girls their age about the war. Some girls had brothers and cousins who went away, and either got killed or came back again, like Uncle Van. No one had ever taught any of them about a Resistance. But she wanted Sonia to keep talking, so she nodded, silent.

"We knew it was dangerous," Sonia said. "Papa was already gone to Dachau—he was a writer. He was outspoken. They took him early, but they left us, because Mama's father had once worked for the government. But they arrested us in early 1944. I was nine."

Roberta breathed as quietly as she could, listening.

"We were sent to prison first," Sonia said. "It wasn't so bad. Mama tried to get us kept there because of her father. But her father was dead by then, and they put us on the train. We went to Ravensbrück."

"What is Ravensbrück?" Roberta finally said, unable to help herself.

"It was a prison camp."

"Like Auschwitz?" That was a name she knew—there had been a newsreel at the cinema once, before the movie started, that showed the gates in black and white, the train tracks. Something about liberation. That had been in the last days before Uncle Van came home.

"Yes, but only for women," Sonia said. "And children."

Roberta blinked, shocked.

Sonia didn't seem to notice. "We were put in a barracks," she said, "Mama and me. We were made to work. There was a work detail that dug all day. There was never an end to the digging—we weren't even making anything, just moving dirt back and forth. Still, they made us do it. In the heat, in the cold, without food or water. Whoever fell during work detail was left there to rot. Women fell every day."

Roberta felt her heart rise up and start beating in her

neck, squeezing it in dread. *I'm not ready to hear this. I'm not.*

"We stood every day in the *Appelplatz*," Sonia said. "That was the main square in the camp. They lined us up and made us stand, for hours and hours. It was supposed to be a roll call, but of course it wasn't. We froze or we sweated under the sun. Whoever fell was left. Mama was all right at first, but as the days went by, she got quiet. Quiet, quiet. I thought it was a good thing, because when you were quiet, you got by and no one noticed you. Then one day, as they made us stand in the *Appelplatz*, she started to scream." Sonia twisted the edge of her bedsheet softly between her fingers, dropping her gaze to it. "She screamed and screamed. She said they were murderers—they would all go to hell. She said the war would be over one day and it would all come out. She said there would be justice, that there would be no silence in the end. She said that the murderers would someday see, that they would someday face their Maker. They took her away and I never saw her again. I heard one of the women say that they executed her, they shot her in the back of the head, but I didn't know if it was true. If she'd just stayed quiet . . ." She dropped the sheet. "If she'd just stayed quiet. But she did not. And then it was just me."

"Could you get away?" Roberta whispered.

Sonia turned her head and looked at her. "When we arrived, they told us that if we wanted, we could see the last woman who tried to climb the fence. Because she was still there." She turned back to looking at the wooden slats again. "She was."

Roberta could not speak.

"Today, it was like I was back there," Sonia said. "It doesn't happen often. The war ended, and they brought us all out of there, and I came here. I'm fed and taken care of. I don't think about it. But today, it was like Weekly Gardening had never existed. I was ten again, on work detail. It's hard to explain. It was more real to me than you are right now."

Roberta put her head in her hands. Her temples were throbbing, and she wished now she'd gotten her own chalky white aspirin pill from Miss Hedmeyer. Her eyes were hot and she wanted to cry, but the tears were jammed in her throat, hard and painful. Had Uncle Van seen these things? Was that why he'd tried to use his gun in the garage? She made herself take a breath. "And the other day? In the dining hall?"

"That was . . ." Sonia searched in her mind, tried to find the words. "We had *blockovas*," she said, "block leaders. They were prisoners who were promoted, assigned to oversee other prisoners."

"Women?" Roberta asked, shocked again.

"Yes. A few were nice, and tried to sneak us things, but most were not. They wanted favor. They had leave to beat you, report on you. If you misbehaved, you were sent to the punishment block. Solitary confinement, and worse."

Roberta thought back to that day in the dining hall, Alison punching Sherri, Sherri's nose bleeding, the chaos and the noise, Lady Loon shouting, *It's Special Detention for you, my girl. Do you hear? Get moving. Move!* It made sense now. A horrible, nightmarish kind of sense.

She circled back to the main problem. "What are you going to do?" she asked the other girl. "This can't keep happening. You'll get sent to Special Detention." Katie, the strongest and boldest of them, had been sent to Special Detention, and she'd been so shaken she refused to talk about it. Roberta wasn't sure Sonia would survive it. "You could be expelled," she said. "You have nowhere to go."

Sonia's chin went hard; her eyes clouded. "It won't happen again."

Roberta wasn't sure about that. But as Sonia drifted to sleep, she sat still, her mind dwelling on the problem, poking at it from all sides. Sonia was tired, drained, but Roberta was resilient. So was CeCe. So was Katie.

They'd gotten this far, all of them. Without breaking, without dying. Sonia wasn't alone.

Together, they could do something. Together, they could carry on.

They sat on the floor of their room that night, all four of them, gathered around CeCe's radio. With the sound low so Susan Brady wouldn't hear, they listened to a show about cops chasing a murderer, and a rendition of "Three Little Maids" that made them all laugh. Then another show, this one about cowboys, before it got late enough that everything went off the air and CeCe turned the radio off. And then they talked.

In the dark, when they'd all been listening for hours, already relaxed, it suddenly became easy. The words flowed, weaving over one another, making up the pattern as they went along. Roberta told about Uncle Van, about the day she had opened the garage door and found him, sitting on a wooden chair, weeping, a pistol in his mouth. She told them of the days afterward, the silence in herself that she couldn't break, the doctors, Uncle Van's blood-shot eyes. He hadn't been able to look at her. Roberta felt a new lump in her throat as she told it, remembering. She wished now that she'd crawled into Uncle Van's lap and put her arms around his neck and never let go. But she'd been thirteen, and everyone had been horrified and silent, including her, and she hadn't known what to do.

"Where is he now?" Katie's low voice came through the dark when Roberta finished.

"He's still at home," Roberta said. "He sees doctors. Mother says he isn't well, that Dad wants to put him in a hospital." She forced the words out. "They're fighting. Mother and Dad. I could see it on Family Visit Day—they wouldn't look at each other, talk to each other. They're ashamed of me and Uncle Van both. I know Dad works a lot. Mother's eyes were red, and she says . . . she says it isn't a good time to come home."

The others talked now as Roberta subsided. A weight had lifted from her chest. Each girl spoke while the others were quiet, listening.

It went like that, night after night. Katie, with CeCe as an accomplice, began pilfering extra food from the dining hall at supper, sneaking through a door into the kitchen and taking it while CeCe kept watch. They snacked on the extra food every night after dark; they pretended that it was for all of them, but by tacit agreement they gave most of it to Sonia. With the lights out and the cold winter coming outside, they ate and listened to the radio and told their stories, one by one, detail upon detail. Katie and Thomas, the boy who'd attacked her and told her to hold still. CeCe and her mother's accident at the beach. Roberta told them, hesitantly, about the song she'd heard on the hockey field, the same song Uncle Van had been playing in the garage that day, as if someone or something had drawn the memory straight from her mind. And the next night Katie told them about Special Detention, and the spiders, and the messages in the textbooks. And the scratching at the window, the voice begging to be let in.

Sonia spoke rarely, but when she did, the others went silent, listening, from the first word. She told them slowly, doling out piece by piece, about Ravensbrück— the layout of the barracks and the other buildings, the women and the other children she'd met there, the weather, the cold, the food, the day-to-day comings and goings of the prison, the stories the women had told. It was slow and it was hard to hear, but the girls listened to all of it, and as Sonia spoke, Roberta fancied that perhaps she felt better. That sending the experience out of her head and into words made it less immense, less impossible. They set up a signaling system for her to use if she felt another episode coming on, but Sonia didn't use it.

They were trapped here at Idlewild. But Idlewild wasn't everything. It wasn't the world.

Someday, by God, Roberta thought, *I'm going to get out of here. Someday we all will. And when we do, we will finally be free.*

chapter 18

Jamie's parents lived in a bungalow that had been built in the 1960s, covered with vinyl siding in the 1970s, and never touched since. It sat on a stretch of road heading out of downtown Barrons, where the houses had been built close together with neat square yards crowned by wooden porches.

Jamie's father, Garrett Creel Jr., opened the door as they climbed the front steps. He was still massive at sixty, broad-shouldered and tall, his ruddy face emphasized by his short-cropped sandy hair. He could have worn a sign around his neck that said I AM A RETIRED POLICEMAN and no one would have batted an eye. He clapped his son on the shoulder and gave Fiona a kiss on the cheek. His lips were dry and chapped, his hand clammy, and Fiona gritted her teeth and smiled as she greeted him. The house wafted with the radiant smell of roast beef.

"Come on in, come on in!" Garrett bellowed. "Diane, they're here."

She came around the corner into the front hall, a small woman in a helmet of permed curls that had been in vogue somewhere around 1983, making a beeline for Jamie, who had just handed his coat to his dad. "*There* you are," she said, as if he were somehow delinquent, even though he'd obediently answered her summons to dinner and arrived right on time.

She pulled Jamie down to her—he was much taller than she was, mirroring his father's height, if not his heft or his looks—and kissed him with a loud, possessive smack, then held his face so he could not look away. She did not look at Fiona yet, and the way she held Jamie's face, he couldn't look at her, either.

"Your hair is still too long," she said to her son, patting his dark blond strands. "And this beard. What is this?" She touched it with possessive fingers. "Your father spent thirty years on the force with a haircut and a clean shave."

Jamie smiled, waited her out, and straightened when she let him go. "Mom, you remember Fiona."

"Yes, of course." Diane tore her gaze from Jamie and turned to Fiona. "*Finally.* I've made pot roast."

Fiona nodded. She could do the girlfriend thing. It just took some practice, that was all. "It smells delicious," she said.

Diane gave her a tight smile. "Catch up with your father," she told Jamie. "Dinner is almost ready."

Garrett was already handing them each a beer and shepherding them into the living room.

"So here you are," he said, squeezing Fiona's shoulder. "Jamie's mother has been asking for this forever. You two have been together for how long now?"

Jamie shook his head. "This isn't an interview, Dad."

"Of course not. Just never thought I'd see the day I had Malcolm Sheridan's daughter in my living room, that's all."

He said it jovially, with an unmissable undertone of disbelief, and there it was. The history that always pressed down on her, the past that never left. She was with Jamie partly because she never had to talk about it with him, but that was when they were alone. She realized now, standing in this outdated living room, listening to Jamie and his father swap news of the force, that with his family the history would always be thick. She also realized that she'd known it for the past year, which was why she'd put off coming to dinner.

As if to prove it, Garrett swigged his beer and turned to her. "I hear you were at Idlewild, Fiona. Trespassing. Climbed the fence and everything."

Fiona clutched her untasted beer. "I beg your pardon?"

"Dad," Jamie said.

Garrett laughed. "You look surprised. I'm good friends with Jack Friesen, who owns the security company they hired out at Idlewild. He told me about the little incident with you."

"I'm writing a story," Fiona managed before Jamie could take up for her again.

"Are you, now?" Garrett asked, and when he looked at her, she saw the face of the man who had testified in court twenty years ago. He'd been younger then, thinner, but his face was the same. He'd been hard then and he was hard now, beneath the florid good-old-boy look. "That seems like a strange story for you to write."

She shrugged, keeping it light. "Not really."

"I'd think the last place you'd want to be is at Idlewild when they found another body. But I guess I'm wrong."

"Dad," Jamie said again. "Enough."

They adjourned to dinner, which Diane was serving in the small formal dining room, set with nice china. Outside the window, the Vermont night settled in, and in the darkness all Fiona could see was their own reflections in the glass.

"I talked to Dave Saunders today," Garrett said to her as he put pot roast on his plate. "He did the autopsy on that body you found."

Jesus, she'd thought he was retired. Retirement obviously meant nothing to Garrett Creel. "What did he say?" she asked him, sipping her beer and watching Diane's face pinch. She likely hated talk like this at the supper table, but with a cop for both a husband and a son, she would have to put up with it in pained silence.

"There isn't much," Garrett said, sawing unconcernedly at his meat. "Died of a blow to the head, almost certainly. Something long, like a baseball bat or a pipe. Two blows that he can see, probably one to knock her out and one to make sure she was dead. No other injuries. She was a teenager, but small for her age. Dead at least thirty years, based on the decomposition. Has been in the well all this time, as far as he can see, since there was no evidence of animals going at her."

Diane made a small sound in her throat that her husband ignored.

"Anything else?" Jamie asked, spooning potatoes onto his plate. He was as inured to this kind of conversation at dinner as his father was. "Did he mention any old injuries, things she might have suffered years before she died?"

"Nope," Garrett said. "Why?"

Jamie glanced at Fiona and said, "We found some evidence that she may have been in a concentration camp during the war."

Garrett paused and looked up, surprised. Then he whistled as Diane made another displeased sound. "Really? When did you learn this?"

"Just before we came here," Jamie said. "I thought maybe the autopsy would show—"

"I'll ask Dave to look again, but he didn't see anything," Garrett said. "Concentration camp, maybe you'd see broken bones, broken teeth." He stabbed his fork into a bite of meat. "She would have been a young girl then. If she was starved, maybe that's why she didn't grow very big. Malnutrition. It's amazing she wasn't gassed."

"Garrett, please," Diane was forced to say.

"Sorry, Mom," Jamie said, but he turned back to his father and said, "Her family didn't make it."

"Well, that's a hell of a thing," Garrett said. "To go through all that just to get killed and dropped in a well. Who would kill a girl like that? Sounds like something a Nazi would do, except she came all the way across the ocean to get away from those bastards." He shook his head. "I was always proud that my dad went over there to help us beat those sons of bitches."

"Garrett," Diane said again, and Fiona dropped her gaze to cut her meat.

After supper, which felt interminable with tension, Diane busied herself in the kitchen again, cleaning up, and Jamie helped her. Fiona was left alone in the family room with Garrett as a football game played on mute on the TV. She stared at the screen silently, utterly uninterested in football, until she glanced at Garrett and realized he was looking at her.

And suddenly, she was finished being polite. Just finished. "Listen," she said to Garrett, knowing the words were a bad idea even as she said them. "Jamie isn't in the room. I know you don't want me here. I'll admit, I don't want to be here, either. Having dinner with the man who found my sister's body isn't my idea of fun."

He blinked at her, momentarily surprised, but there wasn't a shred of sympathy in his expression. "What you don't understand," he said, "is the influence you have on him. The kind of influence he doesn't need."

It took her a second to follow. "Jamie?" she asked. "You think I have an influence on Jamie?"

"He can't move up if he's dating you," Garrett said. "No one trusts a cop who's in bed with a journalist."

It was probably true, but Jamie had never said anything about it to her. He'd never shown any resentment. He'd also never shown any burning ambition to move up, which was probably what was bothering Garrett. "That's his decision," she said.

Garrett shook his head. "People don't always make the best decisions," he said. "So few people understand that you have to look out for your own best interests. All the time. Sometimes I think Jamie understands that least of all."

She stared at him. This conversation was surreal. "Jamie is a good man."

"What do you know about it?" he asked softly, and suddenly she knew, in a perfect premonition, that he was about to hurt her. That he was about to hurt her hard. "Tim Christopher was a good man, too, before his life was ruined."

For a second, she had no words at all. "What did you just say?" she managed.

"I've always wondered," Garrett said. "A witness who saw them arguing, and a drop of blood on his leg? That's circumstantial evidence." He shrugged, but the look he gave Fiona was deep and sharp. "Maybe he was railroaded. Don't you ever wonder?"

"Stop it." The words came out like someone else's voice. "Just stop."

"I'm not the only one," Garrett said. "Because you can't leave it alone."

There was the snap of the dishwasher closing in the

kitchen, the rush of water. Diane laughed at something Jamie said.

"It's been twenty years," Garrett said softly. "You think Jamie doesn't tell me?"

Fiona felt her dinner turn in her stomach, a rush of acid up her throat.

"Wandering around on Old Barrons Road," Garrett said. "Climbing the Idlewild fence. Deep down, you wonder about it just the same as I do. You're a mess, sweetheart."

His gaze was fixed on her, the same gaze he'd used to pin liars and wrongdoers in thirty years of policing. "I was one of the first called out to that field," he told her. "Some kids called it in. I had just come on shift. The only other cop on shift was Jim Carson, and he was barely twenty. No way would I let a kid like that be the first at a body. I took him with me, sure. But I knew it had to be me."

Fiona was silent now, unable to look away.

"Everyone remembers," Garrett said. "Everyone remembers, but no one remembers it quite like I do. Before the circus descended, when it was just Jim and me and the crows in the quiet of that field, looking down. I looked at her and thought, *Whatever this is, this will be the worst thing this town has ever seen. This will be the beginning of the end.*" He blinked. "It really was, wasn't it? It really was. Tim's life was over. The Christophers left. People locked their doors after that."

"You told Richard Rush to lie," Fiona said. The words were hard, but they came. The idea she'd had since she'd read the article and talked to Mike Rush about his father. "You went into his shop and you made him do it somehow. You told him to say that Tim Christopher was there at nine o'clock. And he did. But he must have retracted it for some reason, because it never made it to court." *When I saw that article and asked Dad about it, he got angry,* Mike Rush had said. *My dad only ever gave me the belt three times in my life, and that was one of them. He told me never to ask about it again.*

"Are you going to do this?" Garrett asked her, his eyes on her, never leaving her. "Are you going to do it, twenty years later? Those are serious words, Fiona. I suggest you take them back."

But she wouldn't stop, not now. "Why did you make him lie?"

"What's going on here?"

Jamie stood in the doorway, watching them. His gaze flickered to his father, then to Fiona.

"Thanks for coming, son," Garrett said, his voice cold. "I think the evening is over."

Jamie was quiet the entire drive home, his jaw tight. Fiona looked briefly at him, at the lights of passing cars washing over his profile, and then she looked away, watched out the window.

He didn't speak until he pulled up in front of her apartment building, and then he put the SUV in park without turning it off. "It was something to do with Deb, wasn't it?" he said, still staring ahead. "What you and my father were arguing about. It was something to do with this obsession of yours that won't go away." He paused. "You made him angry. What did you say to him?"

She stared at him. "No one is allowed to make the great Garrett Creel angry—is that it?"

"You have no idea what you're talking about," Jamie said, and his voice was almost as cold as his father's. "What did you say to him, Fiona?"

And suddenly she was angry, too, so furious her hands were shaking. "I told you this was a bad idea. I warned you it wouldn't work."

"You said you'd try. A couple of fucking hours. You didn't even *try* to get along."

"Is that what everything is about with you?" she asked, lashing out at him, taking out all the anger she couldn't unleash on Garrett. "Just getting along?"

"Those are my parents." His voice was rising. "That's my *dad*."

"Jamie, you're twenty-nine."

He stared at her. "What the hell is that supposed to mean?"

"He baited me. He started when we walked in, and he twisted the screws when he was left alone with me. He defended Tim Christopher, Jamie. This was what he wanted to happen." And she'd given in to it. She'd walked right into the trap. What did that say about her?

"Dad wouldn't do that," Jamie said. He ran a hand through his hair. "Maybe you misunderstood. God, I don't even know what I'm doing anymore."

"You're dating a journalist," she said. "You're a cop,

and you're dating Malcolm Sheridan's daughter. Your family hates it. I'm sure your fellow cops hate it. Your sacred brotherhood. And I didn't misunderstand anything. Tell me, do you and your dad ever sit around over beers and shoot the shit about my sister's case?"

Jamie went still and said nothing.

"You knew," she said to him. "That night we met at the bar. You knew who I was. You knew more about my sister's case than I did. Your father was the first on the scene with my sister's *body*. How did you think this would work, Jamie? Why the hell did you talk to me at all?"

"Don't put this on me," he shot back, furious. "You've always known, Fee. From that first night, you knew who my father was. He was chief of police in 1994. You knew he worked that case. You sat through the entire fucking trial, all the testimony, read the papers. So why the hell did you talk to me?"

The silence descended, heavy and tight.

This is why, Fiona thought. *This is why I haven't done this, ever. Not with anyone. Why I've always said no.*

Because there was always Deb. And there always would be. Easy or no easy.

She looked at Jamie and wanted to tell him that his father had made Richard Rush lie about Tim Christopher's alibi. There was no way to prove it. Garrett would deny it, and so, she was sure, would Richard. There was only Mike Rush's word, and Mike had already said he wasn't interested in invoking his father's anger. Mike hadn't known he was talking to Deb Sheridan's sister when he told the story, because Fiona had lied to him. She had lied without a second thought, and if she had to do it over, she would do it without a second thought again. And again.

But she wouldn't tell Jamie. There was no point. He was a cop; his father was a cop; his grandfather was a cop. There was no need to make him believe. There was just hurt and anger, and confusion. Even if they patched it up, she'd hurt him again. Or he'd hurt her. Again.

"Jamie," she said.

"Don't." He scrubbed a hand over his face, then dropped it again. "Fee, we can't do this. Just . . . for now, okay? There's too much shit going on. Just for now."

She stared down into her lap. The anger had gone as quickly as it came, and now she felt shaky and a little ashamed. But Jamie was right. She couldn't do this right now. Not even for Jamie.

Still, the idea of getting out and going home alone made her ill. For the first time, she wondered: *When will this be over?*

But she already knew the answer to that. So she got out of the car.

When he drove off, she stood watching for a moment, her hands in her pockets.

When his taillights disappeared, she turned and climbed the stairs to her apartment.

chapter 19

Barrons, Vermont
November 2014

Malcolm had given her a phone number, of a woman in England who was at the helm of a research project focusing on Ravensbrück concentration camp. The woman answered after the phone rang for nearly a minute. "Ginette Harrison," she said in a clipped upper-crust accent.

"Hello," Fiona said. "My name is Fiona Sheridan. My father, Malcolm, referred me to you?"

"Yes," Ginette said. Fiona heard the whistle of a teakettle in the background, as if she'd just dialed the direct number into a BBC show. "Fiona. I remember."

"Is now a good time?" Fiona asked. "I have some questions about Ravensbrück, if you have a moment."

"Well, yes, I do," Ginette said. She sounded a little bemused. Fiona tried to guess her age from the sound of her voice, but with that dry English accent, she could have been anywhere from thirty-five to sixty. "Pardon, I know I sound surprised," she said. "It's only that it's just after nine o'clock in the morning here, and Malcolm told me you live near him, in Vermont."

"I do," Fiona said.

"That means it's about four o'clock in the morning there, does it not?"

Fiona looked around her dark apartment. She was sitting on the sofa, wearing a sleeping shirt and a pair of women's boxer shorts, surrounded by the boxes from Idlewild. She'd given in and called England after fruitless hours of trying to sleep. "It is," she admitted. "I just . . . It seemed urgent that I talk to you. Did my father tell you we found a body here?"

"Yes." There was a rustling, as if Ginette Harrison was sitting down somewhere, getting comfortable. Perhaps she was putting sugar and milk in her tea. "A girl found in a well?"

"She disappeared in 1950," Fiona said. "It was presumed she was a runaway."

"I see. And no one looked for her?"

"According to the police record, no. Not after the first few days."

"I see," Ginette said again. "I'm intrigued. Not because I'm a ghoul, but because if you've found a verified Ravensbrück inmate, I'd like to add her to my research."

"What do you mean?"

"The records from Ravensbrück were destroyed," Ginette said, her voice clipped with calm anger. "They were incinerated right before the Russians liberated the camp in 1945. Records survive from many of the other camps, but Ravensbrück was obliterated. Willfully forgotten, if you will."

"Everything?" Fiona asked, her heart sinking.

"I'm afraid so, yes. The Nazis dumped all of the prisoner records into the crematorium, alongside the bodies, before they left ahead of the advance of the Soviet army. And when the Russians took over the camp, they made no effort to preserve anything that was left."

"I see." Fiona looked around at the boxes from Sarah London's shed. *Willfully forgotten.*

"Much of my research is focused on filling in those blanks," Ginette continued. "I have spent years trying to find survivors, or any written records the survivors left. There are very few, and what still exists is hard to find."

"Hard to find?" Fiona asked. "The history of concentration camps is taught in schools. I thought there was a large body of work, much of it written by survivors, or sourced from survivors' interviews."

"Most of the women who survived Ravensbrück didn't speak of it," Ginette explained. "They did their best to go back into the fabric of their lives and forget, which was all they wanted. A few wrote memoirs, but they're long out of print. I've gathered what I can, especially from the few women left alive who are willing to talk about it. But Ravensbrück is a footnote. That leaves your dead girl as a footnote, too, I'm sorry to say."

"How could that be?" Fiona said. "How can an entire concentration camp be a footnote?"

Ginette Harrison sighed. "It was a women's camp, for

one. And when the war ended and the Cold War began, it landed on the wrong side of the Iron Curtain. No one in the West had access to the site for decades. Scholars, survivors, writers—everyone was split, East from West. By the time the Cold War ended, many of the survivors had died. No one wrote about it except for a handful of scholars who have kept the hope alive that the story can be rebuilt. One of them is me."

Fiona heaved herself onto her back on the sofa and ran a hand through her hair. She was tired, so tired. "So there is no chance that I'll find a record of Sonia Gallipeau, who was there as a child, most likely with her mother."

"I'm sorry," Ginette said. "Almost none. Malcolm gave me the name Emilie Gallipeau, but that doesn't match any of the records I've found. Tens of thousands of women died at Ravensbrück, you understand—in the gas chambers, or worked to death in the slave labor camp, tortured, executed, or simply starved. Most of those women became anonymous when the records were burned."

Fiona stared at her ceiling in the dark, her eyes burning. It was incredible that tens of thousands of people could vanish from history without a single record. "Were the women Jews?" she asked.

"Very few, in fact," Ginette said. "They were prisoners from countries occupied by the Nazis, communists, members of the Resistance, Gypsies, captured spies. There was also a certain type of prisoner the Nazis termed 'asocial.'"

"Asocial?"

"Prostitutes, destitute women, addicts and alcoholics, the mentally ill. Women the Nazis simply didn't want society to support anymore, or women considered of low morals."

"Jesus Christ," Fiona said. "How horrible."

"So you see why so few survivors left records," Ginette said quietly. "Some of the women at Ravensbrück were highly educated, but many were not. Many were simply powerless."

"And some were children."

"Yes," the other woman agreed. "Some were children."

Fiona thought about this, still staring at her ceiling. The story itself was a horror so large it threatened to overtake everything in its path. She had to try to control it, not to let the nightmare send her off the path of what she was really after. She had to remember Sonia. "What happened to the camp itself after the war?"

"It was mostly demolished over time," Ginette replied. "The Soviet army took it, and there was no effort at historical preservation. Most of the buildings are long gone. There is a memorial there now in what buildings were left, including the crematorium. In the last days of the war, the Nazis who ran the camp fled, though some of them were captured, along with guards. There were two Ravensbrück trials in 1946, and the women—"

"The *women*?" Fiona interrupted. "The guards were women?"

"They were," Ginette said. "The camp commander was

a man, a member of the SS, reporting directly to Himmler. But the guards were women. Some were recruited from women's prisons where they worked as guards, and some were from the local countryside, women who wanted a job." She paused, listening to Fiona's silence. "It's a tad upsetting, isn't it? We like to believe that women wouldn't do such things to other women—send them into the gas chambers with their children, put them in the ovens. But I'm afraid there is no question that they did."

"Sorry I interrupted," Fiona said. "You were talking about the war crimes trials."

"Yes. Even those were forgotten for decades during the Cold War. The records were sealed. There were a number of convictions, at least, and executions of guards. Many guards were never caught. It was the same with every concentration camp. There is a memorial on the site now, though Ravensbrück is out of the way, several hours from Berlin, over back roads. It was intentionally built on a remote site, on a lake with only a small rural town nearby."

"It seems incredible now, that everyone let it go. That there wasn't more outrage."

"That's because you think like someone of the modern generation," Ginette Harrison said, and the gentle English chiding in her voice gave away that she was older than Fiona had thought, perhaps over fifty or sixty. "To do the research I do, you must understand the mind-set of those times. There was no Internet, no way to raise outrage via a Twitter campaign, no digital cameras with which one could take a photo and send it worldwide in seconds."

And that left Ravensbrück abandoned and dismantled, forgotten. "This girl," Fiona said, trying to stay on track again. "Sonia. The body we found. The coroner didn't find any old injuries to the bones or the teeth."

"Then she escaped some of the physical torture," Ginette said. "But Ravensbrück, like many other camps, was a battle of endurance. It was a matter of living long enough while those around you died."

"She was small for her age."

"That doesn't surprise me. If she was malnourished at the camp, then it could have affected her growth. I'm not a doctor, however, so I can't say for sure. If she survived Ravensbrück, though, she must have had some strength."

"You said the Russians liberated the camp," Fiona said. She sensed that Ginette Harrison was busy, politely growing impatient, and she wanted as much information as possible. "Did they keep any records?"

"Not that we've located. The Red Cross has some records of prisoners who ended up with them in the chaos, but I already have those, and I went through them. Your names did not appear."

"But she came to America in 1947 with the support of distant relatives," Fiona said. "Somebody, somewhere, gave this girl aid and helped her get in touch with her family in America. She was ten when the war ended. She could not have done it alone."

"It could have been anyone," Ginette said. "A fellow prisoner, a sympathetic family, a hospital. I'm sorry. We have no way of knowing. You're looking for her family, are you not?"

"I'm looking for anything," Fiona confessed. "Anything at all."

There was a pause. "Miss Sheridan, may I offer a purely personal opinion?"

"Please do."

"You have a young girl, far from home. She has come from a camp in which every record was obliterated. Every member of her family has been killed. And now she is alone, in a strange country, with no one looking out for her but the impersonal staff of an uncaring boarding school."

"Yes," Fiona said.

"There is no one to look for her if she disappears. No one to care. And as far as the authorities are concerned, if anyone knew of her background in a concentration camp, frankly, they would assume she was a Jew." She paused. "This was 1950, in a rural area, you understand."

"What are you saying?" Fiona asked.

"I'm saying," Ginette Harrison said, "to put it bluntly, that if one was looking for a victim to murder, one could not find a better candidate."

Fiona swallowed. "You think she was chosen."

"It's a thought that strikes me," the other woman said, and Fiona could tell she was trying to soften her voice. "I don't wish to alarm you. But this girl disappeared without a single trace for over sixty years, and no one ever looked for her. If you were hunting for someone to murder, what better person could you choose?"

chapter 20

Sonia

Telling the story to her friends was freeing, and she could feel the pieces of her mind slowly moving, rearranging themselves. But the best day came when she got the notebook.

It was CeCe's; she'd received it from her rich father, a careless Christmas present perhaps chosen by his secretary and mailed to his bastard daughter at her boarding school. Sonia could hear the command in her head: *Send my daughter something nice. I don't know—just pick something. What do girls like? Here's some money.* And now CeCe had this notebook, an expensive thing, with a hard cover decorated in flowers and thick lined pages inside, making a creamy *flip-flip* sound as you leafed through them, their weight bending and flopping satisfactorily as you ran your thumb along the edge. A good notebook.

CeCe had emptied a drawer one afternoon when she was almost late for physical education, looking for her socks. The notebook had landed on the floor in a pile of detritus, most of it forgotten or never noticed in the first place by its owner. Sonia had picked up the notebook.

"Oh, that," CeCe said, glancing over as she opened the next drawer. "I've never used it."

Of course CeCe hadn't. This was a notebook made for a girl who liked to write, who took each word seriously and put it down with care. CeCe was not a writer, which was why Sonia knew it was a gift from her father. Anyone who knew CeCe even for a few minutes would know this was not the gift for her.

"Here they are," CeCe said, pulling her socks from her bottom drawer. She glanced at Sonia again, holding the notebook. "Do you want it? Take it."

"I can't," Sonia said. "It's expensive."

CeCe laughed. "It isn't my money." She had a harder edge to her now, since she'd told them the story of her mother and the water. But a hard edge, for CeCe, was still soft as butter. "I'll never use it, honestly. Take it. I have to go."

So Sonia took it. She found the pretty pen that had been sent with the book—it was sitting in the pile on the floor that CeCe hadn't put away in her haste. She'd never miss it; she'd likely forgotten she ever received it. So Sonia picked it up and opened the notebook. She dipped her head down into the book's spine, inhaling deeply of the thick papery scent, feeling something strange and calm move down the back of her neck, into her shoulders, her spine. She felt small, prickling sparks in the top of her brain. *What will I write in this beautiful book?*

She carried the book to class for the rest of the day, and that night she put it under her pillow, still blank. She liked it blank right now, liked to know that it was waiting, listening. Just like her friends.

In the end, she told the book the same story she'd told her friends. The only story she knew, really. The only story she had to tell. And she added pictures.

She had been fair at drawing before the war. She'd drawn her mother dozens of times, as she sat reading or sewing. There had been so many things in those days that kept a person still, that required perfect concentration for hours on end. It had been easy to draw portraits. Her mother, her father, the cat who came to the window looking for food. Then, when she got quicker, her teachers and classmates.

That had stopped. But now she uncapped her pen and wrote in her private notebook, and she told it everything, page by page. And alongside the words, she drew pictures. She drew her mother from memory, and then her father. She had to stop for a day after that, but then she got the itch again, and she opened the book and wrote down what she remembered.

She drew Ravensbrück.

Once she started, she couldn't stop, the edges of her memories sawing at her as she sat at her lessons, as she did her homework and ran pitifully around the hockey field and ate her tasteless meals in the dining hall. The memories weren't the overwhelming ones she'd had that had made her sick. These were like a violin bow grinding along the edge of a single string, shrill, waiting for some kind of resolution to make it stop. The only thing that worked was writing.

She mapped the camp. She drew it from several vantage points, looking over the dormitory buildings, looking toward the crematorium with its plumes of smoke. She drew every face she remembered: inmates, women who came and went, *blockovas*, guards, her mother. Her mother. She drew the man who came to inspect them, the tall man with the silver *SS* on his uniform collar and the long black coat. She drew the landscape in summer and winter, the bodies. She drew the face of the first person she'd seen the day the camp was liberated, a man in a Soviet uniform with a wide, fat face. She'd fled from him on sight, running barefoot as far as she could. She'd wanted nothing to do with soldiers.

She drew the bombed-out church she'd slept in that first night. The woman, the fellow prisoner, who had found her and joined her. The family that had taken them in. Their two children, their thin faces, their wide eyes. There were certain things her memory refused to yield up to her—blanks of time, some of them frustrating, some of them possibly merciful. Her mother standing in the *Appelplatz*—she could not recall that, not clearly. What angle had she watched it from? Had she been in front of her mother, or behind? It wouldn't come, and Sonia started to wonder if she'd only heard about it, though she could have sworn she'd seen it. It was all so confusing.

Her friends noticed what she was doing, of course. She told them honestly what she was writing about, but she didn't offer to show them at first. Even now, after so many nights lying on the floor with them, listening to CeCe's radio and talking, she felt shy about what was in the book. But eventually she showed Roberta, and then the others. Roberta was silent and grim when she read it; CeCe, whose notebook it was, shed big, fat tears down her cheeks and hugged Sonia long and fierce when she was finished.

But Katie had read the notebook with an expression that went harsh and white, impenetrable as concrete. She was sitting on the edge of her bunk, the notebook open on her lap as she paged through it in silence. Sonia sat next to her, her feet curled up beneath her, biting the edge of her thumb. It was an offering, giving Katie the book, and she could not read Katie's response while her eyes were down and her lashes lowered. She waited.

Katie used her palms to clap the book shut with a *snap* that reverberated through the room, a big gesture, just like all of Katie's gestures. "You should be a writer," she said.

"What does that mean?" Sonia asked.

"You have talent," Katie said. She looked down at the closed notebook, the whorls of flowers on the cover. "You can draw. You can write. This is talent, Sonia. Talent can be used to make money."

Sonia dropped her thumb and felt her jaw gape open for a second. "You mean like a job?"

"You could be a writer," Katie said again, patiently, as

if she knew it was difficult for the idea to get through. "You could write books, articles. You could be published. Then you wouldn't have to get married."

The girls had talked, more than once, about how none of them wanted to get married. The only waverer was CeCe, who said she'd like to have children but was terrified of the kissing-and-sex part. The other three agreed that they had no use for boys whatsoever, except that they had no idea how to get by in the world without a husband, without being a terrifying spinster like Lady Loon. It was a problem the four of them had yet to solve, not least because their severe lack of information—aside from *Lady Chatterley's Lover*—hampered their ability to make a decision.

"I can't write a book about Ravensbrück," Sonia said. "I can't."

Katie glanced at her, those dark, bewitching eyes missing nothing. Katie was so beautiful it was hard to look at her sometimes: the raven black hair, the pure perfection of her forehead, the gull-wing slashes of her brows, the straight nose and mouth that almost never moved to express a single emotion. If you wanted to read Katie, Sonia had learned, you had to watch her eyes carefully, as the rest of her face would never, ever give her away. "Why not?" Katie said.

"No one wants to read about this." Sonia gestured to the notebook. "It's just the memories of some stupid girl. We could all be dead in a nuclear war tomorrow. It isn't important."

Katie looked at her for a long moment, thoughts

moving swiftly behind her eyes. This was Katie's calculating look; Sonia had learned to recognize it. "Then don't," she concluded bluntly. "You don't have to write about Ravensbrück. But you *can* write. And you can draw. You could write a book about something else."

"About what?"

"Anything you want." Katie handed the notebook back to her. "You could write children's tales, like *Winnie-the-Pooh*. Or something for grown-ups—I don't know. You could write *Lady Chatterley's Lover*."

That made Sonia laugh, which it was intended to do. She felt her cheeks heat at the same time; they'd read passages from the book in some of their late-night radio sessions. "I can't write that," she said, "since we just agreed I'm not going to get married. A writer has to write from firsthand experience."

Katie rolled her eyes, which was also intended to make Sonia laugh. "Firsthand experience is nothing to write home about, believe me. Tom was sweaty and smelled like mothballs."

Sonia laughed, though it was a painful story. She knew that laughing at it was one of Katie's weapons, a way for her to make the experience smaller, easier to manage. "Do you know something?" Sonia said.

"What?"

"When I first met you, I was a little afraid of you."

Katie shrugged; she was used to it. Everyone was a little afraid of Katie; she was beautiful, bold, impossibly strong. "And now?"

And now I love you very much, Sonia wanted to say,

but instead she said, "Now I just think you like to read dirty books, so you want me to write them."

That made the other girl's mouth twitch, that perfect line of lips cracking briefly into an amused smile that she quickly pressed away. "Write about a girl in a boarding school," she said.

The words were tossed off, but they hit Sonia with the unexpected force of a great idea. She thought about it for days, as she leafed through her notebook. She could start drawing her friends, the girls here. She could stop drawing Ravensbrück. She was almost finished drawing Ravensbrück anyway, at least for now.

So she did quick, furtive portraits of her friends, sketches at first when the girls weren't looking, then others from memory. She did not write words, not yet. She didn't know what the words would be. What the story would be. She knew only the faces. The words would come.

One day, she got a letter from the great-aunt and great-uncle who had sponsored her trip over the Atlantic. They wrote her from time to time, and they visited at Christmas, but they hadn't offered to take her in. They were elderly, and they didn't want children. But this letter was different, inviting her for a weekend visit.

Sonia read the letter over and over, shared it with her friends, trying to parse it. What had made them offer a visit so suddenly? What had made them want to see her? Was it possible they were considering taking her from Idlewild and letting her live with them? She was twisted with a crazy anxiety, mixed with a crazy hope. She could not leave Idlewild and her friends, who felt like sisters.

Her relatives had said that they didn't want children. But to live in a house with a room of her own and a man and a woman . . . a yard . . . to get up in her own room and go to school every morning . . .

She accepted the visit and lived in anticipation, wondering what was to come.

It was November 19, 1950.

She would be dead in ten days.

chapter 21

Fiona stomped off the thin layer of slush from her boots as she entered the little café. A thin, wet ribbon of snow had fallen overnight, just enough to make the drive from Vermont hazardous and wet as it melted again. Still, she'd made it to New Hampshire on time for her meeting with Roberta Montgomery, formerly Roberta Greene.

Fiona had taken a chance and called her, asking if she was in fact the Roberta Greene who had once attended Idlewild, and the elderly woman had given a dignified, reserved agreement. Fiona had explained over the phone, her spiel about the restoration of the school and her wish to cover the story, and after a moment of silence Roberta had agreed to a meeting. Roberta was seventy-nine now, and Fiona easily picked her out in the small café, a white-haired woman who sat with perfectly straight posture and still resembled the picture that had been taken with the field hockey team when she was seventeen.

"Thank you for seeing me," Fiona said, pulling out a chair and ordering a coffee.

"I'm sorry you had to drive in the mess," Roberta said. Her voice was educated, naturally cool, as if she rarely got excited. "I don't drive anymore, I'm afraid. I like to sit here, across from the firm." She gestured out the plate-glass window, where across Islington Street a sign was visible on one of the old buildings: MONTGOMERY AND TRUE, ATTORNEYS-AT-LAW.

"You were a partner?" Fiona asked.

"For thirty years. Retired now, of course." Roberta tilted her face toward the window, and Fiona realized she had the quiet, stoic kind of beauty that defied age. "They still let me come in a few times a week and consult. They're humoring me, but what do I care?" She turned back to Fiona and smiled. "Try the cheese croissants. They bake them here, and I eat them every day. I've stopped worrying about fat at my age."

Fiona smiled back at her and did as she was told. The coffee was so strong it nearly took the top of her head off, which was welcome after the long drive. "I'd like to talk to you about Idlewild," she said.

"Yes," Roberta said. "Someone is restoring it, you said."

"You didn't know?"

Roberta shrugged. "I don't suppose you've found much on the history. No one cared about that place."

Fiona studied the older woman. She'd read Roberta's Idlewild file last night: born in 1935, sent to Idlewild in

1950 after witnessing her uncle, a war veteran, attempt suicide with a pistol in the family garage. It was the same story Sarah London had told: *There had been a suicide in the family, I believe, or an attempted one, and she had witnessed it.* Roberta had stopped speaking for a while after the incident, which caused her parents to send her away. There were no notes in the school file, however, that Roberta had any speech problems after arriving at Idlewild. Once again, the laconic nature of Idlewild's files was infinitely frustrating. No one seemed to pay very close attention to the girls they taught, or if they did, they didn't write it down.

"Do you have good memories of Idlewild?" Fiona asked, her first broad volley of the interview.

Roberta's hands curled around the warmth of her coffee cup. "It was awful," she said, "but it was better than home."

"I found a picture at the Barrons Historical Society." Fiona pulled the printout of the field hockey team portrait and smoothed it open on the table, turning it for Roberta to see.

There was a long moment of quiet. Roberta Montgomery—Roberta Greene, as Fiona's mind kept calling her—was one of those people with a gift for silence. Jamie was another; he didn't feel any need to fill the quiet with his own chatter, which was what made him a good policeman. She thought of him with a pang. He hadn't called or texted her since the night at his parents'.

"I remember this day," Roberta said. "It was May. The snow had melted, but it wasn't warm yet. The grass was wet beneath our feet." She pointed to the teacher. "Dear God, that's Lady Loon."

"I'm sorry?" Fiona asked.

"The teacher," Roberta said. "It was our nickname for her. She called all of us *ladies* when she shouted at us." She shook her head. "Irritating, really."

"And the loon part?"

Roberta rolled her eyes, and for a minute Fiona saw the teenager she'd once been. "She was a lunatic," she explained. "She really couldn't handle a bunch of girls like we were. Her real name was Miss London."

"I know," Fiona said. "She lives in Vermont."

"Lady Loon is still alive?" Roberta's eyebrows climbed up her forehead. "Well, she wasn't much older than us, I suppose. I always figured she'd drop dead of a stroke before she was fifty. We girls drove her crazy."

"Mrs. Montgomery—"

"Roberta, please."

"Roberta," Fiona said. "Do you remember a girl named Sonia Gallipeau?"

She did. Fiona could see it stamped on her features the moment the name was spoken. "Yes, of course," she said. "She was our roommate. I knew her well."

"She disappeared in 1950."

"She was murdered, you mean."

Fiona felt her heart beating in her throat. After so much speculation, so much searching, here was Sonia's living history, sitting across from her in a coffee shop. "What makes you say that?"

"Of course she was murdered," Roberta said. Her

gaze had dropped to the photo again. "We always knew. No one believed us, but we knew. Sonia wouldn't just run away, not without her suitcase."

"But she ran away from her relatives' in the middle of visiting them."

"I know," Roberta said. Her voice was calm, yet somehow infinitely sad. "That wasn't like her at all." She paused, and Fiona waited, feeling like Roberta had more to tell. After a moment, the older woman continued. "Sonia had her hopes up about the visit, that her relatives would take her in. And if she learned that they didn't plan that at all—that this was just a weekend visit and nothing more—it would have upset her. She didn't actually run *away*, you know. She got on the bus to Barrons, and her suitcase was in the weeds near the gates. She wasn't going somewhere unknown. She was coming back to the school." She raised her gaze from the photo. "To us. We were her friends. We would have comforted her and understood if she was hurt. I think she was coming back to the only home she knew."

"The headmistress seemed to think there was a boy."

Roberta huffed a single bitter laugh. "There was no boy."

Fiona took a breath. She'd never done this before; never told a person that someone they cared about, even from sixty-four years ago, was dead. Maybe she should have left this to the police, to Jamie. But no, Roberta wasn't Sonia's family. She was only a friend from over half a century ago. "Roberta," she said, as carefully as she could, "I have to tell you something. This hasn't been released publicly yet. But in the course of the restoration at Idlewild, a body was found. In the old well."

Roberta Greene tilted her head up slowly, then looked up at the ceiling, and Fiona watched grief fall over her like a blanket. The old woman blinked, still looking up, and two tears tracked down her parchment cheeks. Her sadness was so fresh, so raw, it was as if none of the years had happened at all.

"Sonia," she said.

Fiona felt the sting of tears behind her own eyes, watching. *You loved her,* she thought. She cleared her throat. "Yes," she said softly. "Sonia."

"Tell me. Please."

"She was hit over the head. She probably died quickly." Fiona had no idea if this was true, but she couldn't help saying it. "She had been in the well . . . Her body had been in the well all this time."

"Oh, God," Roberta said on a sigh.

"I'm sorry."

Roberta shook her head. "After all this time, I suppose there's no chance of the police catching her murderer."

"You knew her best," Fiona said. "Can you think of anyone who wanted to harm her? Anyone at all?"

"No." The older woman picked up her napkin and dabbed at the tear tracks on her face. She seemed to have a handle on her grief now.

"Was there anyone who bothered the girls? Strangers who came to the school or hung around? Anyone who bothered Sonia in particular?"

"We were so isolated—you have no idea," Roberta said. "No one ever came, and we never left."

"What about gardeners? Janitors? Repairmen?"

"I don't know. We never saw the kitchen staff. There were no gardens except the one the girls were forced to maintain. I suppose there were delivery people, for laundry and such, but we never saw them, either. And as for repairs"—she gave a wry smile—"you're making the assumption that anything at Idlewild was ever repaired at all. Unless a girl's father or brother came on Family Visit Day, I didn't see the face of a single man for three years."

"There was a family visit day?" This was news to Fiona.

"Yes, the last Sunday of every month was designated for families who wished to visit."

"Did anyone ever visit Sonia?"

"Her great-aunt and -uncle visited once a year at Christmas, but that was all. Sonia's other family was all dead in the war. In concentration camps."

Fiona felt a thread of tension unspooling in her, to hear her research confirmed so clearly. "There is evidence that Sonia spent time in Ravensbrück," she said.

Roberta's eyebrows rose again. She paused for a long time, and Fiona realized she had truly surprised the other woman. "You've done your research," she commented. "And you're very good."

If it was a compliment, somehow it didn't sound like one; it sounded more like Fiona had discovered something Roberta considered private, intruded on it. "Did Sonia ever talk to you about Ravensbrück?" she asked.

"No one ever talked about the war in those days," Roberta replied. "We were teenage girls. No one talked to us about anything."

That wasn't an answer, Fiona realized. Not at all. "What about your own family?" she asked. "They didn't talk to you about the war?"

"No," came the answer. And then, repeated more softly: "No."

"Did your family ever come to visit you on Family Visit Day while you were at Idlewild?"

"Only a few times over the years. The way I left home was difficult."

"Because you stopped talking after what happened with your uncle," Fiona said.

Roberta blinked at her. "Yes," she said, her voice chilled. "I'm sorry, but may I ask how you know about my uncle?"

"It's in your file."

"My file?"

"From Idlewild."

The other woman's voice grew even colder. "There are no Idlewild files. The records have been lost."

For a second Fiona was pinned by that cold gaze, which had probably been used in courtrooms and judges' chambers for thirty years. It was impressive, and a little frightening, even in an old woman. Roberta was angry, Fiona realized, because she thought Fiona was lying. "The records weren't lost," Fiona insisted. "They exist. I've read them." She left out Sarah London's shed, and the fact that the records were currently stacked in boxes in her own neglected apartment.

"That isn't possible."

"Then how do I know you were sent to Idlewild after witnessing your uncle attempting suicide with a pistol? It wasn't covered in the newspapers at the time." She'd checked, of course. Journalistic habits died hard.

Roberta pressed her lips together, thinking. Then she said, "My uncle Van came home from the war with a severe case of PTSD, though that term didn't exist at the time. He was very ill, but everyone simply told him to move on and it would get better." She blinked and looked out the window. "When I was fourteen, I walked into our garage to find him sitting in a chair, bent over, holding a gun in his mouth. The radio was playing an old GI song. He was weeping. He hadn't known anyone was home."

"What happened?" Fiona asked softly.

"I started screaming. Uncle Van looked up at me, and he couldn't do it. He couldn't blow his brains out while I watched. So in a stupid way, I saved his life." She turned to look at Fiona again. "I couldn't talk after that. I don't know why; I simply couldn't. It was some kind of shock or stress. We had no knowledge in those days to help people. We barely have it now." She paused. "So my parents sent me to Idlewild, and while I was away, they sent Uncle Van to a mental hospital and had him locked up against his will. Instead of having any feeling for him at all, they thought he was a disgrace to the family. I was a disgrace, too, because I'd had to see a psychiatrist, which in those days was a shameful thing to do. I had exemplary parents, as you can guess."

"I'm so sorry," Fiona said. "You didn't think your uncle was crazy?"

"No. I was sad for him, sorry for him. He felt horrible about what I had seen, that I'd stopped speaking, that I was being sent away. It was another burden of guilt on him. My parents' marriage fell apart the following year, and they thought I was better off away at school—that shame again, you see. When I left Idlewild, I went to law school partly so I could legally find a way to set my uncle free. To set men like him free of their ashamed families. To prevent men like my uncle from having their freedom, their assets, their homes and children, taken away. That day in the garage ended up shaping the rest of my life."

"So after everything that happened," Fiona said, "your parents paid for law school?"

Roberta blinked. "If one wants something very badly, I suppose, one can find a way."

Another nonanswer, delivered smoothly and easily. Roberta Greene was a lawyer through and through. "And did you?" Fiona asked. "Get your uncle out?"

Roberta smiled. "Oh, yes. I got Uncle Van out. It took time, but I helped him get a job, set up his life again. There weren't many tools to help him with his problems, but I gave him what I could. Things got better. He got married in 1973, when he was in his fifties. His wife was the woman who had lived next door to him for years and had always secretly wanted to marry him.

They were married twenty years, until he died. I spent much of my career doing pro bono work for other veterans. It was the best part of the work for me."

"Did you have children?"

"Yes. My husband, Edward, died of cancer last year. Our son lives in Connecticut, and our daughter lives in Sydney, Australia. I have no grandchildren. But they are both happy, I think. At least, I tried to raise them to be as happy as they can be. Happier than I was. My husband helped with that."

"What about your other friends from Idlewild?" Fiona asked, hoping that the talkative mood would continue. "Cecelia Frank and Katie Winthrop. Did you keep in touch with them? Do you know where I could find them? I'd like to interview them as well."

But Roberta shook her head. "No, dear. It was over sixty years ago. I'm sorry."

"Miss London told me the four of you were good friends."

"We were. We stuck together. But we fell apart after Sonia died. We were all so certain she was murdered, but no one would listen to us. No one at all."

"What about the headmistress, Julia Patton? She wouldn't listen to you?"

"No. Is there anything about Sonia's disappearance in the files?"

It was said calmly, but Fiona sensed that Roberta wanted to know. Badly. The files were news to her, and she was burning with curiosity, though she hid it well.

"Not much, I'm afraid," Fiona said. "There doesn't

seem to have been much of an investigation. And there was that bullshit theory about a boy."

The words were out before she thought them, and she surprised herself with them. She'd never realized until this minute that the boy theory made her angry. That someone would dismiss the disappearance of a fifteen-year-old Holocaust survivor as an impulsive everyday tramp's hooking up with a boy and running away without saying good-bye, without even her suitcase. She wanted to dig Julia Patton and Garrett Creel Sr. out of their graves and shake them, shout at them. *If you'd only listened, maybe you could have saved her before she died. Now we'll never know.*

She looked up to see Roberta watching her from across the table. There was a faint smile on her lips, as if she knew exactly what Fiona was thinking. "Bullshit, indeed," she said.

Fiona swallowed. She was tired, off her game. She was losing control of this interview, if she'd ever had it. "A few more questions," she said, trying to sound businesslike. "Do you know a woman named Margaret Eden?"

Roberta shook her head. "No, dear, I'm sorry. I don't."

"Or her son, Anthony Eden? They're the ones who bought and are restoring Idlewild."

"Then I feel sorry for them, but no, I don't know them."

"Can you think of a reason they'd want to restore the school?"

That brought the smile again. "People who don't know

Idlewild look at it and think it might be a good investment. They are quite wrong."

Fiona met her gaze straight on. "Why are they wrong?
Is it because of Mary Hand?"

There was not a whisper of surprise, of derision, of
deflecting humor on Roberta's face. Only a softening
around the eyes, which looked remarkably like pity. "She's
still there, isn't she?" she said. "Of course Mary is still
there. You've seen her."

"Have you?" Fiona asked, her voice a rasp.

"Every girl who went to Idlewild saw Mary. Sooner
or later." Spoken quietly, matter-of-factly, the madness
of seeing a ghost turned into an everyday thing.

Fiona could see honest truth in the other woman's
eyes. "What did she show you?" she asked. She hadn't
wanted to admit to Margaret Eden what had happened,
the strangeness of her deepest, most painful memories
made real. But it felt different to tell Roberta. Roberta
had gone to Idlewild; she knew.

"It doesn't matter what she showed me," Roberta
said. "What did she show you? That is the question you
need to be asking."

"I don't understand it," Fiona said. "Who was she?
Mary Hand?"

"There were rumors." Roberta shrugged. "She died
when she was locked out in the cold—that was one. Another was that her baby was buried in the garden."

Fiona thought of the damp garden, the shape she'd
thought she'd seen from the corner of her eye. *No. Not
possible.*

"There was a rhyme," Roberta continued. "The girls passed it down. We wrote it in the textbooks so the next generation of girls would be equipped. It went like this: *Mary Hand, Mary Hand, dead and buried under land. She'll say she wants to be your friend. Do not let her in again!*" She smiled, as if pleased she'd recalled all the words. "I don't know the answer, Fiona, but I lived at Idlewild for three years, and I can tell you what I think. I think Mary was there before the school was. I think she is part of that place—that she was part of it before the first building was even built. We were in her home. I don't know what shape she took before the school was built, but it's what she does—takes shapes, shows you things, makes you hear things. I have no doubt that she was a real person at some point, but now she's an echo."

Fiona's throat was dry. She thought of the figure she'd seen, the girl in the black dress and veil. "An echo of what?"

Roberta reached across the table and touched the space between Fiona's eyes with a gentle finger. "What's in here," she said. "And what's in here." She pointed to Fiona's heart. "It's how she frightens us all. What is more terrifying than that?"

chapter 22

Fiona was shaking when she got back into her car. Her skin was too tight and her eyes burned. *I'm cracking up,* she thought, digging in her purse to find an old elastic band. She pulled her hair back into a tight, rough ponytail and swiped the elastic onto it, listening to it snap. *Ghosts and dead babies and murdered girls. What next?*

She put her hands on the steering wheel, though the car was still parked, and took a deep breath. She was in a paid lot on Islington Street, and someone had papered the lot with flyers while she'd been in the coffee shop with Roberta, slipping their annoying advertisement onto every windshield. The paper flapped in the damp wind. She'd have to get out and pull it out from under her wiper, a task that suddenly seemed exhausting.

The interview with Roberta spun in her mind, and she tried to sort through it. Why hadn't she used her recorder to catch everything? It was habit, yet she hadn't even brought the recorder in her bag this morning. In desperation, she pulled out her notebook and pen and wrote her thoughts while they were fresh.

She knew about Ravensbrück, she wrote. *Sonia must have told her. Deflected my question about it.*

This was the tactic she had to take, she realized, going back over the conversation. Not to note what Roberta had said, because so much of what Roberta had said had confirmed things Fiona already knew. She needed to think about the things Roberta had deflected, as quickly and neatly as if she'd been hitting shots back over the net in a tennis match.

She knew the Idlewild records had been lost, Fiona scribbled. *How? The only way is if she has looked for them.*

That made her think for a minute. It didn't stretch the imagination that as an adult and a lawyer Roberta would have made an inquiry, looking for something about her old friend's disappearance. Once she was no longer a girl, she had used her powers as a lawyer to free her uncle and make his life as right as she could. She might have tried to make things right in Sonia's death as well, especially as she had been convinced Sonia was murdered. Perhaps she had gotten access to the same missing persons file Jamie had pulled from the Barrons police, the one that said nothing at all. The existence of the Idlewild files had been Roberta's only slip; she hadn't known about it, and she had been avidly interested. It had been one of the only times in the interview that Fiona had gotten a peek beyond the calm, careful facade.

So the next question Fiona wrote was the only logical one: *Does Roberta know who did it?*

And then: *Is she hiding it?*

She had been truly grieved when she'd heard about Sonia's body being found in the well—that hadn't been an act. But Fiona made herself go back over that moment, carefully. What Roberta had shown was sadness and pain. What she hadn't shown was surprise.

Fuck. Fuck. Fiona could have banged her forehead on the steering wheel. She had *seen* that, but it had been too fast, and she'd been too caught up in her own shit. She'd been outwitted by a seventy-nine-year-old woman. A woman who had spent thirty years as a successful lawyer, but still . . . *Never assume, Fiona,* Malcolm said in her mind.

From its place on the passenger seat, spilled out of her purse, her phone rang. She jumped, and for a second a wild hope sprang up in her that it was Jamie. But it wasn't—it was Anthony Eden. What did he want? To summon her to another meeting with his mother? She'd had enough of frustrating old women for today. She ignored the call and flipped the page in her notebook to a fresh one.

She wrote a heading: *Potential Suspects.*

It seemed like in sixty-four years no one had done even this basic piece of logic, so she would do it herself. She started with the obvious choice, the one the headmistress had been so convinced of.

A boy.

That meant Sonia had had some kind of illicit romance. She would have had to keep it from the school, because they would surely have expelled her if they knew. It would have had to be a local boy, since in the pre-Internet, pre-Facebook days, there was no way she could have met a boy from anywhere else. It seemed unlikely, but Fiona kept it on the list, because if it was true, then Sonia's roommate and friend Roberta had likely known. And it was believable that she had kept her friend's secret all this time.

She wrote another possibility: *a stranger.*

The tale loosened, wove into a different pattern. This was Ginette Harrison's theory that Sonia had been targeted. The killer-on-the-road theory, a predator passing through, perhaps a deliveryman or some other worker at the school. *I didn't see the face of a single man for three years,* Roberta had said. The truth, or a lie? Why would Roberta cover it up if a gardener had killed her friend? Or, for that matter, a stranger on the road? She had to circle back to the fact that Roberta might be lying to her for reasons Fiona couldn't see.

If Roberta was covering something, that led to: *One of the girls did it.* Perhaps Roberta herself, or CeCe Frank, or Katie Winthrop.

We always knew, Roberta had said. *Sonia wouldn't run away without her suitcase.* The girls could have protested that Sonia hadn't just disappeared in order to appear more innocent. The girls had had opportunity, access to Sonia, and Sonia's trust. There was no gun or other weapon used in the crime—just a rock or a shovel, something the girls would have had access to. It was easy to imagine an argument, an impulse, done in a rage, the body dumped to cover it up quickly, the girls agreeing to cover for one another, never to expose one another.

And the motive? What kind of motive did teenage girls need? Jealousy, rejection, some imagined slight? The ultimate mean girls, and it explained why Roberta had not been surprised, why she had wanted access to Idlewild's records: so she could find any clues to the crime in the files and remove them. Why she had made it clear she had no idea where the other two girls were now, which could be a lie.

It was the theory that fit in every detail, and it was the theory Fiona hated the most. She closed her eyes and tried to think clearly of why.

It was too pat, for one. Cliché, like a thriller movie. What's more sinister than a teenage girl? Angry and duplicitous and full of hate. Everyone liked to picture a witchy coven of teenagers putting their hapless classmate to death, because it was easier and sexier than picturing Sonia being hit over the head by a local man who probably needed the 1950s version of mental health treatment, who had possibly sexually violated her first. But if it had been an accident, a true mistake, instead of a planned murder, then the girls would have been terrified. Covering it up would have been the first thing they'd do.

She hated it. But she had to admit it was possible. It was possible that she'd just had coffee with Sonia's killer—or with a woman who was covering for Sonia's killer, her school friend.

Maybe Fiona preferred picturing a man doing such a

thing, or even a boy, instead of a girl. And that, she had to admit, circled back to Deb's murder. She had always *wanted* Tim Christopher to be Deb's killer. She had always wanted to believe that a man, sinister and big-handed and cruel, had put her innocent sister to death. Because it had fit.

But no one had seen Tim do it. And no one had seen him dump the body.

And for the first time in twenty years, Fiona let the words into her head, like a cold draft from a cracked window: *Could they have gotten it wrong?*

Tim had always maintained his innocence. Of course he had; nearly every convicted murderer did. But what if the wrong man was in prison? What if Deb's killer was still free?

Sonia's killer had walked free. That person was possibly dead, after living a life in which the murder of a fifteen-year-old girl had never been unearthed. Or that person was possibly living, elderly now. It was even possible that person had had a fruitful career as a lawyer, borne two children, and spent her morning playing cat and mouse with Fiona in a New Hampshire coffee shop.

There is no justice, Malcolm had told her once, *but we stand for it anyway. Justice is the ideal, but justice is not the reality.*

If Tim Christopher was innocent, it would kill her father.

Outside, the cold wind kicked up, and the flyer tucked beneath her windshield wiper flapped. Fiona stared at it, suddenly transfixed.

It wasn't a flyer. It was a note.

She got out of the car and snatched it, nearly ripping it in half. She ducked back into the driver's seat and slammed the door, smoothing out the note, staring at it.

Simple handwriting, on a piece of notebook paper, written in ballpoint pen.

Meet me behind the church at eleven o'clock, it said.

And, beneath that: *You're not looking hard enough.*

chapter 23

Katie

Barrons, Vermont
November 1950

"They're probably circus freaks," Katie said, sitting cross-legged on her bunk and watching Sonia pack. "He's the world's fattest man, and she's the bearded lady. That's why they've lived alone so long with no kids."

"You forget I've seen them," Sonia said, calmly folding a skirt and placing it in her suitcase. "They aren't freaks. I met them when I first arrived in America."

"And they forgot about you for three years," Katie pointed out. "Maybe they were just busy building the cell they're going to keep you in."

She didn't know why she was saying these things, passing them off as jokes. It was cruel, unnecessary, considering the true horror of Sonia's past. But she couldn't seem to stop it.

I don't want you to go.

Sonia was unperturbed despite the barbs Katie was

throwing. She was calm and happy, a little flushed with expectation. Like the other three, she had never been away from Idlewild, even for an afternoon, since arriving here.

"You're packing everything," CeCe pointed out, sitting on the floor, playing with the dials on her little radio, even though it was morning, just after breakfast, and they were at risk of getting caught. They only ever listened to the radio at night. "You're only going for two days. Why are you packing your uniform?"

"Because," Katie said when Sonia didn't answer, "she thinks they're going to want to keep her."

"Shut up, Katie," Roberta said. She was leafing through Sonia's copy of *Blackie's Girls' Annual*, and she didn't look up as she issued the reprimand. There was no venom in it.

"They *might* keep me," Sonia said, adding her pitifully small stack of underwear to the suitcase. "Why else did they ask me to visit after so much time?"

She looked up, and the glimpse of hope on her face, naked and bare before she tucked it away, made Katie feel a slice of pain. She was an idiot, she knew. Stupid and petty. She wanted Sonia to be happy, but not by leaving, not by going to live with strangers.

And what if those strangers didn't want to keep Sonia after their visit was over? What would happen to the hope on Sonia's face then?

Sonia had gained a little weight over the last few weeks. She had smoothed out, her eyes less sunken, her elbows less sharp and bony. She wasn't pretty—Katie knew, with the perfect detachment of the beautiful, that no one was pretty next to her—but her skin had a healthier flush to it, her gaze a calmer sparkle. Her uniform skirt was too short now, and it had begun to grow tight around the hips, though her bust was hopeless and probably always would be. *When we're out of here,* Katie mused idly, *I'll get her one of those padded brassieres.* There were no movie magazines—no magazines at all— at Idlewild, but some of the teachers wore bras that made their bodies look like soft rocket ships beneath their blouses. Katie was fascinated by the idea, not because she found it attractive, but because she had an animal instinct that boys would. *If her hips grow out some more, and I get one of those, and I curl her hair . . .* Oh, being eighteen was going to be fun.

Then she remembered that Sonia might not leave here with the rest of them.

"I bet they're monsters," she said, unable to stop herself. Unable to keep the words from scraping her throat as they came out.

"Hush," CeCe chided, looking up from her radio. "Monsters don't exist."

They were all quiet for a moment, no one believing this, not even CeCe.

Katie looked up to see Sonia looking at her, watching her from those calm eyes. She had stopped packing. "I'll be back Sunday," she said quietly.

The hope draining from her friend's face was worse than anything, so of course Katie's perverse mood swung the other way. "It's best if they do keep you," she said. "That way you can find a way to sneak me some dirty magazines."

Roberta laughed, glancing up from *Blackie's Girls' Annual*, and Sonia made a face. "What if they don't have any dirty magazines?"

"You find a way to *get* them, silly," Katie instructed her. "You ask for an allowance."

"I want chocolate," CeCe said, perking up at this.

"Books," Roberta added. "For God's sake, get us something to read besides *Lady Chatterley's Lover*. We've already read the dirty parts to death."

A squawk came from CeCe's radio, and she twisted a button. "Careful with that thing, or we'll lose it," Katie said.

"No one has heard us so far," CeCe pointed out. "I like it. I want to know what shows are on at this time of morning."

"Probably nothing." Katie watched Sonia put her notebook in the suitcase, accompanied by the pen. Her hairbrush, her nightgown. "I don't think they start the shows this early."

The radio squawked again as CeCe turned the dial. Sonia looked at the book in Roberta's hand. "You can borrow that, if you like," she said.

Roberta looked at her. Her calm gaze cracked for a fraction of a second, a flinch that only someone who knew her well would be able to see. Katie read her thoughts perfectly, since they mirrored her own. *You might not come back.* "No," she said, her placid voice recovered. "You take it." She handed it over, and it went into the suitcase with the other things. "If they don't want you, come back," she said to Sonia. "We'll be here."

"You'll be late for class," Sonia observed, closing the suitcase on its painfully few contents and latching it. "Don't you have Latin?"

They *would* be late for class. There was only half an hour of break time allotted after the first class of the day, and it was already stretching past that now. Soon, someone— dorm monitor Susan Brady or Lady Loon herself—would come knocking on doors, shouting that the lazy girls needed to get their things. Still, nobody moved.

"What time is your bus?" CeCe asked for the dozenth time, though they all knew the answer.

"Twelve o'clock," Sonia replied, as she had every other time. "I should start walking to the bus stop soon."

"Do you have your ticket?" Roberta asked.

Sonia nodded. Her relatives had mailed her the ticket when she'd accepted the invitation. She had carefully placed it in the pocket of her wool coat so she wouldn't lose it—as if she had so many things that she was in danger of not keeping track of them. Now, despite her earlier excitement, even Sonia seemed reluctant. She picked up her shoes and sat on the edge of her bunk, slowly putting them on.

The radio in CeCe's hands stopped its static blast, and the harmony of a barbershop quartet emitted from it. A voice came over the music: *"Welcome to* The Pilcrow Soap Sunrise Show!*"

"Sunrise was hours ago," Katie snorted.

"Shh," Roberta said. Sonia continued slowly pulling on her shoes.

The singing continued, sweet and buttery, the notes slipping so easily from one voice to the next. *"Sweet dreams of you, sweet dreams are true . . . sweet dreams of us saying, 'Yes, I do . . .'"* The girls listened in silence, hypnotized, no longer caring about teachers or dorm monitors or Latin. A few sweet moments of peaceful quiet, the kind only the radio could give them, a few moments of nothing but sound from the world outside, where people were living and singing and playing songs. Normal people in a normal world.

Far off, down a hallway, a single door slammed. The radio squawked in CeCe's hand, the singing interrupted.

It blasted briefly; then it was gone again. Silence came from the little box. Not static, not music. Just silence.

"What did you do?" Roberta said.

"Nothing!" CeCe stared down at the radio. "I didn't touch anything."

Steps sounded in the hall. "Someone's coming," Katie whispered, her lips cold and numb with sudden fear.

CeCe shook her head. "I—"

There was the sound of breathing. A breath in, a breath out. From the radio.

Katie felt her temples pulse, her vision blur. She had heard that same breathing, sensed it, in Special Detention.

She's here.

The four girls sat frozen in a tableau, no one moving.

And from the radio, breaking the breathing silence, came the thin, reedy, distressing cry of a baby's wail. It wavered, as if far away, as if weak. And then it cried again.

CeCe dropped the radio with a thump. She kicked it, hard, and it spun under the bed, hitting the wall, the baby's wail cutting off.

A knock pounded on the door. "Ladies!" Lady Loon shouted through the wood, making them all jump. "Ladies! You are late for class!"

There was a frozen moment in which nobody moved. And then Katie leaned over, took Sonia's icy hand in hers, and looked into her face.

"Go," she said.

chapter 24

Portsmouth, New Hampshire
November 2014

There was more than one church in Portsmouth. There were many, and Fiona silently cursed her anonymous note writer. What the hell church did he or she mean? New England was hardly bereft of churches.

She blew out a breath and checked the time on her phone. It was ten forty-five. Should she stay for fifteen minutes and play into this person's game, or should she start her car and drive away? She already faced a wet drive back to Vermont, and she wanted to get back into the Idlewild files, which she'd barely had time to skim through. She wanted to talk to Malcolm. Even, if he'd let her, to Jamie.

Still . . . *You're not looking hard enough.*

Goddamn it.

It was as if whoever it was knew how to reach into her journalist's psyche and flip the switch of her curiosity—

the switch that couldn't be turned off. The switch that would most likely get her killed one of these days. But it was morning in sunny New Hampshire, with the thin wet snow melting and retirees walking by to go into the twee coffee shops beneath pretty awnings.

She hadn't even processed the thought fully before she got out of the car and slammed the door behind her. Inhaling a bite of the chill air, she stepped to the hood of the car—where the note leaver would have stood to tuck the paper beneath her windshield wiper—and did a slow 360-degree turn, scanning the horizon.

When you looked at it that way, it was unmissable. There was a church only several hundred feet away—one of New England's historical specialties, redbrick with a tall, elaborate white steeple, as pretty as a wedding cake. The clock embedded halfway up the steeple showed the time. Fiona left the parking lot and made her way toward it, crossing the cobblestone walks. She got close enough to the front to read the sign and see that it was called the North Church, and that it dated from 1671, the building itself from 1855. The front doors were open, a cloth Welcome sign propped up outside them. Fiona circled around toward the back.

She didn't see anyone—just more tourists and retirees, and a panhandler sitting on the ground, leaning against the church wall, his knees drawn up. That struck her as odd, since panhandlers were rare in tourist areas like this one, most of them moved along by private security or the cops. She looked at the panhandler again and realized he was watching her.

He was a man, thin and stringy as a kid, in his thirties, his long hair combed back from his forehead. On second look, Fiona realized he wasn't panhandling at all; he had no sign or overturned hat. He was just sitting against the wall, looking at her. His face was pale and pitted, his eyes sunken, his clothes of good quality but well-worn. He wasn't homeless, but a man down on his luck, sick perhaps, used to sitting on the cold ground and watching crowds go by.

She walked up to him and held out the note. "Are you looking for me?"

His eyes didn't leave her face as he looked up from his low position on the ground. He watched her for a long time. She saw uncertainty in his gaze, and calculation, and anger mixed with fear. *Be careful with this one,* she told herself.

Finally, he smiled and stood up, bracing himself against the church wall. "Hi, Fiona," he said.

She stepped back, glad now that they were in an open square in daylight, with people around. This had been a mistake. "Do I know you?"

"I'm sorry about the note," he said, watching her reaction. "I didn't know how else to approach you. It seemed the best way."

"Okay, well, I'm here now. How do you know me, and what do you want?"

The man shifted his weight. Now that they were face-to-face, he made no move to come closer. "My name is Stephen," he said. "Stephen Heyer."

She shook her head. He wasn't sick, she realized now;

he was healthy, his eyes sharp and unclouded. The gray of his skin and his matchstick thinness spoke of addiction instead.

He looked away, past her shoulder, as if considering what to say. He really hadn't planned this, she thought. He'd likely thought she wouldn't follow the note. He scratched the back of his neck with a restless hand. "I followed you here from Barrons."

Fiona's blood went cold.

"You met with that woman," Stephen Heyer continued. "I thought maybe . . . But I don't recognize her. I don't know who she is." He looked back at her face, and she saw something naked in his eyes, a desperation that looked painfully familiar. "Does she have something to do with Tim Christopher?"

Fiona took another step back as if she'd been slapped. "Fuck off," she said to him, with all the icy cold she could summon into her voice, denying her fear, her sudden shakiness. She turned and walked away.

She could hear him behind her, trailing her. "Wait," he said. "You've been going to Idlewild. To the restoration. I've seen you there."

What the hell was this? Some stupid game? She kept walking. "Leave me alone or I'll call the police."

"I go to Old Barrons Road, sleep there sometimes," he said, still following her, as if he was compelled to explain. "The old man who used to run the drive-in lets me use his place."

"You go there to get high?" she shot back over her shoulder.

"No, no," he protested. "I have some problems, yeah, but that's not why. That's not what I'm getting at."

Her mind was racing. If he was a Barrons local, he must have known about Deb. He was around her own age, the right age to have been a teenager when it happened. She racked her brain again for the name Stephen Heyer, trying to put it in context, but she was sure she'd never heard it before, that he hadn't gone to her high school. She pegged him as some kind of creep, a ghoul, maybe looking to scare her for money. She did not need this shit. She really did not.

"I've seen you," he said. He was following at her shoulder. He gave off a curiously diminished vibe, as if he was so low on life force that he couldn't be dangerous. Fiona knew by instinct that she didn't have to run or scream; if she got in her car and drove away, he'd simply recede, defeated. So she strode purposefully toward the parking lot. "That red hair," he continued. "It's unmistakable. I've seen you, Deb Sheridan's sister, the journalist, coming back to Idlewild. Looking, looking, right? They're restoring it, and you can't stay away. I figure you must be looking, looking. You think I don't understand, but I do."

Fiona turned and stared at him. He wasn't lying; he was telling the truth, at least as he knew it. "Listen," she said to him. "Whatever you think you know, I do not give a shit. Do you understand? Stop following me, or I'll call the cops. Whatever crazy shit is in your brain right now, I suggest you forget about it. Forget about me. I am none of your business."

"You want answers," Stephen said. He didn't seem

high, but she wondered how long it had been since his last fix. "Closure, right? That's what they call it. The therapists and group sessions and grief counselors. They don't talk about what a load of bullshit that is." He stared at her, and she saw frustration behind his eyes, some kind of crazy pain that spiraled through him, undulled by drugs. He gestured down at himself. "You think I got this way because I got *closure*?"

Her mouth was dry. "Closure for what?"

"You're not looking hard enough," Stephen said, echoing his own note. "I've been looking for closure for twenty years. Just like you. But I looked harder. And I found you."

She shook her head. "I don't know what the hell that means."

"I know how it feels." He was strangely eloquent now, his eyes bright, an evangelist speaking the truth he knew best. "You're all in here"—he tapped his temple—"and you can't get out. It goes round and round. You're thinking, thinking—always fucking thinking. The therapists and the grief counselors, they don't understand. They want you to talk and write things down and share, but nothing makes it go away. I did drugs. You go walking at Idlewild."

It was as if he were hitting her with the words, punching her in the stomach. "Did you know my sister?" she rasped.

"No," Stephen Heyer said. "But I want Tim Christopher dead."

"What—" She tried to get a grip, sound rational. "Are you some kind of death penalty advocate?" Vermont didn't have the death penalty.

"I don't give a shit about the death penalty," Stephen said, his eyes alight. "I just want him dead. Not for what he did to your sister. For what he did to mine."

There are moments when everything shifts, when the world becomes eerily like the kaleidoscope toy given to children, where with the turn of a cheap plastic knob everything changes, becomes different. Fiona looked at the man in front of her and the calm of downtown Portsmouth disappeared; the colors changed; the air smelled different. Everything flew upward, scattered, and landed again. Her head throbbed.

"Who was your sister?" she asked him. "What did Tim do?"

"Who *is* my sister?" he corrected her, his voice bitter. "Helen Elizabeth Heyer, born July 9, 1973. Would you like to meet her?"

Her voice was a rasp, but she didn't hesitate, the words slipping out of her as they always did when she was buzzed like this, restless, the madness in her blood. "Yes," she told Stephen. "I would."

"My car is parked over there," he said, pointing down the street. He smiled when he saw her expression. "How the hell do you think I followed you to New Hampshire? I'm a fucking addict, not a bum. It's a blue Chevy. I'll pull out and wait for you."

"Where are we going?" Fiona asked him, her temples pounding.

"Back to Vermont," he said. "I'll lead the way. You follow."

chapter 25

Barrons, Vermont
November 2014

The Barrons police department was emptying out at five o'clock, the day staff packing up and going home. They kept a dispatcher on at night, but in a town as small as Barrons, that was all that was needed. A few cops were kept on call in case of emergencies, and a duty officer stayed on until midnight in case of evening domestic disputes, noise complaints, or bar customers that got out of hand. The parking lot was nearly empty when Fiona pulled in, though Jamie's SUV was still there.

Holding a file folder in her hand, Fiona walked through the front door and saw the dispatcher sitting behind the front desk. He looked to be nearly seventy, and he was peacefully leafing through a fishing magazine. He looked up with some surprise.

"Help you?" he said.

He knew who she was. Of course he did. If he didn't

know she was Malcolm Sheridan's daughter, dating a fellow cop, she'd eat her journalism diploma. But she said, "I'm looking for Jamie Creel. Is he around?"

"Are you here to report a crime?" he asked.

"I'm here to see Jamie."

The dispatcher slid a clipboard across the desk at her. "You'll need to sign in. Name, address, identification."

It was bullshit. This was Barrons, not Rikers Island. "Just tell me where to find him."

His hairy white eyebrows rose on his forehead. "I'll have to get my supervisor's approval to let a journalist in here."

"If you know I'm a journalist, then you know my name." She slid the clipboard back across the desk at him. "Go ahead and write it down."

She walked past before he could protest.

She'd never been inside here, even when Deb died. The cops had interviewed her at the house, sitting in the living room, her parents beside her. *I last saw my sister on Sunday, when she visited for dinner. No, I haven't talked to her since. No, I don't know where she could have gone.* And then, after the body was found: *No, she never mentioned anyone following her or threatening her. Yes, I've met Tim Christopher. No, I didn't talk to her that night.* They had been exhausted, those cops that interviewed her. Bewildered, maybe in over their heads. Neither of them had been Garrett Creel.

Jamie was at his desk, a tiny cubicle in the open main room of the station, in front of a 2000-era desktop computer. He was in uniform, though his hat was off and the top buttons of his uniform shirt were undone, the white T-shirt he wore underneath it contrasting with the navy blue. He had obviously heard Fiona's voice, because he was already watching her when she came around the corner from the front dispatch desk, and his eyes, flat and wary, watched her come toward him.

"There a problem?" he said.

"Can we talk somewhere?" she asked him.

His gaze stayed on her face for a minute, and she knew he was reading her, the fact that she wasn't here for personal reasons. What did he expect? That she'd bring whatever they had to his work while he was on shift to try to hash things out? He knew her better than that.

His eyes darted briefly to the back of the dispatch desk, and then to the others in the room—a cop putting his coat on, another standing by the coffee machine—and pushed back his chair. "Come with me."

He led her to an interview room, a closet-sized space with two chairs and a table between them. There was no two-way glass, like on TV cop shows. Fiona wondered if Tim Christopher had ever been in this room, if he had ever sat in one of these chairs.

"What's going on?" Jamie asked, clicking the door shut behind them.

Fiona looked at him. Jamie: tall, broad shoulders, dark blond hair worn slightly long and brushed back from his forehead, scruff of gold on his jaw. She'd missed him—but when Jamie wore his uniform, he was less familiar to her, less like the man who had first said *Hi* to her in a bar on a Friday night. The uniform did that, made him a different man. "Do you know the name Helen Heyer?" she asked him.

"No," he said.

"Think," she said. "Assault case. Unsolved. She nearly died."

Jamie put his hands on his hips, forefingers hooked over his hip bones, the classic pose of the cop pulling you over, and narrowed his eyes, thinking. "No, I don't think so. When was this?"

"She was assaulted in 1993," Fiona said. "She was twenty. She's forty-one now."

"I was eight in 1993," Jamie said.

"But it doesn't sound familiar?" Fiona persisted. "She was found just outside the back door of her parents' home. She'd probably been on the back walkway, coming to the door, when it happened. Someone used a weapon on her, likely a baseball bat. Nothing stolen. She was nearly dead when her father opened the back door to take the garbage out, but her blood was warm. It was quick and silent."

Jamie was staring at her. Behind his eyes, she could see him thinking, calculating. Going over the angles. He was telling the truth; he probably didn't know the case she was talking about.

But he knew she wasn't here for a random reason. He knew she was going somewhere. And he was trying to figure out where it was. There was no baffled confusion in his face, just a closed-off determination to figure out what angle she was going to come from, so he could put up a defense before she got there.

"Did she live?" he asked her. "You didn't say 'murder.'"

"She lived," Fiona said, swallowing down the lump in her throat. "She's in a long-term-care hospital in Bowfield. Her cognitive functions were damaged, and she can't care for herself. She can barely form words, can barely do the most basic functions of life. She hasn't spoken a complete sentence since the assault." She held up the file folder she'd been carrying in her hand. "I went to see her this afternoon. No one was ever arrested, Jamie. No one saw the attack, and Helen can't name her attacker. She was supposed to be dead."

Jamie shook his head. "What does this have to do with me, Fee?"

She slapped the file down on the table, harder than she'd intended. *Keep it under control, Fiona. Keep to the facts.* "It's interesting," she said, opening the folder and pulling out the printouts of newspaper articles that she'd made at home in her apartment before coming here. "It was a big story at the time. The police went to the local media to ask for help. Anyone who had seen the crime, anyone who had seen a stranger in the neighborhood, was asked to call in a tip. It was tragic, a pretty twenty-year-old girl beaten nearly to death, her life destroyed on her parents' doorstep, left for her daddy to find when he took out the garbage. Beaten while her parents were inside, eating supper and watching *Jeopardy!*" She spread the articles out. "But not one of these pieces reported what her brother told me this afternoon. Helen had a boyfriend—a new boyfriend. He was big, handsome, rich, and she was excited. His name was Tim Christopher."

Jamie had been looking down at the printouts—the school photo of Helen Heyer on the top page, her lovely oval face, framed by dark hair that she had placed smoothly over one shoulder for the photograph, smiling for the camera—but when she said Tim's name, he looked up sharply. "What?"

"Her parents didn't know," Fiona said. "The relationship was physical, and her parents would have been horrified that their daughter had given up her virginity— but her brother found out about it. She swore him to secrecy, begged him not to tell their parents about Tim. She was swept up by him. She thought Tim was wonderful, most of the time. According to her brother, there were occasions she was quiet and withdrawn because she and Tim had had a fight. But then she'd forgive him, and all would be well again."

Except for the part about not telling her parents, it was Deb, her exact pattern with Tim, except further back in time. Deb had been so excited to be dating Tim. She was twenty, and thought that the world held bigger and better things for her than life in Barrons with her nerdy parents and their middle-class income. She'd seen wide horizons with Tim, probably because he'd promised them to her. And Helen was Deb, a year before Deb met Tim and died.

She watched the knowledge flicker across Jamie's face. She read him closely. He hadn't known about Helen, yet he didn't register surprise or even shock.

What settled into the corners of his eyes was a heavy kind of knowledge, as if he was hearing something he hadn't known but could have guessed would happen. Still, his voice was tense, defensive. "Did they think Tim was a suspect?"

"When Helen's brother told the cops about Tim, they questioned Tim. At his parents' home, not at the station. One conversation, and then they dropped it."

"Then he must have had an alibi."

"He said he was at the movies at the time—alone. Nothing to back it up. He also claimed that he had never met Helen Heyer, had no idea who she was, and certainly was not dating her."

"Maybe he was telling the truth."

She stared at him in shock. "You realize you're talking about the man serving life in prison right now."

"Just because he committed that crime doesn't mean he committed this one." Jamie sighed. "Fiona. I told you, I know nothing about this case. But if there was no arrest, it's because the officers in charge of the investigation didn't find enough evidence to arrest a suspect. It's their job to close cases, their job to chase these things down. You're looking for something that isn't there."

"Isn't *there*?" she nearly shouted. "If the police had done their job, even a little, Tim would have been arrested before Deb even met him. She would be *alive*."

"Assuming Tim did this," Jamie countered, indicating the articles strewn on the table. "This girl was hit with a baseball bat, not strangled. She was left at her parents' house, not dumped in a field. Deb was seen with Tim dozens of times, while this girl was not. What evidence do you have that he was dating her at all?"

"She admitted to her brother that she was."

"Did the brother ever see him?" Jamie asked. "Did Tim come to the house? Meet the parents? Did he talk to them on the phone? The cops would have asked her friends and family if they'd ever seen her with him. Did they do that?"

Fiona was quiet.

"Of course they did," Jamie said. "So she never told her parents about this great boyfriend she was supposedly seeing, and she never told her friends. Just one person knew, her brother. And he was reliable?"

"He was into drugs," Fiona said. "It got worse after his sister's attack. He became an addict. But he wasn't an addict when it happened. Just a teenager messing around."

"For God's sake, Fiona," Jamie said. "You're listening to a story spun by a drug addict? Because that's who you've been talking to, isn't it? The brother."

Damn it. She had known this would happen, that he would be like this, and it made her so angry. "He's telling the truth," she said, fighting the impulse to shout. "He knows what his sister told him. There's nothing wrong with his memory."

"And how did he find you?" Jamie's gaze was hard and cold. "Because he *did* find you, didn't he? He found some way to approach you and reel you in. You're a smart woman, Fee, but when it comes to anyone mentioning your sister's name, you can be completely goddamn stupid."

She stared at this Jamie and she didn't know him. "Fuck you," she spit at him. "That's the cruelest thing you've ever said to me."

"*I'm* cruel?" he said. "Did you plan to go to your father with this? Was that your idea? To rip his wounds open with an unproven theory that his daughter's death could have been prevented? Your evidence is hearsay from a girl who hasn't spoken in twenty years and an addict. You'll kill him with this kind of shit." He took a breath. "But it's all an acceptable sacrifice, isn't it? Your life, your father's life, your own happiness, our relationship— it's all an acceptable sacrifice to you. This case has already taken your parents' marriage and your mother's life. What's a little more misery for the pile?"

The words made her wince—yet she felt that only now, after a year together, were they getting to the heart of it. "You think I should drop it," she said.

"Of course I think you should drop it. Do you know why? Because you should fucking drop it."

"Really? Or does this have to do with your precious police force?" She shoved the words at him. "The cops did a shit job on this case, Jamie. You know as well as I do that it's always the boyfriend. It's *always* the boyfriend. You think someone came up randomly behind her with a baseball bat? Did anyone think that, even for a minute? But we're talking about Tim Christopher, aren't we? Rich, good-looking, his family one of the wealthiest in the county. Oh, no, sir. No way it could be the boyfriend! Sorry to bother you—we'll just be on our way!"

"Goddamn it, Fee!" Jamie shouted. His face was red.

"You want to talk about acceptable sacrifice?" Fiona said to him. "What's an acceptable sacrifice to you? Is it acceptable that Helen's case is never solved, that her attacker goes free, just so that the Christophers aren't bothered with too many questions? Is it an acceptable sacrifice that you brush me off, just so no one asks questions now? So that the force doesn't face any criticism? Everything is smoother, easier, if we just let it go."

He was breathing hard, trying to keep control. "You need to leave," he said, his voice low and furious. "Now."

"You're right," Fiona said. "I do." She picked up her papers, put them in the folder, and walked out the door.

chapter 26

Fiona was hungry by the time she got home to her apartment. She pulled a box of crackers from the cupboard and stood at the kitchen counter, dipping the crackers in a jar of peanut butter and eating them, as she stared at the file that contained Helen Heyer's press and refused to think about Jamie. It was hard to look at the photo of twenty-year-old Helen, with her clear eyes and silky dark hair, and compare it with the face she'd seen this afternoon. Helen at forty-one was vacant, confused, her eyes sunken and the corners of her mouth turned down, her hair graying. She looked at least fifty. She'd sat in the chair in the corner of her hospital room and watched her brother anxiously, rubbing the knuckles of her left hand with her right fingers in a gesture meant to soothe herself.

Jamie was right that almost nothing about the two crimes matched, but Fiona knew it in her gut. They didn't match because Tim Christopher had a temper. The crimes hadn't been planned; he'd simply done what was easiest in his white-hot rage when a girl made him angry. Strangled her in his backseat. Hit her with a baseball bat. Whatever made her shut up for good. He was so careless he'd rubbed Deb's blood on the thigh of his jeans as an afterthought.

The ice in Jamie's voice: *What's a little more misery for the pile?*

Screw it. Fiona opened the cupboard under the sink and pulled out the bottle of wine she kept there for emergency purposes. It had been there since last Christmas, because very few things counted as big enough emergencies for Fiona to drink chardonnay, but screw it. Her sister was dead, her love life was a mess, she had no career to speak of, and she was scooping crackers in peanut butter alone in her apartment. It was time for a glass.

She had just taken a sip, making that involuntary shudder that always accompanied the first swallow, when her cell phone rang. It was Anthony Eden again. She sighed and answered it. "Fiona Sheridan."

"Fiona," Anthony said. "I've been getting calls from the press about the body found at Idlewild. What do I say to them?"

"Calls? From who?"

He listed two names Fiona didn't recognize, probably second-stringers or freelancers. "Word has gotten out," he said. "What do I say?"

Fiona picked up a cracker and jabbed at the jar of peanut butter. She wasn't hungry anymore. "Tell them you have no statement yet," she advised him. "You're waiting for the police to notify next of kin. That's how it works. The next of kin hears it before the media does." Sonia Gallipeau had no next of kin, but the ruse would work for a while.

"All right," he said, sounding relieved. "And one more thing."

"What is it?"

"I hear you somehow found the Idlewild records."

That surprised her. "How the hell do you know that?"

"It doesn't matter," Anthony said. "The records weren't on the grounds when Mother and I bought the property. I thought they were lost. I'd like to have them back."

Margaret, Roberta, and now Anthony—it seemed a lot of people were looking for the records. But she was not in the mood to be nice. "You can't have them," she told him. "I need them for research."

"But they're part of the Idlewild property."

"When they were sent to the dump in 1979, they ceased being Idlewild property," she said. "They became garbage. Which makes them mine."

"Fiona, I would really like those records."

"Then get a court order," Fiona said, and hung up.

She sipped her wine again. He hadn't answered the question of how he knew she had the records. Roberta knew, but Anthony didn't know her. He could have been in touch with Sarah London, or Cathy. Or his mother could have been making an educated guess.

She looked at the boxes, stacked in her living room. They seemed to stare back at her.

She picked up her wine and began the search.

She started with the girls' files. Sonia's and Roberta's she'd already read, so she pulled Katie Winthrop's and CeCe Frank's. Sarah London had said that Katie Winthrop was trouble; her file backed that up. She'd been sent to Idlewild by her parents for *persistent willful misbehavior,* and the school had not improved her much. There were fistfights, cut classes, talking back to teachers, everything a restless teenage girl might do in the days before she could text her friends or put naked selfies on social media. For a cloistered girl with no access to drugs, alcohol, or boys, Katie's exploits seemed painfully innocent (*Hung her undergarments from a window,* read an entry from her last week at Idlewild), but the school's teachers saw her as a plague that could infect the other students. *Isolation is best wherever possible,* one teacher wrote, *as she tends to have an effect on others.* Katie left the same year Roberta did, 1953, and there was no note regarding her leaving, as the teachers were likely too busy sighing with relief.

CeCe Frank's file was surprising. Sarah had said that she had followed Katie around, the sort of girl who fell under Katie's spell. Fiona had pictured an eager follower, an acolyte type of girl. Yet CeCe's actual file showed something entirely different. Her grades were on the high side of average, though Sarah London had referred to her as stupid. She was never disciplined, never got in fights, and never acted out. Sarah had called her pudgy, but she had scored good marks even in physical education, where her teacher praised her dexterity. *Could be an asset to the field hockey team*, went the note, *but does not seem motivated to apply herself.* It now looked like CeCe was the kind of girl who was kind, friendly, and far from stupid, yet never earned an ounce of praise from the adults in her life—and there could be only one reason. Her bastard heritage must have colored everyone's perceptions in 1950. It still colored Sarah London's perceptions now. When Fiona saw nothing in her file referring to who her father was or why she'd been sent to Idlewild, she knew she was right.

She poured herself another glass of wine and took a break from the files to Google the girls. Katie Winthrop was a dead end—twenty minutes of searching brought up nothing that remotely resembled someone who could have been the Idlewild girl. CeCe Frank's name appeared on a list of girls belonging to a college sorority in 1954, but nowhere else. So CeCe had at least gone to college, then. Fiona wondered if her father had paid for that, too.

She returned to the boxes and leafed through the student files, looking for names that jumped out at her, but nothing did. She moved on from the student records to the other boxes: curricula, financial records, mixed detritus taken from the classrooms. She picked up the Latin textbook she'd noticed earlier—the ridiculous *Latin Grammar for Girls*—and leafed through it, smelling its musty old-book smell and looking at the thick yellowed pages, the fonts that weren't in use anymore.

She noticed the handwriting halfway through the book. A line written in pencil along the edge of the page, past the margin of text. She turned the book to read the words.

Mary Hand wears a black dress and veil
She laughed like my dead little brother
Madeleine Grazer, February 2, 1935

A black dress and veil. The words froze the breath in her throat, and she had to close the book and put it down for a second. February 1935. Someone had seen the figure she saw in the sports field in 1935.

What did she show you? That is the question you need to be asking.

She picked up the book again, turned the pages, and saw more words, in a different handwriting, scrawled across the bottom of another page:

MARY HAND HAS ALWAYS BEEN HERE

Jesus. Roberta had mentioned that the girls wrote in the textbooks. If the textbooks were never changed from year to year, it made sense. This was how the Idlewild girls talked to one another, from one generation of girls to the next.

She pushed the box of textbooks aside and dug through the box of Idlewild's own records: bills of sale, staff hiring and firing paperwork, financial sheets. She found what she was looking for almost immediately in a file called "Land History," slim with very few pages in it. She found schematics and building plans, a map of the grounds that was dated 1940. Behind that was a handwritten map, originally done in ink and now very faded. It showed Old Barrons Road, the woods, the ravine. Within the clearing where Idlewild now stood were drawn a square marked *Church* and another marked *Hand House*. The caption at the bottom—also handwritten—said *Map of original landholdings, 1915. Church burned down in 1835 and never rebuilt, though the foundation was still intact.* It was signed *Lila Hendricksen, 1921.*

So this was, or purported to be, what had stood on the site before Idlewild was built. Fiona did a quick check in the staff records: Lila Hendricksen was listed as the school's history teacher from 1919 to 1924.

Fiona tapped her wineglass with a fingernail, thinking. It was easy to imagine Idlewild's history teacher, most likely a local woman, also being an amateur historian. In any case, she'd written her own notes on the history of the place and kept them in Idlewild's files. Fiona's gaze traveled back to the second square on the map. Hand House. There had been an actual Hand family, and they'd lived here before the school came.

She turned the page and found another sheet, this one also in Lila Hendricksen's immaculate slanted handwriting. The page told, briefly and succinctly, the story—and the tragedy—of the Hand family.

The Hands had lived on the land for several generations, eking out a living as small farmers. By 1914 the
family line had dwindled to two parents and a daughter,
Mary. At age sixteen, Mary got pregnant by a local boy.
Ashamed, she kept the pregnancy a secret until she gave
birth one night at home. Her stunned mother assisted
with the birth while her father looked on.

The baby was born dead, though Mary was convinced that her parents had killed it. Fiona wondered if
she was right. In any case, when her parents took the
baby away, Mary quickly became unhinged, and there
was an argument. It ended with Mary's father banishing
her from the house in the cold, where Mary disappeared
into the night.

Her body was found the next morning, curled up in
the ruins of the old church. She wasn't buried in the
Hand graveyard plot, but instead on the grounds of the
homestead, with her baby's body beside hers. Her parents had moved away soon afterward. The land was then
purchased for the use of the school, the Hands forgotten. Mary's grave, Lila Hendricksen wrote, was situated
on the south side of the burned church.

Fiona turned back to the map. She oriented the page,
recalling in her head which way was north. She found
the spot that was south of the square that indicated the
church. Then she pulled out the map of the grounds
that was created in 1940 and laid it next to Lila Hendricksen's handwritten one. The burned church had sat
roughly where Idlewild's dining hall was now. And

Mary and her baby's grave was where the garden currently sat—the garden that was always in shade. *Her baby was buried in the garden,* Roberta had said.

The rumor was mostly true. What was missing was that Mary Hand was buried there, too.

Right next to the common, where the girls had passed by every day for the sixty years the school had been open.

Fiona jumped when her phone rang. She answered it eagerly when she saw who it was. "Dad," she said.

"Well?" Malcolm asked her. "What do you say? Has history come alive?"

She stared down at the maps in front of her, at Lila Hendricksen's record. "What?"

"Ginette Harrison," he said. "The Ravensbrück historian."

Fiona sat back, her rear and lower back aching from sitting on the floor for so long. "Oh, yes." She'd never updated him about that. Hearing his voice now made her think of her day with Stephen Heyer and what she'd learned about Tim Christopher. *Did you plan to go to your father with this?* Jamie had asked. *You'll kill him with this shit.*

"How did it go?" Malcolm asked. "I have great respect for Ginette. I've known her for years."

"Right," she said, gathering her thoughts. She told him what she and Ginette had talked about, going over everything she'd learned about Ravensbrück.

"That poor girl," her father said softly. "We'll never know her life story now. No one will ever know. So much has been lost. It's such a shame."

"It feels otherworldly," Fiona admitted, "the concentration camp stories. Like it happened in a far-off era or on another planet."

"It does," Malcolm agreed. "It seems so far back in history, until they find some decrepit old Nazi war criminal still living under a rock and put him on trial. Then you remember that it's still living memory for some people. Hell, Vietnam is too far back in the history books for most young people, and I remember it as if it were yesterday."

His words made her brain tingle. She remembered Garrett Creel's words as he carved the roast at the dinner table and discussed the murder with his son: *It sounds like something a Nazi would do, except she came across the ocean to get away from those bastards.*

As they kept chatting, she opened her laptop and searched Google for "Nazi war criminal Vermont." She clicked through the results as they moved the conversation off Sonia Gallipeau's life to her search through the Idlewild records—she stayed off the topic of ghosts—and on to more personal topics. He was telling her about his long-delayed visit to the doctor for a checkup, and how much he hated peeing in a cup, when she stopped him. "Daddy." She stared at her laptop screen, a pulse pounding in her throat. "Daddy."

This was how well her father knew her, how many years he'd lived as a journalist: He instantly knew to be excited. "What, Fee? What is it?"

"You mentioned Nazi war criminals," she said. "Well, I looked it up, and we had one here. In Vermont."

She heard a rustle and a click as he likely picked up his old telephone, with its extra-long cord, and hurried over to his own computer. "We did? I've never heard of it."

Fiona scrolled through the article she had up on her screen. "In 1973, a Nazi war criminal was arrested in Burlington. Acquitted after a trial, because the identity couldn't be established beyond a reasonable doubt."

"Is that so? What happened to him?"

Fiona took a breath. "There was going to be a possible second trial in Germany. But before it could happen, she died of a heart attack in her own home."

Malcolm's voice was a surprised shout. "She?"

"Yes," Fiona said, clicking on the photo that accompanied the article. A woman stared back at her: a wide forehead, thick hair tied neatly back, a straight nose, thin lips in a round face. The eyes were perfectly level, well shaped, the pupils dark, the gaze calm and unexpressive. She was coming down the steps of a courthouse, her body already partially turned away from the camera, as if she was already walking away. *Rose Albert,* the photo caption read, *accused of being concentration camp guard Rosa Berlitz, leaving court after acquittal this morning.* "It was a woman," she said to her father. "She was accused of being a guard at Ravensbrück. And she walked free."

chapter 27

Katie

They thought, at first, that maybe Sonia's dreams had come true. That her relatives had kept her, opened their arms and their home to her. That even now she was sitting on her own bed in her own bedroom, scared and excited and planning to go to school.

But by Monday the rumors were that she'd run away, and that was something very different. Sonia would never, ever run away. The girls knew that. She'd done enough running, enough journeying to last a lifetime. All Sonia wanted was safety, a place to be. Even if that place was Idlewild, with the misfits and the ghosts.

Katie sat in English class on Monday afternoon, her pulse pounding quietly in her wrists, her temples. *Where is Sonia?* Her mind spun the possibilities. A broken-down bus; a case of strep throat that hadn't yet been communicated to the headmistress; a misplaced sign that put her on the bus to the wrong destination. She was only twenty-four hours late; it could have been nothing. But her gut told her it wasn't nothing.

She glanced out the window to see a strange car come up the driveway to the main building, slowing and parking by the front portico. The classroom was on the third floor, and from this angle she looked down on the car, on its black-and-white stripes, on the tops of the heads of the two men who got out, putting on their navy blue policemen's caps. *No,* she thought. *They're not here for Sonia.* She wanted to scream.

That night, the teachers told the girls to stay in their rooms, no exceptions. They went from door to door in the dorm with lists in their hands, taking attendance of each girl. (*We stood every day in the* Appelplatz, Sonia had said. *It was supposed to be a roll call, but it wasn't.*) They listened to Mrs. Peabody's steps moving up and down the corridor, the sharp crack of her irritated voice. A girl had run away only last year, and the teachers were angry.

CeCe looked out the window and watched flashlights in the distance as the adults searched the woods for Sonia. Eventually CeCe climbed the ladder into Roberta's bunk and fell asleep, the two girls curled together in their nightgowns, their faces drawn and pale. Katie stayed awake, watching the lights. Watching the woods.

The next day there was still no sign of her, and again the next. A rumor went around that Sonia's suitcase had been found, that Mrs. Patton had it in her office. Katie thought about Sonia packing her suitcase, carefully folding her few stockings, her notebook, the copy of *Black-*

ie's Girls' Annual that Roberta had returned to her. She ground her teeth in helpless anger.

The weather grew bitter cold, though no snow fell yet. The sky was dark in the morning when the girls were roused for morning classes, and it was dark again when they finished supper and left the dining hall, stumbling over the common to their dorm. Roberta went to morning practice in the dark, the girls in their navy uniforms inkblots against the field in the predawn stillness, playing in silence with barely a shout. Katie watched Roberta dress, her skin as pale and gray as she knew her own was, her eyes haunted, her mouth drawn tight. Darkness and silence—those were the two things that dominated the days after Sonia disappeared. Darkness and silence, waking and sleeping. Then darkness and silence again.

After that first night, flashlights were not seen in the woods again, though the girls were kept under strict curfew after supper, roll call taken by the teachers as they sat in their rooms. CeCe was the one who went to Mrs. Patton's office, pleading for the search to continue—*She's not run away,* she said to the headmistress, the woman no girl dared approach. *She can't have run away. She's hurt. Please, we have to help her.* It was hopeless. She'd begged Katie to come with her, but Katie had refused, embalmed in the dark and the stillness, her body numb, her brain hushed, watching everything as if it were a world away. Watching the other Idlewild girls lose the fearful looks on their faces and begin to chatter again.

"She just ran away, that's all," Susan Brady said. Susan was riding high on her importance as the dorm monitor, helping the teachers with roll call every night. She heard things the other girls didn't, things the students weren't supposed to hear. "That's what the police say. They say she must have found a boy. She wouldn't need her suitcase if he bought her all new things, would she? That's what I think. She was quiet, secretive." She shrugged. "Who knows?"

The teachers lost their tense, watchful postures, their anger replaced with the usual everyday irritation again. *Ladies, ladies. Sportsmanship.* Three days, that was all it had taken. Three days, four. Five. Six.

She's hurt.

The girls didn't speak of it.

The girls barely spoke at all.

I'm failing her, Katie thought, the words like constant echoes buried deep in her brain. *She needs me, and I'm failing her.* It was CeCe who had had the courage to go to the headmistress's office, not Katie. It was Roberta who had left early for field hockey practice to search the woods on her own. Katie was powerless—as powerless as she'd been in the moment Thomas had thrown her down in the playground and yanked her skirt, his breath in her face; as powerless as she'd been the day she'd gotten out of her parents' car and looked up at the portico of Idlewild. All her bravery, all her bluster, was a fake. At the end of it all, when it came down to what mattered, Katie was a girl, and nothing more.

Each floor of the dorm had a shared bathroom at the end of the hall; aside from regular washing, the girls were allowed a bath once per week, the days allotted on a schedule. On CeCe's night, seven days after Sonia hadn't come home, Katie was in their room, lying on her bunk and staring at the slats of the bunk above her, enduring the endless stretch of time between supper and curfew, when she heard screaming from down the hall.

She flew out of bed and fought her way to the bathroom, pushing aside the other girls who crowded the door in curiosity. They gave way easily when they saw who she was; she didn't even have to kick anyone in the shins. She got to the bathroom to find CeCe still in the bathtub, hunched over her knees, her arms crossed over her ample chest, her hair hanging wet and plastered to her face, her lips blue, her eyes vacant. She was shaking.

Katie whirled to the other girls. "Get out," she snapped at them, and when they receded back, she slammed the door. Then she turned to CeCe. "What happened?"

CeCe looked up at her, her big eyes pools of terror. Her teeth chattered.

For the first time in a week, everything was so clear in that moment. The puddles of water on the cold, tiled floor. The lip of the big old bathtub that dated back to the day Idlewild was first built. The smell of school-issued soap and shampoo, mixed with a sickly smell of lavender that came from the bath soap Mary Van Woorten's older sister gave her, which she used religiously. The intestinal coils of the hot radiator against the wall. The grid of the drain against the floor, its wrought iron stark and black against the white tiles. The air was chilled, as if a draft had leaked into the room, and Katie felt as if someone had slapped her awake. "What happened?" she asked CeCe again.

CeCe answered, but Katie was so awake in that moment she already knew what CeCe would say. "She was here."

"Mary?" Katie demanded. "In this room?"

CeCe looked away, her teeth still chattering. "I was rinsing my hair. I went under the water. I saw a shape . . ." She shuddered, so hard it looked like she'd been shoved with a cattle prod. "Something held me down."

Katie looked down at her. There was not a whisper of disbelief in her blood, not a twinge of doubt. CeCe's mother had tried to drown her, had held her down. It was the reason CeCe was here.

It was exactly what Mary Hand would prey on.

Katie jerked up her sleeve, bent over the bathtub, and pulled the plug from the drain. As the water gurgled, the door behind them opened with a quiet click—the toilets locked, but the bath did not, not at Idlewild—and Katie turned to shout at the intruder until she saw it was Roberta.

Roberta closed the door quietly behind her and looked from one girl to the other, instant understanding on her face. She grabbed a bath towel and held it out to CeCe, who snatched it and wrapped it around herself.

"Are you all right?" Roberta asked.

CeCe nodded, staring at the floor. Then tears began streaming down her cheeks, and her shoulders shook with a sob.

"Let's get her out of here," Katie said.

But Roberta was staring at the mirror. "Look," she said.

The fog on the bathroom mirror was drying, but

near the top of the mirror the letters were still visible, written by something scratchy:

GOOD
NIGHT
GIRL

CeCe made a choked sound in her throat, and Katie grabbed the girl's robe and threw it over her shoulders. But it was Roberta who leaned over the sink, raised her arm, and scrubbed the words away with a vicious jerk, her jaw set, her fist scrubbing so hard on the mirror it made a screeching sound.

The curious girls in the hall had lost interest and dispersed, and the three girls went back to their room in hushed silence, Roberta's arm over CeCe's shoulders.

Still, CeCe was sobbing when they closed the door behind them. The robe dropped unheeded and she clutched the too-small towel to her, her shoulders shaking and tears rolling down her face. "She's dead," she said, the words sounding like stones she was trying to dislodge from her throat. "We can say it out loud. She's dead."

Roberta and Katie exchanged a glance.

CeCe rubbed a palm over her wet cheek. "Mary killed her."

Bile curled in Katie's stomach. "Not Mary," she said. "Someone did. But not Mary."

CeCe looked up at her, her eyes wide and seared with pain, searching Katie's face. "What do we do?"

There was the helplessness again, creeping down the

back of her neck, but this time Katie fought it. There had to be *something*. But dead was dead. She knew in her bones that Sonia wasn't alive anymore, not after a week. They couldn't save her. Maybe they never could have.

Roberta picked up CeCe's robe from the floor and hung it, then walked to CeCe's dresser drawer and pulled out a nightgown and a pair of underpants. She held them out to CeCe. "Do you know what I don't like?" she said. Her face was pale and sickly, like that of someone who had lost a lot of blood, but her eyes were fire. "I don't like that Mrs. Patton has her suitcase."

Katie swallowed. She was angry now, the fire in Roberta's eyes similar. Those were Sonia's things. Her books, her notebook, her socks and underwear. They'd all watched her pack them, lovingly, hoping she'd never come back here. It wasn't right that a bunch of adults who hadn't known Sonia and had given up on her got to keep the suitcase and forget about it. Besides, it was possible there was a clue in there. "It must be somewhere in Mrs. Patton's office," she said.

"Which is locked," CeCe said. She had taken the underpants from Roberta and slid them on beneath her towel. Her face was still blotchy, but now her mouth was set in a grim line.

"I'll bet Susan Brady has a key," Roberta said.

"To the headmistress's office?" That didn't seem likely to Katie.

"There's a skeleton key," CeCe said, as Roberta held up the towel and she turned away to put on her nightgown. "I've heard Susan brag about it. It opens everything. She isn't supposed to have it, but she's Mrs. Peabody's pet, and Mrs. Peabody gives her things to do that she doesn't want to do herself. So she has to have a key."

Well, well. Things were always so easy when girls—and teachers—were stupid. "All right, then," Katie said. "CeCe, you're still distraught. You need to go see the nurse. Tell Susan that Roberta and I are mad at you and won't take you, and you have no one else."

CeCe had always pretended to be the stupid one, but Katie wasn't fooled. CeCe caught on quickly. "That's no fair," she said, her distress over the bathroom incident fading beneath her outrage. "I want to help. I was lookout for you when you took extra food from the kitchen for Sonia. I'm *good*."

"You are," Katie agreed, meaning it, "but everyone just heard you screaming in the bathroom, so now is the perfect time to get Susan out of her room. So go get her to take you to Miss Hedmeyer. Roberta and I will get the key."

"Get it and wait for me," CeCe insisted. "I'm coming, too."

Katie bit her lip, but she couldn't argue. If the roles were reversed, she wouldn't want to sit out. "Be quick, then," she counseled. "Tell Miss Hedmeyer you have cramps, and she'll give you some aspirin and send you back to your room. Susan will be mad, but just act sheepish."

CeCe shrugged. "Susan thinks I'm stupid anyway."

It was infuriating how many people got things wrong about you when you were a teenage girl, but as she had learned to do, Katie took her anger and made it into something else. She had the glimmer of an idea in the back of her mind, an idea bigger than stealing a key from Susan Brady's room and getting Sonia's suitcase from the headmistress's office. Her anger fed it, like wood being fed into a fire. It would take thought and planning, and time. Katie had plenty of time.

But first she wanted Sonia's suitcase. "Get your slippers on and get moving," she said to CeCe. She pinched CeCe's cheeks so their red splotchiness wouldn't fade yet. CeCe turned her face to Katie, then to Roberta, who dabbed water on her cheeks from the basin. Katie watched in admiration as CeCe closed her eyes for a minute, drooped her shoulders, and let her bottom lip go soft. Then she whirled and ran from the room, slamming the door behind her as if running from an argument.

It was almost too easy. Susan Brady led CeCe to the nurse, Susan chiding and CeCe choking back distressed sobs; Roberta kept watch in the hall while Katie slipped into Susan's room and rifled through her things, looking for the key. She found it in Susan's jewelry box, among the tiny gold earrings and a cheap paste ring. Both girls were back in their room when CeCe returned, having swallowed the requisite chalky aspirin and taken a verbal drubbing from Susan. She quickly dressed and the three of them set out, slipping down the stairs into the common, then to the main hall—the skeleton key let them in just fine—and down the hall to the headmistress's office.

Sonia's suitcase was in a closet at the back of the room, alongside Mrs. Patton's winter coat and snow boots and other confiscated items taken from Idlewild girls over the years: lipsticks, cigarettes, a pearl compact and mirror, a pair of silk stockings, a glossy photograph of Rudolph Valentino—How old was *that*? Katie wondered—and two beautiful priceless items: a small flask of alcohol and a stack of magazines. The girls couldn't resist: Katie pocketed the alcohol, Roberta snatched the magazines, and CeCe took the suitcase. They dropped the skeleton key in the garden, Roberta edging it beneath the soft, wet earth with the toe of her shoe.

Back in their room, they set aside the unexpected loot and went quietly through the suitcase, reverently touching Sonia's things. The case was neatly packed, and Katie knew that no one had opened it since Sonia had packed it at her relatives' house. Not one person— not the headmistress, not the police, not anyone—had bothered to look in the missing girl's things.

Katie opened Sonia's notebook, leafing through the pages as the other two girls looked on. There was Sonia's handwriting, the portraits she'd drawn of her family and the people she'd seen at Ravensbrück. There were maps, and sketches, and pages and pages of memories, Sonia's short life put down in her private journal. In the last pages were portraits of her three friends, drawn closely and lovingly.

Katie had already known that Sonia was dead, but looking at the notebook—which Sonia, while alive, would never have abandoned to her last breath—she *knew*.

This is good-bye, Katie thought, *but not farewell. Someone did this. And I won't stand for it. None of us will.*

The girls closed the suitcase and went to bed.

And Katie began to think.

chapter 28

Burlington, Vermont
November 2014

The small building that had once been the bus station in downtown Burlington was long gone. Anyone wishing to catch a bus had to go to the Greyhound station just out of town at the airport. Fiona stood on the sidewalk on South Winooski Avenue and stared at a Rite Aid that was currently closed down, the sign half-dismantled and the windows boarded. Traffic blared by on the street behind her. This was a section of town populated with grocery stores, laundromats, gas stations, and corner stores, with a gentrifying residential area starting farther up the street. It looked very little like it would have looked in 1950, but Fiona still felt a connection, a quiet jolt of energy, knowing she was standing in the place Sonia Gallipeau had stood on the last day of her life.

She ignored the people walking by, who were giving side-looks to the woman staring at a closed-up Rite Aid, and turned in a circle. This wasn't just a sentimental visit. Fiona was making a map.

Rose Albert. Rosa Berlitz. Had they been one and the same? Was there a way Rose Albert, in her made-up American life, could have crossed paths with Sonia?

It had taken only a little digging, cross-referenced with county tax records, to get addresses. The police record said that the ticket taker had seen Sonia at the bus station, getting on the bus. Fiona was at ground zero of Sonia's case, the last place she was seen by anyone except the bus driver—who was never interviewed—and her killer.

But Sonia *had* gotten on the bus. That was witnessed. And her suitcase was found on Old Barrons Road, a few hundred feet from Idlewild. Fiona had spent a sleepless night going over it, wishing painfully for Jamie, his clever logic, his head for facts. It wasn't easy, figuring these things out alone. And it wasn't fun, either.

But she had come to some conclusions that she thought were the most logical, the most likely. As Sherlock Holmes said: *Eliminate the impossible, and what's left must be the truth.* If she followed the Rose Albert theory, it wasn't *impossible* that a woman who lived in Burlington would coincidentally be standing on Old Barrons Road, in the middle of nowhere, when Sonia Gallipeau walked by. But it was unlikely.

It was more likely that Rose Albert had come across Sonia in Burlington, before she got on the bus.

But that didn't turn any of it into fact. The newspaper reports of Rose's trial had stated that Rose Albert worked as a clerk in a travel agency, four streets away. Perhaps Rose had somehow spotted Sonia from her home, a fifteen-minute walk from the travel agency, while Sonia and her relatives were out enjoying their weekend. Fiona started walking down South Winooski Avenue toward the home where Sonia had stayed.

But half an hour later, she was no further along. The house of Henry and Eleanor DuBois was nowhere near the address where Rose Albert was listed as living. She could not see how Rose and Sonia could have crossed paths in the space of a weekend. It didn't help that there was no way of knowing what activities the DuBoises had done with their great-niece. Shopping? Sightseeing? Walking in the park? Eating out? If Sonia had any new-bought items or souvenirs in her suitcase, it would have given a clue as to where she had gone that weekend, but the suitcase had disappeared from Julia Patton's office after Sonia was murdered, never to be seen again.

She was walking back toward the site of the former bus station, wishing *someone* in 1950 had interviewed the goddamned bus driver, when it struck her so forcefully she stopped on the sidewalk to think.

The bus ticket. That was the connection.

In 1950, you didn't buy a bus ticket online, or from a machine at the bus station, using a credit card. You bought a bus ticket from a clerk at the station, or at a travel agent's. Rose had worked as a clerk for a travel agent, filling out and filing the stacks of paperwork that accompanied travel bookings in the pre-Internet age.

Sonia's relatives had bought her a round-trip bus ticket to Burlington. But when Sonia had run away to go back to school, she must have changed it.

Fiona felt the excitement building in her chest, and she

started walking again, nearly jogging back toward her car. It was easy to picture: Sonia at the travel agent's, changing her ticket while Rose sat at her desk, doing paperwork. Had Sonia seen Rose? Had she recognized her? She must have; Rose must have known that Sonia knew who she was, that she could identify her as Rosa Berlitz. She knew what bus Sonia was taking back to Idlewild. And at some point, Rose Albert must have decided that she'd have to do something permanent about Sonia, or her life would fall to pieces.

It was speculation. It wasn't concrete. There were a million ways it could have been wrong. It was more far-fetched than the theory of one of Sonia's friends simply caving her head in and dumping her in a well.

But if you followed it, it *fit*.

Sonia had been in the same city at the same time as a woman who might have been a guard at Ravensbrück, where Sonia had been a prisoner. She had visited family within blocks of Rose Albert's home and her office. How far apart had they been, guard and prisoner? One mile, at most? The two of them in the same place in America, five years after the war ended. A coincidence, but a documented one. It fit.

Fiona thought back to the picture from the news story—Rose Albert's calm face, her level eyes, her large pupils, her milky skin. The face of Rosa Berlitz, the guard who had put women in the gas chambers, in the ovens. If she had done that, then the death of one teenage girl would have meant nothing. Not in the face of survival. Not if a secret had to be kept.

If it was true, then Sonia Gallipeau's murder wasn't random, or impulsive. She had been chosen and stalked, though not in the way that Ginette Harrison had imagined. She had been under a death sentence from the moment she walked into Rose Albert's travel agency. Followed until she was away from the city and the crowds, until the bus had driven away and she was alone on a deserted road. Rose Albert hadn't even needed to take the bus alongside her prey; she had already known where her prey was headed. She could have traveled ahead to the bus stop in her car, parked, and waited until the bus pulled up and the girl got off.

If you were hunting for someone to murder, Ginette had said, *what better person could you choose?*

H er head was pounding when she got home, since she'd barely slept and she hadn't eaten. The light was still out in the hallway on her floor—it had burned out nearly three weeks ago—and for once she was grateful for the eerie half-light that was usually an alarming security concern. Her thoughts were too heavy, too loud, and she wanted only the darkness of her apartment.

He was there. She hadn't expected him, but somehow when she saw him, she wasn't surprised. Jamie, sitting on the floor, next to her closed apartment door, his back against the wall, his knees up. Out of uniform, wearing jeans and a T-shirt with a flannel shirt unbuttoned over it and work boots, his hair mussed. He watched her come up the hallway toward him, his expression closed and blank.

Fiona stopped in front of his feet and looked down at him in the half-light. "How long have you been here?" she asked softly.

"Not long."

"You have a key."

He looked up at her. The fight was gone from him, the outrage, the bluster. He just looked at her. "It took me eight months to get that key," he said finally.

It was true. He had given her his key long before she'd given him hers, and it had been hard for her even then. Her father didn't have a key to her place; no one did. Not ever. But at long last, she'd given Jamie one.

She'd questioned it; she hadn't trusted it. It had scared her, so much so that she hadn't noticed he'd been careful with it, that he always called or texted her first, that he'd gone slow. She saw that now, so clearly.

"Keep it," she said to him, her voice hoarse.

He looked away. She should have opened the door now, invited him in if he wasn't going to come in himself; part of her knew that. But he seemed disinclined to move, as if whatever he had to say was better here in the hallway, with the broken lights and the ugly industrial carpet. "I came here to explain," he said.

"You don't have to explain."

"I do." She watched him struggle with this. "You were right."

He was going to tell her something buried, and she hadn't thought she could handle any more buried things . . . but she owed him this. "Right about what?"

"Helen Heyer," he said. "I pulled the file."

Her stomach dropped. "What do you mean?"

"They questioned Helen's friends," Jamie said. "The cops working the case. They interviewed her friends about whether she'd ever told them about her relationship with Tim Christopher. What they didn't do was ask Tim's friends."

Fiona was quiet.

"Tim was popular," Jamie continued. He glanced at her. "You know that, of course. He had a lot of friends. They could have interviewed them, found out who Tim was seeing. One of them would likely have known who he was dating, whether he was lying about Helen. It's routine. But they didn't. They interviewed Tim, with his parents in the room. And then they dropped it." He shook his head. "It doesn't prove that Tim tried to kill Helen. The MO still doesn't fit. But . . ." He trailed off. Fiona knew the rest of it without words. The fact that the cops had backed off from the Christophers meant they'd left part of the investigation undone. If any of his friends had admitted that Tim was seeing Helen, Deb would be alive.

Then Jamie made her stomach drop further by saying, "Dad's name is in the file. He did the interview."

Tim Christopher was a good man before his life was ruined, Garrett had said. "My God, Jamie."

"When I was a kid, he used to take me for ride-alongs," Jamie said. "It was what made me want to be a cop. He'd take me on patrol, and not much happens in Barrons, you know? So we'd spend most of the time shooting the shit. I thought being a cop was fun, and Dad was chief, so everyone treated him like a boss. What's not to like?"

He rubbed the bridge of his nose, his eyes tired, and Fiona waited.

"One night we got a domestic call," Jamie continued. "A woman said her husband was hitting her. I was with him. I was ten. He put me in the backseat while he and his partner went inside. I don't know what happened in the house, but after ten minutes they both came out and we drove away without a word.

"I asked Dad what had happened. He told me it didn't matter, everything was fine, because he was good friends with the guy's brother. Then he turned and looked at me in the backseat. *Family comes first, doesn't it, son?* he said. His partner didn't say anything. Not a word. And I was ten, and he's my dad, so I just nodded and agreed with him. I'd thought I'd forgotten about that night until I became a cop. Then I remembered it."

"What are you saying?" Fiona asked.

"It's small things, you know?" Jamie said. "Or so it seems. His golf buddy's speeding ticket gets thrown away. Another buddy's nephew gets off with a warning when he spray-paints the school. The mayor's son gets let go when he's caught driving over the limit. Dad was still chief when I started, and everyone accepted it. We fought about it at first, but no one would back me up, and Dad was close to retirement. I started to think I could just wait it out, and after Dad was gone, I could help the force be different. Do things different. Like those old days were gone."

Fiona remembered Garrett at the family dinner, how he'd known everything that was going on in the force. "Except it didn't work out that way, did it?" she supplied.

Jamie was quiet for a long beat. "He's so fucking power-ful," he said. "And Barrons is so small. I didn't realize how bad it was, how deep it was, until I'd been on the force for years. No one questions the chief, or anything he does, because then you're off the gravy train. Everyone on the force has it easy. Why rock the boat? They tell themselves it's just a slip here and there, never anything serious. No one is getting hurt. You do a favor for some-one; they do a favor for you. Just fill out the paperwork and go home. And I woke up one day and realized I'd been on the force for seven years, and I was starting to think that way, too. That toxic don't-give-a-fuck. I real-ized I had to get away somehow, get out to save myself." He looked up at her. "That was the night I met you."

Fiona stared at him, speechless.

"I knew who you were," he said. "That night. You were right. Of course I knew. But I wanted to talk to you anyway."

"Why?"

He shrugged. "You looked lost, like me. You're Mal-colm Sheridan's daughter. You've lived life. You know this place, but you don't quite buy it, don't quite buy anything. You don't buckle under. You're beautiful. And your shirt was sliding off your shoulder."

She dropped to her knees, put her hands on his shoul-ders. He was warm, tense, his muscles bunched beneath her hands. "Jamie," she said. "Helen Heyer isn't a thrown-away speeding ticket."

He looked at her, right into her in that way Jamie had, as if he knew what she was thinking. "I know," he said roughly, touching his fingertips to the line of her jaw. "I'm not going to drop it, Fee. I'm going to take it as far as it can go. I'm done."

She leaned in and kissed him. He kissed her back, his hands tangling in her hair. This was so easy; this, they knew. She slid forward between his knees and ran her hands down the tops of his thighs through his jeans as he opened her mouth slowly, gently. It felt raw and familiar and real, and she knew how this would go. Sex with Jamie was never rushed; he liked to take his time, go slow, as if he was studying her. She realized now that it was because he was never entirely sure that she would be back. Because he never quite knew which time would be the last time. And neither did she.

She followed the kiss where it led, not caring if any neighbors came down the hallway, not caring that she was hungry and her knees hurt. Not caring about Idlewild or dead girls or anything but the way she could read his pulse beneath his skin.

He broke this kiss and sighed, his hands still twisted in her hair. "We're not doing this," he said. It wasn't a question.

She kissed his neck, feeling the scrape of his beard against her mouth. "No," she agreed. "Not right now."

He let his head drop back, banging it gently against the wall. "Fuck," he muttered.

Fiona pressed her cheek against his collarbone. He dropped a hand to the back of her neck. And they stayed like that for a long, long time.

chapter 29

Fiona woke on the sofa, her throat scratchy and her neck sore. She rolled over, looked at the mess of her apartment in the dark. There were stacks of boxes, papers. On her coffee table were her laptop and a half-eaten box of Ritz crackers. She tapped her laptop to make it wake up so she could see the time in the little display in the corner. It was six a.m.

She stared at the screen, looking at the topic she'd been reading about when she fell asleep, sometime around three. Rose Albert.

Rose's face stared at her. The picture had been taken on the street by an enterprising photographer sometime after Rose had been arrested and granted bail. She was dignified, wearing an old-fashioned skirt and jacket and a fur stole—out of style in 1973, but giving off an air of class. At the time of the trial, she was only fifty-five, with the clear skin Fiona had seen in the other photographs of her, her mouth a firm line, her eyes so perfectly even and dark, her expression shuttered and cool. The photographer had caught her unawares, and she had put a hand to the fur stole as she walked, nearly clutching it. The few accounts Fiona had found of the trial had described her as wearing a fox fur stole. The same one.

The trial itself was not on public record; the transcripts were sealed. It had been a midsized local story in its day, worthy of a dedicated reporter and a photographer assigned to take shots from the street once or twice, but it hadn't been front-page news. Looking at the coverage, Fiona could perfectly follow the logic of that news editor in 1973: They had to cover the story for the local angle, because there were people who knew this woman, but hell, no one wanted to read about concentration camps really. It was too depressing and out of touch. Vietnam was happening; Vietnam was real. A lady in a fur stole who might or might not have been an old Nazi was news, but not big news.

Still, the coverage was well researched and well written, making Fiona nostalgic for the heyday of reporters who were actually on staff instead of freelance, and stories that didn't have to say "You won't believe what happened next" in order to survive in the click-or-die Internet age. Rose Albert was a spinster living in Burlington, an immigrant from Europe after the war. She claimed to have come from Munich, where she had worked in a factory. She did admit to being a member of the Nazi Party, but she claimed that it was only a survival tactic, because under Hitler's regime, those who did not join were suspect. Yes, she had attended rallies, but only so she wouldn't have been denounced by her neighbors and arrested. No, she had not worked in a concentration camp, and once the war was over, she had come to America to start again, and she had been lucky enough to get the job at the travel agency.

Rosa Berlitz, the Ravensbrück guard, was a mystery. She had been recruited from one of the local German villages, a girl with no experience, and had taken to the job at once. She had chased prisoners with the dogs the Nazis had given the guards, who were trained to attack and kill. She had stood by while women were experimented on and sentenced to death, then helped carry out the murders. Who her family and friends were was unknown; what had happened to her after the war, when the Soviets liberated Ravensbrück, was also unknown. Rosa Berlitz had appeared from nowhere, tortured and killed the prisoners of Ravensbrück without flinching, and disappeared again.

There was only one known photograph of Rosa: standing in a line of other guards, being inspected by Himmler as he toured the camp. Himmler was a large figure in the picture, wearing his long coat and Nazi insignia, striding across the grounds. The women were in uniform, ranged in three neat rows, but Rosa's face was in the back row and slightly out of focus, leaving only two dark eyes, a straight nose, a glimpse of white skin. It might have been Rose Albert, and it might not. No other record of Rosa Berlitz was left, nothing that said she had existed at all, except for the memories of the prisoners who had lived under her.

Three survivors had identified Rose Albert as Rosa Berlitz. One had died of cancer the week before the trial began; the other two had testified in court. It seemed there had been too many holes, too much missing information in the trail leading back to Rosa Berlitz, even with survivors' testimony, and Rose had gone free. When Fiona dug further, she found that the two remaining survivors had died in 1981 and 1987.

Rose Albert was acquitted, but later that year she was found dead in her home. The coroner declared the cause of death a heart attack, and she was quietly buried, her death a footnote in the back pages.

Fiona peeled herself off the sofa. She felt hideous, as if she'd gone on a bender, though all she'd done was sit in her dark apartment and read. She put coffee on and got in the shower, but that only made her shiver no matter how hot she turned the water tap. She washed quickly and got out again, then dried off. She gulped her coffee and tried not to think of Jamie, of what he was doing right now. Of Garrett Creel. Of Tim Christopher with a baseball bat, coming up the walk behind Helen Heyer.

Maybe she was coming down with something. Her head was throbbing, and her throat was still sore. She dug in her cupboards and found some ibuprofen, some cold meds, an old Halls. She took the pills and popped the Halls in her mouth, wincing at its waxy old texture and menthol taste. She had no time to be sick, not now. Not yet.

She needed to settle some things.

She put on her coat and boots, pulled a thick wool

cap over her still-wet hair, and walked out the door after grabbing her keys.

The dawn was gray, the wind icy and bitter, which meant only one thing: snow on the way. It was nearly December, and from now until April, Vermont would fight the winter battle as it always did. Old Barrons Road was quiet, though Fiona could see movement on the Idlewild property through the trees. The pause to retrieve Sonia's body was over, and the restoration had started up again.

But she didn't go to Idlewild this time. She found the rough, overgrown driveway on the left-hand side of the road instead of the right, and followed it into the overgrown weeds where the drive-in used to be. She remembered walking along Old Barrons Road, talking to Jamie on the phone. It felt like years ago. But he'd reminded her that the old drive-in had still been open in 1994. On the night Deb died, it hadn't been running any movies, because November was the off-season, but it was still a hangout for kids who liked to drink in an abandoned lot. The police had interviewed as many of those kids as they could find, but none of them recalled seeing Tim Christopher's car parked at the side of Old Barrons Road, which he must have done in order to dump Deb's body.

The drive-in had closed sometime in the late nineties, and like most people, Fiona had assumed that it was an empty lot. Until she'd met Stephen Heyer in Portsmouth, and he'd told her that he'd seen her because he slept here sometimes. *The old man who used to run the drive-in lets me use his place.*

Her car rumbled over the dirt path, brushing the clumps of overgrown weeds. The screen was long gone, as was the popcorn stand, but a sign remained, placed along what was once the driveway where the cars would patiently line up, waiting to pay admission. It was a four-foot billboard, showing a dancing hot dog and a can of soda, doing a jitterbug on cartoon legs. WELCOME TO OUR DRIVE-IN! the lettering proclaimed. Water had damaged the edge of the billboard, and time had faded its colors, but surprisingly the vandals and graffiti artists had left it alone, a relic in the abandoned lot.

Fiona pulled the car just past the sign, to where the open lot was, and put the car in park. She was cold, her spine shivering, though she was huddled in her coat with the heat on high. *Snow coming,* she thought. She looked around. *Where the hell does Stephen Heyer sleep in this place?*

She pulled out her phone, thinking to call someone about something important, but then she stared at the display, bewildered. Her thoughts were moving too fast, spinning out of her hands. *I'm not sick. I'm not.* She thumbed through her contacts and almost dialed Jamie, just to hear the rumble of his voice. But she flipped past his number and dialed Malcolm instead.

She got his answering machine. She could picture it, a literal machine, an old tape-recording answering machine that sat in his phone nook—because of course her father had a phone nook—next to his nineties-era landline phone. The phone rang, and the machine whirred to life, sending Malcolm's voice down the line, asking her to leave a message. And then a loud beep.

"Daddy," she said, "there's something I have to tell you." She told him about Stephen Heyer, how he'd found her, what he'd told her. About how she'd seen Helen Heyer, who had nearly been beaten to death with a baseball bat by Tim Christopher the year before he'd met Deb. She was still talking when the machine cut her off.

She hung up.

You'll kill him with this shit, Jamie had said.

And then her father's voice, when she was fourteen and her mother didn't want the distressing picture he'd taken in Vietnam framed and put on the wall. *Do you think they won't see the real world, Ginny?* he'd said. *Do you think the real world will never come to them?*

Fiona touched her cheeks. There were tears there, though they were cold and nearly dry. She wiped them off with her mittened hands and got out of the car.

The wind stung her face. She walked across the clearing that had once been the parking area of the drive-in, where everyone would have parked facing the screen. Her boots crunched on the dirt and old gravel. The sky lowered, angry and gray. She walked toward where the screen would have been, trying to see past the rise there. She couldn't see anyone or any cars, but she noticed that the abandoned lot was scrupulously clean, free of litter or garbage, which didn't compute with a place teenagers had been using for decades.

At the other end of the gravel she saw it. An old house, set back, nearly hidden by trees. A trailer, parked farther back in the shadows. A pickup truck on the drive. *Hell,* she thought, *someone really does live here.*

"Help you?" a voice said.

She turned to see a man of her father's age, though heavily muscled, his head shaved in a military crew cut. He wore a thick parka, boots, and old army pants, but it was the rifle slung casually across his forearms that Fiona stared at, cradled in his grip a little like a baby.

"I'm looking for Stephen Heyer," she said.

The man shook his head. "He's not here."

Fiona blinked. Her eyelids were cold in the wind. "He told me he sleeps here sometimes."

"He does," the man said, "but not today."

Fiona felt her shoulders slump. This had been her only idea; she didn't have another. "But I need to talk to him."

The man looked at her curiously, and did not move the gun from his arms. "Sorry," he said. "And I hate to point it out, but you're trespassing."

"I didn't know this was private property," Fiona said through her fog. "I thought it was abandoned. Sorry." She looked around. "Where does Stephen sleep?"

"My trailer," the man said. "I have a few people who come by there when they need a place. Some peace and quiet. I've been letting people sleep in my trailer since 1981." He paused. Fiona tried to take in this oddly specific fact, as if there was something about 1981 she should know. It didn't occur to her what he was waiting for until he said, "My name's Lionel Charters."

Oh, right. "Sorry," she said. "My name's Fiona. Fiona Sheridan."

Lionel went still. "What is Malcolm Sheridan's other girl doing in my drive-in?"

That made her meet his eyes. *Malcolm Sheridan's other girl.* "I guess you were here when my sister died," she said.

Lionel nodded and didn't look away. "My uncle Chip started the drive-in in 1961," he said. "When Chip died, I took it over. I ran it until 1997. Not many drive-ins lasted that long." He shrugged. "It didn't bring in much money, especially toward the end, but I don't need much. My wife left in eighty and my son died in eighty-one. Ever since then, it's been just me." He seemed to be looking at her closely, but Fiona had lost her focus again and things were slipping. "I was here that night. I was here every night. I was here when they found her, too. I could see all the commotion when I stood at the end of my drive and looked across Old Barrons Road. The ambulances and such. It was a shame, what happened to your sister."

Fiona swallowed, unable to speak.

"I've heard Stephen's story," Lionel said. "He's wanted to talk to you for a long time. I take it he finally did."

"Is it true?" Fiona asked, her voice a croak. "I'm not a good judge. Did he fool me?"

Lionel was quiet for a moment, and then he shook his head. "Stephen didn't fool you," he said, and the wariness in his voice was almost mixed with kindness. "What happened to Helen was real. If you're wondering if Tim Christopher did it, he did. Just like he killed your sister. I'd swear that on my son's grave."

"Why?" she asked him. "What makes you so certain?"

Lionel looked away.

Something roared through Fiona. The restlessness she'd been feeling twisted hard in her gut, almost painful, and her blood jittered. She felt like screaming. "You saw something," she said softly. "That night. You saw something."

"I see a lot of things," Lionel said, his face hard. "The ghost, for example. I see her." He turned and looked at her. "Do you?"

Fiona felt her face blanch. "She comes here?"

"Not here," Lionel said. "This isn't her place. But over there"—he nodded in the direction of Old Barrons Road and Idlewild—"I've seen her walking plenty of times. Girl in a black dress and veil. The first time I saw her myself, it was 1983. I thought some teenager was playing a prank, dressing up, even though it wasn't close to Halloween. Who knows what teenagers find funny? So I went over there."

"What did she show you?" Fiona asked.

Lionel blinked, his gaze going cold. "That's none of your business. Just like it's none of my business what she showed you. What that girl does is cruel, a violation of everything that's good and right. I never believed in ghosts until that day, and even now, I don't believe in them—except for that one. I believe in that one. And I've seen her walk the road and through the trees, but I've never gone back across Old Barrons Road again. What she showed me, I'll take to my grave."

Fiona's throat was raw; it felt like she'd swallowed razor blades. Still, she said to him, "November 21, 1994. What did you see?"

Lionel shook his head. "This isn't going to help you, girl. Just like what that abomination across the road shows you isn't going to help you. It's only going to cause pain. He's already in prison for what he's done."

She tried not to sway on her feet. *Tell me.*

He sighed. A crow flew overhead, giving off its hoarse cry. A cold wind whistled through the bare trees past the old lot. The first dry flakes of snow landed on Fiona's coat.

"The cops came that night," Lionel said, surprising her. She'd never heard that before. "Said there was a complaint call, but I know I never made it." He looked around. "It was November, and there were four kids here, maybe five, sitting in a circle, drinking God knows what. They'd made a little fire, but it didn't bother me. It wasn't big enough to spread, and I knew that eventually those kids would get cold and go home." He raised his gaze to the dirt-and-gravel drive Fiona had driven up, and lifted one hand from his rifle to motion to it briefly. "I was just telling the kids that no one had better puke in my bushes, when Garrett Creel himself came walking up that path."

Fiona stared at him, shocked now. "Garrett Creel?"

"In the flesh," Lionel said with contempt. "That old fucker never liked me. Never liked that I go my own way, living on my land, and I don't care about his rules. He'd come here plenty of times, asking if I'm growing weed out here or cooking meth or something. As if I'd do that shit after what happened to my boy. But that night was different." He turned back to Fiona. "He came walking up the drive, you see. From the bottom. Parked his cruiser down on Old Barrons Road and walked the rest of the way instead of driving. Why'd he do that?"

Fiona shook her head. She didn't know. None of this had ever been covered in the papers, in the trial. She felt like she was Alice in Wonderland.

"So Creel comes up here, scares the shit out of the few drunk kids who were sitting here, gives them a lecture. Something about lighting fires—suddenly he's Smokey the fucking Bear. He turns to me, tells me I'm liable if anything happens, just the same as if I was sitting there drinking shitty brew with those kids. All bluster. He took his time. He thought I didn't notice, but I did. So when he walked away, going leisurely back down my drive, I cut across the hill over here"—he motioned to the left, where all Fiona could see was overgrown weeds—"and got a view of the road. It was dark, and Creel didn't see me. His cruiser was parked on the side of the road. He got in, and the interior light went on for a second, and I saw Tim Christopher. Clear as I'm looking at you right now. Sitting in the fucking police cruiser with the chief of fucking police. Then Creel turned the car around and drove away."

Her head pounded. This was like a crazy dream. Tim Christopher in Garrett's police cruiser, and twenty years later, through the media coverage and the trial, no one had heard it. "Why would you lie about this?" she asked Lionel. "What reason would you have?"

"Why would I lie about anything?" Lionel said. "Ask around about me, Sheridan girl. Ask your daddy if you want. I'm an open book, always have been."

"Then why wasn't any of this evidence in Tim's case?"

"Because I was told to shut up about it," Lionel said. "Clearly. By people who meant business. Those kids never saw Garrett's car, but they saw Garrett. He lectured them. But when they were interviewed, not one of them mentioned it. Because the people who got to me got to them. It was Garrett's force, and they were Garrett's cops, every last one of them—none of them was honest. Kids are easily scared. I'm not, but I know when to shut up for survival. And that was one of those times." He looked at her carefully. "Besides, they got him. Tim Christopher's been in jail for twenty years. I had to choose the lesser evil." His gaze cut over her shoulder, and she heard the hum of a motor. "Come to speak it, I think the greater evil is on its way."

Fiona turned to see a boxy brown Chevy come up the drive and stop behind her own car, the engine idling. The driver's door opened, and the big, heavy frame of Garrett Creel unwound itself from the driver's seat and stood. He stared at her, squinting through the flakes of snow in the gray light.

"Fiona," he said, his voice mild, ignoring Lionel Charters. "You don't look so good, dear."

Fiona looked at Lionel. His face was unreadable. He said nothing. He still cradled the rifle.

"I'm . . . I'm okay," she said to Garrett, forcing the words out past her sore throat. The wind blew down the neck of her coat, and she shivered.

Garrett shook his head. "I don't think so. You're gray

as a sheet. There's something going around, you know." He nodded. "Something real bad."

Her brain tried to work—why was Garrett here? What did he want? But it was starting to feel like someone had placed hot coals in the spot where her skull met the back of her neck, and she felt sweat trickling down her back the same time as she shivered with cold. "I just need some aspirin," she managed.

"I don't think you should be driving, dear," Garrett said. He hadn't called her *dear* before, and something about it repulsed her. "You look too sick. I'll take you home."

"Garrett," Lionel said.

"Shut up, Lionel, or I'll have you shut down," Garrett said casually. "Those junkies you let stay in your trailer—you think the cops won't find a fucking pharmacy if they raid that place?"

"My trailer is for people going clean," Lionel said. "You know that."

"Going clean?" Garrett said. "Sure, like that son of yours? Died with enough coke in him to kill someone twice his size. Sounds clean to me."

Fiona could feel the hostility radiating from Lionel like a vibration. "Get off my property," he said. "You're not police anymore. You're not anything. This is private property. I own it. Get off."

"You broke our deal, Lionel," Garrett said. "It took you twenty years, but you broke it. You talked. I thought Fiona might find you, ever since she came to dinner at my house, full of accusations. So I've had a few of my friends keep an eye on her as a favor to me. Turns out, I called it right. We're leaving now." He stepped forward, his footsteps loud on the gravel in the cold air. He put a big hand on Fiona's upper arm. "Come with me," he said.

"Wait," Fiona said.

There was a click, and she turned to see that Lionel had raised his rifle, aiming it at Garrett. "You let her go," he said.

Garrett didn't even flinch. "Are you gonna shoot me?" he asked. "You can't aim for shit. You'll hit her first." He pulled Fiona toward his car as she tried to pull from his grip. "Go ahead, Lionel. Shoot at me. Kill Deb Sheridan's sister while you're at it. Then see how quick your little operation shuts down while you're in prison."

He opened his passenger door, and Fiona tried to twist out of his hold, but he had her tight and he shoved her inside with practiced precision. *He's not going to hurt me,* she told herself as he got in the other side. *He's Jamie's father. He was the chief of police. It's daylight, with a witness. He just wants to talk.*

Garrett started the car and reversed out of the lot. She looked out the window and could see Lionel Charters standing there, watching them, still aiming his gun.

chapter 30

CeCe

There was only one Family Visit Day at the end of the year, held between Thanksgiving and Christmas. So on the second Sunday in December, the three girls left in Clayton Hall 3C sat quietly in their bunks, reading and studying in painful boredom. CeCe was miserable; she was having nightmares, insomnia, trouble eating. Her days were a long, slow echo of grief for Sonia, of wondering what had happened to her. Of wondering if it had hurt.

She lay listlessly on her bed and watched Katie, who was leafing through one of their stolen magazines. Katie had been silent for a few days, but now she was acting as she always had, angry and sassy and beautiful and smart. It should have angered CeCe that Katie had moved on from their friend's disappearance in less than a week, but it didn't, for the simple reason that it wasn't true. CeCe had made a study of Katie, of her ways and thoughts and actions, a closer study than she'd done of any topic in their stupid textbooks. Katie was CeCe's master's thesis and her Ph.D.; if there was a test on the topic of all things Katie, CeCe would have passed with flying colors. And Katie had not, in any way, moved on from Sonia's disappearance. She was pretending to be her old self to deflect attention, but it was a deception. Katie wasn't herself at all. Katie was angry.

CeCe watched her friend flip a page. Katie's uptilted eyes were dark and, in CeCe's opinion, ominous. Others saw a pretty girl who had a defiant attitude; CeCe saw a white-hot fury that was banked so deeply, fed so carefully, that there was no way it would ever cease to burn.

Roberta wasn't acting like her old self, either; she'd gone quiet, pale, obviously in mourning for her friend. The teachers gave Roberta kindly concern, instead of the hard mistrust they gave Katie and the irritated lectures they gave CeCe about bucking up. But CeCe saw the anger there, too, in the way Roberta sat still at meals and didn't speak, in the way her jaw twitched, in the way she tore around the hockey field with new viciousness she hadn't had before, as if she wanted to work her anger out through her muscles. The way she ground her teeth at night and jerked her hair into a braid with her deft fingers every morning, yanking at the strands until they obeyed. It didn't take a genius to see the anger in that.

It was fine with CeCe. She was angry, too.

So horribly, horribly angry. She didn't know what to do with it—channel it, like Katie, or suppress it, like Roberta. CeCe's anger was like an overfilled balloon she couldn't tuck away and didn't want to touch for fear it would explode. It suffocated her, closed her throat so she couldn't breathe. She didn't have a sport to play to burn it out, and she didn't have Katie's wicked intelligence to plot whatever it was that Katie was plotting. All CeCe could do was suffer.

The problem was that she didn't have a target, because she didn't know who had killed Sonia. (That Sonia was dead, CeCe no longer had any doubt. She'd known the minute she'd seen the words *GOOD NIGHT GIRL* in the mirror.) Had her great-aunt and great-uncle done it? If so, why was Sonia's suitcase found in the trees? Katie said that Mary Hand couldn't have done it, because Mary was a ghost; but CeCe wasn't so sure. CeCe had seen Mary from the bathtub, her dark, ominous form moving above her, wearing the black dress and veil. She had seen Mary bend down, felt the cold hand grasp her neck, hold her down under the water. Mary might have been long dead, but CeCe had no doubt that Mary was capable of killing a girl and dragging her to wherever she lived, to haunt future Idlewild girls forever. CeCe had no doubt of that at all.

Besides, Mary walked the grounds, the woods, the road. And Mary had known Sonia was dead; she had told them with the message in the mirror.

CeCe pictured Sonia getting off the bus on Old Barrons Road, seeing Mary waiting for her. What had happened? Had Sonia screamed? Had she run?

There was a knock on the door. "Ladies," came Lady Loon's voice. "Cecelia. You have a family visitor."

CeCe groaned and rolled off her bed. "I'm coming," she called through the door.

Roberta poked her face over the edge of her top bunk and looked over at her. "Who do you think it is?" she asked.

CeCe shrugged, noting the lavender half circles beneath Roberta's eyes, which mirrored her own. She'd crawled into Roberta's bunk more than once in the past week, and the other girl hadn't minded. CeCe slept better when they were together against the darkness, Roberta's larger, bonier body sprawled next to her in her thick nightgown. "Joseph," CeCe said listlessly. "My half brother."

Katie's eyes flickered up from her magazine. "Comb your hair," she said. "And straighten your shirt."

"Why?" CeCe asked her.

Katie stared hard at her. "Look good for him."

CeCe shrugged again, but she did what Katie ordered. "I don't see the point. I don't even want to talk to him, not today. He's nice enough, but I don't have the energy."

"Make a good impression," Katie said. "Trust me."

So CeCe brushed her hair out and tied it back neatly, then readjusted her shirt so it didn't look as awkward over her bosom, and added a cardigan. "I hate this," she said as she pulled on her shoes. "I'm lonely without her."

"Me, too," Roberta said.

They'd gone through Sonia's suitcase more than once, but it hadn't yielded any clues. It had only made them miss her more, picturing these same things when they'd seen them in Sonia's dresser or hanging on her hook, her bathroom things, her hairbrush. They could smell her. Their friend seemed so close. She couldn't possibly be dead, could she?

"If Joseph gives you another gift," Katie said, "accept it. Act shy. Do your dumb-cow act. And don't tell him about Sonia."

CeCe nodded. She didn't even have the energy to be angry about the dumb-cow comment, because Katie was right. She should know by now that Katie saw everything. She didn't have to put up the act when they were in 3C; that was why they were friends.

She took the stairs down and crossed the common to the dining hall, where the familiar tables were set up. This close to Christmas, very few families visited; most girls got a visit home during the holidays, at least briefly, which made the December visit extraneous. *You wouldn't want to see your daughters too much,* CeCe thought with unfamiliar bitterness. *How awful that would be, especially when you took the trouble to send them away.*

Mrs. Peabody sat in the corner, yawning and reading a book; she was the assigned supervisor today. Jenny White sat with her parents, the three of them looking quiet and awkward, Jenny looking desperately out the window. Alison Garner was sitting with her mother, who was heavily pregnant and held a toddler in her lap, a little boy who crowed, opening and closing his hands, as he leaned toward his big sister.

And in the corner of the room, by the windows, stood Mary Hand.

CeCe stopped, frozen, her breath in her throat. Mary wore her dress and veil, and stood with her hands dangling. CeCe could feel the girl's stare through the impenetrable black of the veil, imagined Mary's thin, bony face, which no one had ever seen. Her bladder clenched and her palms turned to ice. Her face prickled with the numbness of terror.

Mary moved. She took a step forward, and then another, walking across the room toward CeCe. Around them, nothing happened: Mrs. Peabody turned a page; Jenny looked out the window; Alison's little brother cooed. *Run, everyone!* CeCe wanted to scream. *Run!* But she realized, as Mary took another step, that none of them could see.

She's come for me, she thought. *Just like she did in the bath.* She'd managed to scream in the bath, managed to push her face out of the water and make so much noise that every girl on the floor had come running. But now, with Mary walking across the room toward her, she couldn't make a sound.

Mary's dress moved as she walked, and inside CeCe's head, deep in her brain, she heard a voice: *My baby. My little girl.*

Her mouth fell open helplessly, sound dying in her throat. She glanced past Mary to the window behind her. Of course: the garden. That was why Mary was by the window. Because her baby was buried in the garden.

Someone help me, please, she thought.

My little girl, Mary said, coming closer. CeCe could see the ruched fabric of her old-fashioned dress, the bony remnants of her hands dangling at her sides. *Darling. Darling . . .*

Finally, CeCe screamed.

The sound was so loud, the blood rushing so viciously in her ears, that she barely heard the room's reaction: the scraping of a chair, the exclamation from the teacher, the frightened screeching of the baby. She opened her mouth and let the scream out until it rubbed her throat raw. Warmth trickled down her leg, and she realized vaguely that her bladder had let go. Hands grabbed her, and Mrs. Peabody was shaking her, her voice coming from far away. "Cecelia! Cecelia!"

Cold air slapped CeCe's face, an angry, icy draft. CeCe blinked, turned her head, and stared again.

Mary Hand was gone.

In her place stood a woman. It took a long, agonized second before CeCe recognized her own mother, wearing a dress of winter wool, her coat buttoned to the throat, a scarf around her neck, her usual handbag in her hand. Her hair was tied back as it always was, and a look of frightened concern was on her thin, lined face.

"Darling!" she cried. "Darling!"

The hands in the bathtub, pushing her down.

Her mother's hands, holding her under the water, the salty ocean filling CeCe's eyes and nose and lungs as she struggled to move.

Mary knew everything. Mary saw everything. *Everything.* Even the things you didn't say to yourself, deep in your own mind, ever.

Mary knew the truth, and when she appeared, she

showed it to you. Even when the truth was that your own mother wanted to kill you. That your own mother had already tried. That even though you'd blocked it out, deep down you'd always known.

This was what had happened to Sonia. *This* was what she'd seen when she'd gotten off the bus. She'd seen Mary, and, behind the mask of Mary, the person who would kill her. Just like CeCe had. And Sonia had run, as long and as fast as she could, dropping her suitcase. Except she hadn't run fast or long enough.

CeCe looked at her mother's shocked face, felt the puddle growing on the floor beneath her, listened to the baby scream, and started to cry.

chapter 31

Garrett drove in silence as his car bumped down the drive and onto Old Barrons Road. Fiona leaned back against the seat, pain throbbing up the back of her neck into her skull. Despite the blast of the heater, her hands and feet couldn't get warm.

"What did Lionel say to you?" Garrett said after a minute.

"What?" Fiona managed.

"You know he's an old druggie, right?" Garrett said. "Him and his son both. His son blew his brains out—with coke, but he blew his brains out just the same. Lionel has pulled this 'recovering' bullshit for thirty years, but I know better. Do you understand?"

"He seemed honest to me," Fiona said.

"He's a liar," Garrett said, and she felt him turn toward her. "Fiona, you have to tell me what he said to you. Right now."

She would never forget it as long as she lived. "He said you were in the car with Tim Christopher the night my sister died," she said. "That it was your car." She looked around. Not this car, no. It wasn't this car. Garrett had been a cop then, and it had been a cruiser. "That was why no one saw Tim's car that night," she said, the words forming slowly. "They saw a cop car instead. But that doesn't make sense, because you didn't kill Deb."

"Of course I didn't kill your sister," Garrett said.

"Tim did," Fiona said, repeating it to herself, because this was the truth—despite everything, despite twenty years of searching and doubting, despite the confusion and the pain, despite what felt like hot pokers inserted into her brain, this was the truth that had not changed. She rearranged the facts, and then, in a brief flash, her mind worked and she understood. "All that talk about Tim being railroaded was bullshit. Tim killed her, but it was you who helped him clean it up. Just like you did with Helen Heyer."

Garrett sighed. "It was a long time ago, Fiona," he said, as if she were bringing up some petty grievance. "Twenty goddamned years."

"What was it?" Fiona asked him. Fear was in her throat, on the back of her tongue. She should never have gotten in the car with him. She should run, but the car was moving. He sat with his hands on the wheel, navigating them over the bumpy back road, and he didn't even look angry. "What was the agreement? Tim killed girls, and then he called you to clean it up for him?"

"Believe me, I didn't like playing janitor," Garrett said, "but it had to be done. The Christophers were important people around here. Good people. Tim had a great future. I did favors for them; they did favors for me. That's how it works. They had a lot of pull, and if I didn't help, they'd have replaced me with someone who would. I couldn't exactly turn them down. And in the end, it didn't even work, did it? All that risk, all that danger to cover him up, and Tim has been in prison for two decades." He sounded disgusted. "I risked everything—my career, everything. And just because he got sloppy, they blamed me. After everything I did for them, for Tim. I thought we were friends, colleagues—family, even. They felt more like family than my own wife and son. But Tim screwed up, and suddenly if any of it had come out in court, they'd have hung me out to dry without a second thought. That's what happens when you deal with certain types of people, Fiona. They use you, and they don't thank you. They just get what they want from you for as long as they can."

Fiona stared at him as his words washed over her in waves. "What do you mean, he got sloppy?"

He glanced at her. "I guess I shouldn't have said that, since she was your sister. I'm just trying to be straight with you here. And I need you to be straight with me."

She felt like screaming. "What do you mean, *he got sloppy?*"

"Calm down. I'm not talking about a serial killer here. He had a temper, that's all, and some girls made him mad. Helen . . . I couldn't do anything about Helen, but no one had ever seen him with her, so it was easy to drop

it." He glanced at Fiona again. "But your sister—I knew
from the minute they called me that Tim was done. Her
father was a journalist, for God's sake. Everyone had seen
them fighting, had seen her get in his car. Tim called me
and said she'd made him mad, it had gone too far, and I
had to help him fix it. Someone would be looking for her
soon. I had to think fast, and I didn't have a lot of op-
tions. We had no chance to take her over the state line."

Deb, Fiona thought. *My God, Deb.*

"The Christophers owned Idlewild then," Garrett
went on. "I thought we'd dump her there, quick, and I'd
be able to go back later and do it proper without attract-
ing any suspicion. It was the only thing I could think of
to do. So we moved the body from Tim's car to my
cruiser, and while he dumped her, I distracted Lionel
and the kids at the drive-in. I told Tim to hide her in the
trees, but the idiot had to put her in the middle of the
field like she was a goddamned display. A rush job—he
just dropped her and ran, even after I told him not to.
How stupid can you be?"

Deb, lying in that field, her shirt ripped open. Dropped
like trash in the middle of the field, waiting to be seen.
Mary Hand, Mary Hand, dead and buried under land . . .
Fiona's head hurt so much.

"It was a goddamned clusterfuck," Garrett Creel went
on. "She wouldn't have been found so fast if she wasn't
in the field, and I would have had the chance to move
her. But someone found her. I had to clean it all up—
everything. I had to make sure his footprints were erased
when we searched for evidence in the trees."

"Richard Rush," Fiona said, remembering the man who owned Pop's Ice Cream. "He saw Tim at four o'clock in the afternoon. But you told him to say he saw Tim at nine."

"Fuck him," Garrett spit, angry now. "His shop was in debt, and I promised he'd be square if he did what I said. Instead, he bailed out on me when he realized he'd be called as a witness at trial. Said he wouldn't commit perjury because of his kids. That was Tim's best chance at reasonable doubt, flushed straight down the toilet."

So many details. So many. Garrett had thought of them all. "The kids at the drive-in," she said. "They saw you that night. You came and lectured them while Tim dumped the body."

"That was easier. I tracked them down and told them that if they said anything about seeing me, I'd pin them on drug charges. Underage drinking. I wore my uniform when I sat them down, and I brought another cop with me. Intimidating as hell. Every one of them shit their pants and shut up. Lionel was tougher, but I just threatened to burn down his fucking business, because I knew he didn't have a penny of insurance. And in the end, you know what? Tim went to jail anyway." He glanced at her, his gaze furious, his face red. "People are so stupid, don't you see? Maybe I sound crazy, but for thirty years it was just *so goddamned easy*. Nothing ever came back on me— not once. What is it with people? Why don't they see?"

Fiona looked out the window. They weren't driving back into town; they had turned onto another side road, past the south end of Idlewild.

"Even my own son," Garrett said. His neck was flushed red where it emerged from his parka, and his hands were tight on the wheel. "I always wanted Jamie to be a cop, but he wasn't on the force a year before I realized he wasn't going to be like me. I did my best to raise him right, but he doesn't have the instincts I do. He isn't hard enough. He still thinks he can do right by everyone. Tim had brains and guts, at least until that last night. Until that night, I always thought Tim should have been my son instead of Jamie."

Jamie knows about Helen, Fiona almost said, but she stopped herself. She didn't think Garrett knew yet that Jamie had pulled the Helen Heyer file, that he'd seen a shoddy investigation under his father's name. "Let me out of the car."

"Oh, I don't think so," Garrett said. "You haven't been listening. My son dating a journalist, Malcolm Sheridan's daughter, Deb Sheridan's sister—it isn't going to happen. You're too close. I thought you'd flake out and leave him, let him find a nice girl, but you didn't take your chance. And now look what you've put your nose into, of all things. After twenty fucking years, you could ruin everything for me, for the whole force. For Barrons, because you just can't quit. Jamie will never have the goddamned guts to get rid of you, but I do."

Terror bloomed in Fiona's agonized brain, yet above it she was strangely calm. He was going to kill her; he thought it was the only way to keep his secrets. He needed no other reason. Maybe he'd killed before; she didn't know, and it didn't matter. He was going to kill her now. She could beg and plead and reason, but it wouldn't work. He'd chosen a course, and he was going to follow it. That was reality, right now.

She unsnapped her seat belt, opened the car door, and jumped before she could form another thought.

The road was so rutted that the car wasn't going very fast. She landed hard on her shoulder, the gravel ripping through her winter coat and the knee of her jeans. Her palms were scraped raw, and she rolled wildly into the ditch on the side of the road, thick with wet leaves and ice-crusted mud. She heard the car swerve to a stop, and she got up, climbed out of the ditch, and started to run.

The sky overhead was dark, looming gray, the trees stark black against it. She was on the edge of an open field, and even in the depths of her fever, fear, and pain, she knew instinctively that Idlewild was a mile in this direction and town was the other way. She took off across the field as fast as she could, her boots digging into the soft, half-frozen earth. She could try for the gas station at the top of the hill, but Idlewild was closer, and she remembered seeing workers there when she'd driven past it, machines moving.

He caught her quickly; he was bigger than she was, stronger, his legs longer. He drove her to the ground and jammed his knee into her stomach, his face looming over her. "I knew you would do this!" he shouted at her, his face red, his features distorted with rage. "I knew it!" He put his hands on her throat and squeezed.

Fiona bucked beneath him, trying to get away, but he was so much bigger, so much stronger. Spots bloomed behind her eyes. She beat at him with her fists and stared past his shoulder, where crows wheeled in a sky dark with falling snow, and thought, *I'm not going to die like Deb. I'm not.*

She twisted her hips beneath him and brought her knee up hard into his stomach. When he grunted and his grip on her neck slipped, she kicked him again. And again.

He reared back to hit her, and she smashed a hand into his face, scratching at his eyes. He cursed and his weight slipped, and she scrambled out from under him and ran.

It took him longer to get up—she didn't look back to see why. Gasping for breath, her throat on fire, she sprinted as hard as she could in the direction of Idlewild, adrenaline giving her a burst of speed. The ground was hard and uneven, her boots kicking through tangles of dead weeds, but for once she didn't put a step wrong. She just ran and ran.

By the time she got to the cover of the trees, her chest was on fire, her legs weak. She could hear him shouting behind her, his voice echoing off into the open sky, but she couldn't make out the words. Then, with a chime of terror, she heard the car's engine. He was going to cut her off when she got to Old Barrons Road, and he wouldn't have to do it on foot.

Fiona called up the map in her head. She knew every part of this place, every foot of the terrain. She ran past the trees and down through a steep ditch, the bottom soaked with deep frozen mud, and scrambled up the other side, fighting her way through the undergrowth. Her hands were icy cold—she'd lost her gloves somewhere; she had no memory of it—and her throat burned, but ahead she saw the south end of the fence that bordered the Idlewild property, at the far end of the sports field. She climbed the fence, her numb fingers trying to slip on the chain links, and swung herself over.

She put her hands on her knees and gasped for breath, like an Olympic sprinter. Her head and neck were alive with pain, the aching so awful it throbbed through her jaw and the roots of her teeth. Saliva filled her mouth, and she spit on the ground, hoping she wouldn't throw up. Garrett would drive back up Old Barrons Road; that meant he planned to either climb the fence or get in through the front gates if he could. The gates were sealed with Anthony Eden's fancy new automatic lock, but Fiona had no illusions that Garrett, who was still fit at sixty, couldn't climb a fence. Still, it would take him precious minutes. She had to use them.

She started across the field at a quick jog, her legs protesting. The wind blew hard, stinging her ears and her neck, and after a minute she wasn't even surprised to see the detritus of mourning at her feet—the cheap flowers and handwritten notes she'd seen before. *This isn't her place,* Lionel had said of the drive-in, but here in Idlewild—this was Mary's place. This was where she walked. Fiona knew she was nearby the same way she knew that the crows were overhead and that Garrett Creel was on Old Barrons Road.

"I'm here," she said to Mary Hand, and kept running.

chapter 32

It was easier to ignore the flowers and the cards this time. Easier to watch her boots scuffle through them and kick them aside as she made her way across the field. Now that she knew what Mary was. But the fear didn't go away. *We were all so horribly afraid,* Sarah London had said, but Fiona understood now. That Sarah London had spent thirty years in this place, with this fear. That the girls had lived with it. That Sonia had lived with it, and yet she had come running back, fleeing her killer, dropping her suitcase in the trees. Just like Fiona was running back now.

This place, she thought. *This place.*

The garbage underfoot fell away and she passed the gymnasium, approaching the main building with its rows of teeth. *Come back,* it seemed to say to her, grinning in anticipation. *Come back here as you always have. As you always do. As you always will, over and over. Come back.* She ran toward it without question, drawn to its grinning face.

A backhoe was parked in the gravel in front of the main hall, and a pickup truck was parked next to it, but she saw no sign of workers. Whoever it was she had glimpsed before was gone. She shouted, but her voice was only a hoarse whisper, blown away by the wind. She'd seen vehicles here earlier, movement; she was sure of it. Where had they gone?

The big black front gates were locked; there was no sign of a security guard. Had Garrett already come and gone, finding no way in? How much time had passed? She had no idea, but when she heard a car's engine approaching from the road, she decided not to chance it. She turned and ran to the front door of the main building, trying to call for help over and over.

The front door of the main hall was locked. Fiona stared at the keypad next to it, blinking stupidly, trying to remember the code she'd seen Anthony punch in. She'd watched him do it, watched his fingers move over the keys—if only she could remember. She pulled the memory dimly from her brain and punched in a number combination, her surprise muffled with pain when the light went green and the door clicked open.

She slipped inside, closing the door behind her. A car's engine could be heard faintly outside, and she walked hurriedly across the high-ceilinged main hall, her boots scuffing on the dusty floor. Her breath frosted on the air, and there was no sound in here except a rustling in the rafters—birds or bats.

How did anyone ever learn in this place? she wondered as she walked to the bottom of the main staircase. She stared up at the balconies above, spinning away from the staircase like a wheel, and her head throbbed. She pictured Roberta Greene here, the young teenager with a braid down her back, wearing the Idlewild uniform from the photographs. Going up and down these stairs, textbooks under her arm, her head down. Wondering when she'd encounter the resident ghost. *She's an echo*, Roberta had said.

Fiona put a foot on the bottom step, thinking to go upstairs and look for the work crews from the windows, but something stopped her. She turned.

A girl stood in the shadows of the west end of the hall, watching her. She was small and slight, her face in shadow. She wore a green-and-blue-plaid skirt and a white blouse. The Idlewild uniform.

Fiona's breath stopped. She stood half-turned, her foot still on the step, as the wind blew outside and howled through a hole somewhere in the roof. Dead leaves rustled across the hall's abandoned floor.

She looked at the girl's uniform, her size, and even though she'd never seen a photograph, she suddenly knew.

"Sonia?" she said, her voice a hoarse croak.

The girl didn't move.

Slowly, Fiona lifted her foot from the step and backed away from the staircase. She walked toward the girl.

"Sonia?" she said again.

As she got closer, she could see the girl's face in the shadows. She had a high forehead, clear gray eyes, a small and straight nose. Lips that were narrow and well formed. A face long and heart-shaped, with a chin as clean as a sculpture's, on a neck that was long and elegant. Her hair was mousy blond, thin and flat, shoulder length, pulled back from her forehead with bobby pins. An average-looking girl, with a quiet sweetness and dignity about her, who would someday grow up to be a pretty, strong-featured woman with wisdom in her eyes. Except that she wouldn't, because she'd never make it past fifteen.

She was as real, in that moment, as if she was truly standing there. She watched Fiona come closer, her expression inscrutable, and then she turned and walked into the shadows.

She's leading me, Fiona thought.

She followed. This was the same back corridor Anthony Eden had led her through on their tour, so long ago now. It led, Fiona remembered, to a back door to the common.

From behind her, she heard the front door rattle as someone tried to open it.

She moved quickly. Sonia was gone; maybe she had given the message she wanted to give. Fiona found the back door and pushed it open, just as she heard the front door rattle again far behind her. She slipped out onto the common and eased it closed behind her.

Where to now, Sonia?

The cold air hit her, and she shivered uncontrollably for a second, her body shaking inside her coat, her teeth chattering. *Quiet, be quiet. Don't make a noise.* Sonia was on the far side of the common, walking toward a building Anthony hadn't taken her to last time. She searched her mind for what he'd told her it was. The dorm.

She hurried across the quad after the girl, shaking away the persistent idea that this was madness. It didn't feel like madness. Her throat hurt where Jamie's father had tried to strangle her to death. As flakes of snow hit her hair and her eyelashes, *that* was what felt like madness. This felt sane.

Halfway across the common, she looked back. In one of the windows of the main building there was a silhouette watching her: a slim girl in a black dress, a veil over her face.

Mary Hand, Mary Hand, dead and buried under land . . .

Good Night Girl.

Fiona turned and ran faster.

The dorm building, unlike the others, was unlocked, for the simple reason that the front door was broken. It had been forced off its hinges at some point, the wood rotten, an unintelligible graffiti sign sprayed on the front. Since the restoration had begun, the door had been propped back in place, kept shut by a piece of wood nailed into it and across the doorframe. The wood of the frame was so rotted that Fiona pried the board from it easily, the wood splintering like butter beneath her hands.

She pushed the door open and walked into a building that had obviously been broken into at least once since the school had closed. Broken bottles, splintered glass, cigarette butts, and even worse garbage littered the floor. An old sleeping bag, crusted with something unspeakable, lay in the corner, shredded nearly to pieces by mice over the years. Charred marks on the floor spoke of at least one fire lit in here. Fiona was grateful when she saw Sonia's shadow flit at the top of the stairs, and she quickly moved past it all and started up.

She was nearly at the top when she heard the gunfire.

It was so sudden that Fiona's knees buckled, and she drooped clumsily on the stairwell, gripping the railing. There was one shot, then another, then two in quick succession. They came from somewhere close outside. The sharp cracks reverberated through her aching head, and she opened her mouth to scream, but nothing came from her tortured throat.

Her vision blurred for a minute, and when she realized the shots had stopped, she pulled herself upward again, her shoulders aching. There was no more sound from outside. *Quiet, be quiet. Hide.* She hadn't known Garrett was armed. It was strange that he'd fired shots outside, and not at her. Maybe he was shooting at Mary.

She moved as quietly as she could down the corridor, blinking in the gloom, looking for Sonia. She saw the girl move through a doorway, silent as a shadow, and followed. The door had a number in cracked, faded paint: 3C.

She was in a bedroom. There had been beds in here once—two sets of bunks, by the looks of it—but they were long destroyed, the mattresses gone, the frames splintered and dismantled. An old dresser lay on its side against one wall. The room was musty and smelled like spilled beer and old, cold urine. It had been defaced and defiled and forgotten, but Fiona knew it had been Sonia's room. That was why Sonia had come through the door.

If it had been Sonia's room, then it was the room she'd shared with Katie Winthrop, Roberta Greene, and CeCe Frank. Shivering, Fiona sank to the floor and closed her eyes. This was the room they'd lived in, slept in. She pictured them, though she had no idea what Katie or CeCe looked like, wearing their uniforms, talking and teasing one another and arguing and whispering secrets at night the way girls did. She wondered what secrets had been whispered in this room. She wondered if this was where the girls had felt safe.

She couldn't run anymore. She was too tired. Shaking with cold, she lay on the ground, hoping Garrett wouldn't find her.

Fiona didn't know she'd drifted off until she opened her eyes. She was looking at the ceiling of the bedroom, but the dark stains in the plaster were gone. The smell of beer and piss was gone. She could hear the wind moaning through the room's only window, but no other sounds. Her body ached too much to sit up, but she turned her head and saw that the bunks were in place, the beds neatly made with green-and-blue-plaid wool blankets over them. A hockey stick leaned against one wall. There was a single wooden chair by the window, and a girl sat in it, her face turned toward the glass. She moved, and Fiona heard a gasping sob come from her throat.

It was Deb.

She wore the clothes she'd worn the day she was murdered. Her gray raincoat was belted around her narrow waist, though the black knit hat she'd worn when Tim Christopher picked her up was gone. It hadn't been on her body, and it had never been found. Deb's dark hair was pulled back into a loose ponytail, secured at the back of her neck. She looked at Fiona from gray-blue eyes Fiona hadn't seen in twenty years.

"Don't let her in," Deb said.

Fiona lifted her head from the floor. "Deb," she said.

Deb turned back to the window. "She'll ask," she said. Her voice was reedy, as if heard through the blast of a windstorm. "She'll beg. She sounds so pitiful. Don't let her in."

I'm hallucinating, Fiona thought, but part of her didn't care. Her sister was beautiful, sitting there with her legs in their dark green pants crossed at the ankles, her feet in the sneakers she'd worn on her date with Tim Christopher. She was quietly, painfully beautiful, forever twenty years old. Her body, dead on the field outside, had still worn those shoes.

"Deb," Fiona said again, scrambling to get words out. "Are you all right?"

"No," Deb said, still looking out the window.

Fiona pushed herself up on her elbows. "Are you always here?"

Her sister was quiet for a moment, and then she answered, "Sometimes." She sounded softly confused. "It's all so strange. Like a dream, don't you think?" She turned and pinned Fiona with her gray-blue gaze again. "Please don't let her in."

"Is it Mary?" Fiona rasped.

"It gets so cold out there." Deb looked back out the window. "She sounds so sad."

Fiona opened her mouth again, trying to get Deb's attention. She had so much to say, to ask, but her sister couldn't hear. Voices and shouts came from outside. She blinked and the room wavered. *No,* she thought. *No.* She tried to heave herself up—to touch Deb perhaps, to grab her—but her body wouldn't cooperate. She tried clumsily to get her knees beneath her, realizing her hands were numb. "No," she rasped out loud.

The voices sounded again, closer this time. Shouts. Fiona's leg gave from under her, and she fell to the floor, landing softly on her shoulder, trying to get her arm beneath her. She blinked as the room wavered again.

"I was so afraid," Deb said.

And then the room went back again, to the abandoned shell with its sticks of furniture and awful smell. Fiona lay on her side as tears coursed down her face, cold against her skin. Her teeth chattered.

There was the shuffle of fabric, the rustle of a dress in the room.

Fiona tried to close her eyes, and couldn't.

The hem of a black dress came into her line of vision. It moved through the door of the bedroom as Mary Hand came inside. Fiona curled her knees up against her chest, unable to move, unable to scream. Unable to run. There was nowhere to go.

"I didn't let her in," she whispered to herself. "I didn't."

The hem of the black dress swept the dirty floor, the fabric so real Fiona could see the sheen of the thick black silk. Then Mary came toward her, her feet ghastly and visible below the dress's hem. They were bare, icy white and blue with cold. Thin skin stretched over bones.

Mary took one step, and then another. Fiona screamed, the sound nothing but air forced high from her throat. Then she screamed again.

There was a shout, and someone came through the door. Two people, three. Men. Voices rang through the room. Hands touched her.

Fiona turned her head and saw that Mary was gone.

She closed her eyes and let them take her.

chapter 33

It hurt. Everything did. The world came and went—voices, sounds, hands, hot and cold. Fiona's head was like an overblown balloon, a deafening pounding in her temples. She opened her eyes and saw an unfamiliar ceiling, heard an unfamiliar voice. She closed them again.

She woke and realized she was in a hospital bed. It was the middle of the night, and she was alone. She was painfully thirsty. Someone far down the corridor was talking in a low voice, then laughing quietly. *She can't get me here,* Fiona thought with a hot wash of relief, and then she fell asleep again.

When she woke again, her father was there.

Her head was a little clearer this time. Weak sunlight came through the window; it was day, then. Malcolm was sitting in a chair next to her bed, wearing a short-sleeved button-down checked shirt, faded cargo pants, socks, and sandals. A pair of black rubber boots sat by the doorway—he always wore rubber boots in winter, then sandals inside the house. His longish gray-brown hair was tangled and tucked behind his ears, and he wore his half-glasses as he read the newspaper in his lap. He hadn't noticed she was awake yet.

Fiona stared at him for a long moment, taking in every detail of him. "Dad," she said finally, breaking the spell.

He lowered the paper and looked up at her over the tops of his glasses, his face relaxing with pleasure. "Fee," he said, smiling.

She smiled back at him, though her throat hurt and her lips were cracked. "Am I okay?" she asked him.

"Well." He folded the newspaper and put it down. "You have a lovely case of the flu, mixed with hypothermia, and frostbite was a close call. Plus the bruising on your neck. But they say you'll be fine."

She struggled into a sitting position, and he helped her, handing her a glass of water from the bedside table. "What happened?"

"You called me," Malcolm said, smoothing her hair. "Remember?"

She did, though her memories were disjointed, out of order. "I wanted to tell you about Stephen Heyer."

"Right." He smoothed her hair again. "You left me a long message. I listened to it when I got home from the grocery store. I could tell something was wrong, but I didn't know what the hell to do. While I was pondering it, my phone rang again. This time, it was Lionel Charters."

Fiona put down the water glass. Her hand was shaky, but she focused on keeping the glass upright. "Lionel phoned you?"

"It was the strangest thing," Malcolm said. "I've known who he is for years, of course. You know he runs a kind of informal rehab center in his old trailer? Lionel's son died of an overdose, and ever since then, he's let addicts stay with him while they try to dry out. It doesn't always work. They do drugs out there, and they deal, and sometimes there's trouble. But Lionel's intentions are good."

Fiona just sat, listening to his voice as he stroked her hair. *He's an old druggie,* she heard Garrett Creel say. *His son blew his brains out with coke.* She had so much to say, so many questions to ask. But Malcolm was telling the story, and she was so tired, drifting on his voice. Once Malcolm was on his track, there was no distracting him.

"Lionel is no friend of the media," Malcolm continued, "but he hates the police more. So he called me and said my daughter had just been on his property, looking for Stephen Heyer. That you seemed sick. He said Garrett Creel drove up, and pushed you into his car with him, and he drove off."

"He told me . . . " Fiona said, then drummed up her strength. "He was at the drive-in the night Deb died. He told me . . ."

"I know what he told you," Malcolm said. "I know what Lionel saw."

She tried to swallow hard in her rasping throat. "You knew? About Garrett's cruiser being there?"

Her father's hand had stopped stroking her hair. It

had gone stiff and tense and still. He looked past her at the wall, his eyes unreadable. "No," he said, his voice deceptively calm. "But I know now."

He looked, for a second, like the stranger who had been at Tim Christopher's trial, the stranger who had sleep-walked through her parents' divorce. But then his face softened into mere sadness. Fiona wanted to say some-thing, anything. "Dad," she managed.

"Lionel let you get into that car," her father said.

She couldn't tell if it was a question. "He was aiming his gun," she said. "But he couldn't shoot."

"He told me that, too," Malcolm said. "I told him he should have tried harder. Then I hung up on him and called Jamie."

Fiona thought of Jamie's father, his knee in her stom-ach, his breath in her face. *I knew you would do this.* His hands on her throat. She must have tensed, because Malcolm smoothed her hair again.

"Where is he?" Fiona said. "Where is Garrett?"

"At the moment?" Malcolm said. "I can't quite pin-point. Likely a holding cell. Or maybe he's talking to his lawyer." He patted her shoulder as she leaned into him in relief. "Jamie couldn't reach his father," he said, continu-ing the story, "and he couldn't reach you. So he got backup and drove to Lionel's place. He found his father's car parked outside the Idlewild gates." He sighed. "I didn't go with him, so I only heard secondhand. But from what I know, they went inside, and Garrett shot at them."

"What?" Fiona said, pulling away from him and sit-ting up. Her head spun.

"Hush, Fee," Malcolm said. "The shot nicked Jamie's hand, but that's all."

"I didn't know he had a gun," Fiona said. Garrett must have had it stowed in the car somewhere, probably the trunk, which was why he hadn't used it on her. "Is Jamie okay?"

"He's fine," her father said. "They had to return fire, but no one was hurt. They found you, in one of the bedrooms of the old dorm, calling for help before you passed out on the floor, with his hand marks on your neck. They arrested Garrett. And here we are."

She was shaking; she should call the nurse. They must have her on some kind of medication, something for the pain and the inflammation. She was so tired. "He tried to kill me," she said. "He tried to strangle me in the field off one of the back roads. He was going to kill me and dump me."

"I know," Malcolm said. "The doctors examined your neck. Garrett hasn't talked, but the police will come to take your statement."

"He covered up for Tim. With Helen." The words were jumbling in her head, but she felt the urgency, the importance of getting them out before she sank into sleep again.

"I know, honey," her father said again.

You're going to kill him, Jamie had said. There was no going back. Not from knowing that Tim could have been stopped before he ever met Deb. "I'm so sorry, Dad," she said.

He blinked and looked down at her. "For what?" he asked.

"I shouldn't have gone." The words coming up through her pained throat. "I should have left it alone. But I thought—I started to wonder whether it was possible that Tim hadn't done it. Whether it was possible that whoever had killed Deb was still out there." She felt tears on her face. She remembered Deb, sitting in the chair by the window, but she couldn't tell him about that. She wasn't even sure it was real. "I kept going over the case and I couldn't stop. I couldn't stop."

Malcolm looked thoughtful, and then he stroked her hair again. "You were seventeen when it happened," he said. "You had questions." He sighed. "I didn't have the answers, and neither did your mother. We couldn't even answer our own questions. I'm afraid, Fee, that we left you to deal with all of it alone."

"That isn't it." She was crying now, the sobs coming up through her chest as she heard Deb say, *I was so scared*. She pressed her face into his checked shirt, smelling his old-school aftershave and the cedar smell of the old drawer he'd pulled his undershirt from. "I should have just left it. I'm just so sorry."

He let her cry for a while, and she felt him drop a kiss to her temple. "Well, now," he said, and she heard the grief in his voice, but she also heard Malcolm Sheridan. Always Malcolm Sheridan. "That isn't the way I raised you, is it? To leave things be. It's just you and me left, Fee. That isn't how we wanted it, but that's how it is. And you're my daughter." He let her tears soak into his shirt as her sobbing stopped, and then he spoke again. "Besides, Helen's family never had an arrest, a conviction, like we did. We can fix that, and we will." He kissed her again. "Get some sleep. We're going to be busy."

She wanted to say something else, but her eyelids felt like sandpaper, and she closed her eyes. Sleep took her before she could speak.

The world was disjointed for a while, images passing by like dreams. She had a long, vivid dream of running across the field toward the trees, the dead brush scraping her shins, her breath bursting in her chest, as Garrett ran after her. Crows called in the stark sky overhead. Fiona jerked awake over and over, disoriented, before falling back into the same dream again. She had another dream of waking to the sight of her hand in Jamie's, lying on the bed. His hand was bandaged, her fingers curled around it. She was aware of him, could see the familiar strong bones of his hand, the lines of his forearm, but she did not look up to see his face before falling asleep again.

The fever broke sometime the next day, and she sat up in the bed, sweaty and weary, drinking apple juice, as the police took her statement. Malcolm sat in the back corner of the room, listening, his sandals on over his socks, his newspaper folded on his lap.

She did not hear from Margaret Eden, but she heard from Anthony. When she was well enough to get her cell phone back from her father ("What do you need that thing for?"), she answered his call. He told her he was sorry, and he asked if there was anything he could do.

She had the beginning of an idea, an itch at the back of her mind, and she asked Anthony a question. The answer he gave her put all the pieces together, and she realized it had been in front of her all along.

She had her answers now.

She would go to the Idlewild girls as soon as she was well again. But she had a suspicion that they'd come to her first.

chapter 34

Katie

Barrons, Vermont
April 1951

This was going to work.

There was never a doubt in Katie's mind. Still, she could feel the tense anticipation from the other girls in Clayton 3C. Roberta sat in the chair by the window, pretending to study from a textbook. CeCe pulled off her uniform and put on her nightgown, even though it was only just past lunchtime. She yanked the pins from her hair and scrubbed her hand through it, making it messy.

For her part, Katie straightened her stockings and her skirt. She polished her black shoes to a shine and put them on. She added wadded Kleenex to her bra, then put on her cleanest white blouse, adjusting it so that the fabric stretched just slightly over her enhanced chest. She pulled a cardigan with the Idlewild crest over the blouse and buttoned it demurely to her neck.

CeCe pulled off her shoes and stockings, sitting on the edge of the bed. "I really don't know about this," she said. Her cheeks were pale. *Good*, Katie thought. *That makes it more believable.*

It was Roberta who answered. "Just follow the plan," she said, bending her head to the textbook. In the five months since Sonia had disappeared—since she had died, since she had been killed; they all knew she had been killed—Roberta had gone waxy and hard, rarely smiling, never laughing. Her grades didn't falter, and she played better than ever on the hockey field, but the change was clear to Katie. Roberta had taken her grief and her anger and buried it, let it sink into her bones. She looked less like a girl now and more like a grown woman, and she had become fierce. Katie loved her more than ever.

"You know I'm no good at these things," CeCe said, pushing the covers back on her bed and obediently sliding into it. "When Katie cheated on that test, I nearly passed out."

Katie leaned toward the room's only mirror, smoothing and adjusting her hair, and watched the corner of her mouth turn up. CeCe always got cold feet, but she always did as well as the rest of them. "You were perfect," she said to CeCe, "and you know it."

CeCe flushed; praise from Katie always pleased her, even after all this time. Still, she had to whine a little. "This feels like lying."

"It isn't lying." Roberta looked up from her book and directed her gaze at CeCe, lying in the bed. "We talked about this for months. It isn't lying if it's making someone happy. If it's making all of us happy."

CeCe bit her lip and looked back at Roberta. "Not Katie," she argued. "She doesn't get to be happy."

So that was what was bothering her. Katie should have known. She laughed, touched despite herself. "I'll be happiest of all," she said. It wasn't a lie, not completely; her heart was pounding in anticipation and a queer kind of excitement. She was ready. Was that the same as happy? She didn't know, and in this moment she didn't particularly care. She had just turned sixteen. What mattered was that she got what she wanted.

"It'll be fine," Roberta said, her voice flat.

"If it works," CeCe said.

Katie leaned closer to the mirror, smoothing her eyebrows and lightly biting her lips. They weren't allowed makeup at Idlewild—absolutely not—and part of her wished she had some, at least some dark eyeliner and mascara like she'd seen on movie stars, but she was afraid it would look too obvious. She definitely needed to look like a schoolgirl. "It'll work," she said.

CeCe lay back in the bed, pulling the covers up over her ample chest. Katie caught Roberta's gaze in the mirror's reflection, and they traded a look of understanding.

I'm going to do this.

Yes, you are, and we both know why.

It's going to work. I'm going to make it.

Roberta's gaze softened, the lines around her eyes easing, and she smiled at Katie in the mirror.

There was a knock on the door. "Ladies!" Lady Loon said. "It's Family Visit Day. Cecelia, you have a visitor."

Katie smoothed her expression into one of concern and opened the door. "Oh, no, Miss London," she said. "Are you sure?"

Lady Loon looked frazzled, tendrils of hair escaping from the bun on top of her head. "Of course I'm sure, Katie," she said. "What's the matter?"

"It's just that CeCe isn't feeling very well."

Katie stepped back, and Lady Loon stepped into the room, looking at CeCe on the bed. CeCe moaned a little. She looked positively green, probably from terror, which added to the effect.

"What is the matter?" Lady Loon asked her.

"Oh," CeCe said, licking her lips as if they were dry. "It's my stomach, Miss London. Is it my father who has come to see me?"

Lady Loon clenched her hands, her knuckles going white. "No, it's—your brother, I believe." She hated saying the words, Katie could see, keeping her face straight. Lady Loon did not like referring to CeCe's bastard status, or her brother's, which was what they wanted.

"Oh, no," CeCe groaned, quite believably. "He came all this way. I can't. I just can't."

"It's very rude to turn him away," Roberta commented calmly from over her textbook. "Can you talk to him, Miss London?"

Lady Loon's eyes went wide. She looked positively

horrified. "Me? Ladies, *I* am certainly not going to talk to that man." *An illegitimate bastard,* she didn't say.

"He came so far," CeCe wailed again.

"Maybe one of us can go," Roberta said.

"Maybe," Katie said, as if this had just occurred to her. "Roberta, why don't you go?"

Roberta frowned. "I have a Latin test tomorrow, and I need to study."

Katie rolled her eyes. "Oh, please. Why study?"

That made Lady Loon jump, just as it was supposed to. "Of course she needs to study, Katie Winthrop," she said sharply. "And since you seem to be at leisure, you are to go speak to Cecelia's brother immediately and explain the situation to him."

"Me?" Katie put her lip out just a little, petulant. "*I* don't want to go."

"You'll do as you're told, young lady. Now go."

Katie huffed a put-upon sigh and stomped out of the room. She didn't look back.

He was sitting at a table in the dining hall, waiting. Before he noticed her, Katie took stock. He was twenty-one, according to CeCe. Dark hair slicked back. Nice suit, pressed shirt. A narrow face, gray eyes. He sat politely, no fidgeting. His hands were folded on the table in front of him, and she saw that they were elegant and masculine, the fingers long, the knuckles well formed. *Nice hands,* she thought, gathering her courage. *I can deal with a man with nice hands.*

She glanced to see that no one was looking. Then she folded the waist of her skirt with a quick twist of her wrist, making the length climb an inch above her knees, and then another. She unbuttoned the Idlewild cardigan but didn't take it off, letting it fall open just so, so that he would be able to glimpse the stretched blouse beneath. Then she squared her shoulders and walked toward him.

He was expecting CeCe, so it took him a moment to realize she was coming his way, that she was heading for him. He lifted his chin and looked at her and froze perfectly still.

Katie blinked her tilted, long-lashed eyes at him and smiled. Sweet and knowing at the same time. Abashed, as if he was having an effect on her, yet she didn't quite want it to show.

Joseph Eden watched her come toward him, and his eyes went wide, his jaw dropping open just a little as he watched her thighs move below the hem of her skirt.

"Hi there," Katie said to him, pulling up a chair and sitting across from him.

"You—" He stopped and cleared his throat. "You're not CeCe," he managed.

She smiled at him again. "No, I'm not. I'm her roommate. She's not feeling well today, but she felt terrible that you came all this way. So she sent me instead." She held out her hand and leaned across the table, letting the cardigan fall open just the right way. "My name's Katie," she said. "Katie Winthrop." When he shook her hand in his bigger one—*Nice hands,* she reminded herself—she squeezed it and leaned forward across the table. Now he'd have a hint of cleavage, hidden in the shadows of her sweater and her blouse. "I have to confess, I've always wanted to meet you," she said, lowering her voice conspiratorially.

He blinked. "Me?"

"CeCe talks about you so much." Katie let a dreamy look cross her expression. "Her wonderful brother. We're all dying of curiosity." She lowered her voice again. "Especially me."

He caught her gaze, and she saw the second his shoulders relaxed. He smiled. Hooked, but not quite reeled in. Not yet. "Well, I'm Joseph," he said. "Joseph Eden. It sure is nice of you to come and keep me company if CeCe isn't feeling well. I did come a long way."

She let his hand go and smiled again. He had a nice enough smile, lovely hands, and a good suit. And he wasn't legitimate, but he was Brad Ellesmere's only son, and would someday be his heir.

Katie was counting on it.

You make your own fate, she thought. *You build it every day. This is how it begins.*

"Well, then," she said to Joseph Eden. "We have some time to kill before you go all the way home again. I think we can entertain each other. Don't you?"

chapter 35

She had made her full statement to the police, and the doctors gave her permission to go home, so Fiona pulled clothes from the overnight bag Malcolm had brought for her and spent forty-five minutes putting them on, slowly pulling on underwear, jeans, a T-shirt, and a zip-up hoodie. The fever had broken, but she was still woozy and tired, her muscles made of melted butter. She put on socks and walked to the bathroom adjoining her hospital room, washing up the best she could. Her face in the mirror was ghostly, her skin waxen, shadows under her eyes. Her red hair looked stark under the fluorescent lights and against the pallor of her skin. She tucked it behind her ears and looked down into the sink again.

When she was finished, she walked to the bathroom door and stopped.

A woman stood in her hospital room. Small of stature, but straight of posture. Thick white hair cut short and curled. She wore a wool coat, belted at the waist, her hands in the large pockets. When Fiona made a noise in the bathroom doorway, she turned and looked at her, one eyebrow raised. It was Margaret Eden.

Fiona stared at her. She was light-headed; this felt a little surreal. She said, "What are you doing here?"

"I came to see you," Margaret said.

Even in her ill state, Fiona didn't think for a second that Margaret Eden was concerned about her health. "Why?" she asked.

Margaret stayed where she was, hands in the pockets of her expensive coat, and waited. Finally she said, "Fiona. Do we have something to talk about?"

Fiona stepped farther into the room, steadying herself on the doorjamb. "I know who you are," she said. "Who you really are."

"Do you?" The older woman seemed curious, but unconcerned.

"Yes." Fiona felt her fingers go slick against the door, cold sweat on her palms. "You're Katie Winthrop."

She hadn't known what to expect, but it wasn't the smile that spread over Margaret Eden's face, her features relaxing. Margaret turned her chin, directing her words back over her shoulder. "Girls," she said. "She knows."

Two other women came into the room. One was Roberta Greene, tall and stately, her features composed. The other, the same age as Katie and Roberta, was shorter and rounder, her eyes kind and her hair cropped close to her head. *CeCe Frank,* Fiona thought to herself, *or whatever her name is now.*

"It's nice to meet you, honey," CeCe said, taking Fiona's hand and squeezing it. "Oh, sit down. Katie, she's still ill." CeCe sighed and looked in Fiona's eyes. "She forgets about people's feelings sometimes."

Fiona turned to stare at Katie again. "The first time we met, you told me you'd never been a student at Idlewild."

Katie shrugged. "I lied," she said. "I do that sometimes. When I have to. How did you figure out it was me?"

"I've seen your Idlewild file. It has your full name— Katherine Margaret Winthrop. It didn't click at first. But I asked your son what your maiden name was, and when he said Winthrop, I knew."

That made Katie laugh. "All right, it isn't a state secret. I just don't make my past public, that's all."

"How did you do it?" Fiona asked Katie, walking to the edge of the bed and lowering herself. "How did you change your name? And why?"

Katie still stood, her hands in her pockets. *Beauty, but not the wholesome kind,* Sarah London had said of Katie Winthrop in 1950. *She was a discipline problem from the day she arrived until the day she left.* She looked down at Fiona where she sat on the bed, and in the arched brows and the determined set of her jaw, Fiona could see that girl from sixty-four years ago. "Well, I married Joseph Eden, for one," she said. "I didn't want to be Katie anymore. I wanted to leave everything behind—my family, Idlewild. Not the girls, of course. But the rest of it, yes. My parents had always treated me like an embarrassment, and as Joseph's wife I could forget about them entirely. I was young, and I thought I could start new. I told Joseph I'd always hated the name Katie, and that I wanted to be called by my middle name, Margaret, instead. I told him I wanted to leave that old wayward girl behind and start a new life as his wife." She shrugged. "He agreed."

"Who was Joseph Eden?" Fiona asked.

"He was my brother," CeCe supplied. She pulled up a chair and sat on it facing Fiona, as if they were going to have a chat. Katie stayed standing, and Roberta had walked to the window, where she listened as she looked out. "My half brother, that is. We had the same father."

"Brad Ellesmere," Fiona said.

CeCe blinked. "Is that in my file?"

"Never mind what's in the file," Fiona said. "Katie married your father's illegitimate son?"

"His heir." This was Roberta, speaking from her place by the window. Her voice was low, commanding, and they all looked at her. "He was Brad Ellesmere's illegitimate son, but he was also his only son. Brad Ellesmere put him in the will. He was the Ellesmere heir."

"I see."

"You think it's cold," Katie said. "I can see it in your face, Fiona. You think it makes me a manipulative bitch. I was sixteen when I met Joseph, though he waited until I was eighteen to marry me. I was sixteen, and I needed to make my own life by whatever means I had."

Fiona swallowed. "I'm not judging you."

"Aren't you? You're right. I married him because I

thought he'd be useful. Because I was cold and angry. But do you know what? I ended up liking him. I made him happy. I never thought I'd make anyone happy. We were together for nearly sixty years, and we got along just fine. Not many married couples can say as much." She smiled. "Joseph got me out of Idlewild, away from my family, away from everything. I used his money to send Roberta to law school so she could help her uncle. I used his money to send CeCe to Vassar so she could get away from her horrible mother. So she could stay away from that woman."

"My mother was Brad Ellesmere's housekeeper," CeCe explained. "Having his illegitimate child was a burden to her. It was harder in those days. There was so much shame. She tried to drown me in the ocean when I was six." She rubbed a finger lightly over her lower lip. "She really wasn't stable," she said, her voice almost gentle. "My father sent her for treatment after she tried to kill me, but she checked herself out and left. I went to college and became a teacher so I wouldn't have to go home."

"You're a teacher?" Fiona asked.

"Oh, no, not anymore." CeCe dropped her hand. "I quit once I got married and had children. I'd achieved what I wanted, and I was better at being a mother anyway. I preferred to raise my kids. Katie howled at me, I can tell you, but that was the one time she lost an argument with me."

"CeCe always did want children." Katie was still standing, looking down, watching as Fiona tried to follow the conversation. This was how the girls talked, it seemed, finishing one another's sentences. Completing one another's thoughts after so many years.

"CeCe was a better mother than any of us, I think," Roberta said from her place by the window.

"That's true," Katie said. She had been beautiful once; Fiona could see that now. She was still beautiful. Katie glanced down at CeCe, and Fiona saw the complicated love in the look. "Without that degree, you would have married some country bumpkin at eighteen, not an engineer at twenty-seven."

CeCe reached over and, to Fiona's surprise, took Katie's hand in hers and held it tightly. "She got us out of there," she said to Fiona, still holding her friend's hand. "All three of us. Away from our families, our pasts. Katie set us free."

"That wasn't all of it, though," Roberta said. She was watching them, leaning casually against the window. "There was always a bigger plan behind that one. A bigger goal."

"Sonia," Fiona said. "You wanted to find who killed your friend."

"The police wouldn't investigate," CeCe explained. "That was my fault. I told the headmistress that Sonia had been at Ravensbrück when I tried to explain she couldn't have run away. I was so innocent. I had no idea that would make everyone assume she was a Jew, that it would make the investigation less important, not more. But they asked a few questions, looked in the woods for an hour or two, and filed it away. It was over."

"With money," Katie explained, her voice soft, "we at

least could investigate the matter ourselves." She pulled up a chair at last and sat next to CeCe, crossing her legs elegantly. "I hired private investigators over the years to go over the evidence, but never with any results. The school was still open, and they wouldn't give permission for my investigators to search the grounds. They claimed it was an old case of a runaway girl, and there was no cause. When the school closed, I begged Joseph to buy it, but unfortunately that was the one time he said no to me. He said the land was a terrible investment and he'd lose his shirt. He wasn't willing to lose that much money to satisfy a whim of mine." She smiled at Fiona. "But we did solve it in the end. Ourselves. I'll tell you freely, if you want. Would you like to know who Sonia's murderer was?"

It was the temptation, the same one that had lured her into this case, that had nearly gotten her killed. Katie Winthrop, Fiona realized, was very adept at playing off the expectations of whomever she was talking to.

"I already know," Fiona said to her. "Though when I first looked at it, the most likely suspects were you three." She glanced around at them. "You had access to her, and you certainly had the opportunity. Sonia was killed by something blunt to the head, not a weapon. It was a crime of opportunity, of someone who hated her seeing their chance and getting rid of her."

The women were quiet. Katie looked amused. Roberta stared out the window, her jaw set. CeCe's eyes were wide.

"But I never liked that theory," Fiona went on. "The account I heard was that you were friends with her, that you liked her. Roberta brought her to the school nurse a few weeks before she was killed."

That made Roberta turn her head. "She had a fit in the garden," she said. "It made her think of the digging detail at Ravensbrück. A flashback, though that term wasn't in use at the time. Sonia almost certainly had some form of PTSD. She nearly passed out."

Fiona nodded. "You cared about her. It could have been a lie, but when you talked about her when we met, it didn't seem like it. I should have just assumed that one of you did it and moved on."

"But you didn't, did you?" Katie asked softly. "How terribly clever."

"No, I didn't. I followed another lead." She met Katie's gaze. "I don't know how you did it, but I have the feeling that what I found won't be a surprise to you at all."

"You won't know unless you tell us, will you?" Katie said.

"I did some research," Fiona said. "I learned about a woman named Rose Albert. Also known as Rosa Berlitz."

There was a long, drawn-out minute of silence. Fiona could hear her own breathing, the beeps of machines in rooms down the hall, the clatter of someone walking by dragging an IV stand. Nurses talked and laughed quietly beyond the door of her room. The four of them were still. Roberta still looked out the window, but Katie and CeCe watched Fiona.

"Well." Katie sat back in her chair and pressed her hands together. Her features were composed, even amused, but

Fiona still had the feeling she'd impressed the older woman for the first time today. "This is interesting."

"How did you do it?" CeCe blurted. She looked like she could barely contain herself. "You never saw the picture."

"What picture?" Fiona asked.

"Sonia's drawing. In her notebook." CeCe glanced at Katie, who was giving her an icy look, and made an impatient sound. "Leave it, Katie—she already knows. Why not tell her about the book?" CeCe turned back to Fiona. "Sonia had a notebook. I gave it to her, actually—it had been a present to me, but I never used it. Sonia took it and wrote in it. All of her memories. And she drew pictures— of her family, of Ravensbrück, of the people she knew there. The notebook was in her suitcase when she disappeared."

"The suitcase that was taken from the headmistress's office?" Fiona asked.

CeCe ignored another dirty look from Katie. "We took it, of course. We wanted Sonia's things back. They didn't belong in some dusty old closet, and we thought it might hold a clue. So we took it. But we never found a clue in there, not until 1973."

"That was the year of Rosa Berlitz's trial," Fiona said. "The year Rosa died." A heart attack in her own home, the papers had said.

From her place in the window, Roberta chimed in. "I had a baby in 1973," she said. "My son. I didn't hear about the Berlitz trial. But when I came back to work at the firm, people were talking about it. My firm hadn't handled the case, but it was a landmark in local legal circles. I heard the word *Ravensbrück*, and I started to wonder." She turned and faced Fiona, the harsh light from the window illuminating her still-perfect skin. "I dug up the articles about the trial. A war crimes trial, and it wasn't even front-page news."

Fiona nodded. That was what she'd seen as well.

"I made copies of the articles and mailed them to Katie and CeCe," Roberta went on. "I asked them if they thought it might have some bearing on Sonia, since Rosa Berlitz had lived in Burlington. It was just too much of a coincidence that she and Sonia had been close enough to cross paths. But I'm sure you thought the same thing already."

"It was me who figured it out," CeCe said. "I saw the photo from the newspaper and I recognized her immediately. I was the one who kept Sonia's suitcase, you see, with the notebook in it. We'd all read the notebook, but I'd read it many times over. And the minute I saw Rosa Berlitz, I recognized her face. Sonia had drawn a portrait of her from memory. Rosa had been a Ravensbrück guard."

"Wait," Fiona said. "Rosa Berlitz was acquitted. You're saying you had evidence of her identity, and you didn't go to the authorities with it?"

"We would have gone to the authorities," Katie said quietly. "But we didn't have time. We went to Rosa first."

"All of us," Roberta said.

"We went right to her house," CeCe added. "Knocked on the door, and there she was."

"I have to say," Katie said, "she really wasn't expecting us. She wasn't an old woman, but she was a recluse, especially since the trial. She was not well." She shook her head. "Not well at all."

Fiona found that she was gripping the edge of the bed so hard her knuckles were white. "What did you do?" she said. "The obituary said she died of a heart attack. What did you do?"

Katie smiled at her. "We asked her questions. About Ravensbrück. About Sonia. About everything." She shrugged. "She didn't want to admit anything at first, but we were persistent, and Roberta has a lot of experience with witnesses on the stand in court. She was magnificent. I suppose you could say we bullied Rose a little bit, but that's a matter of opinion, isn't it? In any case, we made her believe that it was over, that we already knew everything there was to know. We made her believe she could be indicted not only for the Ravensbrück crimes, but for Sonia's murder as well. She looked sick— she wasn't well, as I say—and then she started to talk."

"She admitted to it?" Fiona asked.

"Yes," Roberta said. Her voice was bitter. "She knew where Sonia was going from her bus ticket. Sonia had changed the ticket at her agency. She went to the stop in her car, parked, and waited. When Sonia got off the bus, she followed her into the woods and killed her with a rotted beam from the old fence. Then she dumped the body, walked back to her car, and drove away. She was very, very sorry."

"That dried-up old Nazi bitch," Katie said darkly.

"Yes, she was," CeCe added. "She wouldn't tell us where she'd dumped the body, because she knew that would seal her case. It was her word against ours, and once a body was recovered, it was over. But we weren't leaving. We asked and asked. We were so angry after all these years. She got agitated."

Fiona had to ask it. "Did you kill her?"

It was Katie who answered that one. "Did you think we killed her?" she asked. "What a picture that paints. All of us standing over her, choking her—suffocating her, perhaps—in revenge. The coroner misdiagnosing it as a heart attack. The three of us sending Sonia's killer to hell." She nodded. "I like it. That isn't how it happened. But I can't say I find the picture distasteful."

"No, we didn't kill her," Roberta added. "She had a heart attack. A real one. While we were there, asking over and over where we could find Sonia's body. I think the fear and the stress just overpowered her. She fell on the floor. We thought she was faking at first, but she wasn't. She really was dying."

"It was a disaster," CeCe said. "She was the only one who knew where Sonia was buried. I was so upset."

Fiona stared at her. "So—what did you do?"

"She died," Katie said, her voice cold and sharp. "We left. That was all."

"You just left her there?"

Roberta snorted, the most unladylike sound Fiona had ever heard the older woman make. But it was Katie who answered.

"If that piece of Nazi garbage had killed your sister," she said, "and then spent *decades* living free while she rotted in a well—what would you do?"

The room was quiet. Fiona couldn't answer.

Katie Winthrop rose from her chair and touched Fiona on the shoulder. "I'm not a bad person," she said. "None of us are. But this was Sonia's killer. We'd spent our lives trying to find her when no one cared, when the police stopped looking. I think, of all people, you would understand."

"Jesus," Fiona breathed.

"You see what we were up against," Katie said. "We had to be hard. We've always had to be hard. It was either that or break."

"I have one more question," Fiona said.

"Go ahead," Katie said. "You've earned it."

"Idlewild." Fiona made herself say the word. "The restoration. Was it ever real?"

Katie shook her head, giving her the truth. "I bought Idlewild because I knew Sonia was buried there somewhere," she said. "She had to be there. I intended to go over every inch and find her. Anthony never knew. He just thought I was misguided. He disapproved from the first, just like his father did. But that was because he didn't know what I really wanted."

"And now you've found Sonia," Fiona said.

"I have," Katie said softly. "I'm going to give her a proper burial. And then, my dear, you can rest easy. I'm not going to restore Idlewild. I'm going to take that place, with all of its ghosts, and I'm going to bury it. I'm going to dismantle every stick and stone until there's nothing left, and then I'm going to leave it to rot, just like it wants to."

chapter 36

Barrons, Vermont
December 2014

Fiona stayed at her father's house her first night out of the hospital, on the twin bed that was still in her old bedroom, and then she went home. She was shaky and tired, but the worst of the flu was over, and her neck was beginning to heal. She went back to her small apartment, laden with groceries from Malcolm, and looked around at the stacks of boxes from Idlewild Hall. Then she went to bed.

She thought maybe she'd stay there. That maybe she'd run out of whatever had driven her for the last twenty years, and without it she had nothing left. The jittery feeling she always got in her bloodstream was gone, and she thought she'd sleep for a week. But instead she stared at the ceiling, her mind ticking over—more slowly, more deliberately than it used to, but ticking all the same. Within an hour she was up again, wearing old boxers and a stretched-out T-shirt, eating crackers and canned soup, her feet up on a box of Idlewild records. She pulled out her laptop after a while and checked her e-mail.

There was a small avalanche in her in-box. Jonas hoping she was okay. Journalists from the local press covering the story of Garrett Creel's arrest and looking for a statement. Hester, one of the sisters from the Barrons Historical Society, sending her links to the story in the local press. There was nothing from Jamie.

It was midmorning, quiet in her apartment building, most of the residents gone to work. Fiona clicked on the links Hester had sent her and scanned through the news stories.

Garrett Creel had been charged with kidnapping and attempted murder for his attack on her, as well as firing at a police officer, who happened to be his own son. He was scheduled for a bail hearing the next day. The articles on the newswire gave a brief summary of Fiona's background, of Deb's murder and Tim's conviction, of the fact that Fiona was dating Garrett's son, but no motive for the attack was given. And there was no mention of Garrett Creel covering up evidence of Tim's crimes and the murder of Deb in 1994.

It wasn't completely surprising. The police would keep the internal investigation under wraps for as long as they could. There were always potential leaks in internal police cases, but it took a diligent journalist to dig them out. This story was a small one—a retired chief of police attacking a thirty-seven-year-old woman and trying to choke her to death. A family dispute. Even a lovers' quarrel, maybe. Something seedy. She set aside the requests from the journalists in her in-box without answering them. She would decide whom to talk to, and when.

She picked up her cell phone, stared at its string of notifications, and suddenly felt tired. She wished Jamie was here.

He hadn't texted. He hadn't called. He'd been at the hospital—she hadn't imagined that. She wondered what he was doing, how he was taking his father's arrest. She pictured that cozy, time-warped house without Garrett in it, Diane knocking around it by herself.

As she was staring at her phone, it rang in her hand. An unknown number. On impulse, she answered it.

"Hello, Fiona" came the rich, familiar voice of an elderly woman on the other end.

Fiona felt her stomach tighten. "Hello, Katie."

Katie Winthrop sighed. "No one ever calls me that," she said. "Except Roberta and CeCe. And now you. The hospital tells me you were released. How are you feeling?"

"Fine, I suppose."

"I just talked to Anthony. He's suspicious that something is up. He asked me why in the world you wanted to know my maiden name."

"Then you should tell him the truth, don't you think?"

"I just might," Katie said. "I'm old enough now. I'm tired of being Margaret. I think it's time to be Katie again. But that isn't what I'm calling about. I'm calling about the Idlewild files."

By reflex, Fiona stared around her darkened apartment at the files stacked against the walls. "Anthony already tried," she said.

"Yes, he did. Now I'm going to try and bargain with you. I want the files. I already own the school and the property. I want the files, too."

"What for?"

"Because it's my history," Katie said. "It's our history, me and the girls. Sonia's history. And maybe I'm a maudlin old lady, but I think it might have answers."

"It's a bunch of old textbooks and personnel files," Fiona said. "I don't think you're going to find the answer you want."

"Then I'll be disappointed, I suppose. But I'm willing to make an offer," Katie said. "What do you want, Fiona?"

Fiona stared down at her bare legs, her bare feet, as the words echoed home. *What do you want, Fiona?*

She wanted all of this to be over. She wanted to be different. She wanted her life to be different. She wanted the chance to do it all over again.

She wanted money, a career that felt real. She wanted Jamie back.

But what she said was "I want Sonia's diary."

There was icy silence on the other end of the line.

"You thought I'd ask for money, didn't you?" Fiona said. "I suppose everyone asks you for money. But that's not what I want from you."

"What exactly do you want with the diary?" Katie asked.

"There's a historian in the UK who is writing about Ravensbrück," Fiona said. "The records from the camp were burned before the Soviet army liberated it. The survivors' histories are few. She's trying to put the pieces together, to tell the story. Sonia's diary would add to the history."

"I'm willing to consider it," Katie said. "I'll ask the girls. But we aren't prepared to give the diary away permanently. We'll lend it or give a copy. But we're in that diary—she drew all of us. It's personal to us."

"I think she can work with that."

"I'm burying her, you know," Katie said. "Sonia. Now that the coroner is done with her and she has no relatives, I've asked that she be released to me. I'm going to have her properly buried in Barrons Memorial Cemetery, with a headstone. There will be a small ceremony next week, if you'd like to come."

"I will," Fiona said. "And I'm still going to write the story about the case, about her disappearance and the discovery of the body."

"I see," Katie said. "And will your story mention Rosa Berlitz?"

"It might." It would. Of course it would. Whom did she think she was dealing with?

"Do your worst," Katie said, resigned. "I'm old now. I have lawyers."

"I will. Thanks. And there's one more thing."

"What is it?"

Fiona reached into one of the file boxes and pulled out the file in which Lila Hendricksen, Idlewild's history teacher, had put together the map of the Hand house and the church before Idlewild was built. "When you get the files, there's one in particular you'll want to read. It's the history of Mary Hand—the real Mary Hand. She was an actual person, and her house was on the Idlewild grounds before the school was."

There was another cold silence, but this one was tinged with fear. "My God," Katie said. "Is she buried there?"

"With her baby, yes," Fiona said.

"She's in the garden, isn't she?" Katie was excited now. She didn't wait for a reply before she said, "I knew it. That damned garden. Well, it's my garden now, which makes her mine, too. I'm calling the girls."

"Katie—"

"I'll take care of it," Katie said, and hung up.

chapter 37

The Barrons police headquarters looked the same as it always had, squat and industrial. Fiona crunched through the icy crust of last night's snow through the parking lot and up the walk to the front door. She passed the picnic table where she'd sat the first day she'd told Jamie about the Idlewild story.

Christmas was a few weeks away, and someone had pulled out the department's box of wilted decorations. A too-short garland made of tinsel sagged over the door when Fiona walked through, and a small plastic Christmas tree, topped with a Snoopy, sat on the dispatch desk. The old cop on dispatch looked up and nodded at Fiona as she came through the door. "Back interview room," he said. "The chief's waiting for you."

Fiona tasted copper in the back of her throat at the

words. *The chief's waiting for you.* It wasn't Garrett Creel; it was Barrons' current police chief, Jim Pfeiffer. Still, she wasn't quite used to hearing those words. She nodded and kept walking.

The open office had a low hum of activity that went quiet as she passed. Jamie's desk was empty, his coat gone, his computer off. Jamie was on leave while his father's case moved through the system.

People watched her as she walked by. This was the effect of being the person Barrons' beloved longtime police chief had assaulted and nearly killed, the person that had caused his fall from grace. She kept her gaze forward and walked back to the station's interview room.

Jim Pfeiffer was fifty, fit and vigorous, unremarkable except for the black-framed glasses he wore that made him look more like an engineer from 1960s NASA than a modern-day cop. He shook Fiona's hand and offered to take her coat before he closed the door of the interview room.

"Sit down," he said, not unkindly. "I thought we should talk in private."

Fiona sat. "I already gave my statement," she said. "Several times, actually."

"Yes, I'm aware," Pfeiffer said. "There are a few other things I'd like to go over." He smiled. "First of all, how are you doing?"

Fiona smiled tightly back at him. "I'm just great. Thanks. Your entire force hates me because your former boss tried to kill me, but that's okay. I sleep great at night knowing he's out on bail."

Pfeiffer leaned back in his chair. "That's how the system works, Fiona. The judge made a ruling."

A judge who was one of Garrett's golf buddies, likely. But Fiona kept quiet.

"We've been getting some calls from the media," Pfeiffer said. "Chief Creel's arrest was public record, but I've been fielding inquiries that contain inside information." He stared at her from behind his glasses. "Specifically, we've been getting calls about a case from 1993, the assault of a girl named Helen Heyer. There seems to be some belief starting up that the Heyer case has to do with Tim Christopher."

"Is that so?" Fiona asked.

Pfeiffer sighed. "Please, Fiona, drop the act. We all know the Heyer case was one of your crazy theories before all of this happened."

"Yes, of course," Fiona said. "I had a crazy theory, and Garrett tried to kill me to shut me up. But my theory is crazy. Sure thing."

"It will go through the standard channels of investigation," Pfeiffer said, the exact phrase he'd used at the press conference. "But we don't appreciate media muckraking over this."

"Then talk to the media who are doing the muckraking, not me."

"Except it *is* you," Pfeiffer said. "It isn't you making the calls, but it's you feeding them. Please don't insult me by suggesting otherwise."

Fiona stared down at her hands and said nothing. She'd known from the first that none of it would be followed up properly—not Garrett's cover-up of Tim's assault on Helen Heyer, not Garrett's attempts to cover Deb's murder. Her father had raised a journalist, not a fool.

So she'd called Patrick Saller, the journalist who had written the original article about Deb's murder for *Lively Vermont* in 1994. Patrick was freelancing now, and Fiona had offered him everything she knew about the police corruption case that was about to unfold—a case that tied back to Deb's murder, to the piece Patrick had written, even back to the interview he'd done with Richard Rush in which he'd stated that Tim Christopher had eaten ice cream in his shop at nine o'clock. Saller had remembered every detail of the case, and of his own piece, and had jumped on the lead.

But she wasn't telling Pfeiffer that.

"Okay," Fiona said. "You'd like the media to leave you alone. Anything else?"

Pfeiffer shook his head. "I'm not getting through to you, am I?"

"Like I said, you need to talk to the reporters who are calling you, not me."

"There's a Web page," Pfeiffer argued. "It's called the Tim Christopher Truth page. There's a bunch of garbage on there about police misconduct on these two cases. Christopher's lawyer has caught wind of it. He says he might sue."

"Interesting," Fiona said. *You can't sue someone you can't find,* she thought.

"There are social media pages. There's some hippie lawyer involved, working pro bono. Someone's made a podcast. Fiona, this is crazy."

"Well, there are a lot of crazy people out there," Fiona agreed. "None of them are me."

Now he was angry. "It's you and your father, and you know it."

Fiona suppressed a smile. Malcolm might not have known much about modern technology, and he couldn't have made a Web page or a Facebook post to save his life, but it didn't matter. Malcolm knew everyone. No one could muster the right people to get a message out more quickly, or in a more sophisticated way, than Malcolm Sheridan. He had Patrick Saller on his side, as well as a retired civil rights lawyer from his Vietnam days. He also had the support of Jonas Cooper, Fiona's editor at *Lively Vermont*, who knew a few tech geeks from the local community college.

And when it came to exposing the attempted cover-up of his daughter's murder, Malcolm was both connected and motivated. Lighting a fire under the cops was his God-given talent.

"I wouldn't care about all of this," Pfeiffer said. "People post shit on the Internet all the time. My problem is that yesterday I got a call from BCI. They're opening an internal investigation into Garrett Creel and four of my other cops for criminal misconduct."

Fiona tried not to show her shock. That was new to her. She didn't think even Malcolm had any sway with the state police's Bureau of Criminal Investigation. That was why they'd come up with the Internet campaign.

"This is just the start," Pfeiffer said. He had a head of steam now. "There will be more names. I'll have to put more guys on leave, which makes me understaffed. I have to pay for overtime, which shoots my budget to hell. Morale is going to be a problem. I'm hardly swamped with recruits here. I still have to get up every morning and work in this community."

"And this is my fault?" Fiona said. "He covered for my sister's killer, and then he tried to fucking kill me."

"I get it. I do. It makes me mad. But I have to catch the next Tim Christopher who comes along."

"Then your cops shouldn't have tried to cover for the first one." Fiona pushed back her chair. "We're done."

"Call off your dogs, Fiona," Pfeiffer said.

"I told you, they're not mine."

"Just answer me one question."

"What is it?" she asked.

"I read your statement. You say Garrett told Tim to dump the body in the woods, to buy time before it was found. Yet Tim dumped it in the field. His words, according to you, were 'He dropped it and ran.'" Pfeiffer paused. "That doesn't seem to fit, does it? Tim was cool enough to call Garrett that night, cool enough to go along with the plan." He looked at Fiona through the lenses of his glasses, and she could see he hadn't missed a detail of this case. "Why do you think he botched it up so badly? Why did he lose his nerve?"

Fiona had actually thought about this; it was true the facts didn't fit. Unless you remembered that this was Idlewild. "I think something scared him," she said. "I think he dumped her and ran because he was afraid."

Pfeiffer's brows rose. "Tim Christopher was so scared he ran?"

"Yes."

"What could scare him that badly?"

She'd thought about this, too. Lain awake wondering about it, actually. What had Mary Hand shown him? What sights, what sounds? Tim Christopher, a murderer— what had she reached into his mind and shown him that was so frightening he'd dropped Deb's body and run?

She shook her head at Pfeiffer. "We'll never know," she said. "But I really hope it was horrible."

Her breath puffed before her as she walked away from the station. When she rounded the corner of the building, heading for the parking lot, she stopped when she saw the figure leaning against her car. Her heart pounded, and suddenly she felt light-headed, as if the sudden jolt of happiness could make her fly away.

"Jamie," she said.

He moved off where he'd been leaning and stood straight, his hands in the pockets of his coat. The cold wind tousled his hair. He looked paler than he had the last time she'd seen him, but his vitality hadn't dimmed, and he held her gaze with his own, his look dark and worried. "Hey," he said. He cleared his throat, looking her over. "Are you . . . okay?"

She was quietly, surprisingly elated to see him; what should have felt complicated suddenly didn't feel complicated to her at all. But Jamie was tense, his posture hard. "Sure," she managed. "I'm fine now. How are you?"

"All right, I guess," he said. "I saw your car by accident. It was an impulse. I guess I can't stay away from this place. I'm not stalking you."

"Good to know."

He glanced past her to the station. "You've been to see Pfeiffer?"

"I was summoned." Fiona crossed her arms. "He's pissed about the BCI investigation. He blames it on me. But I think he's going to figure out pretty quickly who's behind it."

He looked at her for a long moment, and she watched the wariness drain from his expression like water. "I didn't instigate it—given what's happened, they opened the investigation themselves. But I'm cooperating, Fee. I'm giving them everything I know."

"About your own father?" she asked gently.

"He covered for Tim. He tried to kill you. He shot at me." Jamie shook his head. "But I told you before all of that. I was already done. And I meant it." He gave her the ghost of a smile. "I guess it's safe to say I'm not going to be a cop anymore."

"So what will you do?"

"I don't know. I'll have to think of something. Maybe

I'll take up woodworking, or buy an apple orchard." He took his hands out of his pockets, and she saw the bandage on his hand. "I hear journalism is a particularly lucrative career, except I can't write for shit."

That made her laugh, the sound brief before it died again. He didn't have to be a cop to do good, to help people. Maybe in time he'd realize that. "Jesus, Jamie," she said, rubbing a hand over her forehead. "What a mess. How is your mother handling it?"

"Not good," he said, looking grim. He glanced at her. "She blames you, at least for now."

Of course she did. She was a cop's wife, a cop's mother. *His mother hates me and his father tried to kill me,* Fiona thought. *This is never going to work.*

As if reading her mind, Jamie said, "So what now, Fee?"

She looked around at the cold, empty street, beneath gray skies that threatened more snow. At the police station behind her. At the man in front of her.

What now?

And then she took a gamble.

"Do you want to go for coffee?" she asked him.

He thought it over, and then he answered.

But he didn't have to. She already knew what the answer would be.

epilogue

As the machines moved in and the crew worked, the small knot of men circulating, Fiona aimed her camera at the damp square of dirt and took another shot.

"There's nothing to see yet, you know," Katie Winthrop said at her shoulder.

Fiona didn't answer her. For the first time in their brief acquaintance, Fiona was seeing the indomitable Katie Winthrop nervous. The old woman was bundled deep into her coats and scarves, her hands ensconced in thick mittens, her elegant feet lost in a pair of winter boots. She was talkative and fidgety, edgy and emotional. Today, Fiona could clearly see the troublemaking fifteen-year-old who had once driven her teachers crazy.

Anthony was hovering in the background, fretting over his mother, ready to offer her tea from a thermos. Fiona paid no attention to him as she watched two of the dig crew consulting, then calling a third man over for his opinion.

"God, I hate this place," Katie said.

"So do I," Fiona said, her gaze still on the crew. "Everyone hates this place."

It was a dark December day, the sun long hidden behind the cold clouds, and the dim light made Idlewild look even worse. Behind them, shadows loomed under the row of deep eaves that lined the main hall, making them look even more like cavernous teeth. Having the building behind her gave Fiona the chills, as if it would move while she wasn't looking. The plastic that had been stretched around the old garden flapped mercilessly in the winter wind. Everything seemed to be waiting.

Not long now, Fiona thought, watching the men.

"Oh, thank God," Katie said. "The girls are here."

Fiona glanced around briefly to see Roberta and CeCe approaching, bundled just as deeply as Katie was, their arms linked. Jamie accompanied them, making sure neither woman stumbled on the frozen mud of the drive. Roberta looked grim, but CeCe gave a polite wave.

"Good God," Roberta said when they got close. "This place is even worse than I remember. Is it going to take long?"

"What is that smell?" CeCe asked. "Oh—it's the garden. Now I remember." Her expression went hard as the memories hit. "Disgusting."

It was. Even in the frigid cold, as soon as the crew had overturned the first layer of frost-crusted earth, a damp, hideous smell had come from this square of land, as if it exhaled bad breath in their faces. The crew had said something about drainage and clay and pH, but Fiona hadn't bought it. The smell was Mary and her baby. It always had been.

Jamie moved to stand next to Fiona's shoulder. "Are you okay?" he asked her softly.

"This is nice of you," Fiona murmured back. "You didn't have to come."

She turned, and their eyes met for a long moment. He gave her half a smile as her throat went dry. "I wanted to," he said.

Fiona tore her gaze away and stared ahead again.

"I'm taking you for a beer after this," he said. "I don't care if it's early."

"Okay," she said, feeling her cheeks warm. It felt like a first date.

"Katie," Roberta complained as Fiona focused her camera on the garden again. "Your son is trying to give me tea."

"Take it," Katie said. "It makes him happy."

"I'd rather have hot chocolate," CeCe said. "It would cheer me up. I like hot chocolate better. I don't really want to see a dead body. Oh, no. I'm talking too much, aren't I? I do that when I'm nervous."

She went quiet, and Fiona knew that either Katie or Roberta—or both—had taken her hand.

Without CeCe's chatter, there was only the flap of plastic and the wind again. The work crew, hired by Katie, had been here for five hours already, and the light would fail soon. But the square they were examining wasn't very big, and the soil was loose and wet despite the weather. They'd already gone deep, the small backhoe parked by men working by hand with shovels. Finally, the crew foreman made his way around the hole in the ground to Katie, a serious look on his face.

"We've hit something," he said. "Wood."

A coffin. Mary's parents had left her outside to die, but they'd buried her and her baby in a coffin.

It took another forty minutes, but the coffin was uncovered and lifted from deep under the old garden. It was rotted, rough, makeshift, clearly homemade. The stench that accompanied it, even in the brisk winter wind, was so bad that the men of the work crew raised their scarves over their noses and mouths.

Fiona smelled it, too, but she kept her hands on the camera, taking shots as the coffin emerged from the ground. She had written most of her piece on Sonia Gallipeau, the sad story of her life and death. Jonas was going to use it as part of his relaunch of *Lively Vermont*—at long last, he was changing the magazine's focus from soft-pedaled tourism stories to the kinds of in-depth local coverage he wanted to run. He'd sold his half of their house out to his ex-wife, taken the money, and invested it in the magazine while he lived in the room over his elderly mother's garage. Strangely, he was in a better mood than ever since he'd done it. *I feel like I'm twenty again,* he'd said.

Part of his jubilation came from the fact that the cover

story of the new *Lively Vermont* wasn't going to be about Sonia Gallipeau at all. It was going to be an exclusive article by the legendary Malcolm Sheridan, excerpted from his forthcoming book about the 2008 financial crash. Jonas had worked out a deal for the first new writing from Malcolm Sheridan in twenty years, and even living in his mother's garage couldn't dampen his joy.

Don't get too comfortable, Malcolm had warned Jonas as they sat in Malcolm's living room, Fiona looking on in amusement. *I'm retired. I'm not writing for you all the damn time.* But Fiona knew better. Her father was writing—that was what mattered. The Tim Christopher cover-up, as painful as it was, had shaken something loose. It had reawakened her father's desire to get out into the world and get something done. Just as it had reawakened hers.

Fiona was writing, too. Sonia Gallipeau was just the beginning. She was going to write real stories for the first time in her life. Her focus was going to be the unsolved cases, the missing loved ones who were never found, the cold cases that stayed unsolved. She was going to write about what mattered, whatever the cost. And Jamie was going to help her, lending the expertise gained from ten years as a cop.

As soon as the Idlewild bodies were buried.

There was no story about Mary Hand. That wasn't why she was here, taking pictures. She was taking pictures because, after so many years of suffering in silence, someone needed to document this.

"I hope no one is going to be sick," Anthony said. He was standing next to CeCe, watching the coffin come out of the ground, and he was clearly talking about himself.

The girls were quiet, the three of them lined up, watching. They had stood exactly this way at Sonia's memorial service four days ago, a solemn line of old women in vigil for their friend. Sonia was buried properly now, in a cemetery beneath a headstone bearing her name.

The coffin was placed on crude wooden struts, and the crew foreman approached again. "What do we do?" he asked Katie. Fiona lowered the camera. She felt Jamie take her hand in his.

Katie blinked at the foreman as if waking up. "Open it," she said.

Anthony stared at her. "Mother," he said. "I don't think we can just do that."

Katie looked at the foreman. "Can we do that?"

The foreman looked back at his crew, then shrugged. "We should probably call the cops," he said, "but it doesn't matter to me. A coffin this old, it's just a few old bones."

"What do you think, former policeman?" Katie asked Jamie.

Jamie's gaze was fixed on the coffin. His hand was warm on Fiona's. "I say open it," he said.

"Then do it," Katie told the foreman.

Roberta pulled a handkerchief from somewhere in her winter coat and held it to her nose. "What are we going to do with her?" she asked Katie as the crew foreman walked back to the grave.

"We'll bury her," Katie said. "Properly, like we did with Sonia. Mary and her baby. Then she'll go away."

"I don't want to see it," CeCe said, but she didn't move.

Fiona heard something behind her and turned.

There was nothing there.

She turned back, but she heard the sound again. A footstep.

There was a rushing sound in her ears, and a strange smell that was almost nutmeg. Fiona peered into the shadows and saw Mary standing at the edge of the trees in her dress and veil, watching them. She was holding a tiny, swaddled baby in her arms.

From behind Fiona, the crew foreman said, "Hand me that crowbar." There was a cracking sound of wood. CeCe cried out.

"Jesus," Jamie said.

Still, Mary watched. Fiona stood frozen, her hands still on her camera.

"My God," Katie said softly. "Oh, my God. It's her."

Mary didn't move.

"I guess we'll call someone," the crew foreman said.

"You're right, Katie," Roberta said. "We'll have to bury her. We'll have to bury both of them."

In Mary's arms, the baby moved sleepily. Fiona blinked. Mary vanished into the shadows of the trees.

And then there was nothing but the windblown field, the blank winter sky, the breath of cold wind. And silence.

acknowledgments

Thanks to my editor, Danielle Perez, for believing in this book and championing it from the first. Thanks to my agent, Pam Hopkins, for helping me through the process of writing something new and scary. My mother, brother, and sister keep me grounded, and my husband, Adam, keeps me (mostly) sane. Molly and Sinead read an early version of the book and talked me off a ledge, and Stephanie read a later version and talked me off still more ledges. Thanks, guys.

For research on Ravensbrück, I am indebted to the work of Sarah Helm, first in *A Life in Secrets* and then her heartbreaking work on Ravensbrück itself, *If This Is a Woman*. Any errors are my own. Any readers looking for fiction about Ravensbrück should read *Rose Under Fire* by Elizabeth Wein.

And thank you to every reader who has ever sent me an e-mail or a Facebook message, every book club that has picked up one of my books to read, and every blog or reviewer who has bothered to write about my work. This simply does not happen without you.

the Broken Girls

—————◆—————

Simone St. James

questions for
discussion

1. Discuss the relationship between Sonia, Katie, Roberta, and CeCe. How would you characterize their friendships? Why do you think the author chose to write about four girls with such different backgrounds?

2. Why do you think the author chose to write from multiple perspectives? Did you enjoy one character's voice more than the others? How did the alternating points of view affect your reading of the book?

3. Discuss the character of Mary Hand. Do you think she is a malevolent ghost? What do you make of her past? Why do you think the author chose to include a supernatural element, and how effective is it?

4. Mary shows different things to each girl. What do you think they mean? Is she trying to scare the girls or is there a deeper purpose? What does she show to the other characters and why?

5. From the beginning, Fiona is determined to identify the girl in the well and uncover the truth of what happened to her. Why is this case so important to Fiona?

6. Why do you think the author chose the title *The Broken Girls*? Do you think Fiona is "broken"? If so, do you think this is true for the whole novel or do you believe she changes? What about the four girls in the 1950s?

7. How would you characterize Fiona and Jamie's relationship? Do you think it's healthy? How does it change throughout the course of the novel? Use specific examples from the book to illustrate your points.

8. Journalism plays an important role in the book. Why do you think the author chose to make Fiona a journalist? Her journalistic investigation often intersects with the police investigation. Do you think the media plays a positive or negative role in police work of this kind?

9. How are the themes of voice and silence explored in the novel? What do they mean for each of the women? Use specific examples from the book to illustrate your points.

10. Why do you think the author chose to set the novel at a boarding school? How does the remote location add to the atmosphere and plot? How would the story be different with a different setting?

Keep reading for an excerpt from
Simone St. James's latest chilling novel

THE SUN DOWN MOTEL

Available now from Berkley

Fell, New York
November 1982
Viv

The night it all ended, Vivian was alone.

That was fine with her. She preferred it. It was something she'd discovered, working the night shift at this place in the middle of nowhere: Being with people was easy, but being alone was hard. Especially being alone in the dark. The person who could be truly alone, in the company of no one but oneself and one's own thoughts— that person was stronger than anyone else. More ready. More prepared.

Still, she pulled into the parking lot of the Sun Down Motel in Fell, New York, and paused, feeling the familiar beat of fear. She sat in her beat-up Cavalier, the key in the ignition, the heat and the radio on, her coat huddled around her shoulders. She looked at the glowing blue and yellow sign, the two stories of rooms in two long stripes in the shape of an L, and thought, *I don't want to go in there. But I will.* She was ready, but she was still afraid. It was 10:59 p.m.

She felt like crying. She felt like screaming. She felt sick.

I don't want to go in there.

But I will. Because I always do.

Outside, two drops of half-frozen rain hit the windshield. A truck droned by on the road in the rearview mirror. The clock ticked over to eleven o'clock, and the news came on the radio. Another minute and she'd be late, but she didn't care. No one would fire her. No one cared if she came to work. The Sun Down had few customers, none of whom would notice if the night girl was late. It was often so quiet that an observer would think that nothing ever happened here.

Viv Delaney knew better.

The Sun Down only looked empty. But it wasn't.

With cold fingers, she pulled down the driver's-side visor. She touched her hair, which she'd had cut short, a sharp style that ended below her earlobes and was sprayed out for volume. She checked her eye makeup— not the frosty kind, like some girls wore, but a soft lavender purple. It looked a little like bruises. You could streak it with yellow and orange to create a days-old-bruise effect, but she hadn't bothered with that tonight. Just the purple on the delicate skin of her lids, meeting the darker line of her eyeliner and lashes. Why had she put makeup on at all? She couldn't remember.

On the radio, they talked about a body. A girl found in a ditch off Melborn Road, ten miles from here. Not that *here* was anywhere—just a motel on the side of a two-lane highway leading out of Fell and into the nothingness of upstate New York and eventually Canada. But if you took the two-lane for a mile and made a right at the single light dangling from an overhead wire, and followed that road to another and another, you'd be where the girl's body was found. A girl named Tracy Waters, last seen leaving a friend's house in a neighboring town. Eighteen years old, stripped naked and dumped in a ditch. They'd found her body two days after her parents reported her missing.

As she sat in her car, twenty-year-old Viv Delaney's hands shook as she listened to the story. She thought about what it must be like to lie naked as the half-frozen rain pelted your helpless skin. How horribly cold that would be. How it was always girls who ended up stripped and dead like roadkill. How it didn't matter how afraid or how careful you were—it could always be you.

Especially here. It could always be you.

Her gaze went to the motel, to the reflection of the gaudy lit-up blue and yellow sign blinking endlessly in the darkness. VACANCY. CABLE TV! VACANCY. CABLE TV!

Even after three months in this place, she could still be scared. Awfully, perfectly scared, her thoughts skittering up the back of her neck and around her brain in panic. *I'm alone for the next eight hours, alone in the dark. Alone with her and the others.*

And despite herself, Viv turned the key so the heat and the radio—still talking about Tracy Waters—went off. Lifted her chin and pushed open the driver's-side door. Stepped out into the cold.

She hunched deeper into her nylon coat and started

across the parking lot. She was wearing jeans and a pair of navy blue sneakers with white laces, the soles too thin for the cold and damp. The rain wet her hair, and the wind pushed it out of place. She walked across the lot toward the door that said OFFICE.

Inside the office, Johnny was standing behind the counter, zipping up his coat over his big stomach. He'd probably seen her from the window in the door. "Are you late?" he asked, though there was a clock on the wall behind him.

"Five minutes," Viv argued back, unzipping her own coat. Her stomach felt tight, queasy now that she was inside. *I want to go home.*

But where was home? Fell wasn't home. Neither was Illinois, where she was born. When she left home for the last time, after the final screaming fight with her mother, she'd supposedly been headed to New York to become an actress. But that, like everything else in her life to that point, had been a part she was playing, a story. She had no idea how to become a New York actress—the story had enraged her mother, which had made it good enough. What Viv had wanted, more than anything, was to simply be in motion, to go.

So she'd gone. And she'd ended up here. Fell would have to be home for now.

"Mrs. Bailey is in room two-seventeen," Johnny said, running down the motel's few guests. "She already made a liquor run, so expect a phone call anytime."

"Great," Viv said. Mrs. Bailey came to the Sun Down to drink, probably because if she did it at home she'd get in some kind of trouble. She made drunken phone calls to the front desk to make demands she usually forgot about. "Anyone else?"

"The couple on their way to Florida checked out," Johnny said. "We've had two prank phone calls, both heavy breathing. Stupid teenagers. And I wrote a note to Janice about the door to number one-oh-three. There's something wrong with it. It keeps blowing open in the wind, even when I lock it."

"It always does that," Viv said. "You told Janice about it a week ago." Janice was the motel's owner, and Viv hadn't seen her in weeks. Months, maybe. She didn't come to the motel if she didn't have to, and she certainly didn't come at night. She left Vivian's paychecks in an envelope on the desk, and all communication was handled with notes. Even the motel's owner didn't spend time here if she could help it.

"Well, she should fix the door," Johnny said. "I mean, it's strange, right? I locked it."

"Sure," Viv said. "It's strange."

She was used to this. No one else who worked at the motel saw what she saw or experienced what she did. The things she saw only happened in the middle of the night. The day shift and the evening shift employees had no idea.

"Hopefully no one else will check in," Johnny said, pulling the hood of his jacket over his head. "Hopefully it'll be quiet."

It's never quiet, Viv thought, but she said, "Yes, hopefully."

Viv watched him walk out of the office, listened to his car start up and drive away. Johnny was thirty-six and lived with his mother. Viv pictured him going home, maybe watching TV before going to bed. A guy who had never made much of himself, living a relatively normal life, free of the kind of fear Viv was feeling. A life in which he never thought about Tracy Waters, except to vaguely recall her name from the radio.

Maybe it was just her who was going crazy.

The quiet settled in, broken only by the occasional sound of the traffic on Number Six Road and the wind in the trees behind the motel. It was now 11:12. The clock on the wall behind the desk ticked over to 11:13.

She hung her jacket on the hook in the corner. From another hook she took a navy blue polyester vest with the words *Sun Down Motel* embroidered on the left breast and shrugged it on over her white blouse. She pulled out the hard wooden chair behind the counter and sat in it. She surveyed the scarred, stained desktop quickly: jar of pens and pencils, the black square that made a clacking sound when you dragged the handle back and forth over a credit card to make a carbon impression, puke-colored rotary phone. In the middle of the desk was a large, flat book, where guests were to write their information and sign their names when checking in. The guest book was open to November 1982.

Pulling a notebook from her purse, Viv pulled a pen from between its pages, opened the notebook on the desk, and wrote.

Nov. 29

Door to number 103 has begun to open again. Prank calls. No one here. Tracy Waters is dead.

A sound came from outside, and she paused, her head half raised. A bang, and then another one. Rhythmic and wild. The door to number 103 blowing open and hitting the wall in the wind. Again.

For a second, Viv closed her eyes. The fear came over her in a wave, but she was too far in it now. She was already here. She had to be ready. The Sun Down had claimed her for the night.

She lowered the pen again.

What if everything I've seen, everything I think, is true? Because I think it is.

Her eyes glanced to the guest book, took in the names there. She paused as the clock on the wall behind her shoulder ticked on, then wrote again.

The ghosts are awake tonight. They're restless. I think this will be over soon. Her hand trembled, and she tried to keep it steady. *I'm so sorry, Tracy. I've failed.*

A small sound escaped the back of her throat, but she bit it down into silence. She put the pen down and rubbed her eyes, some of the pretty lavender eyeshadow coming off on her fingertips.

It was November 29, 1982, 11:24 p.m.

By three o'clock in the morning, Viv Delaney had vanished.

That was the beginning.

Fell, New York
November 2017
Carly

This place was unfamiliar.

I opened my eyes and stared into the darkness, panicked. Strange bed, strange light through the window, strange room. I had a minute of free fall, frightening and exhilarating at the same time.

Then I remembered: I was in Fell, New York.

My name was Carly Kirk, I was twenty years old, and I wasn't supposed to be here.

I checked my phone on the nightstand; it was four o'clock in the morning, only the light from streetlamps and the twenty-four-hour Denny's shining through the sheer drapes on the hotel room window and making a hazy square on the wall.

I wasn't getting back to sleep now. I swung my legs over the side of the bed and picked up my glasses from the nightstand, putting them on. I'd driven from Illinois yesterday, a long drive that left me tired enough to sleep like the dead in this bland chain hotel in downtown Fell.

It wasn't that impressive a place; Google Earth had told me that much. Downtown was a grid of cafés, laundromats, junky antique stores, apartment rental buildings, and used-book stores, nestled reverently around a grocery store and a CVS. The street I was on, with the chain hotel and the Denny's, passed straight through town, as if a lot of people got to Fell and simply kept driving without making the turnoff into the rest of the town. The WELCOME TO FELL sign I'd passed last night had been vandalized by a wit who had used spray paint to add the words TURN BACK.

I didn't turn back.

With my glasses on, I picked up my phone again and scrolled through the emails and texts that had come in while I slept.

The first email was from my family's lawyer. *The remainder of funds has been deposited into your account. Please see breakdown attached.*

I flipped past it without reading the rest, without opening the attachment. I didn't need to see it: I already knew I'd inherited some of Mom's money, split with my brother, Graham. I knew it wasn't riches, but it was enough to keep me in food and shelter for a little while. I didn't want numbers, and I couldn't look at them. Losing your mother to cancer—she was only fifty-one— made things like money look petty and stupid.

In fact, it made you rethink everything in your life.

Which in my crazy way, after fourteen months in a fog of grief, I was doing. And I couldn't stop.

There was a string of texts from Graham. *What do you think you're doing, Carly? Leaving college? For how long? You think you can keep up? Whatever. If all that tuition is down the drain, you're on your own. You know that, right? Whatever you're doing, good luck with it. Try not to get killed.*

I hit Reply and typed, *Hey, drama queen. It's only for a few days, and I'm acing everything. This is just a side trip, because I'm curious. So sue me. I'll be fine. No plans to get killed, but thanks for checking.*

Actually, I was hoping to be here for longer than a few days. Since losing Mom, staying in college for my business degree seemed pointless. When I'd started college, I'd thought I had all the time in the world to figure out what I wanted to do. But Mom's death showed me that life wasn't as long as you thought it was. And I had questions I wanted answers to. It was time to find them.

Hailey, Graham's fiancée, had sent me her own text. *Hey! You OK?? Worried about you. I'm here to talk if you want. Maybe you need another grief counselor? I can find you one! OK? XO!*

God, she was so *nice*. I'd already done grief counseling. Therapy. Spirit circles. Yoga. Meditation. Self-care. In doing all of that, what I'd discovered was that I didn't need another therapy session right now. What I really needed, at long last, was answers.

I put down my phone and opened my laptop, tapping it awake. I opened the file on my desktop, scrolling through it. I picked out a scan of a newspaper from 1982, with the headline *POLICE SEARCHING FOR MISSING LOCAL WOMAN*. Beneath the headline was a photo of a young woman, clipped from a snapshot. She was beautiful, vivacious, smiling at the camera, her hair teased, her bangs sprayed in place up from her forehead as the rest of her hair hung down in a classic eighties look. Her skin was clear and her eyes sparkled, even in black and white. The caption below the photo said: *Twenty-year-old Vivian Delaney has not been seen since the night of November 29. Anyone who has seen her is asked to call the police.*

This. *This* was the answer I needed.

I'd been a nerd all my life, my nose buried in a book. Except that once I graduated from reading *The Black Stallion*, the books I read were the dark kind—about scary things like disappearances and murders, especially the true ones. While other kids read J. K. Rowling, I read Stephen King. While other kids did history reports about the Civil War, I read about Lizzie Borden. The report I wrote about that one—complete with details about exactly where the axe hit Lizzie's father and stepmother—got my teacher to call my mother with concern. *Is Carly all right?* My mother had brushed it off, because by then she knew how dark her daughter was. *She's fine. She just likes to read about murder, that's all.*

What my mother didn't mention—what she hated to talk about at all—was that I came by it naturally. There was an unsolved murder in my family, and I'd been obsessed with it for as long as I could remember.

I looked at the newspaper clipping again. Viv Delaney, the girl in the photograph, was my mother's sister. In 1982, she disappeared while working the night shift at the Sun Down Motel and was never found.

It was the huge, gaping hole in my family, the thing that everyone knew about but no one spoke of. Viv's disappearance was a loss like a missing tooth. *Never ask your mother about that*, my father told me the year before he left us all for good. *It upsets her.* Even my brother, the eternal pain in the ass, was sensitive about it. *Mom's sister was killed*, he told me. *Someone took her and murdered her, like that guy with the hook. It creeps me out. No wonder Mom doesn't talk about it.*

Thirty-five years my aunt Viv had been missing. My grandparents—Mom and Viv's parents—were dead. There were no pictures of Viv in our house, no mementos of her. The year before Mom died, when I was home for the summer, I'd found a story online and seen Viv's face for the first time. I'd thought maybe enough time had passed. I'd printed the clipping out and gone downstairs to show it to her. "Look what I found," I said.

Mom was sitting on the sofa in the living room, watching TV after dinner. She took the clipping from me and read it. Then she stared at it for a long time, her gaze fixed on the photograph.

When she looked back up at me, she had a strange look on her face that I'd never seen before and would never see again. Pain, maybe. Exhaustion, and some kind of old, rotted-over, carved-out fear. In that moment I had no idea that she had cancer, that I would lose her within a year. Maybe she knew then and didn't tell me, but I didn't think so. That look on her face, that fear, was all about Vivian.

Her voice, when she finally spoke, was flat, without inflection. "Vivian is dead," she said. She put down the clipping and got up and left the room.

I never asked Mom about it again.

It was only after Mom died that I got mad. Not at Mom, really—she was a teenager when Viv disappeared, and there wasn't much she could have done. But what about everyone else? The cops? The locals? Viv's parents? Why hadn't there been a statewide search? Why had Viv been allowed to vanish into nothingness with barely a ripple?

The first person I asked was Graham, who was older and remembered more than I did. "Grandma and Granddad were divorced by then," Graham said. "When Viv disappeared, Grandma was a single mother."

"So? That meant she didn't look for her daughter? Granddad, either?"

Graham shrugged. "Grandma didn't have much money. And Mom told me that she and Viv used to fight all the time. They didn't get along at all."

I'd stared at him, shocked. We were sitting in my mother's rental apartment, in the middle of boxing up her things. We were taking a break and eating takeout. "Mom told you that? She never told me that."

My brother shrugged again, leaning back on a box and scrolling through his phone. "They didn't have the Internet back then, or DNA. If you wanted to find a missing person, you had to get in your car and go driving around looking for them. Grandma couldn't take time off work and go to Fell. And Granddad was already remarried. I don't think he cared about any of them all that much."

It was true. Mom hadn't had a good relationship with her father, who had left their family to sink or swim. She hadn't even gone to his funeral. "What about the cops, though?" I said.

Graham put his phone down briefly and thought it over. "Well, Viv had already left home, and she was twenty," he said. "I guess they thought she'd just taken off somewhere." He looked at me. "You're really into this, aren't you?"

"Yes, I'm really into this. They didn't even find a body. It isn't 1982 anymore. We have the Internet and DNA now. Maybe something can be done."

"By you?"

Yes, by me. There didn't seem to be anyone else. And now that Mom was gone, I could ask all the questions I wanted without hurting her feelings. Mom had taken all of her memories of Viv with her when she died, and I'd never hear them. My anger at that was helpless, something that the therapists and counselors said I needed to work through. But my anger at everyone else, my outrage that my aunt's likely abduction and death were written off as just something that happened—I could work through that by coming to Fell and getting my own answers.

I clicked the other scanned article I had on my computer. It was headlined simply *MISSING GIRL STILL NOT FOUND*. The details were sketchy: Viv was twenty; she had been in Fell for three months; she worked at the Sun Down Motel on the night shift. She'd gone to work and disappeared sometime in the middle of her shift, leaving behind her car, her purse, and her belongings. Her roommate, a girl named Jenny Summers, said Viv was "a nice person, easy to get along with." She was also described—by who was not cited—as "pretty and vivacious." She had no boyfriend that anyone knew of. She was not into drugs, alcohol, or prostitution that anyone could tell. Her mother—my grandmother—was quoted as being "worried sick."

She was a beautiful girl, gone.

On foot. Without any money.

Vivian is dead.

Viv's case hadn't received national or even statewide media attention. The local Fell newspapers weren't digitized—they were still physically archived in the Fell library. When I started digging, all I found were true-crime blogs and Reddit threads by armchair detectives. None of the blogs or threads were about Vivian, but a lot of them were about Fell. Because Fell, it turned out, had more than one unsolved murder. For such a small place, it was a true-crime buff's paradise.

The second article was in Mom's belongings. I'd found it when I'd gone through her dresser after she died, tucked in an envelope in the back of a drawer. The envelope was white, crisp, brand-new. Written on the back, in Mom's lovely handwriting, was: *27 Greville Street, Apartment C.*

Viv's address, maybe? The piece of newsprint inside the envelope was nearly disintegrating, so I'd scanned it and added it to the first one I found.

Vivian is dead.

Mom had wanted no memories of her sister, no discussion of her, and yet she'd kept this article for thirty-five years, along with the address. She'd even put it in a new envelope sometime recently, recopied the address, which meant she'd at least pulled the article out of the old envelope, maybe read it again.

Viv was real. She wasn't a spooky tale or a ghost story. She had been real, she had been Mom's sister—and somehow, looking at that crisp white envelope, I knew she had mattered to Mom, a lot, in a way I had lost my chance to understand.

This was all I had: two newspaper articles and a memory of grief. Except now I had more than that. I had a little money and I had a very clear map from Illinois to Fell, New York. I had an address for Viv's apartment, maybe, and the Sun Down Motel. I had no boyfriend and a college career I had no passion for. I had a car and so few belongings that they fit into the back seat. I was twenty, and I still hadn't started my life yet. Just like Viv hadn't.

So I'd left school—Graham really was blowing this out of proportion—and got in my car for a road trip. And here I was. I'd look around town and dig up the local articles in the library. I'd go see the Sun Down for myself, since my Internet search said it was still in business. Maybe someone who lived here had known Viv, remembered her, could tell me about her. Maybe I could make her more than a fading piece of newsprint hidden in my mother's drawer. Her disappearance was the big mystery of my family—I wanted to see it firsthand, and all it would cost was a few days out of school.

Try not to get killed. That was my big brother, trying to scare me. It wasn't going to work. I didn't scare easily.

Still, I closed my laptop and tried not to think about someone hurting the girl I'd seen in the photo, someone grabbing her, taking her somewhere, doing something to her, killing her. Dumping her somewhere lonely, where maybe she still was. Maybe she was only bones now. Maybe that person, whoever they were, was dead now, or in prison. Maybe they weren't.

Vivian is dead.

It wasn't fair that Vivian was forgotten, reduced to a few pieces of newsprint and nothing else. It wasn't fair that Mom had died and taken her memories and her grief with her. It wasn't fair that Viv didn't matter to anyone but me.

I was in Fell. I didn't belong here. I had no idea what I was doing.

And still I waited, without sleeping, for the sun to come up again.

Ready to find
your next great read?

Let us help.

Visit prh.com/nextread